The Best New England Crime Stories Anthologies:

Snowbound (2017)

Windward (2016)

Red Dawn (2015)
Rogue Wave (2014)
Stone Cold (2013)
Blood Moon (2012)
Dead Calm (2011)
Thin Ice (2010)
Quarry (2009)
Deadfall (2008)
Still Waters (2007)
Seasmoke (2006)
Windchill (2005)
Undertow (2005)
Riptide (2004)

SNOWBOUND

BEST NEW ENGLAND CRIME STORIES

An Anthology

Edited by
Verena Rose, Harriette Sackler
& Shawn Reilly Simmons

The Dames of Detection
d/b/a Level Best Books
18100 Windsor Hill Dr.
Olney, MD 20832
www.levelbestbooks.com

Trade Paperback
ISBN-13: 978-1947915015
ISBN-10: 1947915010

Manufactured & Printed in the United States of America
2017

INTRODUCTION

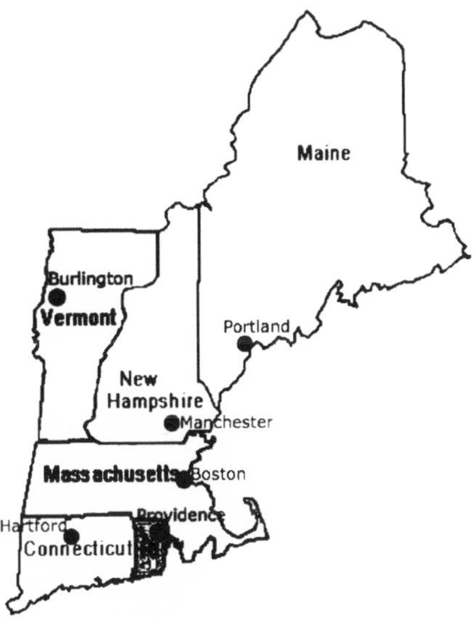

In our second year as the editors of the Best New England Crime Stories, the Dames of Detection d/b/a Level Best Books is very proud to present SNOWBOUND. We are also continuing our tradition of arranging the stories by state—not alphabetically, but rather like a trip through New England starting with Connecticut and then continuing on through Rhode Island, Massachusetts, Vermont, New Hampshire and ending in Maine.

Therefore, SNOWBOUND opens with two stories representing the state of Connecticut: Lucy Burdette's story about a not so noxious Nanny and Chris Knopf's UGLY about life in a mental facility.

The state of Rhode Island also is only represented by two stories, but never fear they are great ones—FARM TO TABLE by Shawn Reilly Simmons, about a wayward traveling salesman, and the Al Blanchard Award winner, THE MURDEROUS TYPE by Andrew Welsh-Huggins a cautionary tale about May-December relationships.

Massachusetts is represented by the greatest number of stories in SNOWBOUND with an astounding 17 of the total 38 stories. This section of the book starts with Michael Bracken's A.K.A. BOB JONES where $2 bills play an important role, followed by Patricia Dusenbury's UNSTRUNG QUARTET, Maurissa Guibord's THE EXPLORER, an historical with a twist, LD Masterson's ALL THAT SPARKLES, Emilya Naymark's A VERY LUCKY BOY who as it turns out may not have been, Alan Orloff's RULE NUMBER

ONE a story about the art of the double-cross, Trish Perrault's GOOD TO BE HOME, but is it? Another historical from Keenan Powell entitled THE BANSHEE OF ADAMS, MASSACHUSETTS with an understated theme, POISONING PENELOPE by Suzanne Rorhus highlights author rivalry, and Steve Roy's GEORGE SAYS. Emily Dickenson features in Harriette Sackler's EMILY, Lida Sideris' story THE NUT JOB demonstrates how looks can be deceiving, Shelagh Smith gives us CORWYN'S HOLLOW where you'll meet Gilly, Queen of the Faerie Mists. You won't want to look in a mirror after reading Mary E. Stibal's JUJU. Hiding in plain sight figures prominently in OUT OF TIME by Robin Templeton, and our last historical in Massachusetts is by Gabriel Valjan entitled SAVING GRACE. Bev Vincent crossed the borders of Massachusetts and Vermont with STICKY BUSINESS, a story about hapless criminals

Next on our road trip is Vermont where we begin with Maia Chance's MAIDSTONE about the perils of being a maid, and Dayle Dermatis explores the parent-child relationship in VOICES CARRY.

Sharon Daynard opens the New Hampshire section of the book with her story of wifely ire, GHOSTING MRS. MUIR, and in another story of wifely ire we have BLACK ICE by Connie Hambley. AN OMINOUS SILENCE by Edith Maxwell takes place on a snowbound train in 1890, and rounding out the New Hampshire stories we have our third story of wifely ire, AFTER I DO by Peggy McFarland.

The final, and largest, state on this trip around New England is Maine. Maine has the second largest number of stories represented in this anthology with a total of ten. Domestic abuse features in Christine Bagley's story ON A WINTERS NIGHT, Bruce Robert Coffin's TO-DO LIST highlights the perils of assisted living, the inaccuracies of prejudice are an important theme of BLESS AMERICA'S VISITORS by Charlene D'Avanzo. Judith Green's OFF HER MEDS has a very interesting twist at the end, a small-town theatre group features prominently in Janet Halpin's MRS. FEATHERPATCH AND THE CASE OF THE SKEWERED HAM, and in a tale with lots of twists and turns is Rosemary Herbert's A TWIST OF FORTUNE. In LUNCH BREAK by Travis Kennedy the protagonist works hard to stay alive, a granola bar wrapper figures into the solution of Lorraine Sharma Nelson's TOTALLY MISUNDERSTOOD, a suspicious church donation causes investigation in David Rappoport's THE ANONYMOUS DONOR and finally, two cats, then two more plus an owl feature prominently in THOSE AMBER EYES by Verena Rose.

We complete the anthology with a story that takes place in New England but with no specific state. HARD AS GRANITE by Charlotte Broadfoot is a scary story of the possibilities of child abuse.

The editors are very proud of this group of stories that became SNOWBOUND. There is something for everyone to enjoy and we know you will agree.

The Editors at Level Best Books:
The Dames of Detection,

Verena Rose
Harriette Sackler
Shawn Reilly Simmons

THE AL BLANCHARD AWARD

Al Blanchard was one of the original organizers of the New England Crime Bake conference, a president of Mystery Writers of America, New England Chapter, and a member of Sisters in Crime. He was known for encouraging new authors, for being a dedicated writer and mentor, and for being a fan of all things mystery. The very popular regional gathering of mystery writers he and a few others conceived of all those years ago is still going strong today.

After his tragic death in 2004, the Crime Bake Committee established The Al Blanchard Award in his memory to honor the best short crime story either by a New England author or with a New England setting. Stories are judged by committee separate from the submissions for the Level Best anthology.

The Dames of Detection d/b/a Level Best Books are very pleased to be the editors of the Best New England Crime Stories anthologies, and it's an honor for us to continue the tradition of publishing The Al Blanchard Award-winning story. Congratulations to Andrew Welsh-Huggins for winning this year's award with his story "The Murderous Type."

Verena Rose
Harriette Sackler
Shawn Reilly Simmons
Editors & Co-Publishers
Level Best Books

TABLE OF CONTENTS

NEW HAMPSHIRE page 286

RHODE ISLAND page 322

VERMONT page 340

NEW ENGLAND page 360

CONNECTICUT

DOROTHEA AND THE CASE OF THE NOXIOUS NANNY

by Lucy Burdette

Dorothea found the final disgusting house centipede in the damp powder room in their basement. This one was a whopper, the king of creep: three inches long, and a yellowish color, with two sets of antennae and maybe two hundred legs, all wiggling in hideous synchrony.

He sprinted across the linoleum floor. She gripped the jar with the holes poked in the lid ready to scrape him in, trying not to look at the other fifty or so centipedes writhing frantically inside. She lunged forward. The big centipede darted onto her leg and up over her knee, finally disappearing inside her jean shorts. She screamed, leaping to her feet, slapping at her thighs, feeling those horrible spindly legs everywhere. Finally the bug dropped out and she stomped it flat with her sneaker, shivering in horror as the legs continue to wave. She nudged the wiggling carcass into the jar.

She was finished. No more.

She stored the jar on a small shelf behind her father’s workbench and texted her friend Ben.

Got enough to do her in. Keep you posted.

Ben texted back. *Courage.*

Upstairs in the kitchen, the new nanny was waiting with a glass of beet juice, laced with powdered ginger. "Made fresh for you, Miss Dorothea," she said, the extra chins below her mouth quivering. She took a step back, folded her arms so the hanging flaps of skin were tucked close to her ribs. "We haven’t gotten off on the right foot, now have we? I can see you are accustomed to running the show. Thank goodness I am here to turn things around."

She chuckled as she patted the wisps of hair that curled around her perspiring forehead, the shade of Dorothea's flesh colored crayon. "Before you go outside today, I want you to practice your cursive. My nanny friends tell me children don't learn this skill these days, but I think it's important. Children who take notes using longhand learn much better—this is a scientific fact. So please write 100 times: "I will make my bed every morning and I will not argue with Nanny Ruth." She grinned and pushed a lined yellow tablet in front of Dorothea, and then set a blue pen and the glass of noxious beet juice beside it.

“I’m going for a quick constitutional walk around the block,” she told Dorothea’s parents as they came into the kitchen. “Back in a jiffy. Have a wonderful day.”

Once she was gone, Dorothea slapped the pen on the table. "No one writes longhand anymore," she complained. "We text. We type. Besides, there's no school today. It's not fair that I have to sit inside and do this dumb made-up homework."

But her father, who usually backed her up because he wasn't that fond of Nanny Ruth either, hated whining even more. He kissed Dorothea and her mother on the cheek and left for work.

"Texting, that's so sad," said her mom, who was getting organized for a major work presentation. Besides, she was a little bit afraid of Nanny Ruth so Dorothea doubted she'd ever take a stand against her. "I think it's a wonderful idea really. Then you can write the loveliest thank you notes for birthdays, and Christmas and "– her face brightened – "when you get married."

But Dorothea hated boys, so that wasn't happening. Except for Ben next-door, but she'd known him since he was two days old so he didn't count. Obviously, she wasn't making any progress by petitioning her parents to dismiss the nanny, so she'd have to go ahead with Plan Centipede.

When her mother had driven away, Dorothea retrieved the jar of bugs, went into the nanny's bedroom (strictly forbidden), and dumped the centipedes in her underwear drawer. She shivered with disgust and delight as they dispersed among the unmentionables. They wouldn't all stay put, but enough, she hoped, to freak the nanny out and get her to resign.

ΩΩΩ

When it came, the scream she'd imagined sounded more like a terrified horse's whinny, or the time her rabbit got killed by a fisher cat who'd managed to unlatch the hutch in their backyard. Both animals had screamed like murder victims right under her window.

Nanny Ruth's shriek was well worth the trouble over the last three days of collecting those odious bugs. The first scream was followed by a series of satisfying thumps and bangs and more screams—or screamlets, she thought with a wicked smile, as they were "eeks" and "scats" and "buggers" and even a "dammit," more than full voiced screams.

ΩΩΩ

In the week leading up to this, Dorothea had tried getting rid of the nanny with grown-up discussion, as her parents had been telling her since she was two years old to *use her words.* "That woman is noxious," Dorothea said, thinking the big vocabulary word might score some points. "And Ben gets a key to his house and he takes care of himself until his mother gets home," she explained.

"That's so sad," said her mom, rubbing her belly that now looked like a basketball or more like a watermelon—the big kind not the little round ones. "And it's dangerous too, especially with that man who's moved in at the end of the block. You remember what I told you—under no circumstances, ever, are you to go near his house."

Dorothea sighed. "I remember." Her mom was a defense attorney in New Haven and tended to think the worst would always happen.

"Besides, we are really going to need Nanny Ruth when your brother is born," said her dad.

And that ugly truth showed how much Dorothea mattered in this family: She was twelve years old and didn't need a nanny, but the baby would.

So they all had to pretend to like Nanny Ruth and listen to her old fashioned, out of touch advice about raising a nice young lady (Dorothea), because they were afraid she'd quit.

When she told all this to Ben last week, they came up with a masterful plot. They would do something so horribly disgusting that Nanny Ruth would resign on the spot. Then her mother could quit her job and take care of the dumb baby herself. End of story. The baby, ugh. The idea made her sick to her stomach.

A text buzzed through on her cell.

Ben: Did she find them?

Dorothea: Didn't u hear the scream? LOL

Ben: Meet at treehouse?

Dorothea was in so much trouble already that she might as well go, even though Nanny Ruth had told her she couldn't set foot outside until she was finished. Ben would have sugar and marshmallow cereal and High-C and little packets of M&Ms, nothing like the dreadful healthy snacks Nanny Ruth prepared. She'd never known any kid who had to drink freshly squeezed beet and ginger drinks every morning, but Nanny Ruth insisted this recipe was the perfect tonic for anything that ailed you—even if you didn't know you had it yet.

Dorothea hid her noxious red drink behind the spice rack on the counter and then ducked out the back door, slipped through the hole in the bushes marking the two yards, and climbed hand over hand up the boards that had been hammered into the big oak. "Anybody home?" She poked her head into the opening, smelling the heavenly combination of sawdust, peanut butter, chocolate, and a little mildew from the piece of carpet taken from Ben's cellar. Ben was sitting in one of the frayed lawn chairs they'd retrieved from some trash set by the curb a month or so ago. They both agreed that the green stripes looked exactly right with the paisley rug.

"Come on in," Ben said, "and squawk!"

While Dorothea described what had happened, they watched her house from their tree perch, which was high enough so they could see over Dorothea's one-story ranch and out to the street. The big oak tree had leafed out just enough that they felt completely invisible. It seemed like forever as they waited, hoping that Nanny Ruth would call a taxi and climb in with all her luggage, including that horrible vegetable juicer she'd inflicted on the family ever since she moved in two weeks earlier.

"Maybe it will take her a while to pack," Dorothea finally suggested. "It always takes my mom ages. She keeps changing her mind about what outfits to bring."

"But she wouldn't be choosing outfits, she'd be packing everything," Ben said.

They waited and waited and waited. They saw all the usual things that went on in the neighborhood: the creaky old woman down the street walking her dog who was even creakier and slower, the woman from the next block over pushing a stroller with a brand-new baby in it and dragging a screaming toddler by the wrist, and the Heinz 57 dog as her mother called him, meaning mutt, trotting down the street and nosing into all the garbage cans. At the very end of the block, in the driveway of the house her parents said she should never ever go near, the new owner backed his muscle car out of the garage and began to wash it.

"Holy cow," said Ben, pointing to a dark blue car that was inching down the street from the other direction. Exactly at the time it stopped in front of the house next to Dorothea's, Nanny Ruth came out of the front door with two matching turquoise suitcases and her juicer, packed up in its original box.

She glanced up one side of the block and down the other, as if she was looking for a taxi. Two people—a man in faded black jeans and a skinny woman with super bleached blonde hair—got out of the blue car and came up the sidewalk to Nanny Ruth.

“They don’t look like cab drivers to me,” said Dorothea.

“Maybe she called an Uber,” said Ben.

“She’s not that cool,” Dorothea said.

They chatted for a few moments, but Nanny Ruth shook her head and folded her baggy arms over her chest. As the strangers continued to talk, their faces got angrier. Nanny Ruth’s face got red too and she waggled her finger at the woman. Finally, the man gripped her elbow and pushed her back into the house. The woman grabbed the luggage and dragged it inside.

Dorothea had a sinking feeling, a coldness in the pit of her stomach. If she hadn't been such a brat about the creepy crawlies, Nanny Ruth would be dusting the living room the way she did every morning instead of fighting with these two strangers.

“What should we do?” Ben asked.

“Let’s wait a little bit and see what happens,” said Dorothea with more confidence than she really felt. Her mother was always telling her she was too dramatic—she should slow down and take some deep breaths before she freaked out. Two times this year she’d called the police after she’d heard funny noises when her parents were out for quick dinners. One time they’d found the Heinz 57 dog in the garbage. Another time it was only the door slamming on the screened-in porch after the wind picked up.

But a few minutes later, the two people left the house with Nanny Ruth pinned in between them, this time without her stuff. The woman got into the backseat of the blue car, and the man shoved the nanny in behind her, slammed the door, and then roared away.

“I'm going to call my mother,” said Dorothea.

“Should we take a look around first?” Ben asked. “If you call, she'll want to know exactly what happened so she can decide whether to come home or phone the cops. Maybe those were her friends and they talked her into leaving her position as a nanny.”

“Maybe,” said Dorothea. “But why did she go off without her luggage then?” They hadn't looked like the sort of friends she'd want.

They climbed down the rungs of the treehouse ladder, slipped through the opening in the mountain laurel bushes between their houses, and stepped through the back door into Dorothea's kitchen. Everything looked normal here. The nanny had cleaned up the coffee cups in the sink and put away Dorothea's cereal box, and even found the hidden beet juice and stowed it in the refrigerator.

Dorothea and Ben tiptoed through other rooms, but found nothing out of place. No sign of the luggage. Dorothea met Ben's gaze.

"We're going to have to check her bedroom." Just saying that gave her the cold feeling again in her stomach, but she led Ben down the hall. When Nanny Ruth had moved in, one of the first rules of the house was that her room was her room, her private business. No entry, no admittance, no way, not ever. The only time Dorothea had broken that rule was to stow the creepy bugs in her bureau. But this was an emergency. Wasn't it? She turned the knob on the nanny's door and pushed it open.

The room had been torn apart, the clothes from Nanny Ruth's suitcases strewn across the floor like leaves after a bad storm. Toiletries and her jewelry had been emptied into a big mess on the desk, and the juicer taken from the box and thrown to the ground. The drawers of her bureau hung open, and even the bed had been stripped. There wasn't one part of the room that hadn't been ripped to smithereens.

"Holy macaroni," Ben breathed.

Dorothea pulled her cell out of her shorts pocket and dialed her mother's work number. Once the secretary answered, she said: "Good morning, I need to speak to my mother."

"She's in that super important meeting," cooed the secretary, "you know the one she's been working on for months and months with all the first year associates? I promise I'll have her call you later as soon as she comes out."

"Later is not fine," said Dorothea, "this is important. I need to talk to her now, please."

"No can do. Can I help with something?" the secretary asked, the sweetness in her voice dropping away.

Dorothea couldn't imagine that woman being of any use at all. "Have her call me the instant she comes out. Please."

"Of course."

Dorothea punched the off button. Was there another grown up who would be more help? Her father, a New Haven judge, was never available during the day. And Ben's mother worked as a supervisor at the biggest Costco in Connecticut—he'd been told the only time he should call was if he was bleeding—a lot—or the house was on fire. She ticked off the neighbors in her mind. The old woman was too old and too deaf to help. And the mother could barely manage her own kids.

The new man, she thought. And she explained her idea to Ben. "We'll just run down the block, stay on the sidewalk and shout to him, ask if he saw anything funny."

"Maybe he memorized the license plate or something," Ben said. "If he was a criminal in his other life, he'd know what to look for."

They walked slowly up the block, watching the man soap his car and then squat down to wash the hubcaps. Up closer, he didn't look as scary as her parents made him sound. His hair was combed, and he wore a newish pink shirt tucked into ironed khaki shorts, and worn boat shoes like the ones her dad liked. That gave Dorothea the courage to call out to him from the curb.

"Excuse me?"

He stood up from the crouch he'd taken by the back left wheel, and walked over to the house to turn off the hose. Then he came down the length of his driveway. Both she and Ben shuffled a few steps away.

"Did you need something from me?" he asked, pushing his sunglasses onto his forehead. "I'm not much for cookies and I don't read magazines if that's what you're selling."

"We're not selling anything, sir," Ben said in a small voice. "We just wondered..."

"We wondered if you happened to notice the kidnapping at my house," said Dorothea. She pointed down the block. "We think my nanny was taken by two people in a blue car. And everything in her room has been torn apart." Her lip began to quiver and she bit it so she wouldn't cry.

"Like they were looking for something valuable," Ben added. "And they took her when they didn't come up with the goods."

Dorothea hoped the man wouldn't assume they were asking because he had experience with crime. Although truthfully, that would be a plus in this situation.

"Tell me more about the car," said the man. "What made you think she'd been kidnapped?"

"They each had a grip on one of her arms, Sir," Ben said, looking to Dorothea for confirmation. "And then they threw her in the back seat and drove away."

"Did you recognize the people you think kidnapped your friend?" The skin around his eyes crinkled into worried lines. "By the way my name is Lewis, not sir."

"She's not really my friend," said Dorothea, thinking of the beet juice and the creepy crawlies and getting that cold stomach pit thing again. "But we didn't recognize the bad guys."

Lewis wiped his soapy hands off on a clean rag that had been draped over his bucket. "Let's go take a look."

If there was one thing her parents would hate more than her going into this man's house, it was probably bringing him into theirs. But she couldn't think of how to tell him, and besides, she had a good feeling that he could help.

The three of them hurried up the block to Dorothea's house and Ben charged up the front steps.

"Wait!" barked Lewis. "Before you go rushing in somewhere, you have to think. What did you see? What can you picture in your mind's eye? What made you believe this woman was taken against her will?"

So they explained about Ben's treehouse, and ended up inviting Lewis to come with them so he could see for himself how they managed to spot the

Nanny Ruth situation. Dorothea sensed that Ben was a little down about inviting him into his lair – the only grown up who'd ever been inside was his dad. And he'd been gone for months and months.

Lewis squeezed through the hole in the floor and scrambled to his feet. "Nice pad, kid." He tousled Ben's hair. They showed him how they could see Dorothea's sidewalk if they stood near enough to the side opening, and exactly where the blue car had been. "Okay, I got the overview," said Lewis, "what came next?"

So they took him in the back door to Dorothea's kitchen where she explained that everything seemed to be in order. She even admitted that she had hidden the beet juice, hoping that it would start to smell and get the nanny in trouble. And as long as she'd gone that far, she figured she might as well admit to the creepy crawlies. She thought Lewis was trying not to laugh, but it could have been disapproval just as well.

"Did she leave any notes? Any messages?" he asked.

"I get it!" said Dorothea. "Sometimes a hostage leaves a message behind that only a certain person would understand."

Lewis nodded.

She rushed over to the refrigerator, where the family left messages for each other, and sure enough a note in Nanny Ruth's sloping handwriting was stuck to the surface with a Garfield the cat magnet.

Dear Dorothea, I know how you loathe beet juice and practicing longhand. So I hope today you will eat some cake when you are back from the bank, and play with Ben as long as you like. And just be grateful you're having a brother—sisters are not so nice.

"Oh my gosh," said Dorothea. "I can't believe she wrote this, even though it's in her handwriting. She would never ever tell me to eat cake. Or play with Ben as long as I liked."

"What about the bank?" asked Lewis.

"That makes no sense at all; I never go to the bank unless I'm dragged there with one of my parents."

"What about the sister/brother thing?"

Dorothea made a terrible scrunched-up face. "Mom's having a baby. But we've known all along it's a boy; they even have the dumb name picked out."

"So she was trying to tell you something," said Lewis. "Probably several things. Do you see the way the handwriting changes a little at the end of the note?"

Ben said, "It's like they were making her hurry or maybe she got scared."

"Good observation. Now let's go see her space," said Lewis.

The three of them looked over the nanny's bedroom again, with Lewis reminding them not to touch or move anything. "You said you were here before?" he asked Dorothea. "Did you notice anything missing?"

Dorothea shrugged. "First of all, it doesn't look like they took her jewelry. The box was dumped on the desk. But then it looks like costume jewelry, the kind of stuff my mom used to let me play with. If they thought there might something valuable, wouldn't they scrape it all into a suitcase or a pillowcase and take it away to sort through later?"

"Possibly." Lewis pointed at the drawer that still had a few pieces of underwear in it. "This is where you put the centipedes?"

Dorothea felt her face get hot and she nodded.

"Think back to when you delivered the bugs, was there anything unusual in the dresser? Anything besides the undies?"

After a few moments of serious thinking, Dorothea shrieked. "There was a little red cardboard envelope taped to the side of the drawer. Like the key my dad takes when he goes to the safe deposit box."

"Is it there now?" Lewis asked. "Remember, don't touch, just look."

Dorothea peered into the dark recesses of the bureau and finally shook her head.

"I bet Nanny Ruth was taken to the bank by those people, probably to empty her safety deposit box."

"Good guess," said Lewis. "We've done as much as we should by ourselves. You need to call your mother now, tell the secretary you must speak with her," he told Dorothea. "And I'll call the cops. For all we know, the bad guys could come back here for something else. And trust me, you don't want to be here if that happens."

Which made Dorothea intensely curious about Lewis's experience in the crime world. She double lifted her eyebrows at Ben to see if he was wondering the same thing. A tiny nod of his chin confirmed that he was.

"Should I mention you?" she asked Lewis.

"Let's see how it goes. If she asks, you tell the truth."

Lewis waited while Dorothea called her mother, this time insisting to the secretary that she be brought out of the meeting. Her mother sounded annoyed and flustered, and then more and more concerned as Dorothea told the story.

"What makes you think she was kidnapped?"

"First, we saw her get dragged off. Second and third, she left me a weird note on the refrigerator and her room has been tossed. And fourth, the safety deposit box key for her bank is not in her drawer."

Her mom paused for a moment of cold silence.

"Young lady, we will have a talk later about how you knew she had a key in her drawer. And your use of the word *tossed.* Right now I want you to go to a neighbor's house, you and Ben both. Whoever's home, I don't care which neighbor it is. Just text me when you're there." She hung up.

"That means you," Dorothea said to Lewis, who had clearly overheard the whole conversation.

"She won't be pleased," he said with a grin.

They trooped down the block to his house and sat on his front stoop while he fetched bottles of root beer and a bag of chips. Within minutes the sound of sirens split the air and two police cars screeched to a halt in front of Dorothea's house, followed shortly by both of Dorothea's parents.

ஓஓ

Later that night, after the cops caught the bad guys outside the bank, and Nanny Ruth was saved, she was invited to eat dinner at the family supper table. Ben and his mother had been included too, and even Lewis. The nanny looked a little pale, and nervous, and she flinched at any unusual noise. Like when Ben accidentally dropped his fork onto his plate of meatloaf and mashed potatoes.

"How did you know these people anyway?" her father asked. "And what was the business about brothers and sisters in your note?"

Nanny Ruth sighed deeply and dabbed her lips with a napkin. "The blonde woman is my half sister. She's been involved with robberies and drugs in the past. The way she'd been contacting me at my last job—I had a terrible feeling about what might happen. That's why I answered your ad. I thought it would be best to get away from her. And I rented a safe deposit box to keep my valuables in. I'm so sorry to get you all involved."

"It wasn't your fault," said Dorothea's mom.

While her father served big slabs of chocolate cake and scoops of ice cream, Dorothea asked her mother how she knew Lewis. Her mom looked at Lewis and nodded. "You tell her."

"I'm a detective. On vacation right now. Your mother doesn't care for me because…" He looked back at her and held out his hands.

"I shouldn't have been so hard on him and scared you into thinking he was a bad guy," said Dorothea's mom. "He's super good at what he does and that made me mad because he kept putting my clients in jail. I lost a lot of court cases because Detective Lewis was so good at noticing things. And relentless about pursuing an unanswered question." She took Dorothea's hand between the two of hers and smiled. "We're awfully glad you asked for his help."

When the cake and ice cream had been eaten, and the dishes stowed in the dishwasher, and the guests had gone home, Dorothea's mother propped her feet up in the television room and her father sat down to rub them. Nanny Ruth beckoned to Dorothea.

"I'd like to thank you personally for helping me today. Lord knows what would have happened if you two kids hadn't been so clever. Come with me."

Dorothea followed her down the hall and into her room. Everything was back in order, and the luggage had been stowed away. "I understand that you're too old for a nanny, and I've been a little too bossy. I had a little brother when I was your age too. And I want you to know he's my best friend these days. It's hard to picture now, but life will get better and you'll probably love him to pieces."

She smiled and pulled Dorothea into a tight hug. "Thank you. Now, I have something of yours that I think I should return." She opened the bottom drawer of her bureau and handed Dorothea a jar of horrible multi-legged centipedes, all flinging themselves against the glass, trying to get out.

Dorothea couldn't help it, she screamed. And then they both started to laugh.

Clinical psychologist **Lucy Burdette (aka Roberta Isleib)** has published 15 mysteries, including the Key West food critic series. Her 8th Key West mystery will be published in 2018 by Crooked Lane Books. She's been short-listed for Agatha, Anthony, and Macavity awards, and is a past president of Sisters in Crime. She lives in Madison CT and Key West FL. www.lucyburdette.com.

UGLY
by Chris Knopf

With all the caterwauling going on all night, you'd think you were in one of those circles of hell. A circle so bad, it didn't even get into the book. This was the biggest problem for me, a guy who liked the quiet and solitude of that hole under the railroad tracks they pulled me out of for purely bureaucratic reasons. The cops stuck me in the mental ward because the New Haven train station complained about me lurking around, and the do-gooders rejected me because I always ran away from their boring halfway houses, so here I am. In limbo, Virgil's hangout, though I've never seen him walking the halls.

My friend Harry was even more bitter about it than me, though it was in his nature to be negative and suspicious, which weighed on me, though sometimes he was the more sensible one.

And being invisible, he didn't have to endure the drugs. That's my other beef with mental hospitals: Drugs, drugs, drugs, morning, noon and night. The dirty little secret (not that little or secret) was the real purpose of this pill joy: to keep us all quiet and easy to get along with, neither of which always happened anyway, obviously given all the noise.

I'm not prone to boastfulness, but I did get good at holding those pills just beyond my epiglottis, so when I opened my mouth to prove I'd swallowed, I'd get the green light. Then I'd just hack up the pills and stick them in a hiding place after the pharmaceutical enforcers left the room.

If you think this is easy to do, just try it sometime.

Otherwise, I admit it was nice to have a soft bed, heat and food that didn't come from a dumpster, though it could taste better. Also a place to relieve yourself other than a patch of gnarly bushes that filled up faster than you'd think.

Life's full of trade-offs, Harry would tell me, and I had to agree. Though I'd trade all those amenities to be back in my house under the tracks. Homeless and deranged is a matter of perspective, which these jokers with all their authority didn't seem to understand.

I can talk as well as the next guy, but my approach to the situation was to keep my mouth shut. Once you utter a word, you end up in little rooms with nice people trying to communicate, which I really didn't want to do. The other advantage is your fellow patients usually leave you alone, since they have enough on their minds to bother with a guy who doesn't say a single thing.

You might wonder, what about human companionship? But I have Harry, even if he can sometimes be a lousy companion.

Needless to say, the prime directive from the day they put me in here was to get the hell out again. The problem was the shrinks, who had the power of God over us people forced there against our will.

You know about Catch-22. The shrinks will sign off on your release if they think you're being honest with them, but if you're honest and tell them you have a friend like Harry, that only I can see and talk to, they make you stay and fill you full of drugs. Makes no sense, but there you have it.

The noisiest character in the whole place lived next door. He was even shorter and skinnier than me, and had a lot of issues, but the important factor was Tourette Syndrome. This is the thing where people can't help shouting out things they really shouldn't. Curse words, insults and random nonsense that makes everybody uncomfortable. It was a crappy deal for Tourette, which everybody called him, but the main problem was one of the male nurses, a guy named Buck.

I think his name says it all. You can picture a burly son-of-a-bitch with a sweaty face and long, dark blond hair that never got enough brushing. The other nurses knew he acted like a dick, but liked that he could put down any of us patients should our animal spirits get the best of us. He always came fast and hard, and knew the restraining holds that were most effective, and legal. Not that he ever pulled that stuff on me. I'm not that stupid.

Every time Buck walked by Tourette's room, Tourette would yell "Ugly!" And sometimes "Knuckle dragger!" or "Peanut brain!" Since he never called anybody else those exact things, Buck took notice. He'd stop and stare into Tourette's room, but that was all he could do, since yelling crazy stuff was sort of the norm around here. But Harry and I both knew Buck was building up a serious dislike for Tourette, and wished like hell the little guy would knock it off.

Still, I liked Tourette. And so did Harry, which made all the difference. We played chess in my room. He was really good, and I mostly lost, but it was a nice way to spend the time. He was twitchy, and sometimes had an unprintable way of expressing himself, but he could also speak like a normal person, and didn't mind that I didn't speak back. I think Tourette liked me, too, since he often made me take back a move, and explain why it was a bad idea. Along the way, I learned he'd been president of the chess club at Yale, my alma mater that I left in my junior year due to flying creatures and an unadvisable tendency to talk to Harry when other people were within earshot.

This is why keeping my own counsel seemed the best course of action.

During one of our games, Buck poked his head in my room and Tourette yelled "Spit bucket!" I so wished he hadn't done that, and I was right, because the next time Buck came in the room, closed the door behind him, and grabbed Tourette by the throat. His hand was so much bigger than Tourette's neck, it fit all the way around. He shook Tourette like you'd imagine a dog with a rat. I thought Tourette was a goner, but his eyes stayed open, and he just stared at Buck, no fear, just this blank look.

"Keep it up, dude," Buck said. "Next time we're minus one whacko."

Buck looked at me as if to say we'd be minus two whackos if I said anything, and since I said nothing and just nodded, he knew I understood.

Buck left, but before he was through the door, Tourette yelled "Ugly," loud enough to hear down the hall. Buck stopped for a second, but then kept going and I was able to breathe again.

This is how it stood for a couple weeks. Tourette and I played chess and he never failed to say things around Buck that Harry and I knew were only leading to trouble. I thought Buck had made peace with the whole thing, since he'd look in on us, listen to Tourette, then just move on. Until one night, when he took the trouble to walk into the room and toss the chessboard into the air. This was disappointing, since I was about to put Tourette in check. Though all was saved when Tourette put the board back on the table and returned our pieces to their original positions, as far as I knew. I went on to checkmate him, so I guess he got it right.

But unfortunately, things went down hill from there. The more Buck took issue with Tourette's comments, the worse they got. Not just referring to the man's appearance, but anatomical things and speculations on his sexuality. And I wasn't the only one to hear this. I'd catch the other nurses hiding smiles, and exchanging knowing looks with each other. And some of the other patients would repeat what Tourette said, though only when Buck was way down the hall.

One night, really late, I heard noises coming from Tourette's room. They were muffled, but enough to wake me up, since I'm a light sleeper. Actually, I think it was Harry who noticed first, coming to me in a dream and telling me something bad was going on.

But then it stopped, and even though I listened hard, I heard nothing but the old man four doors down who snored louder than a lawn mower with a bad carburetor. So Harry apologized and we both went back to sleep.

The next morning, I stopped at Tourette's room on the way to the showers, like I usually did, and he didn't answer my knock on the door. So I knocked harder, and nothing. A nurse was coming down the hall, so I grabbed her and pointed at his room, doing this stupid mime act to make her take a look.

She used her key to get in and there was Tourette, hanging by a torn piece of bedsheet jammed with a knot behind the top of his closet door.

This caused a big stir for a few days among the patients who had a firm enough grip on reality to appreciate what had happened. Official-looking people in suits and ties came and went, and spent a lot of time in Tourette's room with the hospital big shots talking to each other in voices too low to make out the words.

None of the shrinks or nurses said anything to me, so I didn't know what they thought about it. Since I didn't talk, none of the patients tried to share their opinion, but I did get a lot of funny looks, mostly kind and dismayed.

I missed those chess games. I don't know what happened to Tourette's chess set, since they cleared out his room right after it happened. There was another box of pieces in the recreation room, which I got all set up, and sat staring down at the board, but nobody took the bait.

After a week of this, me and Harry got so bored we started getting on each other's nerves. So at his suggestion, I made myself figure out what else I could do. This was hard, since I was stuck in a mental hospital, and there was only so much they offered in the way of suitable activities. I had no artistic talent, so painting and messing around with modeling clay was out. I liked music, but couldn't play anything, and you can't go around singing if you never talk. I tried the library, but the Dewey Decimal system confused and terrified me, and the atmosphere felt too much like college, where I'd first encountered primordial creatures emerging from difficult textbooks.

Then Harry reminded me I'd been a biology major, and was particularly good in the lab, manipulating organic material and mixing up precisely-measured concoctions. In the recreation room there was a sign-up sheet for vocational training, which could also be a ticket out of this place, since it made it easier to dump people like me back on the street. One option was food prep in the hospital kitchen. My heart soared and Harry gave me a high five.

This became my happiest time in that place. I fit in like I'd trained for this my whole life. The kitchen people would just give me an assignment, like chopping up salad fixings, or scrambling dozens of eggs in a big pan, talking to me in loud voices as if I was deaf, and stupid, but they meant well. And the better I did, the less they bothered with me, assuming I'd get the job done.

One of the big events at the hospital was Employee Appreciation Night. The idea was the management, medical staff and administrative people would get dressed up, and the kitchen would go all out on a big fancy meal. A real banquet. Topflight ingredients, four courses and table service, speeches by the big shots and a string quartet from Yale to offset the decorations made by the patients' art classes, which otherwise would have spoiled the mood.

When you don't speak it's hard to communicate, but I got across that I wanted to be part of the team making dessert, the fun part: cream-filled tarts.

The hardest thing about that job was not eating all my work product, but I was so busy and excited by the process I burned off the excess sugar.

When it came time to bring out our creations, the night was coming to an end and the wait staff, comprised mostly of mental patients, was beginning to falter. Since the kitchen people were either exhausted themselves, or recruited into cleanup duty, a lot of us were standing around, resting or socializing, depending on individual capabilities. The head chef asked for volunteers to help serve the last of the desserts and fill coffee cups.

I was still plenty jazzed up, so I raised my hand, and soon had a big tray full of tarts to bring out to the gathering. Though inexperienced at this, I think I did okay loading up a manageable tray, both enticing and well-balanced, so I wouldn't drop the thing into somebody's lap.

It was dazzling to see all the people at big round tables, talking and laughing, and listening to the string quartet, now joined by our hospital band, which wasn't bad if you got past the piano player who had his face nearly resting on the keys.

The chef hadn't given me much in the way of direction, so I was free to find tables awaiting the privilege of dessert. I took my time searching around, since I had an objective of my own. And sure enough, there was a table filled with people I knew – shrinks, maintenance guys and nurses, including Buck.

Each one of them got a fruit-topped tart that I'd made myself, and it was gratifying to watch them dig in and clear their plates. It looked like we'd done our job at this point, so I just hung around the kitchen door and watched all the fun.

This is why I was there when Buck stood up suddenly, grabbed at his throat, and fell over. The people at his table just looked at him writhing around for a moment, which I found amusing, since handling emergencies was supposed to be part of their jobs. Maybe it was the context.

But it wasn't long before there were shrinks and nurses all over him, tearing open his jacket and shirt, and thumping on his chest. He made it harder for them by flopping up and down, but this is what happens when there's a seizure involved. People in that part of the room started to notice, but the band kept playing, oblivious.

I went back into the kitchen to help with the cleanup, so I didn't see the whole thing, though I heard the next day that Buck didn't make it, having overdosed on the psychotropic drugs that flowed freely through the hospital.

I hoped the big shots took notice, since those things are really dangerous if mixed together and taken in large quantities, and almost tasteless if stirred into the cream filling of a tasty tart.

"Ugly," said Harry, and I didn't argue.

Chris Knopf's "Kill Switch," included in *Rogue Wave: Best New England Crime Stories,* was short-listed for the 2016 Derringer Award. "A Little Cariñoso" appeared in the April 2017 edition of *Alfred Hitchcock's Mystery Magazine.* "Crossing Harry" is included in Akashic's *New Haven Noir,* released August 2017. *Tango Down,* eighth in Knopf's Sam Acquillo Hamptons Mystery Series, will be released in December 2017.

MAINE

ON A WINTER'S NIGHT
by Christine Bagley

Cassie walks down the hill from her attic apartment heading toward *The Wharf* where she bartends nights. Icicles, like crystal daggers, hang from the eaves of former sea captains' homes along the waterfront. She wonders if they drop, at just the right moment, would they actually kill someone—someone like Jimmy Glover? Her face burns with rage and the strong winds of a bone cold winter.

Cassie never liked Jimmy Glover, not his hundred-dollar haircut or his thousand-dollar suits. She despised the way he snapped his fingers at her when he wanted a drink. Three quick snaps that said, "Let's go baby." Cassie would start washing glasses or check on another customer just to tick him off.

Last night, Chester Joyce, a lawyer from Boston and an old friend of Cassie's father, came into the bar and told her there would be no charges against Jimmy Glover.

She'd pounded the bar and whispered angrily, "But I've seen her bruises. The week before she died, she was using a popsicle stick for a splint on her ring finger. Said she jammed it in the basement door. Jimmy Glover is a cokehead and he treated her like a dog. Ask anyone in town if he didn't smack his wife around when he was jacked up."

"I know Glover's history, Cassie. But Francesca never filed a complaint or restraining order against him. The DA said there was no physical evidence, no witnesses, and no murder weapon that pointed to anything other than an accidental fall."

"So he walks?"

"Yes."

Cassie shook her head and said, "No friggin' way."

As she nears *The Wharf*, Cassie hears the seagulls screeching, and wishes she were one of them so she could scream as freely. She thinks about Francesca's last moments, if she'd known she was going to die, if she'd tried to fight back. Cassie knows in her gut that Jimmy pushed her down the staircase of their mansion on Seaview Lane. Cassie wipes a rogue tear from her cheek as her grief spills over.

The streetlights are just coming on, and the town is bathed in pink and orange hues. Dusk is Cassie's favorite time of day, and she tries never to miss standing at a window, or being outside at sunset. The French call it *entre le chien le loup*—between the dog and the wolf.

Francesca's death has evoked all the other losses in Cassie's life; a mother whose death she was too young to mourn, and a father, shot in the line of duty when she was nineteen.

Her boots crunch on the snow and it reminds her of someone munching on a cookie with their mouth closed. Her steps are quick and determined, and her hands are balled up in fists inside her mittens.

Francesca Paredes was the best friend she'd ever had, the one who filled all the gaps in her life, and knew her better than anyone. Knew that obtaining a graduate degree in art was the most important thing in Cassie's life, and that she'd lost her virginity at fifteen, to a guy ten years older, in the back seat of a Honda Civic at East Harbor Lighthouse. Francesca's mother couldn't speak English and called Cassie, *caro*, made her *caldo verde* soup with chunks of sausage, kale, and potatoes because she thought Cassie was too thin. The last time she'd seen Marta Paredes, it was she who was too thin and Cassie's heart broke.

ooo

Halfway down the hill, Cassie can smell the fish that permeate the docks. She thinks of how different her and Francesca had been both physically, and in their attitudes. Franny had been tall, dark, and graceful, and she had looked at the world with a "people are basically good" philosophy. Cassie is short, strong, and mouthy, with the motto "Like everyone, but trust no one."

Opening the heavy wooden door to *The Wharf,* Cassie is hit with the aroma of fried haddock, boiling lobsters, and freshly-made chowder. Dan, the owner, is filling paper cups with coleslaw and looks up when she walks in.

"How were classes today?" he asks. Cassie attends Mass School of Art in Boston where she is studying for a Masters in Teaching and Art Education.

"Okay," she says, hanging her coat on the hook. She removes her beanie and shakes out her short blonde hair. When Cassie smiles, she can light up a room with her green eyes and playful demeanor. But since Francesca's death, she's been sullen and her eyes look empty, as if they're out of order.

"You doin' okay, Cassie?"

She shrugs.

"You know, they say what goes around comes around, ever hear that?"

"Sure." Cassie ties on a navy blue apron with the words *The Wharf* written in white across the front. She grabs a pack of paper cups and takes out a giant tub of tartar sauce from the fridge.

"The whole town feels bad about it, Cass. I don't think he'll show his face for a long time."

"Paul will be happy," she says flatly. Paul has been waiting tables at *The Wharf* for years and is openly gay.

"What do you mean?"

"Jimmy used to call him Paula in front of everyone. I saw him elbow Paul in the jaw one night when he was putting his coat on. Said he was sorry while he smiled right in Paul's face."

Dan's face turns red.

"Guy's a monster," she says, setting the tub of tartar sauce down with a bang.

ooo

The cousins sit on a bench at Fort Cushing, overlooking East Harbor. Eve, the taller one, wears a long black coat, a black beret pulled down across her forehead, and her silver hair trails in the east wind. Beside her sits Ellie, a flashy redhead with wavy hair parted on the side reminiscent of Rita Hayworth. Eve and Ellie walk around town with an air of wonder, as if they're high on life. Everyone in town knows the cousins and makes up stories about them. Some say they're not cousins at all, and that they're stoners because they're too happy for a couple of old Yankees. Retired, both women live in a condo on the first floor of the McAdams Mansion.

"I don't know Eve, that's a little dicey even for me."

"Ellie. It isn't like we're goody-two-shoes. Come on, remember the boat?"

"How could I forget? We stole it while Tommy Hatch was in Europe and drove it out to Misery Island." Ellie pauses. "Why didn't we just ask Tommy if we could borrow it?"

"What fun would that have been?" asks Eve. "It's always about the drama for us."

The wind picks up and Eve removes a strand of hair from her eye with a gloved finger.

"We never got caught, did we? Pulled that little boat back into the harbor that same night and no one was the wiser. Even refilled the gas tank. Just saying."

"Just saying *what*," says Ellie, turning to look at Eve.

"We're up to it."

"But you're talking about a whole other level – way beyond petty theft."

"That's right. We're not getting any younger, Ellie. All the work we do at the Abuse Center doesn't mean a hill of beans if we can't stop the abuse."

"I don't know, Eve." Ellie shakes her head and takes a deep breath. She watches as a small lobster boat putters into the harbor. "Can't we just add some nasty stuff to your scones and make him really sick?"

"It's not enough for what he did."

"Let's walk," Ellie says, pulling up the collar of her red peacoat. She loops an arm through Eve's when they pause at the wood railing and look down at the sudsy foam of the ocean sloshing over the rocks.

After a while Ellie inhales the cold salt air and lets it out slowly. "I don't like it Eve," she says, "It's way too risky, and I don't see how just the two of us can pull it off. We're not exactly nimble anymore."

"We'll just have to find a way. I cannot, in good conscience, let this go, Ellie."

"Well then, God help us both," says Ellie, with a grim face.

ɷɷɷ

Pete the Lobsterman is hauling a crate of lobsters into the back of his gray pickup, which is covered in salt, dings, and scrapes, as if he drives blind in a rubber truck. He is a small man with sturdy legs and a face like an old leather pocketbook. But his eyes are knowing, electric blue with a mischievous twinkle for the right person.

"Well if it ain't the Gold Dust Twins," he says to Eve and Ellie as they approach.

Eve smiles. "How's the catch today?"

"Pretty good for an old man with old traps," says Pete, hauling the last crate onto his truck. He looks over at Ellie and says, "How ya doin' Irish? Need any lobster for your bisque?"

"I'm well, Pete, and thanks I've still got some from the last time. How are you?"

"Oh much better now," he says, and there it is, that special twinkle.

"Did you hear they're not going to prosecute Jimmy Glover?" Eve asks.

"Ya, I heard. That kid's a bad seed," says Pete shaking his head and leaning against the truck. "I remember when that little weasel threw my son off his boat at Brown's Island. Left him there for two days. If it wasn't for Buddy Larsen who saw him waving and picked him up, who knows how long he would have been marooned. It was Buddy who told me about it. I wanted to deep-six the guy," says Pete. "But I don't have the nerve."

Eve looks up at the sky like she's checking for snow, and Ellie bends down, pretending to tie her shoelace.

ଡଡଡ

On the way home from work that night, Cassie passes the cousins' place where Francesca sought refuge when Jimmy was out of his head. She would never go to Cassie's apartment or her mother's because that's where he'd look first. Cassie knows the cousins are involved with the Women's Domestic Abuse Center in Lynn, and that they had encouraged Franny to get a restraining order. They even talked with their social workers and lawyer friends for advice, and the bottom line had always been, "Leave him." But Franny kept thinking he'd change.

She'd tried to defend him by blaming the pressures of his job as a stockbroker in his father's firm, and the expectations of being the only son of the oldest family in East Harbor, whose surname is still engraved on park benches, monuments, and bronze plaques at Hendley Hall.

Cassie mounts the stairs to her attic apartment, which is one enormous room with three windows at each end. Her artwork covers her wall space, and her drawings and sketches are scattered everywhere.

Her books are stacked against the wall like a game of *Jenga,* since two bookcases are not enough to house them all. Every night, no matter how late, Cassie reads a short story before bed. Tonight, she is reading Poe's, *The Cask of Amontillado,* and afterward she stares at the exposed beams of her ceiling. She hears the tower clock at Hendley Hall toll twice, and she reflects on Montreso and revenge.

ꝏꝏ

John Roddick dated Francesca Paredes for three years before Jimmy Glover came on the scene, loved her in a way he hadn't loved since. John knew that Jimmy had swept her off her feet just to prove he could, that, and to spite his overbearing parents. The Glovers had expected a well-educated, snowy white debutante for a daughter-in-law, like Vanessa Pedrick, rather than a poor, high school graduate who worked in retail.

John had known Francesca was in trouble soon after Jimmy and Francesca had married. He'd tried to intervene, calling her cell to see if she needed help or money to get away from him. The last time John had seen Francesca, Jimmy had dug his nails into her arm at a party because she was talking to him.

"Hey Jimmy. Take it easy, man we're just talking."

"Ya? Well don't get any ideas, Roddick, you lost, remember?"

"Screw you, Glover."

"Screw *me*?"

John should have seen it coming. He should have realized Jimmy was using, and looking for a fight. When Jimmy put his fists up to his ears and started dancing on his feet, John remembered he'd been on the Harvard boxing team. Before he knew it, three quick jabs landed on his jaw and then the knockout punch. When he came to, Jimmy and Francesca had left. In his heart, he'd known she was doomed, that sooner or later Jimmy would cross the line. He just didn't know what to do about it.

John rises from the couch to take a hot shower, the first in over a week. He hadn't opened his frame shop downstairs since Francesca's death, hadn't even answered his phone. He is unshaven and smells like a brewery. Guilt and regret fill his head and have crippled his thinking. It is time to come out of his haze, because if he doesn't, he will go insane. A half hour later, he picks up his cell and punches in a number.

"Hey Dan. It's John Roddick. Is Cassie there?"

ꝏꝏ

A few days later, Cassie meets John for coffee at *The Wren*, where they have the best homemade donuts around. His eyes are bloodshot and she can smell alcohol seeping from his pores. But he is still that rugged looking guy with soulful brown eyes and slender fingers, who played the slow version of the *Rocky* theme for her, on the piano in the high school auditorium.

"I've been trying to call you," she says, licking donut powder from her fingers. It is the first time in weeks that she's eaten breakfast. "I even knocked on your door the other day."

John wastes no time. "I heard he hasn't left the house since it happened."

"I know. I went by and all the shades were down. His Beamer was in the driveway still covered in snow from the blizzard the day of Franny's funeral. I wanted to throw a snowball with a rock in it through his window."

"I'd like to do more than that."

"Meaning?"

John leans in and looks at Cassie, his eyes moving back and forth as if trying to see into her mind.

"In the biblical sense?"

Cassie questions him with her eyes.

"An eye for an eye."

She nods. "We're on the same page then."

They are sitting in a far corner of the coffee shop, and he looks around to make sure no one can hear them.

"Bear with me 'cause I'm just tossing around ideas right now. But what if we could get him in my boat and drown him out by Egg Rock," he says.

"I was thinking of something like that, but won't his body eventually wash ashore?"

"Maybe, maybe not. Who cares? There's a hundred people in East Harbor who'd like to see Jimmy Glover dead. You think anyone's gonna care?"

"His parents will. They'd never let it go."

Cassie stares into her coffee. John looks out the window.

"I think if we make it look like a suicide, it'll be more believable," says Cassie in a low voice. "Remember their wedding at Castle Rock?"

"Yep," he says, frowning.

"Well, it would make sense that he killed himself where they got married then everyone will think he had remorse and couldn't live with himself. There'll be less questions that way."

"How?"

"We'd need to get into his house, have someone he wouldn't suspect would hurt him open the door for us. Like the cousins."

"The cousins?"

"Franny used to run to them whenever Jimmy was out of his head."

"Really?" John looks surprised maybe even hurt that Francesca hadn't run to him. "Okay, then what?"

It was like Cassie was working from one of her sketches, carefully penciling in the details. "Maybe the cousins could bring Jimmy some of Eve's homemade scones as a gesture of sympathy. When he opens the door, you're behind them and barge in, deck Jimmy, and we put him in the back of his car."

"And the cousins will go along with this?"

"I won't know until I ask. I've got a small painting I did of Francesca and I was thinking of bringing it over anyway."

John gazes out the window and says softly, "You have any more of those?"

"Of course."

John's heartache is palpable, and Cassie wonders why the hell Franny hadn't married *him*? Why hadn't she trusted Cassie that Jimmy was an animal?

He clears his throat. "So we've got Jimmy in the car. And then?"

"We drive him up to Castle Rock and shove him off the cliffs. It's like a 50-foot drop and the water's no more than 35 degrees this time of year. If the fall doesn't kill him the cold water will."

John leans back in his chair. "And if the cousins agree, they could be waiting in their car to drive us home."

"You got it."

"What if he wakes up before we shove him over?"

"Then we knock him out again. I'll bring my heavy-duty Maglite just in case."

ϱϱϱ

On her way to work that night Cassie stops in at the cousin's house. There is no sunset to speak of only a silver sliver in the west. But she still pauses and gazes at the illumination, as if it is an entryway to the other side. Can Franny see her? Does she know what she is about to do?

"Come in, Cassie," says Eve. "We've been thinking about you."

The cousins' condo is French cottage charming, with antiques and deep cushioned sofas, gold-framed oils of flowers and stonewalls, and an over-abundance of designer throw pillows. They have a spectacular view of the harbor, empty now except for a few buoys and fishing boats. The smell of Eve's scones adds to the homey feeling and Cassie understands why Franny sought safe haven here.

"Sit down, dear. I've just made some fresh cranberry scones and Italian roast coffee," says Eve.

"Thanks." Cassie hands her the wrapped five by seven oil on panel she'd done of Francesca. It had taken her hours to prime the wood, but the glazing technique she'd used had made Francesca's face look even more lovely than it had been in real life. Ellie enters the kitchen wearing a silk-flowered robe, and black leggings with red flip-flops. She gives Cassie a warm hug.

"Ellie, Cassie brought us a present."

When Eve unwraps the framed painting both women gasp. Francesca is looking over her left shoulder, black eyes staring straight at the onlooker with full red lips and a vibrant smile. Cassie painted her long dark hair in shades of black and charcoal to add more dimension.

"Cassie. This is stunning, and such a remarkable likeness," says Eve.

"Thanks."

"Are you still going to art school?" she asks.

Cassie nods.

"Francesca told us how talented you are, didn't she Ellie?"

"All the time," says Ellie still looking at the picture. Shaking her head, she says, "She was *so* beautiful."

The three women sit at the round pedestal table in the dining room, sipping coffee and nibbling scones. The cousins keep looking at Francesca's picture, which Eve had propped on the table. When Cassie works up enough courage she says, "I need to talk to you about something."

"Don't look so scared, Cassie," says Ellie, "It's only me and Eve, honey."

"I know but this is really serious."

"Oh, just spit it out dear," Eve says, pushing a cranberry back in her mouth.

"It's about retribution."

Ellie nods. "Jimmy Glover?"

"Yes. Are you interested?"

"As a matter of fact we are," says Eve, looking at Ellie.

Cassie feels her body uncoil and her heartbeat slow down.

"How far are you willing to go?" asks Eve.

"All the way. And there's someone else who's in on this."

"Oh? Who?" asks Ellie.

"John Roddick."

"Of course," says Eve.

"Do you have a plan?" Ellie asks.

"We do, but we really need the two of you."

When Cassie finishes explaining the plan, Eve and Ellie agree to visit Jimmy Glover, scones in hand, and drive the getaway car. All they want to know is when.

Three days later, in the middle of a Nor'easter, Cassie Allen, John Roddick, and the cousins leave their homes to carry out the murder of Jimmy Glover.

ꝏꝏ

The first part of the plan goes well. It is ten thirty on a Tuesday night and the snow is coming down hard and fast. John and Cassie are crouched down in the back seat of the cousins' big gray Buick. They drive slowly through East Harbor, as the windshield wipers work furiously to keep the glass cleared. They pull into the driveway and park the car at the side entrance of Jimmy's sprawling colonial. John and Cassie get out and hide behind his Beamer, which is covered in snow and looks like an igloo. They watch as Eve and Ellie ring the bell.

Cassie pulls out her Maglite and hands it to John. "Just in case," she says.

When Jimmy opens the door, he looks like death reheated. He is wearing a hooded Harvard sweatshirt, hands in the pouch, and the dark circles under his eyes remind Cassie of *The Walking Dead.*

Jimmy lets the cousins in and as he starts to close the door, John creeps up the stairs and barges inside. With one vicious, pent-up-anger punch, he knocks Jimmy down—but not out. Jimmy gets up and swings at John but he is drunk and misses. John takes the Maglite from his jacket pocket and swings it hard at Jimmy's head. Jimmy slumps to the floor and doesn't move again.

Meanwhile, Cassie is feverishly scraping snow off Jimmy's car. But the snow is hard underneath and does not come off easily. Cassie's heart is pounding, knowing that the success of their mission depends on Jimmy being in the water by midnight, at high tide.

The cousins find Jimmy's car keys on the kitchen counter and follow John, who hoists Jimmy over his shoulder.

"Wait a minute," says Eve. "If we're going to make it look like a suicide, he'll need a coat."

John lowers Jimmy to the floor and the three of them manage to get a coat from the front hall closet and put it on Jimmy. John pauses to look at the staircase where Francesca died.

Ellie is the last one to leave and wipes the wet snow from the floor. All of them are wearing gloves so there will be no fingerprints. But she forgets the scones and has to go back in the house and then wipe the floor again.

John has laid Jimmy's body in the back seat of the car then gets in the front seat and turns on the heater to help melt the snow. Cassie is still in a panic, scraping the windows from two storms' worth of snow. John drums his fingers on the steering wheel. "Should have brought another scraper," he says angrily. Finally, he yells out the window, "Cassie! Forget it! Let's go!"

Cassie gives it a few more scrapes then jumps in the front of Jimmy's car beside John while the cousins follow in their Buick. Few people are out on the roads and those who are, could barely see who's driving. For that, they are greatly relieved.

On the way to Castle Rock, Cassie keeps turning in her seat to see if Jimmy is still out. "You clocked him good, John, he looks like he's dead already."

Jimmy's head is facing Cassie and his mouth is hanging open. His normally perfect hair is in greasy cowlicks and his sweatpants smell like whiskey and urine. He looks vulnerable, lacking the air of superiority he normally carries around. His appearance makes Cassie uncomfortable because she almost feels sorry for him.

She looks outside as they cross the causeway to the tip of East Harbor's peninsula. It is nearly a whiteout and John has the high beams on. Under the light of the postern lanterns, Cassie can see the snow coming down sideways. The cousins are close behind, their two bright headlights like stalking FBI agents in a gangster movie.

The closer they get to Castle Rock, the more Cassie's stomach feels like her intestines are seizing up. Her teeth chatter, but it is not from the cold. She looks at Jimmy again and thinks she sees him move.

When they make it to the entrance of Castle Rock, the cousins remain in their car with the engine running. John and Cassie pull Jimmy from the car, and lug his dead weight between them toward the edge of the cliff. A blurred moon slips behind a cloud as though unable to witness the execution.

Cassie is watching John, who is breathing heavily.

As they near the precipice, Cassie peers down and sees the waves crashing into the rocks in a spiral spray. Jimmy's head is hanging on his chest while they support him under the arms, and Cassie hears him mumbling. But the wrath and fury Cassie has been harboring since Francesca's death, is slowly being replaced by alarm as the realization of what they are about to do strikes her full in the face. And then she feels Jimmy start to straighten up.

"Are you ready?" John yells, his voice sounding miles away.

Suddenly, Cassie lets go of Jimmy and, when she does, Jimmy turns and gives her a backhander that knocks her to the ground. She rolls away, thinking of Francesca tumbling down the stairs and scrambles to her feet. Through the swirling snow she screams, "Is that what you did to Francesca, Jimmy? Is that how you killed her?"

"Shut up you dumb bitch," he shouts, staggering towards her.

Cassie sees John moving behind Jimmy's left shoulder, as Jimmy wobbles. And that's when John rams him from the side. But instead of stopping short at the edge, Jimmy holds on to John and they both plunge over the cliff.

"No! Oh God, no!" Cassie falls to her knees and crawls to the brink of the crag. The moon emerges as she looks down into the abyss of the swirling Atlantic. Jimmy's body is gone, and she wonders if he's been pulled straight to hell. John is splayed across a rock, half-in and half-out of the water, eyes wide open.

ععع

Cassie wakes up the next morning wrapped in a thick quilt on the couch at the cousin's condo. They'd heard her screams and found her sobbing face down on the edge of the cliff. Over two feet of snow fell that night, enough to cover their tracks and Jimmy's car, which the police found the next day.

ععع

The cousins grew frail very quickly after that night. In the spring, Eve developed pneumonia and had to be hospitalized. Ellie took a bad fall and broke her hip. Within a year they moved into an assisted living facility in Swampscott. Eve no longer cooks her scones and has lost her thirst for adventure of any kind. Cassie visits them now and then, and they sit together in the common room hardly talking. What is there to say?

Cassie left East Harbor after she graduated from art school, and splits her time between teaching and volunteer work at the Women's Domestic Abuse Center. Two easels stand by the window in her new apartment in Marblehead, and hold watercolors of John Roddick on his boat, and the cousins sitting on the bench at Fort Cushing. An unfinished night scene of a snowstorm on Castle Rock, sits on another drawing board.

John Roddick's body washed up on Dexter Beach two days after that night, but Jimmy Glover's body has never been found. There have been times when Cassie swears she's seen Jimmy walking by the seawall that connects East

Harbor to Marblehead. He is wearing a cashmere coat, collar up, with his hands in his pockets. Her stomach churns, and she starts to shake until she realizes it's not him.

One day, she was sitting at the bar at *The Wharf* visiting Dan when she thought she saw Jimmy coming through the door. She was so stunned she knocked her beer over.

But the worst part is the dreams—when she is startled awake by a knock on her door, and Jimmy is standing there and says, "Hello Cassie—remember me?"

Christine Bagley holds an MFA in Creative Writing from Lesley University in Cambridge. Since 2011, she has been teaching writing to foreign national physicians and scientists at the Schepens Eye Research Institute-Massachusetts Eye and Ear, affiliates of Harvard Medical School. She is the former editor of the *Medical Services Review* for Massachusetts General Hospital, and Eye Contact for the Schepens Eye Research Institute. She was also a fiction contributor at the 2016 Bread Loaf Writers Conference in Middlebury, Vermont. Bagley is the author of four published short stories: "The Elevator," "The Madness of Ida Mae," "The Burren," and most recently, "On a Winter's Night."

TO-DO LIST
by Bruce Robert Coffin

Perfect Harmony is a quaint little home for the aged, nestled in the hills of Western Maine in the town of Farmington. Formerly owned by a wealthy family that had fallen on tough times, the Victorian with the Mansard roof is the only thing remaining of what was once a thousand acre property. The immaculate building, painted an inviting shade of yellow with white trim, was built in amongst a grove of hardwoods, mostly maple and oak. At this time of year, the red and gold leaves are so brilliant that anyone coming up the drive might mistakenly think the old girl was on fire.

None of the twenty-one residents of Perfect Harmony, twenty-two before Mary Keating drowned last month, actually hail from Farmington. Most aren't even from Maine. We were all placed here by relatives no longer wanting to care for the elderly and deteriorating patriarch or matriarch of the family. It's been three years, six months and twenty-four days since my own kin deposited me here, not that I'm keeping track. They dumped me in the middle of nowhere to live out my days without so much as a by-your-leave. Oh, I still get the obligatory bi-monthly visits from two of my three daughters but most times the grandchildren can't be bothered to come, which of course means that I don't get to see my great grand-babies either. Unless pictures on a cell phone count. In my book, they don't.

Harmony is located about as far from civilization as a place can be. The population of Farmington is about 4200 people and at fifty-six square miles that averages out to seventy-five people per square mile. If Farmington truly is in the middle of nowhere then Harmony is ten miles farther than that. By my calculations, it would likely take me two days to reach the town proper if I set out on foot, attempting to make a break for it. Even so, I have thought about it.

Please don't think of me as a complainer, au contraire, I'm far from it. The rest home is actually quite nice. The building is beautiful and spotless, the grounds are neatly manicured and most of the staff are cheerful and kind. Most, but not all. There's one member of the staff who is the sole origin of our misery. Terry Moscone, or Terry the Tyrant as he's known to us, is Satan reincarnate. I'm convinced of it. He need only sprout horns and a tail to complete the imagery. More akin to a fire plug than a real man, he's short and stout with a cheesy little rat stash, the Lilliputian version of Hitler. Terry's what Jerry Seinfeld might describe as a close talker. I'm not sure which is worse his annoyingly squeaky voice or his putrid breath. He's either misplaced his toothbrush for the past decade or he fancies a nice shit sandwich.

Terry the Tyrant is a sadist. How can I say this so matter-of-factly? Because it's a God-given fact. There are no two ways about it. The little bastard enjoys inflicting pain and he's good at it. He's been terrorizing the residents at Harmony since I've been in residence and, if the stories are true, a great deal longer than that. Terry is one of two night-duty nurses. Both nurses work four twelve-hour shifts a week, covering three shifts by themselves and one overlap on Wednesdays. Meaning that for three nights every week, Sunday through Tuesday, he has the run of the place, controlling everything and everyone. Terry the Tyrant owns us. And he never lets us forget it.

Every other week or so one of Harmony's residents suffer some kind of accident. I imagine the occasional legitimate sprains or broken bones do happen in other facilities where the elderly are housed, but at Harmony it's usually the fault of the Tyrant. I mentioned Mary Keating because she was my best friend. Mary lived on the second floor in the room next to mine. She drowned in the tub one Sunday night while we were alone with Terry. I never saw or heard anything but I know what happened just the same.

We've all fallen victim to Terry's temper tantrums at some point. When he gets mad he becomes cruel, breaking sentimental items, stealing money, or eating our food, mostly the desserts. Terry loves desserts. But he derives his greatest pleasure from hurting us. Mary confided in me once that Terry had forced himself on her. She'd gotten so upset when I suggested that she break the silence and report him that she never spoke of it again.

By now you're probably wondering why none of us have complained to the staff or to our families. I can only speak for myself, but frankly, I'm terrified. Not about what he'd do to me but about what he might do to one of the others. That's the most twisted and evil thing about Terry the Tyrant, he doesn't hurt which-ever resident he's mad at, he'll hurt another, then make sure we both know why it happened. If I told anyone what Terry's been up to I might just lose another friend to a drowning accident, or a fall down the stairs. I simply can't risk it.

Dick Jameson is a retired veterinarian who lives directly across the hall from me. Tall and lanky, he's in pretty good shape for a man in his late seventies. He's always reminded me of the actor Don Ameche, even has that same mischievous glint in his eyes. Dick is kinda sweet on me. He calls me his Susie Sunshine. Nothing has ever happened between us, it's against house rules anyway, but we're both widowed and I have to admit I sort of enjoy the attention. Always the gentleman, Dick opens doors for me and pulls out my chair at the dinner table. Now that Mary’s gone, he is my closest friend. We can talk about anything.

One night last week Dick and I were working on a puzzle in the upstairs lounge with several other residents of Harmony, among them were June and Al Paulson. June and Al aren't related they just happen to share the same last name. June is a wheelchair-bound retired school teacher. Al was a career military man, former prisoner of war in Vietnam, or as he calls it, the Nam. Mercifully, it was one of Terry's nights off and Nurse Wendy was working. Wendy's a peach, always smiling and joking with us. I'd guesstimate her to be late fifties, about the same age as my eldest daughter. The four of us were discussing how lucky we were to have Nurse Wendy as a caregiver when the topic of Terry reared its ugly head. Al told us that he'd experienced the same physical and psychological torture that Terry inflicts on us while in a POW camp. I have to admit the stories he shared sounded all too familiar. As I was listening to him, I looked at the others. They weren't watching Al, they were staring at me. It suddenly dawned on me that this conversation was for my benefit. The others had already discussed whatever this was about.

I turned toward Dick. "Why are you telling me this? What's this all about?"

"Well, I guess it's sort of an intervention," he said.

"Intervention? I'm not an alcoholic or anything."

June spoke up. "We've all been talking, Sue, and we finally decided to broach the subject with you."

"Who's been talking? What subject?" Their mysterious behavior was making me uncomfortable and upsetting my stomach.

"All of them," Al said. "Mrs. Havorsham, Fred Nutting, Nettie Banks, Maya Reynolds, everyone. You're the last."

"I'm not so sure I want to hear whatever it is you're trying to tell me."

"Go on, Al," Dick said.

Al leaned in close. "At night, in the Nam prisoner camps, we'd pass the time by whispering to each other through the walls. We made up stories about our great escape and what we'd do to our tormentors if we ever got out."

I looked at Dick. He was grinning. They all were.

"Don't you see what Al's getting at, Susie?" Dick asked.

"You're talking about escaping? Leaving Harmony?"

"Not exactly," June said.

"Retribution," Dick said.

"Pay back for all the misery that sawed-off demon has put on us," Al said.

My upset stomach became too much and I excused myself. What they were talking about was hurting another human being, or worse. I couldn't be a party to something like that.

But what about Mary? my inner voice asked. *Remember what you told her? Stand up. Fight back. You can't let him get away with this. He'll just keep hurting others.*

I *had* said those things to her. All talk when I'd wanted Mary to speak up, but now, when given the chance, just a nervous Nellie. Probably why they'd come to me last. I was disgusted with myself for being so weak. Thankfully, my bathroom break bought me some time to think it through, and the more I thought about it the more I warmed to the idea. Maybe they were right. Maybe we had to do this, before he killed someone else, someone like Dick. I hated to admit it, but that knot in my stomach began to feel more like excitement and less like fear.

Ten minutes later, feeling quite a bit better, and with a renewed sense of purpose, I returned to the activities lounge. All three of them looked up anxiously as I entered the room and sat down. In my absence, they'd managed to assemble most of the covered bridge, leaving only the sky pieces.

"Well?" June asked.

"We've made it very clear to everyone," Dick said, taking my hand. "Either we're all in or it won't happen."

"I'm the last?"

June nodded.

"Twenty yeas," Dick said. "Your vote is the last Susie. What say you?"

"Are you in?" Al asked.

Unable to maintain my stoic façade any longer, I cracked a huge smile. "Oh, I'm in." I looked toward the door to be sure no one was listening, then turned back to face them. "Tell me more."

They laid out their entire plan. It would take place on Sunday after visiting hours were over and after the last of the day staff had departed, when we'd be alone with Terry the Tyrant.

We spent the remainder of the week planning every aspect of the event. The event. That's what we called it in case any of the staff overheard. The residents who took muscle relaxants as part of their daily medication all went without, willingly enduring the spasms and pain. We held several more puzzle sessions to aid with the planning. Terry wasn't due back until Sunday night and we vowed to be ready.

It was exciting to witness the youthful exuberance infecting us all. I'd never seen Dick or June look so vibrant. I felt like a school girl myself, nearly bursting with anticipation. My only regret was that Mary wouldn't be a part of the event. But I planned to do something special in her honor.

Finally the big day arrived. Sunday seemed to drag like no other. It wasn't my month to be visited so I read to pass the time. We'd requested tapioca pudding be served for dessert that night. Tapioca was Terry's favorite. Most of the residents took their nighttime meals in bed and Terry was infamous for stealing their pudding. It was a perfect way to deliver his medicine.

Terry was in rare form when he came on duty at seven o'clock. I could see the chip on his shoulder the moment he walked in. A half hour later the last of the day workers left. Dick and I watched from the porch as they drove away down the long dirt drive.

By eight o'clock Terry was yelling at some of the residents telling them to go on up to bed. There was a televised football game he wanted to watch and he didn't want to be bothered. I stayed in my room with the door open pretending to read, listening as he made the rounds. I could hear his oohs and aahs about the tapioca.

At eight-forty-five, Dick, Al and I crept downstairs to the recreation room where the big screen television was blaring. Terry was lying face down in the middle of the floor, eyes open but physically incapacitated. The medication worked. I turned off the TV and headed to the kitchen, to begin preparations. Al and Dick went to fetch the others.

I was gathering some necessary items when Dick and Al raced into the kitchen.

"Someone's coming up the driveway," Dick said breathlessly.

"Who?" I asked, as if it mattered.

"I don't know who," Al said. "But we've gotta hide Terry. Quick."

The three of us hurried into the rec. room and began dragging Terry toward the kitchen. We dragged him by his feet and watched with amusement as his head bounced over each threshold. He was surprisingly heavy for such a little shit. We tucked him into the walk-in cooler then returned to the rec. room. I turned on the television then sat next to Dick on the love seat. Al sat in one of the wingback chairs. I'd just lowered the volume, using the remote, when Harmony's front door opened. It was Julie, one of the day shift workers.

"Hi Julie," I said, trying hard to sound like I wasn't out of breath. "Didn't expect to see you so soon."

"I'm such a ninny. Forgot my purse."

"Happens to me all the time," Al said.

"You lose your purse a lot, do you?" Julie asked, giving him a sly grin.

Al blushed. "Well, of course I don't have a purse, but if I had one I'd probably lose it."

"Real smooth," Dick whispered, after Julie was out of sight.

"Sorry," Al said. "I babble when I'm nervous. Sue me."

Julie returned less than a minute later, purse in hand. "Well, good night. Don't get into any mischief."

"We won't," I said.

We let out a collective sigh of relief at the sound of her car starting.

Dick got up and looked through the window. "That was close."

I switched off the television and headed back into the kitchen. Dick and Al returned to the elevator to enlist the help of the others.

By nine-thirty every resident of Perfect Harmony Home for the Aged had gathered in the rec. room, giggling like children. Mrs. Havorsham sat in her wheelchair clapping and calling Terry names. In her lap she held a large wooden spoon and a bar of soap. Others were holding things like rolling pins and meat tenderizers. Several of the residents possessed butane lighters, used for igniting the grill.

Terry the Tyrant had been stripped down to his boxers and tied tightly facedown across the top of the coffee table. He looked like a roasted pig on a platter. His mumbled pleas for help went unheeded. It would've been difficult to hear him anyway, what with our vocal gaiety.

We'd nominated Al to be our spokesperson, mainly because the event had been his idea in the first place. He stood in the center of the room, high atop a wooden stool, a bathrobe-clad master of ceremonies.

"Ladies and gentlemen, ladies and gentlemen, may I please have your attention."

The room slowly quieted until the only noises were mumbled protests from the guest of honor.

Al donned his reading glasses and pulled from his pocket a brief prepared speech, penned on a recipe card. "Thank you all for being here tonight. I'd like to start by recognizing those of you who've made great sacrifices this week, going without your medication in order to make this night possible. We owe you a debt of gratitude."

Several people yelled out in agreement. "Here, here."

Al turned his attention to the Tyrant whose eyes widened. "And speaking of sacrifices, I think it's safe to say that no one has sacrificed or suffered more than we all have at the hands of Mr. Moscone." This was met by loud boos. "While his sacrifices, in repentance for all the suffering he's inflicted, lie ahead." The crowd cheered.

"Terry the Tyrant, as he's so fondly known, has set the bar mighty high indeed. Terry, it is my sincere hope, our sincere hope, that this lasting tribute will be worthy of your admiration. Many of us took naps today so that we'd have the energy necessary to put on a good show." He paused and removed several sheets of paper from his pocket. "We've compiled what you might call a to-do list. A recipe of retribution for all of your years of cruelty."

More protests from the Tyrant. More enthusiastic cheers from the residents.

Al turned his attention to Mrs. Havorsham. "Dear Eunice, at ninety-six years young, we'd like you to have the great honor of kicking off the event?"

"It would be my pleasure," she said excitedly. "What should I do first?"

"Whatever you'd like. You may choose something from the list or simply use your imagination."

"Ooh, I've got one. Would you please place this bar of soap in his mouth for me?"

Dick did as she asked, jamming it firmly between Terry's teeth.

"Thank you, Dick," she said. Mrs. Havorsham then proceeded to run over Terry's splayed fingers with her wheelchair. He screamed out in pain. The room cheered. Her face lit up like a Christmas tree.

Item by item, our lengthy to do list was checked-off while Terry lay there helpless and screaming. Nettie, Maya and I served coffee and snacks to the residents, who took frequent bathroom breaks. The fun continued until almost three in the morning. There wasn't a part of Terry's exposed body that wasn't either bruised, bloodied or broken. And, in a fitting tribute to Mary Keating, I made sure that there were parts of Terry not on display in similar condition.

It was Dick who first noticed that Mrs. Havorsham had slumped over in her chair. She didn't appear to be breathing.

"I think she's dead," Dick said.

I checked for a pulse. Nothing.

"Doc told her she had a weak ticker," Al said. "Think all this excitement might've been too much."

We all gathered around her, sad at losing our friend but thankful that her final memories had been such happy ones. It was my idea to return Mrs. Havorsham to her room.

Terry was still breathing, but barely. He was making a ragged wheezing sound that didn't sound too promising. We untied Terry and put his clothes back on him before leaving him face down on the floor. It was time for the final act. Dick informed the group that it was a little chilly outside so we each dressed warmly, knowing that we'd be out there a while. Those of us that could stopped by Mrs. Havorsham's room to pay our last respects.

By four o'clock we were all outside on the lawn, a safe distance from Harmony, comfortably seated in both lawn and wheel chairs. We watched as Al and Dick ran out the front door laughing like school boys.

"Did you do it?" I asked.

"Oh, we did it alright," Dick said with a big smile on his face.

At six-thirty we heard the first of the approaching sirens. Most of Harmony's windows were blown out and roof had begun to cave in. The flames were beautiful hues of red and gold. I looked down the line at our group. Everyone was smiling and peaceful, glad to be free of our tormentor. Happy for the first time in a long time. I watched as Al got up and adjusted June's shawl. He bent down and tenderly kissed the side of her upturned face.

"What shall we tell the authorities?" June asked.

"We'll tell them that Terry died trying to save poor Eunice," I said.

Dick took my hand in his. "That's exactly what we'll say."

Bruce Robert Coffin is a retired detective sergeant from the Portland, Maine police department and the bestselling author of the Detective Byron Mystery Series from HarperCollins. His short stories have been featured in several anthologies including The Best American Mystery Stories 2016. He lives and writes in Maine.

BLESS AMERICA'S VISITORS
by Charlene D'Avanzo

Across St. Mary's reach, a blood-orange sliver punched out of the sea and stained the horizon crimson. Dawn, four twenty-three. Any other day, lobsterman Barney McRae would've witnessed the celestial event. He'd squint like always when the sun was fully up.

But Barney wasn't lookin' east. His eyes fixed on the horror sprawled inside *Bless America*'s cabin, Barney backed away like a Maine lobster facin' dog sharks. The stern coaming jabbed his back so bad Barney thought he'd been gaffed. He clutched his chest and slid down the transom onto his butt.

At the landward end of St. Mary's pier, Nadia Almasi drank in the dawn, a beatific smile gracing her face. This is why she had brushed her lips against Amhed's cheek, slipped out of bed, and had driven an hour east in the dark. Too much death in the ER. She needed rebirth.

Movement on the boat at the end of the pier caught Nadia's attention. Her gaze shifted and she stiffened. No mistake. At the back of a lobster boat, a man grimaced, gripped his torso, and dropped down out of view. Was he having a heart attack? If so, she only had a few minutes to help him. Nadia ran the hundred feet to the end of the pier, clambered into the boat, and fell to her knees beside him.

She placed a hand on the man's shoulder, her touch so gentle it hardly registered. "Sir? I'm a doctor. Can I help you?"

Barney swiveled his head in her direction. The woman confused him. She was dressed like any American—green parka, khaki pants. But her eyes were almond-shaped and skin the color of dark honey. Not American. A foreigner. Arab maybe. Or from India. "I'm okay. Jus' hit my back."

"I thought you were having a heart attack."

"Nah. Heart's good. You might want to check on him." He glanced toward the cabin.

Nadia turned toward the front of the boat and sucked in a quick breath. The body lay on its stomach, head facing them. The neck appeared to be greenish-red—possible evidence of advanced lividity, but it was difficult to see in the dim light. She skirted a coiled rope on the deck, stopped at the cabin's entrance, leaned over, and lightly touched an outstretched hand. The skin was cold. This person had been dead a long time. She went back to the older man.

"He dead?"

"Yes. Can I check your pulse?"

"Don't worry 'bout me. Just a little shook up is all."

Nadia did a quick assessment. On his cheeks and between shags of white hair tumbling down his forehead, the older gentleman's skin was ruddy. Flashing gold teeth when he opened his mouth, he didn't slur his words or droop a lip.

"What's your name?"

"Barney. Barney McRae."

"I'm Nadia Almasi." There was a large box to his right. "Let's get you sitting up."

Nadia squatted in front of Barney and gripped his broad shoulders. The red flannel shirt gave good traction. Like two lobster pots on the same line, they rose together.

Stiff but steady and on his feet again, Barney made his own way to the tackle box. With a grunt, he lowered himself onto one end. Nadia neatly perched herself on the other.

Both stared at the dead person for a few seconds.

"Do you know who that is?" she asked.

Barney stared at the ground and gripped the edge of the box, knuckles white. He licked his lips. "Could. Not sure. Can't see the face."

Nadia said, "The police. I'll call them."

It was a whisper. "They'll think it was me."

She turned to face him. The old man's lips trembled. "Why?"

Barney thrust his chin at the cabin. "Frickin' right theah."

Nadia pulled a phone from her coat pocket and pressed 911. Barney stole glances at her while she talked. He'd freaked out, no doubt 'bout it. Had to admit the doctor lady helped him some. 'Twas easier havin' company with the dead. But he hated feelin' like he owed a person, never mind somebody from away. Not from New York or anywheres close. *Away*. Foreign country. Iraq, Iran. Someplace like that.

When the sun reached thirteen degrees off the horizon, the corpse was on its way to the morgue. The medics had detected no evidence of heart attack for Barney. Officer Matt Martin asked the two witnesses to accompany him to Clark's Harbor station for questioning. Barney could ride in the back seat of Martin's cruiser, while Nadia followed in her car.

Clark's Harbor was on the other side of the bridge from St. Mary, only ten minutes if you drove fast. Martin didn't speed, naturally, so Barney had time to brood on the way.

He had never been interviewed by the police before. The time when they were lookin' for that kid didn't count because Fred Hamilton only came to the door to ask a couple questions. Barney'd told Fred that 'course he was sure he didn't see 'im. Christ, in St. Mary a boy with one of them Mohawk haircuts'd stand out like a blue lobster in a tank packed with brown ones. That was before Hamilton retired and moved down ta Florida.

Barney shifted in his seat and ran a sweaty palm down his trousers. Talkin' to police 'bout a dead body, 'spose anyone'd be nervy. He sure wished 'twas Fred 'stead a this Martin fella.

Inside the municipal building, Officer Martin led the way down the stairs to the police department. Barney held onto the rail so he wouldn't trip if his bad knee failed him. He glanced up at the door marked "Town Hall Desk." A month earlier, he'd paid for one of those stickers you put on your license plate. As usual, Anne Gillette teased how he was the oldest bachelor in St. Mary. Barney wished like hell he was up there right now. He'd even accept Anne's hamburger casserole offer.

With a grunt, Barney put two feet on the linoleum floor and let go of the railing.

"Mr. McRae, I'd like to speak with Mrs. Almasi first," Martin said. "We have one interview room. So I'll need you to wait in our little coffee area."

Perfumed with burnt joe, the room held a two-foot-square wooden table, one chair, and a counter with a tiny sink and the coffee maker. Below deck, *Bless America* had four, maybe five times more space. Barney circled the room, peered into the sink, squinted up at the slider basement window, circled again. Finally, he leaned over, held onto the table, and lowered himself onto the plank chair.

In the interview room Officer Martin explained the process to Nadia. He'd ask a few questions about where she lived and so on. Then he'd ask her to describe what she saw and did that morning. The tape recorder would keep track of what was said, and he'd make observations in his notebook.

"I understand," she said. This officer was polite and professional. Nothing like the men who bullied them in Iraq.

Matt glanced at his phone, pressed the start button on the tape recorder, and noted the time, date, plus who was in the room. He started with the basic—where she lived.

Nadia reached into the little pocketbook on her shoulder, pulled out her wallet, and handed him her driver's license. Then she placed both hands on the interview table and looked at the downy-faced blond man straight on. "My husband and I became American citizens three years ago. My children were born here. Amhed—that's my husband—was a reporter stationed in Baghdad. We left Iraq before the war because he saw what was coming. We've been in the U.S. for eleven years. I'm a doctor. I learned English in a private school when I was a young girl."

Matt nodded. That explained her perfect speech. He also appreciated her candor. "Do you have an office near here?"

"I'm an ER physician. Jonesboro hospital."

"Thank you, ah, Dr. Almasi. Now please describe what you saw this morning."

"Well, I was watching the sun come up when I noticed a man in the lobster boat tied up at the other end of the pier." She placed her hand over her heart. "He clutched at his chest and disappeared from my view. It looked like symptoms of myocardial infarction, so I ran down the pier to help him."

Matt looked up from his notebook. "What happened next?"

"I asked if he'd had a heart attack. He said that he did not. His coloring looked good, and he showed no symptoms of stroke or infarction."

"Did Mr. McRae say anything that explained his behavior?"

"He didn't need to. I saw the body on the floor inside his cabin."

"Please describe what you saw."

Nadia gave a detailed account of the body including possible evidence of lividity and overall appearance and positioning. Matt penciled a sketch as she spoke. The woman was observant and precise.

"Did Mr. McRae say anything else?"

"He appeared to be frightened—his voice quivered, you know. He said people would think he'd killed the dead man because it was in his boat. After that I called 911."

Down the hall, Barney shifted on the wooden seat and clutched the black mug he'd found in the sink. He stared up at a window that offered only a view of the sky. Fair weather clouds drifted by. Twice already he'd gotten up and stuck his head out the door. He stood to go when someone walked down the hallway, but it was only another cop wanting a cup of coffee.

Matt said, "Thank you, Dr. Almasi. Now, please explain why you were in St. Mary so early this morning."

"Well, as I said, I'm an ER physician. Yesterday was especially bad. Car accident. Three teenage girls. One died on the way to the hospital, the second one in the OR. The third is in intensive care in pretty bad shape. I didn't sleep too well last night. I don't know, watching the sun come up seemed like it might help."

"Have you done this before? Gone to St. Mary to see the sunrise?"

"Amhed and I drove down to the little town one morning last month. I recalled how pretty it was, so I thought I'd go back to see the sun come up. It's unlikely I'll do it again, though."

"And why is that?"

"Well, it didn't turn out to be a peaceful morning, did it?"

Nadia had nothing more to add.

"Thank you Dr. Almasi," Matt said. "If you remember anything else, please call me." He handed her a Clark's Harbor Police business card with his name and phone number.

"I will."

She tucked the card in her wallet as he walked her down to the coffee room. He signaled to Barney who set down a mug of coffee and pushed up to his feet.

In the interview room, Officer Martin sat opposite Barney McRae, three feet of metal table between them. As the policeman explained the process once more, Barney got his first good gander at the man. He figured the guy was about Corrine's age if she'd lived more than six months.

Martin pressed the tape recorder's button. "Okay, Mr. McRae, let's begin. Like I said, I need some background information before we talk about this morning. Let's start off with how you spell your name."

"B-A-R-N-E-Y."

"Excuse me. Is Barney your real name or a nickname?"

"Oh. Name's B-E-R-N-A-R-D M-C-R-A-E."

Barney gave his address on Spruce Hill Road and said he'd lived in St. Mary forty-five years.

"How old are you, Mr. McRae?"

"Sev'ty five."

"Married?"

"Wida"

"And your occupation?"

Barney straightened up. “Lobstaman. Fifty odd ye-ah. Still got some pots out.”

“Thank you. Now, Mr. McRae, as precisely as you can, tell me what you saw this morning and when you saw it.”

“’Twas sunup. I walked down ta my boat and there t’was.”

“What was?”

“The—er body. “Twas on its belly, right in my cabin like ya saw.”

As Barney spoke, Matt appraised the man before him. Matching head of white hair and bush beard. Wild black eyebrows that gave him a look of perpetual surprise. Mainer through and through. Seemed truthful, but the old bird could be craftier than he appeared. Matt had been fooled before and wasn’t about to let it happen again.

“Can you tell me anything about the body as you first saw it? Take your time.”

Barney closed his eyes, forced the memory, popped his eyes open, and wiggled his eyebrows. “The head. It faced me. Um, the eyes was shut. ’N it had clothes on. Don’t recall what they looked like though. Whitish maybe. That’s all I remembah.”

“Did you touch the body, Mr. McRae?”

“Ba Jesus, no. Backed ’way sa fast I stabbed my back on the stern coaming.”

“All right. What happened then?”

“Well, that girl walked up. Wanted ta know if I were okay.”

“Go on.”

“She, um, said she were a doctor, ’n helped me ta my feet. I walked over ta the tackle box ’n sat.”

Matt nodded again. “And after that?”

The policeman studied Barney’s eyes. There it was, that flicker of indecision.

Barney scratched the back of his head and regarded the ceiling. A fly bounced off the fluorescent light. What the hell, he thought.

He eyed Martin and raised his chin. “Well, I tol’ her I was worried someone’d think I’d did it.”

“Did what, Mr. McRae.”

“Killed ’em”.

“Why would anyone think that?”

Barney could feel the heat travel from his lobes to the top of his ears. He had very big ears. He glanced toward the door.

“Firs’ off, the—ah, body—’twas in my cabin. Also, I, um, warned off a guy couple weeks ago.” Barney met Martin’s gaze. “He deserved it, ya know. But I didn’t do nothin’.”

“Who did you warn off and why?”

“’Nother lobsterman out on Tuck’man Island. Last name Ames. Guy thinks he owns the ocean.”

Matt lowered his gaze and doodled on his notepad. He didn't want his expression to reveal that the dead man had a Maine license with the name William Ames.

"Please explain why you, ah, warned off Mr. Ames."

Barney frowned. Jackass Will Ames didn't deserve the "Mr." title. "Ames dropped pots my side the island again. Bastard knows that's McRae terr'tory. Has been since my granddad claimed it."

Martin nodded again. Anyone who lived near St. Mary knew about the hostility with some of the Tuckerman Island lobstermen.

"Let's return to the dead man on the deck of your cabin. Do you have any idea who he is?"

Barney sat back in the metal chair and crossed his arms over his coverall suspenders. This "Mr. McRae" business was getting on Barney's nerves. "Nah."

Matt took a chance. "Could the body be Mr. Ames?"

Barney licked his lips. "'Spose so or someon' that size."

"Anything else about the dead man in your cabin?"

Barney blinked. "No."

"Is there anyone you think might be able to help us out here?"

Barney shook his head. Martin didn't ask another question. Barney shifted in his chair, looked up at the ceiling, down at his hands. With every click of the clock on the wall he got more and more nervous.

Finally Barney couldn't take it. He leaned in and gripped the edge of the table. "You can't be thinkin' I kilt that man. I'm a good Chris'tan, fer one thing. 'N not sa stupid as ta put 'im in my boat if I did."

Matt doodled three question marks in his notebook. If Barney didn't kill Ames, who did, why did they place the body in McRae's boat, and when?

"I'm only getting information, Mr. McRae. When were you last on your boat? Besides this morning, that is."

"Yestidy, 'bout noon. Checked my pots 'n came back to the peah."

"Do you usually dock your boat at the St. Mary pier? Don't you have a mooring?"

"'Course I've a mooring. With the game hip 'n knee, it's a whole lot easier ta get in 'n out of the boat from the peah. Nobody minds I do it."

Matt nodded and wrote "docks at pier, common knowledge" in his notebook.

Barney narrowed his eyes. "So you, ah, suspectin' me?"

Matt repeated, "I'm simply gathering information, Mr. McRae."

"Why would a man put som'on he's offed 'n his own boat!"

Matt tapped the table with the eraser end of his pencil and plastered his best blank look on his face.

"I weren't even goin' out taday."

Matt placed the pencil in the middle of the table, slid his phone to the side, and looked up at Barney. "Okay, you weren't going out today. Why were you on your boat this morning?"

"Sun-up. I like ta watch it, ya know."

"And you usually do that from your lobster boat?"

"Ah, no. Sun's bettah from the othah end o' the dock. I wanted ta check on somethin' in the boat."

"What was that?"

Barney studied the items on the table for a moment, then licked his lips. "Um. What the deadhead lef'."

"Excuse me?"

"This deadhead good-fer nothin' guy who come out yestidy. He calls las' night askin' me ta check fer somethin' he coulda lef' behind. He'd meet me at the boat sun-up."

"Are you saying that you took someone out with you yesterday. Someone you didn't know?"

"That's it. Guy comes up sayin' he never been on a lobstah boat, ya know, 'n offers ta pay two hundred dollas cash if I take 'im out. So I did. Stupies' thing I ever done."

Matt scribbled this intriguing piece of information in his notebook.

"Did this person show up this morning? And what did he say he left onboard?"

"'Is phone, that's what. No, jerk nevah showed 'n there was no phone."

"What was this person's name and where does he live?"

Barney blinked. "Um, gave the name 'a Alice Cooper. I 'member 'cause Alice's a girl's name. Said he lived 'n Portland and ta call 'im Al."

Matt nearly groaned. The old guy didn't know that Alice Cooper was a famous rock star. He'd follow up but'd bet his shirt no male named Alice Cooper lived anywhere in the state.

He thanked Barney for his cooperation, gave him his card, and repeated earlier instructions about Barney's statement. "Also, Mr. McRae, I want you to call me right away if you remember anything else, even if you think it's not important."

Barney followed the policeman down the hallway. It looked like he was home free, but he wasn't quite out of it yet. The policeman stood in the coffee room's doorway and apologized to Nadia for the wait. Behind Martin, Barney ran thick, stubby fingers through his hair. Nadia smiled as she passed him, but Barney didn't notice.

"I assume you'd like a ride back to St. Mary, Mr. McRae?"

Barney gave a quick nod.

"And please, don't leave the area without contacting me first."

"Ayup. What about my boat?"

"You won't be able to use it for a day or two. Sorry."

Matt drove back over the Clark's Strait bridge and dropped his charge at the single-pump gas station with the rusted flying red horse. The old man limped down the hill, shoulders hunched against the wind.

ΩΩΩ

To Barney's dismay, folks kept asking about the corpse in his cabin. He was good when he finally got out on his boat, but pull up to the pier and they'd appear from nowheres. You'd expect that kind of behavior from the four other St. Mary lobstermen, Chet who ran the gas station, and Audrey the mail lady. But the rev'rend from Clark's Harbor? Besides that, three nuts pretended they knew Barney. He was darn sure they didn't.

Four days after finding the dead body, Barney stood in *America First's* stern, hand on hip. He frowned at his trap hauler. Damn roller got itself stuck again. He'd chuck the thing and hand-haul his pots, but with his hip that wasn't gonna happen. Footfalls on the wooden pier interrupted those thoughts. The other St. Mary lobster boats'd left the harbor hours earlier, so he figured he'd one more dumbass ta deal with.

Barney squinted, stroked his chin. No mistakin' it, the foreign lady doctor was walkin' his way. 'N she had an ankle biteah with 'er.

"Good morning, Mr. McRae. May we come aboard?" With a smile, she looked down at the knee-high child standing beside her. "This is my daughter Safia."

"'Spose."

"May I hand Safia over to you?"

Before Barney had a chance to decline, Nadia lifted her daughter over the gunwale. Barney held out his arms and clamped two sun-spotted hands around the child's waist. He stood frozen in that exact position until Nadia clambered onto the stern deck, released Safia from Barney's grasp, and set her down onto the deck.

"'Tis early," Barney said, even though it wasn't especially so.

Nadia gestured towards the east. "Yes, but a lovely morning. I, ah, hope I'm not interrupting your work."

Barney shrugged. "What is it you're wantin'?"

Nadia leaned back against the port gunwale, Safia at her side. Barney did the same on the starboard side and crossed his arms.

"Do you read the local paper, Mr. McRae?"

"The St. Mary Gazette now 'n then."

"So you don't know what's happening where I live west of here."

"Sure don't."

"It's getting pretty bad for us. Even neighbors we've known for years act different—as if we're terrorists out to hurt them." She bit her lip. "It's even happening to Safia in school. Children treat her differently."

Safia lifted her chin and held the blue eyes of the ancient man. "They whisper and point. I thought we were *friends*." Safia bit her lip and dropped her head.

Barney rubbed his neck. Lil' newt deserved bettah. "Sorry ta hear it."

"Children in Safia's class can invite a visitor to talk about the kind of work they do. We thought you might be willing to describe what it's like to be a lobsterman."

Barney held out a hand. "Hol' up. You can't be wantin' me ta do that."

"I did hope you would consider it, Mr. McRae. You're a Maine lobsterman whose family, I assume, has been here for generations. If you visited Safia's class at her invitation—can't you see how impressed her friends would be?"

The plea in the child's eyes 'bout broke his heart. But not quite.

Barney stalled. "My, ah, car's broke."

"I'll pick you up, drop you at the school, and drive you back home."

Barney looked out across the harbor.

"At least think about it, Mr. McRae. Here's my card. You can call me anytime."

Barney nodded. Nadia climbed out the boat, reached back for Safia, and lifted her out. Hand in hand, mother and daughter walked down the pier and up the St. Mary hill. Barney stuffed the card in his coat pocket and watched until they were out of sight.

ଡଡଡ

The following day, Officer Matt Martin stepped onto the concrete step of Barney McRea's cottage. He looked around for a buzzer, found none, and knocked on the weathered pine door. The raised wood grain chafed his knuckles. Matt's nose was uncomfortably close to the door, so he stepped back to wait. He was about to knock again when Barney yanked open the door and squinted at him.

"Oh, it's you. I tol' all I knew already."

"I have some information I thought you'd be interested in, Mr. McRae."

Hand on his hip, Barney said, "Well, out with it man."

"Sir, I'd rather speak with you inside."

Barney stepped aside, let Martin pass through, glanced down the driveway, and shut the door. Matt appraised Barney's domain in three seconds. Pine plank walls and floor, darkened with time. Veteran black wood stove, braided rug dotted with spark scars. Open kitchen shelves that held plates and glasses alongside cereal boxes, flour, sugar, and canned coffee. Snug, dim, old Maine.

Barney lowered himself onto the wood chair at the far side of the kitchen table. He nodded at another in the corner by the door. Matt retrieved the chair and placed it opposite the old man. He ran a hand across decades of cuts on the tabletop. Barney leaned back into his chair and crossed his arms over his suspenders. It didn't look like the policeman was going to arrest him, but you never knew.

Matt looked up from the table. In shadow, the old Mainer was hard to read. "Mr. McRae I'm here to tell you that we've arrested the man we believe killed William Ames. The news will be out tomorrow, but I wanted to tell you in person."

Barney raised one shaggy eyebrow. He knew that the dead person in his cabin was Will Ames. The police had released the name and asked anyone with information to step forward. But he had no idea who killed Will.

After a moment, Matt went on. "We arrested William's cousin Noah."

Flicker. "Figures."

"Why do you say that, Mr. McRae?"

Barney leaned forward, ten fingers on the table. "Tol' ya they're a bad lot. Ames. Noah he's two, three years younga 'n Will. Two of 'em been like two lobsta togetha in a tank since they was kids. Only one come out alive."

Matt nodded. Lobsters were notorious fighters. Unless you put rubber bands around their claws, one would kill and eat his tank mate.

"Noah Ames came up on our radar quickly. Your friend Dr. Almasi gave us a crucial tip."

Barney bit his lip at the "friend" but kept mum.

"The day after we interviewed both of you, Dr. Almasi called with something she'd recalled overnight."

Matt took Barney's blink as "go on".

"Driving home late from the Emergency Room on the eleventh, she was stuck behind a slow moving food truck in that curvy stretch of the shore road where it's difficult to pass. The truck braked at the road turnoffs, as if the driver was trying to read road signs."

"Huh," Barney said.

"The truck turned right onto St. Mary Road, and Dr. Almasi was able to resume normal speed. Only she wondered why a food truck would drive into St. Mary, especially close to midnight, because there are no food stores in town."

Barney nodded. That he had to drive all the way to Clark's Harbor for food was a constant irritant.

Officer Martin continued. "She thought the information might be significant because the body was found the next morning."

Barney grunted.

"With Dr. Almsai's information we were able to trace the truck to Noah Ames."

Barney had to ask. "How's that?"

"Clearly printed on the back in large letters were 'Sure Food' and 'Market Fresh'. Most important, she recalled three letters on the license plate. 'SAA.' Because her daughter's name is Safia Alya Almasi."

Barney coughed. "She gotta good mem'ry."

"License plates can be hard to trace, but we had a lucky break."

Matt studied the lobsterman. You'd expect someone in McRae's position to be pleased with news of the arrest. If he was, the old guy didn't show it.

Officer Martin stood, said he'd keep Barney informed, and let himself out. Barney eyed the door until he was sure the policeman wasn't going to return. Then he let out the breath he was holding and fell back into his chair. Given what Martin just told him, he had to think on what'd happened.

First off, Noah Ames killed Will, his own cousin. Then he dumped the body in Barney's cabin ta shift the blame. Bastard Noah Ames set 'im up.

Barney stroked his beard while he pondered it all. Ovah 'n ovah, Will broke the key rule—don't mess with a lobsterman's traps. He'd been warned a hundred times but kept stealin' crittahs that weren't his. 'Twas sinful. Nothin' else ta call it. 'Course whether the jerk deserved ta die, that was somethin' else.

Noah settin' Barney up, there was no forgivin' that. Noah and Barney'd been at it in the lobstah war fer decades. But dumpin' a body on 'im?

By-the-Jesus, Noah musta had a real good laugh when he dropped dead Will onto *Bless America's* deck.

Barney slapped a hand on the table and jumped up so fast his chair crashed to the floor. Back and forth, he paced the twenty-foot width of his cabin, his anger growing with each step. He smashed a clenched fist into his palm until the hand went numb.

Cool it, he said ta himself. Don't want a heart 'tack or somethin'. The thought reminded him of that doctor lady. What was her name? Nadia? She might've saved his life after all. If she hadn't got stuck behind Noah's truck, 'membered the license 'n all, he jus' might be in jail right now.

Jeezum Crow.

Barney slid the chair back into place, sat back down at the table, and clasped his hands like he was praying. He hadn't been in church since Helen died, but if there was a time ta go back 'n give thanks, it'd be now.

Church. His favorite statue in Sacred Heart of Our Lord was Mary at the annunciation. She looked scared to death. Safia's pleading eyes reminded him of that.

Barney limped over to the peg rack by the door, rifled though his coat pockets, and pulled out Nadia's card. With a quick nod, he ran a fingertip across her phone number.

If that's what it took ta thank the good Lord, well, he was gonna do it.

Charlene D'Avanzo is an award-winning environmental educator with forty years experience as a marine ecologist. Her Oceanographer Mara Tusconi Mysteries introduces readers to the beauty of Maine's seawaters plus grave threats facing them. D'Avanzo lives on Little John Island in Yarmouth, Maine.

OFF HER MEDS
by Judith Green

She loved to walk on the beach first thing in the morning. With Cuddles pulling at his leash, making little dashes at the seagulls which flew up, squalling disdainfully, at the last moment, she walked at the edge of the water, letting the waves lap at her bare feet and gazing out at the far, faint line of the horizon. The air so fresh, and the blue, blue sky above her, and all that space, shared only with a few other dog-walkers, who nodded, smiling, as they passed by farther up in the dryer sand.

Now Cuddles barked, that short, excited yap that meant he'd found something. Another seagull? *You'll never catch one*, she thought. But no, he was straining toward something floating in the water, just beyond the line of the breakers. A bit of flotsam—or was it jetsam? She'd never learned the difference. The thing tumbled forward in the froth, and the wave drew back, leaving it deposited neatly on the hard, wet sand. She could see now that it was a man's running shoe, white, its sodden laces drooping. *Oh, well*, she thought, *someone's unhappy at losing that*, and she grasped at the leash to pull Cuddles past.

But Cuddles would not come. He pulled with all his miniature-terrier might, avid for the running shoe, actually dragging her toward it. What ailed the beast? Why all this yapping over a lost running shoe?

Then she saw. Inside the shoe there was a foot. A severed, human foot. The bloody stump of an ankle protruded from the opening.

"Omigod! Omigod!" She yanked the dog away and stumbled up the beach away from the thing. She fumbled for her phone, dropped it in the sand, snatched it up again. Dialed 9-1-1.

"York County Sheriff's Department. What is your emergen—"

"There's a shoe! A foot! I mean, there's a shoe with a foot in it. On the beach. By the water—"

"Ma'am, may I have your name?"

"It's Cecilia Richardson. I'm at Long Sands, kind of in the middle, and there's a shoe. A running shoe. My dog found it. It has a foot in it, cut off at the ankle. A human foot."

"All right, Ms Richardson. A cruiser is on the way. You can—"

She pressed *end.* She couldn't bear to stay near the thing. Pulling the dog by his leash, she headed up across the beach to the road.

She called Alan. His voice, when he answered, was still rough with sleep; she could hear the coffeemaker chortling in the background, and knew that he hadn't yet had his first cup. "I'm at Long Sands," she told him. "I've called the police."

"*What?* What's the matter?"

She told him about the severed foot in the running shoe. "They're sending a cruiser."

"Hold still!" Alan's voice was muffled. He was probably pulling a shirt on over his head. "I'll be there in a moment."

He pulled up at the edge of the sidewalk moments before the police car arrived. An officer, a young man with thick, black hair which fluttered in the summery on-shore breeze, climbed out of the cruiser, dodged the excited dog. "Are you Cecilia Richardson?"

"Yes, yes! And there's the shoe—"

Both men turned to look as she pointed down the beach. At that moment, a wave arched over the sand and crashed down over the shoe. As the water withdrew, the sand gleamed wet. And empty.

"The shoe! The wave took it! Hurry!" she shrieked.

The young officer took off running. Alan followed more slowly. She could see the shoe bobbing beyond the breakers, further out now as another wave crashed on the beach and withdrew.

The young officer hesitated, then made as if to step into the waves. Alan put a hand on his arm, pulled him back away from the breakers. Stood talking to him.

The shoe was getting further away! Why didn't the officer go after it? She trotted down the beach, the dog rollicking at her side, then pulled him up short. She could hear Alan's voice, snatches of words as he spoke to the officer. "Hospital—" and "off her medications—" and "saw something in a documentary—" And the officer nodding, the two men standing with their arms crossed over their chests, mirroring each others' poses in mutual masculine understanding.

So that was how it was going to be. She would be written off as a hysterical female. Just because she'd been put on medication—*temporarily*—after her miscarriage. Anyone would have been sad. Didn't Alan understand that? Hadn't *he* been sad, too? But now they wouldn't believe her about the shoe. Men!

They turned now and saw her standing there. The young officer approached her cautiously. "Thank you for your report, ma'am. I've, um, got your contact information from your husband, so we'll be in touch if we need anything further."

"But what about the shoe? Don't you need—"

"I'll speak with my higher-ups." The officer stared down at his feet, shuffled them in the loose sand. "Maybe we can send a boat..."

"Come on." Alan took the dog's leash from her, tucked his other hand under her arm and pulled gently but insistently. "Let's go home."

Meekly, she followed his car through the side-streets toward their house. He'd taken Cuddles with him. Didn't he even trust her with the dog? In their tiny kitchen, she let him guide her into a chair, and sat like an invalid while he poured her a cup of coffee, brought her a bowl of yogurt, sliced a banana into it. Then brought her the plastic week-at-a-time pill container.

Well, of course she hadn't taken her pills yet this morning. She was supposed to take them with food. So why would she take the pills *before* her before-breakfast walk on the beach with the dog? Off her medications, indeed!

"There *was* a foot in that shoe," she said at last.

"Mm," he said.

"Taking medicine doesn't mean I'm crazy!"

"Of course not," he said. He was using his soothing voice. "Listen, I've got to get ready for work. You'll be okay here alone?"

"I've got Cuddles," she snapped, and splooshed a spoon into her yogurt.

She spent the morning online, poring over every local newsfeed she could find, searching for any indication of an accident, a murder, any event that might have produced a body without a foot. She considered calling the hospital to see if anyone of that description had been admitted lately, but of course they wouldn't tell her. HIPAA, and all that.

How long had that—that *thing* been in the water? How long would a running shoe float? She thought of experimenting with one of her own shoes in the bathtub, but decided against it. She couldn't reproduce the conditions of the ocean. Salt water was more buoyant, for one thing, and the action of the waves…

Waves. Currents. She needed to find out where the running shoe might have come *from.* The waves that washed up on Long Sands...where did they start from? Back to the computer. She studied charts of the prevailing currents in the Gulf of Maine, tide tables, weather reports. It was all so confusing.

But she had to find out. She had to prove that it was at least possible that there had been a foot in that shoe. She hated it when Alan used that big-man-looking-after-a-poor-weak-woman tone of voice on her. It didn't help that he was the sole breadwinner. Oh, why had she given up her job when she became pregnant? If only...

She got up from the computer and wandered through the living room and down the hallway, and opened the door.

The air in the room was still and cool in the semidarkness of the drawn curtains. She stepped carefully across the carpet to push open the drapes and lift the sash, letting in salt air, and the chirp of birds in the back yard, and a sturdy beam of sunshine to stripe the floor at her feet. That was better. She breathed deeply, once, and turned to face the room.

The crib stood in the corner, its hand-crocheted blankets neatly folded at the foot. Over the changing table, with its pad covered in a cheery waterproof gingham, a mobile hung with tiny animals now fluttered and turned in the moving air. The rocking chair, too, bobbed slightly, as if rocking itself. A plush teddy bear sat on the end of the changing table, holding its little arms out as if waiting to be held.

She picked up the bear and settled wearily into the rocking chair, gazing out the window at the apple tree in the back yard. She must have dozed a little, because suddenly there was Alan, standing in the doorway with Cuddles at his ankle, both of them peering in at her as she sat with the teddy bear in her arms.

"Oh." His voice was flat. "That's where you are."

She stood up hastily, and put the teddy bear back into its usual spot on the changing table. "I was just...airing out the room. Let me get this window closed. Did you have a good day at work?" She knew that her voice sounded too bright. Brittle. "What would you like for supper?"

"Whatever," he said.

He trailed after her into the kitchen and stood there while she rattled open the cupboards, then yanked open the refrigerator, seeking inspiration for dinner. He looked over at the laptop, still open on the kitchen table. He shook the mouse to bring the computer back to life, and the chart of currents in the Gulf of Maine reappeared on the screen. He sighed.

She knew he wouldn't say anything. He never did.

At first he thought they ought to turn the baby's room into a study, or a guest room. But he wouldn't talk about that anymore, either. Men.

She settled on spaghetti, and put a pot of water on the stove to boil, then began to brown the hamburger. A jar of Paul Newman's sauce, a bit of salad—using the lettuce from the Farmer's Market before it got any limper—and *voila.* Dinner.

He ate his dinner in silence, sitting across the table from her. As he coiled the last of the spaghetti on his plate around his fork he asked, "Did you take your medications?"

She flipped open the lid on the *Wednesday* section of her evening pill container and showed him that it was empty. "There's ice cream for dessert," she said.

She ought to do better, she thought the next afternoon. Something nice for supper. She had a butternut squash from the Farmer's Market, and, scrolling through recipes, she settled upon caramelized onions to go with it. Lovely.

She left the onions cooking slowly on the stove and wandered into the living room, where she leafed through a magazine, and then into the baby's room. She gazed out the window for a moment, then went to the bureau and lifted out a stack of tiny undershirts. She laid out the shirts, then refolded them neatly, and—

Snap! Crackle! She whirled around. Black smoke roiled from the kitchen doorway, filling the living room. Oh, God, the onions! Choking, gasping for air, she grabbed Cuddles and dashed through the thick smoke and out onto the porch. "Call the fire department!" she shrieked to a neighbor tending to her flowers next door.

She sobbed in the neighbor lady's arms as the fire truck arrived, siren wailing, and people gathered on her lawn. The firemen charged up the steps--

"I think we've found your problem, ma'am." One of the firemen stood in the open doorway, holding the pan of onions, now a blackened mess, by the handle.

One of the neighbors must have called Alan at work, because suddenly there he was, in among the firemen in their enormous slickers and rubber boots who were milling about in her kitchen, taking turns looking at the frying pan, now back on the stove, and patting Cuddles, who was barking joyously at all the commotion.

Alan followed the firemen out to their truck, which loomed at the curb, surrounded by little groups of chattering neighbors. She stood on the front steps, watching the firemen roll up their unused hoses, and she heard it. Oh, yes, she heard it. Alan murmured something to the men, and they nodded their understanding, and one of them repeated his words just loud enough that she heard it: *probably off her meds...*

Cheeks flaming, she spun on her heel and marched into the house.

She busied herself opening all the windows in the house to let out the sludgy smell of overcooked onions. She heard the fire truck roar to life and pull away, and the chattering of the neighbors as they bid each other farewell and dispersed. She heard the front door open and close, and Alan's quiet footsteps as he followed her into the bedroom.

She lifted the window sash high, then fiddled with the curtains as an excuse to keep her back turned to him. "Aren't you going back to work?" she asked.

He didn't answer right away. Then he said, "I'm thinking of retiring."

"Retiring?" She turned to look at him. He looked exhausted, his shoulders drooping. When had he got so bent? "Why on earth would you do that?"

"You need me here," he said.

"What, to keep an eye on me? Don't worry. I'm safe enough. After all, I've got Cuddles." And at the sound of his name, the dog yipped his impatient *Don't just stand there—pat me!* bark.

Alan sighed. He lifted his shoulders and let them drop. Then, without another word, he turned and walked toward the living room. The front door opened and snicked shut, and a moment later she heard his car start up.

Men.

ꝏꝏ

He was in his chair at the table that night before she'd even had a chance to set out the plates and silverware. Wordlessly, he watched her bring the water glasses to the table, and set a casserole on a hot pad in front of his place, then fetch the rolls and butter. At last she sat down, and looked at him.

"What?" she asked.

He waited a beat. "Tonight I want to *watch* you take your meds."

"Just because I blew it and called the fire department? What if there *had* been a fire? What then? If I'd spent a lot of time standing around to analyze the situation, then it might have been too late, and there goes the house!"

"Yes, okay, I get your point," he said quietly. "But if you don't take your meds, you—you *see* things."

He was wrong, of course. She felt so much better without them. And, in fact, without them she was beginning to see...well, see *him.*

"Take your pills," he said. "Please."

"Oh, all right! Just let me get some food in me first." She spooned a heap of mac-and-cheese onto her plate, ate three forkfuls, then reached for the evening pill container. She flipped open the *Thursday* section, took out the two pills which had been nestled together in the tiny, square space, and popped them into her mouth. She swallowed noisily, then opened her mouth wide to show him the pills were gone. "Okay?" she asked. "Okay?"

"Okay," he said, and reached for the dish of mac-and-cheese.

Slowly, as if she hadn't a care in the world, she lifted another forkful of food to her mouth. She knew from practice exactly how long she had before the coating melted off the pills under her tongue. While Alan was busy serving himself, she maneuvered the pills onto the fork with her tongue, and then, as she dipped the fork once more toward the food on her plate, into her lap. She knew that the paper napkin in her lap would stick slightly to the wet pills, but not much. It wouldn't matter.

The dog looked up at her imploringly. "No, Cuddles," she said. "No begging at the table."

ooo

As soon as he left for work the next morning, she went into the baby's room to open the window, let the room air out. The stack of tiny undershirts still sat on the top of the bureau, and she lifted the uppermost one and buried her face in it. Smoky? No, she breathed in the scent of Ivory Snow. But perhaps she should re-wash the clothes anyway. She opened the second drawer, checked the tidy stacks of diapers, ran her hand over the soft fabric. Yes.

She lifted out one of the stacks and held it in the crook of her arm while she lifted the corner of the newspaper she'd used for a drawer liner. As she tucked this morning's pills into a fold in the newspaper, she looked at the familiar photo of Jimmy Carter's inauguration. Lord, how many inaugurations had there been since then? She ought to reline with drawer with fresh paper, she thought. But she was used to Mr. Carter. He had looked avuncular even back then, like a good old grandpa, and he had changed reassuringly little since.

She checked the collection of pills. It had grown into quite a pile. She never had to worry that Alan would find them. He never came into the baby's room. He had at first, sometimes, but he didn't seem to care anymore. All he seemed to care about was these stupid pills.

Well, let's see how *he* liked taking them!

She fetched a small bowl from the kitchen, and carefully lifted the newspaper to slide the pills into it. She'd never felt so clear-headed. Off her medications, indeed.

She sat down in front of her computer and scrolled through recipe after recipe...it needed to be perfect. Ah, here: curried chicken with cashews. Curry to hide the flavor, cashews for extra crunch. Just right. She'd claim an upset stomach at dinnertime, just nibble on a bit of plain chicken, offer him the extra sauce.

But first some fresh air. "Come on, Cuddles. Walkies!" she called.

"Thought you'd never ask," Cuddles said.

She knelt down and threw her arms around his neck. "Oh, Cuddles, what would I ever do without you?"

"Let's go to the beach," he said.

"That's sounds perfect," she said. "A walk on the beach, and then I'll cook dinner." She clipped the dog's leash to his collar and, humming a little tune, she headed for the door.

Judith Green lives in western Maine, where she is the seventh generation of her family on her hillside, with the eighth and ninth generations living just down the road. The former Adult Education director for an 11-town district, she published 25 high-interest/low-level books for adult new readers. Her Level Best Books story "A Good, Safe Place" was nominated for an Edgar. She is currently working on a mystery novel set in small-town Maine.

MRS. FEATHERPATCH AND THE CASE OF THE SKEWERED HAM
by Janet Halpin

"I don't know how I ever let you talk me into this."

"You can't chicken out now," Tom said, steering his Jeep Patriot down one of Kindness, Maine's steeper hills, slick with snow and sleet. "You go in there, stab someone, and you're done."

He shot me a grin, a wicked grin that made my fifty-eight-year-old heart go pitter-pat. Tom McManus, chief of police in this tiny seaside town, tall and buff and a teensy bit gruff, could talk me into anything. Up to and including committing murder.

Well, not real murder. He'd sweet-talked me into starring in a fundraiser for one of his aunt Honoria's many charities, a dinner theater murder mystery set in an English country manor, circa 1928. Me, Antoinette Picasso, longtime star of TV's *Mrs. Featherpatch Cooks Up a Murder*, winner of three Emmys, two Golden Globes, and one Golden Raspberry award, playing a murderer at a ham and bean supper, twenty bucks a plate.

During a snowstorm. Hell, not a snowstorm, a fricking nor'easter. In October. It was for a good cause, I guess, the town's historical museum. Don't get me wrong, I love history, but if it wasn't for Chief McSexy's wicked smile, I'd be watching the storm ravage the Maine coast from the warmth and comfort of my hotel room.

"Tom, are you sure the show will even go on in this weather?"

He just smirked.

"The entire state of Maine seems to be snowed in," I warned.

He smirked again.

"We won't have an audience of more than three people," I insisted.

I got the third in the smirk trifecta as he turned into a parking lot--packed full of cars. I mean, bumper to bumper, practically stacked on top of one another.

Tom laughed, no doubt at my shocked expression. "We're Mainers, Toni, we don't let a little weather stop us."

"You know, there's a reason us flatlanders call you Maine-iacs."

"Not to our faces," he said. "Admit it Toni, you're coming to love Maine."

True. Since we'd met last spring, I'd practically lived here. I was looking for a nice little summer place for when I wasn't working. Tom was a big part of that, but seriously, where else but Maine could a lobster addict like me spend her golden years? *If* I could make it through the winter.

Tom popped out of the Jeep, opened my door, and we leaned into the wind-driven snow, sleet and maybe even a little hail, slip-sliding up to the hulking old Grange building that had been converted into the Kindness Historical Museum.

Tom helped me up the steps, which had been salted and sanded but were still icy as hell. We entered a spacious hall with a high ceiling, wide floorboards, and pictures of the town's forefathers dotting wood paneled walls. The place smelled of ham roasting and beans baking. Rectangular tables ringed the room, jammed with people chatting, laughing, sipping red wine out of clear plastic cups and nibbling on squares of cheese speared onto toothpicks, as if the storm of the century wasn't raging outside.

Tom took my coat and hung it on a rack stuffed full of LL Bean's finest outerwear. His aunt Honoria, a spry old lady who could fit into my pocket, bustled up to us, twittering like a sparrow on speed. I put her age between seventy and a hundred, couldn't be sure and didn't want to ask. One never asks a lady her age if one wants to stay in good with the family.

"Oh, Toni, thank you so much for doing this!" she bubbled. "When Tom told me you'd volunteered to be in our little show, I was beside myself with excitement."

I was drafted, but didn't argue the point. "This is quite a turnout, considering everyone needed dogsleds and snowshoes to get here," I said.

"They've all come out to see you. I'd like to introduce you to everyone before the show, if that's okay. Oh, you're not hungry are you? We won't be serving for a few minutes, but the kitchen will make up a plate for the cast."

I held up my hand. "I'm good. I had a lobster roll before coming."

"Two lobster rolls, I believe," Chief McTattletale said.

I shushed him. Guilty as charged, but did the whole world need to know about my lobster addiction?

I gave Tom a push. "Why don't you go make trouble someplace else, while I meet and greet the fans. Honoria?"

She looped her arm through mine, leading me around the room, stopping at each of the tables so I could chat, pose for selfies and autograph programs, shopping lists and random slips of paper. Some celebs--like my ex--would rather have their eyes poked out with a stick than get up close and personal with the general public. I am not one of them. Happy fans meant good ratings, good ratings meant a renewal and a renewal meant job security for me, an actress who had the gall to be over fifty in a world where woman weren't allowed to age beyond thirty. Besides, all the *ooh-ing* and *ahh-ing* fed my ego.

As I schmoozed, I looked around for my castmates, easy to spot since they were already in costume, dressed up like they were at a *Downton Abbey* dinner party. A big-bellied man in a Friar Tuck robe, the vicar, obviously, hunched over a table, shoveling in a plate of beans. The butler, an Abraham Lincoln clone minus the beard, stood near the fireplace, shooting a death stare at a handsome piece of man meat in a dress suit and hair so shiny I could see my reflection. Mr. Handsome was with two women in flapper get-ups, the younger blonde in a fringed dress that barely covered her unmentionables, the older blonde wearing a headband with a feather.

The three were having an argument. I listened in. Partly because I'm nosy—hey, I'm old enough to freely admit my flaws—but mostly because, as an actress, I sought to improve my craft by studying character and conflict. And there was lots of conflict oozing out of that trio.

"You *promised* me you'd leave her and run off with me!" Younger Flapper shrilled.

"You promised *me* you wouldn't bounce any more bimbos between the sheets," Older Flapper cried.

Mr. Handsome laughed a laugh I'd score a ten on the nasty scale. "I promise I'm gonna dump you both if you don't shut up!"

Honoria sailed up to me and tugged me away before I could hear the exciting conclusion.

"Let's go elsewhere before that creep sees me," she said.

"Who? Mr. Handsome? What's your beef with him?"

She steered me toward the tables on the other side of the hall. "His name's Joey Brown. Cheats on his wife, cheats on his mistress, cheats his clients. And he's the world's pushiest real estate agent. He's been trying to get me to sell my land for two years. I've told him to leave me alone a hundred times but the obnoxious little shit doesn't take no for an answer."

Why were the ones who were good-looking on the outside so rotten on the inside? I glanced at Chief McHunky, being fussed over and fed root beer barrels and other Depression-era candies by Honoria's elderly friends. Except him. He was practically perfect inside, outside and upside down.

I continued on, flitting from table to table. I signed and selfied and chatted until my temples throbbed and my cheeks ached from smiling. After what seemed like a decade, Honoria finally took pity on me and whisked me away to an alcove at the back of the room near the kitchen, where my cast mates had assembled.

"Everyone, this is Antoinette Picasso," she said, breathless and impressed, as if announcing I'd walked on the moon. Which I'd done on the SyFy channel's *Zombie Moonwalkers II*, but that was beside the point. "Toni, this is the director, Kevin Steel." She nodded to the Abe Lincoln clone. "And these are the rest of the Kindness Players. They volunteered to help out today too, like you."

Yeah, volunteered. If thirty years of TV, film and stage work had taught me anything, it was how to read people, and the last thing this crew wanted to do was be here. Especially the obnoxious little shit of a realtor and his blonde flapper adversaries. They shot stinging glancess at each other that brought new meaning to the phrase, *if looks could kill*.

Honoria, oblivious, ran through a quick introduction of the cast--the ingénue, played by Sally Seaforth, the young blonde flapper, followed by Doug Dingle, playing the vicar. He was chowing down on more beans. I hoped they wouldn't kick in before the final curtain. We were in awfully tight quarters and I had a sensitive nose. Sally's *eau-de-cheap* perfume was already making me sniffle.

Next came Priscilla Plum, the forty-something blonde flapper, playing the dowager.

"I wanted to get cast in your role," she said, pouting at me.

And I wanted to sail into my golden years as a size two, but, as the man says, you can't always get what you want.

"Last, and certainly least," Honoria said. "Priscilla's husband, Joey Brown." She imbued the guy's name with maximum loathing.

I shook hands all around, even pouty Priscilla, then Honoria said, "Well, I've got to see to the dinner prep, so I'll leave you to it. Break a leg, dearie."

She hiked up to her tiptoes and gave me a peck on the cheek that made a jaded old cynic like me melt, and then she skedaddled.

"Honoria, wait," Joey called after her. "I wanna talk to you!"

"Drop dead," she lobbed at him as she disappeared into the kitchen.

"Joey, can you keep your business affairs to yourself? My players need to concentrate," the director, Kevin, said with a considerable amount of acid. Or maybe that was bile. I could never keep those straight.

"Won't be your players for much longer, if I have my way," Joey said with an evil grin worthy of Simon Legree.

Kevin froze him with a look and I notched up one more on the obnoxious little shit realtor's enemies list.

We did a short, extremely tense run-through of lines and blocking as the high school kids drafted into service delivered plates heaping with ham and beans to the audience. Honoria had sent me the script, so I had my lines down pat. The play, creatively titled, *Murder at the Manor*, written by Kevin, was basically an Agatha Christie rip-off. The bad parts Agatha had tossed in the circular file long before her work saw an editor. It was so terrible, I expected most of the audience to flee the theater and hurl themselves into a snowdrift to escape the second act. If the hammy performances didn't kill them during the first.

Run-through complete, Kevin tossed me my costume, a knee length sequined dress that had apparently been marinating in mothballs for a year, and I navigated through the phalanx of teens clogging the steamy kitchen to the restroom to change. I nearly collided with Sally on her way out. She'd been crying.

I came out a few minutes later and stopped short when I heard, "I could kill you for this!"

That was definitely Doug. He had a voice like a foghorn. I peeped around the corner and saw him near the ice machine, another plate of beans in his hands. Goodness, I did *not* want to be around when that gas giant went supernova. But I *did* want to be around for this explosion--the argument he was having with Joey.

"That house you sold my mother?"Doug said. "The stairs *collapsed.* She'd only been there a week! She broke her back."

"Listen, Doug. These things happen, it's the price of home ownership." Joey's voice was as smarmy and oily as my agent's when he tried to convince me guesting on *Naked & Afraid* was a great career move.

"You *knew* it was a dump," Doug cried. "*You* talked her into it when you knew the place was falling apart. She broke her back, man! You gotta make it right."

"Not gonna happen. *Caveat emptor*, as they say, buyer beware." Joey stiffened and sliced me a side eye. "Did you get all that Mrs. Featherpatch, or do you want me to raise my voice?"

Goodness, he really was a little shit. I stepped into the kitchen, smoothing my dress. "No, I can hear you just fine, unfortunately."

Kevin was at the mirror, slathering on makeup. He glanced back and shot me a grin. Then he and the others followed me back to the main hall, where the show was about to begin. Honoria waved to me from her table, the seats filled with the cast of *The Golden Girls*, plus Tom, looking outsized and uncomfortable in that sea of blue hair and pastels.

The heavy drapes were drawn across the windows. The cast assembled on our makeshift stage, the clear area in the center of the hall, and we took our marks. The house lights went out, the spotlight flared on. Jazz-age music from a boom box set the scene, wild applause greeted my first line, and the story of Lord and Lady Crumbumble's ill-fated weekend party began.

Creaky dialogue and even creakier exposition laid out each character's conflicts and motivations with the subtlety of an elephant stomping into a tea party. The acting was overwrought, except Sally, who was pretty decent. Clearly Joey had ingested an entire hog before donning his tuxedo--he was the biggest ham who ever trod the boards. Next to me. I threw myself into the role of Lady Crumbumble so hard it's a wonder I didn't hurt myself. I never got to play the killer, so I was emoting for all it was worth.

The end of the first act neared, when the spotlight would turn off then back on, and I would be found standing over my husband's body, skewered by a knife to the heart. It was really just a toy knife Joey, playing the murdered Lord Crumbumble, would squeeze in his armpit, but it'd do. Not like we were working with a twenty million dollar special effects budget.

Various threats to kill Lord Crumbumble were delivered, the music faded out, thunderstorm sound effects piped up--can't have a cliché manor house murder without a cliché storm--and the spotlight winked out.

Sally screamed, on cue. She'd scream again in roughly thirty seconds and the light would pop back on. I had to hurry. I heard Joey crashing about, getting into place on the bar table where I'd find him spread-eagled and dead. I waded through the dark toward the sound. I brushed against someone, probably an audience member hurrying to the can, but I didn't let it disrupt my focus. Just ahead, Joey gasped and sighed, his death gurgle the most convincing acting he'd done the whole show.

I found the table. Quite painfully--I bashed against it, lost my balance, and fell, flailing in the darkness. Sally screamed again. The spotlight popped on. And there I was, belly-flopped on top of that obnoxious little shit of a realtor.

I blinked at the knife inches from my nose. It wasn't a toy. It wasn't in Joey's armpit. And Joey wasn't acting. He sprawled on the table, his tuxedo jacket open, blood sopping his snowy white shirt, his eyes lifeless and staring--a carving knife sticking out of his chest.

I gasped. Joey Brown was dead.

ꝏꝏ

Tom pushed me into a chair, far, far away from the body. He shoved the glass of water Honoria gave him into my hand.

"Sit, stay," he said as if my name was Fido, then he hustled back to Joey's corpse, stalking around the body like a lion on the hunt. He yanked his phone out of the back pocket of his jeans and dialed his detectives or the state police, or whomever the state of Maine required he call in to investigate a murder.

I drank my water, agreeing with the *sit* part of Tom's command. I was too shaken up to stand. Numb, a little fainty, even. I mean, Mrs. Featherpatch found a body nearly every episode. Last count, she and her sensible shoes had stumbled over five hundred corpses, murdered in nearly as many ways. But me? Except for the occasional wake, I generally steered clear of the dearly departed.

"How are you feeling?" Honoria asked, gently squeezing my shoulder.

I drank the last of my water. "Better, thanks."

She wrung her hands. "Who do you think did such a thing?"

That was the question of the moment. I scanned the room. The once buoyant audience now sat subdued at their tables. The wait staff clustered near the fireplace. The Kindness Players gathered in the alcove. Everyone seemed to be in shock, but one of them was faking it. One of them was a killer. A real cold customer. Daring too, to stab a man with a hundred people in the room. What if the spotlight had come back on a few seconds early?

"I don't know, Honoria, but from what I saw and heard today…" I looked toward the alcove again. "There were quite a few people who didn't like the man."

"What happened? Do you want to talk about it?"

Not really. I'd already told Tom, and would have to go over it again for the investigators. But, I guessed I should get my story straight, so I ran over my part in the gruesome affair in as much detail as I could remember. I left out the part about Joey's death gurgle. I'd be hearing that in my sleep from now on. And when I was awake.

"I hurried to hit my mark in the dark, heard Joey crash onto the table, then brushed against someone before… Well, you know the rest."

"That person you bumped into is important," Honoria said. "It's *got* to be the killer. Could you tell if it was a man or a woman?"

I rubbed my throbbing temples. "I don't know. It happened fast, and I was focused on getting to Joey--" Something popped in the back of my brain. Not an aneurysm, thankfully, but a memory. I stiffened. "Honoria, I think I know who the killer is." I bounced out of my chair. "I have to talk to Tom."

I hustled across the room and she followed.

"Yeah, see you in fifteen minutes," Tom said, ending the call and shoving his phone into his pocket. He directed a scowl at me. "Thought I told you to sit." He shifted that glare to Honoria. "And I told *you* to keep an eye on her."

I waved off his concern. "Do you always have to play Chief McBossypants?"

He grit his teeth in a give-me-strength way. Tom wasn't fond of my teasing nicknames, so of course I lobbed them at him every chance I got.

"Tom, I wouldn't be bothering you if it wasn't important. I think I can help you solve the case."

That earned me an eye roll. "This is real life, not your TV show."

"Hey, after fourteen years wearing Mrs. Featherpatch's comfortable shoes, I know a thing or two about detective work. For instance, the knife, the murder weapon, it came from--"

"The kitchen," he finished. "I already checked. There's a carving knife missing." One side of his mouth quirked, practically a smile from Chief McGrumpy. "Seems I know a thing or two about detective work too, Mrs. Featheringtonshire."

I scowled--I despised his teasing nicknames for me only a little less than he did mine, because, seriously, they were ridiculous.

"Do you want to hear what I have to say or not?"

He shrugged, but I knew he was interested. He had a tell, a twitch of his left eyebrow that meant he was curious. It was adorable, and most informative.

"I remembered something about the person I brushed against, a detail that can help pinpoint the killer."

Tom shifted into cop mode. "What? You know who it is?"

"Not exactly. But if I can talk to my castmates for a few minutes, I'll know for sure."

He scowled. "You mean question the suspects, point fingers, tease out motivations, in other words, go full-on Mrs. Featherpatch."

Tom said that like it was the worst idea in the world, which it probably was, but it worked a dozen times on my show, so why wouldn't it work here?

"Why not? Who knows, you might have a confession before your investigators get here." I batted my eyes at him. "Sound like a plan?"

"Sounds like a bad plan, but who am I, a highly trained officer of the law, to argue with the great and powerful Mrs. Featheryawn?"

He was goading me, but this wasn't the time or place for that. Later, when we were alone, he could goad me to his heart's content.

I turned to Honoria. "You want to come with?"

"Absolutely!"

"One question," Tom said. "What exactly are you going to ask that'll get a confession out a killer?"

"Oh, the questions won't matter. That's just a distraction." I took his arm and steered him across the room. "I'm going to find the killer by sniffing them."

ººº

I draped one of my TV character's cotton cardigans over my shoulders--metaphorically, of course--and entered the alcove as Delphinia Featherpatch.

"Gather round, people," I said in her clipped, efficient way. I even clapped my hands.

The Kindness Players did as ordered, forming a circle around me. Sally dried her teary eyes with a paper towel, Kevin eyed me, rubbing his hands together, a dry-eyed Priscilla chewed on her pinky nail, and Doug shuffled over, eating a cookie.

"I have a few questions," I said, pacing around the circle. "Questions about Joey. Each of you here had a beef against him, each of you here had a reason to want him dead."

I stopped in front of Doug Dingle. His vicar's costume was stained with beans and ham grease. "Including you, Doug. You had a hell of an argument with Joey in the kitchen, near the knives. I believe you threatened to kill him. Why?"

"Chief McManus, why are you letting her do this?" Kevin cried, shooting Tom a beseeching look.

Tom leaned against the wall, arms crossed. He eyed Kevin and lifted an eyebrow. "Why? Because I'm the chief." He nodded to me. "Please continue, Mrs. Featherlily."

Oh how I loved this man. I'd marry him and have his babies if my old uterus hadn't closed up shop for good. Guess I'd just have to settle for marrying him.

"Thank you," I said, turning back to Doug. "Can you tell us what the argument was about?"

As he sputtered through an explanation about the collapsing stairs and his sainted mother's grievous injury, I got as up close and personal as I dared with a guy who'd eaten his weight in beans today. He ended his tale of woe with the most clichéd line in all of detective fiction: "I didn't kill him, I swear."

I believed him--he passed the smell test. Failed the test, really. I was looking for a particular smell, a scent I'd picked up on the person I'd brushed against in the dark. Joey's killer. And it wasn't Doug.

"What about you, Honoria? Joey had been harassing you. You went into the kitchen before the show, you had access to the knife." I gave her a sniff. Her scent was all old lady, lilac sachet and peppermint candies. "Where were you when the lights went out?"

Tom straightened. "Hold on, Toni--"

"Hush, Tommy, it's a fair question," Honoria said. "Don't think it hadn't crossed my mind, dearie. Joey was a pesky fella, *always* bugging me to sell my property when I didn't want to sell. Made me mad enough to spit nails. But I have eight acres on the oceanfront, other realtors have been banging on my door too. I haven't murdered them, and I didn't murder Joey. I plead not guilty. At least, I'm not guilty of *this* crime."

Tom did a double take and so did I. Forget about the chief, I wanted to marry this lady.

"And for the record," she said, gushing and blushing. "I'm *delighted* you think I could be a murderer."

I let that hang, then swung on Sally. "What about you?" She twitched in alarm, making the fringe on her dress swish. "You were furious with Joey." I turned to Priscilla. "You too. I saw you both arguing with him earlier. What about?"

They exchanged glances, silent a second, and then both volcanoes erupted.

"He told me he was going to leave her--" Sally jabbed a finger at Priscilla. "He was gonna run away with me and she was pissed. That's why she killed him!"

"I did not! Joey told me he was going to dump you and come back to me. You killed him!"

Neither one of them killed him. I had to abandon Sally's airspace because her perfume nearly knocked me over. I would've noticed if Joey's murderer had been drenched in that stink. And one sniff of Priscilla's whiskey breath let her off the hook too.

That left only one suspect.

"Kevin," I said, pausing a long time before going on. "You and Joey had a tense moment earlier, something about the Kindness Players not being yours anymore if he had his way. What did that mean?"

Kevin swallowed. I could hear him gulp. "Nothing. It was a joke."

"It wasn't a joke," Doug said, munching on his cookie. "Joey was threatening to fire Kevin from the theater. Joey's on the board, uh, *was* on the board, and he said Kevin was doing a lousy job."

"No, that's not true," Kevin cried.

"Face it, Kev, you're no Spielberg," Priscilla said.

"Ticket sales have been *way* down this season," Sally said.

Honoria weighed in. "The board only made you director because you're Muriel's nephew and she's richer than Midas. You remember Muriel, Tom, she backed her car into the Cumberland Farms and you had to take her license away."

Tom grunted. He watched the action, all dour and scowly, but I suspected he was enjoying himself.

"You're all insane!" Kevin cried. "That's not a reason to kill a man—Mrs. Featherpatch, *what* are you doing?"

Sniffing him of course. And getting my answer.

"You know," I said, straightening Kevin's coat lapels and stepping back. "A long time ago I smoked. Forget drugs or corruption, Hollywood's biggest scandal is there's so many smokers in the land of 12-hour a day workouts and trendy juice cleanses. I quit when I got pregnant with my first child. Well, tried to quit. Nicotine is potent and addictive. Took me a full year to be free of demon tobacco."

Tom's eyes just about rolled out of his head and into the parking lot at that. *Get to the point*, he mouthed.

I did have a point, and it was a doozy. "Anyway, I kicked the habit, but to this day, twenty-five years later, just one sniff of that tobacco smell can ignite a craving so fierce my mouth waters. And *that's* what I smelled when the lights were out. When I bumped into Joey's killer." I looked the murderer right in the eye. "When I bumped into you, Kevin."

I fell silent. Tom didn't say a word. Kevin's castmates glared at him with accusing eyes. Honoria pressed her palm to her mouth.

"All right, I killed him," Kevin said, his voice loud in the silence. "He was always lording it over me. In school, *he* was the quarterback, I was the water boy. He went to Bowdoin College, I ended up at Bates. *Bates!* He was a rich realtor, I'm a bank teller. And believe me, he didn't hesitate to rub it in." He glared at each of us in turn. "Then I got named director. For once in my life, I was better than him. I was on top. I was the director, he was just an actor. He was gonna take that away from me. I had to stop him. You see that, don't you?"

"Not really," Tom said, securing Kevin's hands behind his back with a zip tie he pulled from his pocket.

I followed cop and perp to the door, where Tom shoved Kevin into a chair to wait for the police to arrive. Sirens wailed outside--they were close.

Tom turned to me. "So, Joey was *just* an actor. I'm dying to hear your thoughts on that."

"Never mind that, what's the deal with the zip ties? Do you carry an emergency supply?"

"Have to, with you around. Bodies seem to drop at your feet. I like to be prepared."

"Seriously, Tom, you think it could happen again?"

"Maybe." He kissed me. "Probably."

I slid my arm around his waist. "Well, Chief, if it does, Mrs. Featherpatch will be there, and together we'll solve the case."

Inspired by the genre fiction that enthralled her as a kid, **Janet Halpin** writes dark, humorous short stories and novel-length mystery, YA, S/F and WWII-set paranormal and time travel. She lives with her family in the Massachusetts suburbs.

A TWIST OF FORTUNE
by Rosemary Herbert

Her head wrapped turban-style in a colorful scarf so that just a few wisps of her white hair showed, and her hands on a duck egg in lieu of a crystal ball, Helen Snowe, of Troy, Maine, closed her eyes. She closed her lips, too, to stifle a chuckle. She knew she could not be tight lipped for long in her role of fortune teller.

What could she say to sound oracular? Perhaps it did not matter to the sulky, agitated teen who sat before her and who would no doubt be clueless as to the meaning of that word in any case.

It had been a lark to scoot over in advance of this blizzard on the request of her neighbor and friend, to tell fortunes at a birthday party attended by a gaggle of six giggling teens. The sixteenth birthday party had been planned to include going to a movie theatre and local eatery, but now the teens were about to be snowed in at the birthday girl's farmhouse, insulated from the boys they no doubt desired to meet during the party outings.

Yes, it had started out as a lark. But now, faced with this particular teen—the only girl who did not join in the laughter—Helen found that she was taking her role seriously.

What to say to her?

Fearful that she might knock the egg off of its makeshift stand—a roll of electric tape wrapped in shiny aluminum foil—by moving her hands off of it with her eyes closed, Helen nevertheless made a blind attempt to swirl her hands mysteriously around the egg. It seemed important to appear lost in thought, and even to be inspired, feats that would be more difficult to achieve with her eyes open.

But her effort was only met with giggles as she knocked her hastily made, sequined sign board that read "Helen of Troy, Psychic" onto the floor.

It was exceedingly difficult not to join in the laughter!

But then she thought of the teen's eyes. They were heavily lined with kohl, but that did not hide the fact that they were also bloodshot. Was this from crying?

Helen let out a deep sigh. The big exhalation, at least, was not an act. She was truly concerned and perplexed. It seemed a bad idea to talk of love, even in a hopeful way, to a girl who must be smarting from some emotional wound. Perhaps a boyfriend had dumped her this very day. Perhaps there was trouble or sadness at home.

Now the teen sighed, apparently with impatience.

Helen must say something. But what?

Dipping her scarf-wrapped head, Helen peeked at the egg enough to wave her hands carefully around it.

"I begin to see..." she said, and was gratified to hear an expectant gasp and one giggle from the group.

Closing her eyes again, she called to mind psychics and fortune-telling gypsies in old black-and-white films.

"My vision is in black and white," she intoned, inspired.

She opened her eyes, with head still bent toward the egg, and looked up at the girl, who now gazed at the fortune teller raptly.

It was obvious now what to do. This child needed encouragement, hope.

"Yes, the vision is coming into sharper focus now," she said, deepening her voice and trying to endow it with an edge of excitement.

The girl leaned forward over the egg. Except for the giggler, her friends moved to the edges of their seats.

This was really quite fun! But what about the troubled girl? She must choose her words carefully.

"Oh dear!" Helen said. "The vision is fading!"

Even the giggler joined in the gasps of dismay.

The birthday girl's mom winked at Helen.

Helen peered at the egg more closely and gently draped the fingers of one hand over the top of it.

"It's coming into focus again," she said, to the relief of all, including herself.

Helen knew that being too specific would be a mistake. A general, hopeful prediction would do the trick. It must be something that would affirm a positive direction for the girl's future.

Helen kept her left hand on the top of the egg. With her right, she ventured to gently cover the teen's clasped hands.

She gazed intently into the adolescent's eyes.

"You will go far," she predicted, in a solemn tone.

The teen sat still, as though riveted.

Helen considered and then said something more. "Fortune will smile on your undertakings. You will be a winner!"

The girl's reaction was immediate.

"I know!" she cried with a strange kind of jubilance.

ooo

It was with horror the next day that Helen read a text message from the birthday party host. "Zoe disappeared!" her friend wrote. Opening the link in the message, Helen saw the headline:

TROY TEEN MISSING
AFTER BLIZZARD BIRTHDAY PARTY

A photo in the online edition of the *Troy Tattler* showed the kohl-eyed girl whose future Helen had predicted. The news story revealed that the girl had strayed from the birthday party sleepover sometime in the early hours of the morning, after the other partygoers had finally fallen asleep. Her footprints—or perhaps those of Helen, who had left the party to cross to her neighboring house early in the storm—were mere indentations in the snow on the relatively protected porch of the farmhouse where the party was held. But the footprints disappeared entirely in the open expanse of lawn and meadows where snow had drifted during blizzard conditions.

"She had seemed to enjoy herself at the party," the birthday girl's mom and party host had "tearfully" told a reporter. " I just can't fathom why she would go out in that storm!" she reportedly "wailed."

The birthday girl had refused to comment.

But one of the partygoers—was it the giggler?—was all too ready to share a thought.

"That psychic told Zoe just what she wanted to hear," she said. "Zoe told me so."

Helen answered an urgent knocking at her door. Standing there were two tabloid reporters. One was a local man, known for magnifying the straying of a goat into an event worthy of national interest. In fact, he had gotten a gazillion hits online for such stories—probably more for the inflated headlines and romping-goat videos than for the power of his prose.

The other reporter was a woman. Dressed in outerwear that was stronger on style than substance, she was certainly not a local.

The first reporter barged into Helen's house. "Duane Dutremble, *Troy Tattler*," he announced, stamping his feet so that snow fell in big, wet clumps on Helen's hardwood floor.

The other reporter shook her head at this pushiness and gave Helen a comforting, commiserating smile. "Liz Higgins, *Beantown Banner*," she said, extending her velvet-gloved hand to shake Helen's in a genteel manner. "I gather you are Helen Snowe. I'm pleased to meet you."

"The *Beantown Banner*!" Helen exclaimed. "What's a Boston reporter doing here?" she asked.

"We are everywhere that things need solving, I hope," the news gal said with evident pride.

In fact, she was staying at the neighboring farm for a feature on Maine Maple Sugar Weekend, an event that this March blizzard was nixing.

Duane Dutremble stamped his feet some more.

The Boston reporter's shiver was not lost on Helen.

"Perhaps you should come in," Helen offered.

"What the heck did you say to that girl?" Dutremble demanded of Helen, as Liz Higgins used her own scarf to soak up the local hack's snow puddles.

Stifling a sob, Helen turned to Liz.

"Do I need a lawyer?" she asked in some desperation.

"You can begin by ejecting either or both of us, while you collect yourself," Liz whispered. "You don't have to comment," she added.

It was a risk to give this advice but Liz decided to bet on Helen's need for help, in hopes that Helen would keep her on site.

"I'm not commenting!" Helen told the local man. "And I would like you to leave," she said firmly.

"Just one question," he said.

"No. Please get out. Now!" Helen said, as Liz nodded reassuringly.

"You!" Dutremble said, shaking his index finger at Liz and then thrusting his middle finger skyward. "The big city reporter!" he growled. "You'll see that we Mainers only spill the beans to our own!" he said, stomping out of the house.

"Do I need a lawyer?" Helen again asked Liz, as she filled the kettle and lit the old gas stove burner under it.

"Perhaps you can tell me more, so I can help you evaluate what to do next," Liz said, peeling off her gloves, and then removing her coat, hat and boots.

"I meant well!" Helen cried, ushering Liz to a sofa. She wrung her hands. "It was all a lark. I am no psychic, even though I pretended to be one. But that girl was troubled, I could see it. I tried to say something encouraging to her. That's all. Now the newspaper says she likely ran away and I…." Helen sobbed. She sat down heavily beside Liz.

Taking both of Helen's hands in hers, Liz leaned forward. Her gaze spelled empathy.

"I told the poor thing that she would 'go far,'" Helen admitted, breaking into tears." And now she's run away! In a blizzard!"

Just then, the kettle screamed in unison with a police siren.

"You've committed no crime," Liz said firmly as Helen stared with horror at the door, where a loud knocking ensued.

Liz removed herself to the kitchen to silence the kettle. And to listen.

A loud bang left Liz wondering if the two officers who announced themselves had slammed the door shut or if the wind had done it.

"Would you like to sit down?" she heard Helen say, her voice filled with trepidation.

"Thank you, ma'am, but you sit. We'll stand," one officer said.

Looming over a witness was hardly a way to gain confidence, Liz thought, as she sat down out of sight on a kitchen chair, listening at the same time as she took notes.

"We understand you spoke with the missing girl, Zoe Zuckerman," the same officer said. He went on to recap what the police already knew, that the girl's absence had been noticed by the host mom at daybreak, just an hour or so after the rest of the partygoers had finally fallen asleep. At the time, the snowfall had been its fiercest, and the wind had been extreme, wiping away any sign of footprints. The police knew that Helen had played psychic and offered the girl a prediction about going somewhere, according to one of Zoe's friends.

"Where did you tell Ms. Zuckerman that she would be going?" demanded the second police officer.

"Nowhere!" Helen said agitatedly. "Nowhere specific."

"Did you have any idea she was planning to run away?"

"Of course I didn't!" Helen exclaimed. "Are you sure that she ran away? What if she's somewhere out there, just lost in the snow? Oh, this is too horrible!" she cried.

"Are you qualified to counsel teens?" the police officer went on.

"I was acting, just acting, playing the role of a fortune teller," Helen said. "It was supposed to be for fun, nothing serious."

"Well, ma'am, it seems one girl took your words serious enough. She took them to heart."

Helen sobbed. "What are you doing to find her?" she demanded.

"Well, we're talking to you, for one thing."

"Telling fortunes for fun at a birthday party is not a crime," Helen said, but she did not sound convinced.

The policemen lingered long enough to assess when Helen had returned to her home on foot, and to learn what the weather conditions were like then. They asked her to remain available for further questions if need be.

At that point Liz surprised the lawmen by emerging from the kitchen. They were more astonished when she introduced herself as a Boston reporter.

"You'll find that the locals aren't exactly talkative to people from away," one officer said. "And a reporter from away—well, good luck to you!"

Liz and Helen learned that a ground-and-air search was planned once the storm abated, but that was not forecast to happen anytime soon. Outside the window, the wind still howled, whipping the waves of still-falling snow, and the gales were expected to continue until at least sunset. Members of the close-knit community were advised to hold off on any impulse to find the girl "so we won't have another tragedy on our hands," one officer said, handing Liz another strong line for the report that she was writing.

After the lawmen left, Liz poured tea and served it to Helen. Then she rapidly produced her report of events. Knowing that her story portrayed the anguished woman in a good light, she broke her rule and offered to read it to Helen before pushing the button and sending it to her editor. Comforted at being given this special consideration, Helen consented to being photographed thigh-deep in snow on her porch—and to the use of shots Liz had taken while the police were still on site. The story would go up online instantly, with the photos helping to ensure placement on the front page of the print edition.

While she took the portrait on the porch, something in the yard had caught Liz's eye. Now, with Helen opening up so well to her questions, Liz decided to take the chance to let her story source relax before pressing her more. Helen gladly assented to letting Liz shovel the entry and a path to the wood pile, while she rested.

Of course, Helen could not rest, as calls came in from the reporter Dutremble and Maine's big newspapers, the *Portland Press Herald* and *Bangor Daily News*. Just outside the door, Liz was glad to hear Helen repeat to each, "I have no comment." Liz made her way to the woodpile when it seemed Helen had turned off her phone.

Even without shoveling snow down to the ground, digging a path to the woodpile was laborious in the blowing snow. But it paid off when Liz reached the item that had caught her eye, a hot-pink strap of some kind poking through the snow. After photographing this, Liz dug carefully with her velvet-gloved hands, following the long strap deep into the drift. There she found, sparkling with some gaudy pink and silver sequins apparently snared randomly in the weave, a small, crocheted bag about the size of a change purse, just large enough to hold an ID card and a small amount of money. Her fingers frighteningly inflexible and numbed with cold, she struggled to take more photos before pocketing the purse and staggering a few more yards through thigh-deep snow to gather an armload of firewood from the pile.

Inside, Helen's kindness came to the fore as she stoked the wood stove and pulled a chair close to it for Liz. The reporter was grateful for the bowl of lukewarm water that the Mainer brought for her to plunge her hands into to stave off frostbite. She also thanked herself for the reporting experience that had allowed her to trust her instincts and wait to press her source further.

When her hands were at last warmed and dried, Liz pulled out the purse, only to hear Helen gasp.

"Those sequins! They are the same color as the sequins on my sign! My silly 'Psychic' sign," Helen explained. "Look!" she said, crossing the room to a desk and returning with two small jars half-filled with sequins. "The sign fell on the floor. Maybe she set the little purse down there."

"*If* it was her purse," Liz said. "There were five other girls at the party, correct? Did you notice any of them wearing a purse like this? It is the kind that is worn with that long strap across the body."

"No, they were all snuggled in for a sleepover. You know how girls dress these days. Some already had on pajama pants, with fleece or other tops on, not matching. One even had bare shoulders, wearing a tank top even on a freezing-cold night. No one was wearing a purse, although of course some were watching their cell phones for messages. Probably from boys."

"There is no cell phone in this purse, no ID, but there is a photo. Not of a boy but a baby goat."

"Must have been born last spring or awfully recently," Helen remarked. "Goats aren't often born in the dead of winter. Funny, that's a black-and-white goat. You don't see them much around here. Come to think of it, there is one that took a prize at the county fair, though. Looked like someone threw a pot of ink at a white goat. Very special markings."

"Sounds like a good newsroom mascot," Liz said, opening her iPad. Her screensaver, which pictured the *Beantown Banner's* front page, caught Helen's eye.

"Would you look at that!" Helen exclaimed. "Your picture of me is in black and white! Probably a good thing, because my eyes were red from crying," she said ruefully.

"The page designer probably thought it would be a more powerful statement of the blizzard, emphasizing the whiteness," Liz said, distractedly, continuing her online search.

"And the whiteness of my hair, too!" Helen said. "My, do I look my age!"

Liz looked up from her screen. "What was Zoe's reaction when you predicted that she would go far?" Liz inquired.

"Strange. Excited-like," Helen said. "It was like I hit on something that she knew was true."

"That can happen when someone wants to hear something significant from a fortune teller. It's human nature," Liz said.

"Yes, but the other girls were more giggly when I told them theirs. Zoe was, well, I guess I'd say *intense*. I should have given her a more ordinary prediction about prom dates and things, like I did the others, but she seemed so unhappy, so worried."

"Did she seem to take you more seriously than the other girls did? Is that what you mean?"

"Not at first. She seemed pretty unbelieving so I kinda hammed it up a little to get her to believe in me. I never told fortunes before and she was the first one."

"What did you do to ham it up, Helen?"

"Well, I closed my eyes and I sighed. I hoped I sounded mysterious!" Helen laughed. "It was really pretty silly."

"Did you do anything else?" Liz asked, returning her eyes to her iPad screen.

"Well, let me see. I said something about my vision for her fading in and out. She really seemed to sit up and listen when I said it had become clear again, black and white."

"Can you tell me where this barn and these goats are located?" Liz said, passing the iPad to Helen.

"Why, that's one of Duane Dutremble's goat videos!" Helen laughed. "Why would you be watching that?"

"Look who's lurking in the stall over there," Liz said, pointing to a figure in the background of the romping-goat video."

"It sure looks like Zoe," Helen said perplexedly. "She looks so wholesome without that eye makeup."

"The father of those romping goats had gone missing last autumn, right?"

"The sire, yes."

"And he is a blue-ribbon goat, right?"

"Yes, that's so. He's an Alpine. They come from Switzerland and do well in Maine's cold winters. He was black and white, not brown and white like Avery's other goats. They didn't even have to find that goat. He was returned to his stall."

"Seems it was a non-story," Liz mused. "But was it? And who is Avery?"

"It's Avery Dostie who owns the farm and the goats in that video. A couple of miles away from here. The Zuckermans, Zoe's family, live the next farm over from him. It's way too far to head for in a blizzard. Come to think of it, the Zuckermans keep goats, too."

Liz turned her gaze to the window.

"Is there any shed, barn or other outbuilding somewhere out beyond the woodpile?" she asked.

"There is! Zoe could have dropped her purse on the way to that! But it'd be hard to get to in this snow. We'd sure get frostbite digging our way out there."

"Well, here's where being a reporter from a big city newspaper from away can be an advantage," Liz thought. "If my hunch is wrong, I'll only be living up to Mainers' expectations…" she said aloud.

"But if it's right, you'll save the day!" Helen crowed.

"Well, I might save a stray teenager," Liz smiled. She pulled out her phone and called the Town of Troy Police Department.

"Just a hunch, huh?" the police chief said.

"Well I found a purse in the snow that might belong to the girl."

"All right then," the chief said. "But can you get Helen to make a heck of a lot of hot chocolate?"

ΩΩΩ

Liz pulled on thick hand-knitted mittens borrowed from Helen as she climbed on the horse-drawn sleigh that was usually reserved for rides during Maine Maple Sugar Weekend. Too deep for snowmobiles, the drifts looked likely to halt the horses in their progress, too. But this was the only hope for covering the distance between the farm that neighbored Helen's house—the same place where Liz had been set to report on the now-canceled maple sugaring event—and the old shed where Zoe might be sheltering from the storm.

But they did not have far to go. That's because a farm girl called Zoe knew better than to set out in a blizzard to cuddle her beloved goat.

ΩΩΩ

It was the goat's bleats that led the big city news gal to call a pause before setting out with the sleigh. It was the woman from away who found Zoe and her black-and-white kid safely nestled in the loft of that horse barn.

And it was the big-city reporter, yes, that gal from away, who got the local girl to spill the beans.

"I'm sorry I worried everybody. Am I in trouble?" Zoe asked.

The teenager held her baby goat close and suckled it with a bottle. Liz seated herself in the hay next to the teen and told her who she was.

"This is your secret goat, isn't it?" she asked gently.

"I guess you can say that," the teen said. "But I didn't steal her! You can't put it in the paper that I stole her!"

"We only put the truth in the paper," Liz said, "and now it's time for you to tell it. You did not steal this kid but it is also not entirely yours, is it? You did purloin farmer Dostie's big, black-and-white Alpine, didn't you?"

Zoe remained silent.

"Do you understand what I'm asking?"

"I have read Nancy Drew. I know what 'purloin' means. It means to steal! But I didn't steal Mr. Dostie's goat!"

"Well, let's just say you 'borrowed' him ," Liz said. "You were the one who took and then returned farmer Dostie's goat last October?

"How do you know?"

In her agitation, Zoe clutched her kid closer.

"Does your kid have a name?" Liz asked, keeping in mind the need for the information in her news story.

"Lois," the girl said. "Like Lois Lane in Superman. I figure she's black and white like a newspaper, and Lois Lane's a reporter. But you probably know that."

"Well, Lois is certainly getting plenty of news coverage!" Liz laughed, reflecting on how the goat's name was a gift to a newspaper reporter. "She's just a couple of weeks old, isn't she?"

"She is. Am I in trouble?" Zoe asked again. "How did you know that I borrowed that goat?"

"Farmers around here no doubt know that a goat's gestation time is around 150 days. But even city reporters can find that out. Just like I learned that the only black and white goat in the area belongs to farmer Dostie, and it went missing for a few days last October, about 150 days before Lois was born. You borrowed farmer Dostie's goat to breed with a goat from home, didn't you? You are holding the evidence of your actions in your arms, Zoe Zuckerman. Now, can you fill us in on how you kept Lois a secret?" Liz went on as an older man arrived in the barn door.

"Yes, I did borrow Mr. Dostie's goat, but I put him back where he belonged! I was right that breeding him with our goat would give me a black-and-white one! After she was born, I hid Lois in an outbuilding on our farm and snuck out at night and before school and whenever else I could to feed her. I knew I looked all red-eyed and tired so I started using this ugly eyeliner to hide that," Zoe said. "Luckily," she continued, "I could get a ride to the party with my big brother. He was in on the secret. Our Mom and Dad pretty much leave the goats to us, but I was still worried they would wonder where the black and white one came from. During the party, we were going to hide Lois in that old shed, but when it looked like it was gonna snow, we hid her in this barn instead. All through the party, I was so worried! Lois needs me to feed her! And I was really scared someone would go in this barn and find her," she admitted. "Oh, God, am I in trouble?" she asked again.

The man in the doorway stepped forward. It was Avery Dostie.

"Young lady," he began. "I think you know what you did was wrong. People usually pay for the services of a prize-winning billy goat," he said. "Would you hand me your kid, please?"

With tears spilling from her eyes, Zoe complied with the request and put the goat in the big farmer's arms.

The farmer examined the goat approvingly.

"I think I know how you can pay for your misdeed," he said.

"You won't take Lois from me, will you? Oh, please!" Zoe pleaded. "I knew it was wrong to borrow your goat but I wanted so bad to breed a blue ribbon winner of my own!"

"No, Miss Zuckerman, I will not do that, even though I can see you've got a prize-winner here," the farmer said. "Instead, I will ask you to provide your services next fall to help me decide which goat pairs have the best chances for producing more blue-ribbon kids. You seem to have quite a knack for this. Do we have a deal?"

Wiping away her kohl-stained tears, Zoe stood up. She stood tall. She took farmer Dostie's outstretched hand and shook it firmly.

"Deal!" she said. "I just knew it was all gonna turn out right," she said, after a moment. "The fortune teller told me fortune would smile on me. She said it was black-and-white and I would be a winner!"

Rosemary Herbert is the author of *Front Page Teaser: A Liz Higgins Mystery*, which draws on her experience at the *Boston Herald*. She is editor in chief of *The Oxford Companion to Crime & Mystery Writing* and co-editor, with Tony HIllerman, of *The Oxford Book of American Mystery Stories* and *A New Omnibus of Crime*. She wrote "A Twist of Fortune" in her Maine island cottage during a fierce snowstorm.

LUNCH BREAK
by Travis Kennedy

It was a sunny Monday morning, warm for January in Maine, and Charlie Cushman had staked out a strip of parking spots on Silver Street to smoke cigarettes and steal shit from cars.

Charlie came from a long line of dirtbags and was dumb as a stump among polite society, but he had a Realtor's eye for criminal mischief. Silver Street was quiet that day, and mostly under construction. Metal-framed tunnels covered the sidewalk on the sunny side of the street, and thick wooden panels were affixed to the framework to keep the frigid winter wind away from the work happening inside. The city had installed computerized parking meters a few years earlier, and so the construction firm had to build a box inside the wooden tunnel where commuters could buy parking tickets to leave on their dashboards. It was like a clapboard ATM, hidden from sight.

When Charlie spotted it, he knew immediately that fortune had smiled on him. He would watch patiently from the shade of a dark stoop as his marks goose-stepped across the icy sidewalk, and ducked into the tunnel to negotiate with the machine. They never bothered to lock their cars, and were out of sight for at least twenty seconds. Charlie only needed ten or so to grab anything worth stealing.

By noon he had collected more than forty dollars, a tablet computer, a glass pipe, and a new pack of cigarettes. All told, Charlie had been having a pretty splendid morning; until he grabbed the wrong backpack out of the wrong pickup truck.

That's when he became my problem.

ººº

At roughly the same time Charlie was making the worst decision of his life, I was a few blocks away in a bar called The Last Resort, about to get my ass kicked.

The Last Resort was a dive bar in a dive neighborhood up the road from the post office, one of the only square blocks in Portland where gentrification hadn't started to settle in yet. It was also the regular hangout of a thug named Ricky Pickett, who had taken an eighteen-wheeler loaded with 4K televisions that didn't belong to him.

Ricky was the defacto leader of a little swarm of angry rednecks who were moving heroin from across the New Hampshire border into the rural towns, stealing the occasional delivery truck, and allegedly vanishing some of the local competition in the sandpits out in Baldwin. He was a brute of a guy, over six feet tall and at least 250 pounds. He had been a portly fellow his whole life, which I could have some sympathy for; but his was the mean kind of fat, which came with an impressive amount of torque.

Daryl Walsh, the guy who owned the trucking company, was an old friend of my father. He had earned a reputation for staging robberies of his own trucks in the 1980's, but he's been running the shop clean since Vanilla Ice was on the radio. I stopped by the Last Resort on my lunch break as a favor to Daryl, with the humble goal of negotiating the truck's safe return. But things didn't work out that way.

"You don't even have to say you took it," I told Ricky from across the bar. "They just need it back. They'll even pay a finder's fee, this one time. But as a show of good faith they need you to send back the driver's wallet, the poor guy is freaking out."

Ricky's cold eyes settled on me. "Time for you to go," he said. His voice was high and gravelly, and he spoke in short bursts, like he was trying to talk while holding his breath. I had no way of knowing how many of the other deadbeats at the bar might back him up if he needed it, and Ricky had graciously offered my last opportunity to tuck my tail between my legs and leave the room without violence. Any sane man would take it.

I let out a long sigh, and elected insanity. "Don't be stupid, Ricky," I said, leveling my eyes on his. "I'm doing you a favor. You think they don't know you stashed the truck in that old salt shed in Standish? They'll take it on their own, and burn the place down for good measure unless you give me the wallet right now with an apology." The hiding spot was a guess, but the little flicker in his eyes told me I was right. His cheeks flushed red. In theory I could have left then, but stubborn principle had taken over the negotiation. "Now quit wasting my time. I only get an hour for lunch."

The bartender wordlessly made his way to the back room and shut the door. Ricky climbed off of his barstool, holding my gaze. He pulled an old wallet from his duffel bag and tossed it on a four-top table between us.

"Go ahead and take it," he said, his eyes dancing with wicked anticipation.

I took a step toward the table; so did Ricky. I reached slowly toward the wallet, and Ricky did a little fake lunge toward me, getting me to pull my hand back. He grinned, and I grinned back. I reached again, closer this time; he lunged again, enough that he leaned across the table and swept his arms together, trying to catch me. We had established a pattern now, which was to Ricky's clueless detriment.

For the third time, I leaned toward the table slowly. Ricky hovered on the balls of his feet, waiting for me to get my hands too close. I waited there for a moment - just long enough for his balance to get shaky - then lunged forward quickly. Ricky did the same. I reared back hard and he lost his balance over the table trying to catch me. I grabbed my side of the table and pulled it down, letting the wallet slip onto the ground at my feet. Ricky's end of the table swung up, and met his face in the middle. He let out a loud grunt, and a stream of blood flew out of his nose as he fell backward. His hands went to his face and he dropped onto his knees.

"Oh my God, Ricky, are you all right?" I scooped the wallet off the floor. "I was trying to grab the wallet like you told me to, Ricky, why did you do that?"

A couple of guys got up from the bar like they were going to do something about it all, but I was at the door already. I held up a commanding finger. "You think they sent me alone?" I bluffed. "Come on out and see." They stood still, angry but anxious, like a pack of junkyard dogs on invisible chains.

"Our friends will appreciate how sorry you are about the whole mixup," I said as I leaned against the door. "You're welcome, by the way." Pickett pushed himself up onto his elbow and glared at me.

"You're a dead man," he sputtered, as I showed myself out.

Now when you collect death threats at the clip I do, you develop a sense for how immediate the danger is on a case-by-case basis. Sure, in the heat of the moment ole' Ricky probably meant it; but he might not have the attention span to track me down later. Guys like him get in fights every week. As long as I kept my eye out for his crew and stayed clear of The Last Resort for a while, it might blow over.

However, Ricky was now the third person in Portland planning to kill me. Mondays, right? Fortunately they weren't working together, or I would probably be dead already.

ΩΩΩ

I was a fat kid, growing up.

I've found it's easier to be honest about what motivates my behavior if I disclose my childhood shame up front. So I was a fat kid, in a rough neighborhood. I got teased a lot and beat up sometimes, and the girls didn't like me; so I didn't have much interest in playing outside with the other kids. I would usually rush home from school as quick as I could, and settle in my room with a sleeve of Chips Ahoy and a crate of comedy videotapes. No matter what was happening in the world outside, I could vanish for a couple of hours with Eddie, Chevy, Steve Martin, Pryor, Carlin and old Saturday Night Lives. Their world was the only safe place I had.

By Junior High, the teasing turned into beatings. Meanwhile, my self-medication through junk food and comedy began to manifest itself in bad skin and an uncontrollable, hair-trigger smartass mouth, all of which contributed to more abuse. It was a vicious cycle, and finally my old man got me into boxing in hopes of putting a stop to it. This was a miserable experience for most of that first year; but it got me exercising, and learning a little self defense. I replaced the cookies with apples, and my skin cleared up. The summer before Junior year I grew half a foot, and suddenly I wasn't a fat kid anymore. I kept boxing, and worked in mixed martial arts. And when I was 17, I picked up the old man's side business.

My father worked in street maintenance for the city; but he seemed to spend most of his time solving problems for people from the neighborhood. I don't really know if he was a fixer, or a vigilante, or a little of both, depending on the day; but guys I used to call "Uncle Jimmy" or "Uncle Donny" were always coming by the house looking for help with one thing or another, and we never seemed to have trouble with money.

I had the same knack for problem solving as the old guy I guess, and twenty years after he died I'm still doing it. My name is Shawn MacIntosh. I'm 37 years old. Don't go falling in love with me; I might not be around for long.

ooo

My phone started ringing when I was a block away from the Last Resort, and I winced when I saw it was my little sister, Jasmine. She never calls just to chat; Jasmine finds her way into more jams than rhubarb.

"I'm friggin' dead, Shawn," she said, before I could get out a hello.

"Okay, let me hear it."

"Some jackhole stole my bag out of Jeremy's truck this morning. I seriously need that bag back now, or I'm done for. Like dead."

"What did the police say?"

"I can't call them," she said under her breath.

I sighed. "Of course you can't. What's in it?"

"Just stuff of mine, all right?" She snapped back, with the attitude of the fifteen year old girl she never grew out of. "No drugs. I swear. But I was doing a favor for these guys from Providence."

My skin went cold; I was pretty sure she wasn't talking about a couple of fratboys from Johnson and Wales here. "What were you doing in Providence?"

"I wasn't IN Providence," she hissed, and then remembered she was asking for a favor. "I've been picking up shifts at the club. These guys came in last night. They looked mobbed up a little but they were nice, right? They knew this guy Tony I used to go out with, and asked if I wanted to make some money. All I had to do was drop a bag off in a trashcan behind the car wash on Forest Ave this morning. They gave me five hundred bucks, and said they would know if I didn't do it."

"Did you look in it?"

"Of course I did. I didn't want to get caught with five pounds of crank or whatever. It was full of cash. I stopped counting at four grand. I didn't even want to touch it. So I put it in my backpack from when I was still stripping because it's Kevlar and has a lock on it, and Jeremy was gonna drop it off for me, but some prick stole it when he stopped on Silver Street to get a coffee."

"Pretty nice of Jeremy, putting himself in that position for you."

"He didn't take it, Shawn! Just find it, all right? I'm seriously dead if you don't."

"Jasmine, if there's more than four thousand dollars in that backpack whoever took it is probably halfway to Boston by now."

"Not if he can't get the lock open."

"All right. Dammit. I'm heading over to Silver Street now."

"You're the best, Shawnie," she said. "The combination is my birthday. Let me know when you find it, okay? Love you!" She hung up before I could say anything.

From the sound of things, Jasmine had agreed to deliver a payment from the Providence mob, and it vanished midway. She was right: if it didn't turn up, she was dead. Clearly, I was not going to have time for a sandwich before I had to get back to work.

I steered toward Silver Street among an unnaturally busy crowd of pedestrians who were walking to lunch in the January thaw, past upscale restaurants that had been holes in the wall two years ago and will be recycled into something entirely different by the time I finish this sentence. I carried a faint hope that the culprit might still be around; but the street was empty. A city police cruiser rolled by slowly. Jasmine hadn't called them, so somebody else must have—which meant our thief was robbing cars there for a while. This was helpful.

So here's where someone in my position gains a certain edge. Sure, Portland PD could take statements, and swing by Silver Street to keep an eye out; maybe even ask around a little. But what the police, God bless them, couldn't do was walk two blocks up the road and just ask Rodney Black who did it.

Rodney was parked in his white Mazda outside the Nine Ball Club, waiting for customers. His parents called him Rodney, but everyone else called him Black Friday because every couple of weeks he would get his hands on a wholesale volume of weed from his uncle and sell it at doorbuster prices. The Mazda's windows were tinted so black that I couldn't see inside, but the engine was running and his after-market subwoofer was banging so loud I could feel my fillings shaking.

I rapped on the window, and it slid down to reveal Black Friday in all his 140 pound glory. The air in the car was heavy with the reek of his uncle's potent strain of cannabis, and the scrawny ginger was hiding behind massive sunglasses and a flat-rimmed Celtics hat, baked beyond reason.

"Big Mac," he let out a slow smirk. "You buying? Since when?" He slid his sunglasses down below his glazed eyes, revealing genuine concern. "Dog, The munchies though! They're a powerful thing." Years ago, I had come to accept that around here I'll always be the neighborhood fat kid.

"I appreciate that Rodney, and I'm good," I said. "You know Maine legalized it though, right?"

"I'm still cheaper," he shrugged. "No taxman, man. So what do you want? This is my rush hour."

"Listen, someone was picking cars on Silver Street today. You have any idea who?"

Friday squinted at me. "What do you care, he take your EZ-Pass or something?"

"I'm not asking for me. A friend of mine." I stressed the word "friend" and winked, hoping he would assume I was working for the mob or something.

"Yo like, something really expensive? Cause if I'm gonna rat out a guy it's gotta be worth my while."

"You're doing him a favor. He'll want to return what he took. It's hot. Like, it could get him killed hot."

"What?" Friday blurted out a laugh and pounded on his steering wheel. "That's classic! A'ight bruh, I'll tell you who, but you gotta tell me what this is all about."

"Deal," I said. "After I sort it out."

"Cushman, dog."

"Charlie?" I rolled my eyes. "Or his dad?"

"Charlie. He was sitting on that street all morning. Came over and bought a dime, said he just got a new bowl. Then he went right back over there." He mechanically dug into his glove box for a pipe and crammed a pinch of weed into it.

"Okay. Thanks," I said. "Any idea where he got up to?"

"I'm sure he's drinking away his profits somewhere," he shrugged as he lit a plastic lighter to the end of the bowl and pulled in an absurd amount of smoke, then let it crawl out slowly through his nose. "Some people have no self control, right? You owe me a beer."

"Right," I said as the window rolled up. I stretched and got my bearings, taking a moment to suck in the clean winter air through my nose. It had never tasted so refreshing after hovering around Black Friday's Mazda. The sun was warm on my face, enough that I almost convinced myself I could smell the saltwater and hear the seagulls in the harbor on a spring day.

I was probably high.

When I opened my eyes, my little meditation evaporated and reality sunk in: there were at least a dozen bars I could think of between the waterfront and the edge of the city where Charlie might take his winnings in the middle of a weekday. I didn't have that kind of time on my hands, so I took another deep breath and called the grocery store on Munjoy Hill.

I was trying to track down Jack Nealon, the closest thing Portland has to a Don. Organized crime has deep roots in Maine, believe it or not; the state was a logical entry point for bootleggers from Canada and Europe during prohibition, and the families put guys up here to lay down roots. Only a handful of them stuck around after the Eighteenth Amendment was repealed, but they left behind an entire infrastructure designed to move illicit materials. If there's one universal truth, it's that there will always be swift business for people who are willing to take a risk moving something valuable from one place to another.

The guys running operations today aren't your Jersey Tracksuit Italians; they're more likely to wear Carhartts and hang out in bait shops, moving who-knows-what from Canada to points south and stringing together your garden variety RICO hijinks to pay for the boats and ATVs. Jack was somewhere in the middle; he was a French-Irish guy from up the coast and still had an active lobster license, but he dressed sharp whenever he left the house and could recite the first 40 minutes of Goodfellas by heart. He also ran the biggest sports book in the state, and hosted high stakes poker games for the New York lawyers in the summer. He did well for himself.

Charlie had been working off a revolving debt to Jack for most of his adult life with side jobs, so the old man knew how to find him on short order just about any time of day. This was a complicated call to make, however, because Jack Nealon was the second person in Portland trying to kill me.

A few weeks ago, a cokehead named Butchie Clark who had been working security for some of Jack's projects went rogue and kidnapped a kid from the private school downtown. What he didn't realize is that it's a French-speaking school, so he couldn't communicate with the little guy about who his parents were and how rich they might be. A stripper who lived next door sniffed out trouble, so she told Jasmine, who told me; and when I couldn't get in touch with Jack, I called it into Portland PD. I had no choice. When they got to Butchie's house, he had locked the kid in a closet and was dousing the place in gasoline. Butchie's dead now.

Jack was better off, and I'm sure he knew it. But I had taken Butchie off the man's payroll, through the police, no less. Jack has a sensitive ego about these sorts of things. It started filtering back to me through the Scumbag Information Network that he had a spot picked out for me at the bottom of Casco Bay; but it was kind of a playful death threat, like maybe he would kill me someday or maybe we would end up laughing it all off and going in on a timeshare together.

Jack didn't use cell phones, but he kept a regular office in the back of the grocery store on Munjoy Hill. There was a long pause after I told the kid who answered the phone my name, while he ran out back to find out if Jack was taking my calls. It dawned on me that Jack might just tell the kid I should go ahead and pound sand, but eventually his deep voice greeted me.

"Portland Police Department," Jack grumbled.

"Yeah, Jack, I know. I'm sorry. But listen, Charlie Cushman screwed up big, and you're gonna want me to find him ASAP."

He was quiet for a beat. Finally he caved to curiosity. "Explain."

"He borrowed the wrong book from the library," I said, and waited while Jack processed the code I was using. "He's gonna need to return it or the late fees will be pretty severe."

"The hell do I care?"

"They're probably under the impression he was using your library card," I said, and waited. I heard Jack exhale hard and curse. I was stretching it a little, but it stood to reason that when word got out Charlie had robbed Providence, everyone would assume he did it for Jack. It was a crappy coincidence for the old man, but exactly the kind of collateral damage you need to budget for when you employ a broad circle of dumb assholes. "So they might come to you to collect on it," I said, "and they'll be grumpy if they have to drive all the way up from Rhode Island."

There was a devastatingly long silence on the other end of the phone while Jack decided what to do about me. "He's at the Last Resort," he finally said, and hung up.

This was not my day.

ꝍꝍꝍ

I peeked through the glass door of the bar and saw no sign of Pickett or his crew, which was an uncommon win in my column. I entered cautiously, and kept my back to the wall as I surveyed the room. Charlie was sitting at the bar, nursing a beer. The bartender saw me approaching, and an expression of pure terror washed over his face that quickly morphed into weary resignation. I was probably not his first death wish.

"You can't be in here," he said.

"I just need two minutes," I told him, and slapped a twenty on the bar, then clamped a hand on Charlie's shoulder. "Give my friend here a glass of your finest whiskey." The bartender sighed and shook his head; but consummate professional that he was, he gave Charlie a generous pour and took down a second glass for me.

"I'm good," I waved him off. "Lunch break. Charlie, I need to talk to you." I motioned to a booth, and Cushman rolled his eyes but reluctantly followed with his whiskey. He slumped into a seat across from me. "I'm gonna make this quick," I said. "You stole a bag from a truck on Silver Street today." He sat up straight in his chair, prepared to protest, but I waved him off.

"Listen to me. That bag is a mob payment. It's been missing for two hours, which they are definitely going to notice."

"Christ," Charlie groaned. He slumped into his chair and dropped his head in his hands. "Do they know I took it?"

I shrugged. "I figured it out in ten minutes." He spit out a stream of obscenities and stormed over to the bar, where he retrieved the bag from under his stool and dropped it on the table.

"Take it and get out," he said. I would have been happy to, but we both knew I needed to make sure the cash was still there. I put Jasmine's birthday into the lock and unzipped the bag. Charlie's curiosity got the better of him then, and he peeked in alongside me.

It was stuffed full of drug money bills, all ratty and wrinkled and sorted in elastic bands. On top of the pile was a large brass key with a note taped to it. Charlie snatched it up before I could stop him.

"Supply compromised," he read out loud. "Withdraw 200K from First County B&T in Lyman. Go underground." Charlie read the note back to himself a couple of times, until he figured out what it meant. "First County? That bank closed, like ten years ago. The whole business park is empty. Oh my God!" He whispered. "You know what this is? It's two hundred grand sitting in a safe that nobody's gonna miss!" Charlie grinned and rubbed his hands together anxiously.

"Wait, dummy," I said. "This is Providence's money. They'll know it's missing, you took it from their drop route. When word gets out..."

"Providence?" Charlie scrunched his eyes. "Why would Providence send a bunch of cash to their drop? They're having loyalty problems up here."

"What?"

"God, MacIntosh, for a guy who's supposed to be connected you're clueless," Charlie said, and chugged the whiskey in one nervous gulp. "These dealers from Providence have been moving H up here for months now, and a couple of weeks ago it started disappearing between their dropoff and pickup."

"Who's taking it?" I asked.

"Who do you think?" He smirked.

"Wait. Jack?" I was stunned. Charlie didn't say anything, but he wasn't carrying an unsustainable poker debt for nothing. "Jack Nealon doesn't deal heroin, Charlie. That doesn't make sense."

"Exactly, he doesn't," Charlie said, and tried to sip from the empty glass. "It's going right into an incinerator. Eventually they'll either give up or get reckless enough to get pinched. Either works for him."

Now it made sense. The Providence guys didn't know who was robbing them. Which meant they didn't know if they could trust their usual courier, so they recruited my dimwitted sister to drop off their bait bag. Whoever was taking the heroin was somebody's stooge, and they would probably be dumb enough to follow the bag to their trap in an abandoned bank. If Nealon's guys took the bait, a gang war would break out across Southern Maine within hours.

While Jack and I weren't exactly best buddies, he was the devil I knew. He didn't let his guys deal drugs. He sponsored the little league teams through his restaurant. He almost never resorted to violence. Besides, Charlie had already derailed their plan, and I was left literally holding the bag. *What the hell was I going to do with this thing?*

"You've gotta be kidding me," a scratchy voice said from over my shoulder. It was Ricky Pickett, emerging dramatically from the men's room to solve my problem. Black specks of dried blood still clung to his nostrils and dark patches had formed under both of his eyes.

"Ricky, you didn't go to a hospital?" I was legitimately shocked. "For God's sake, I broke your nose dead to rights! You need to get that thing looked at."

Ricky stumbled toward me, and his friends materialized from the pool room with cues in hand like a bunch of extras in West Side Story. The bartender vanished to the stockroom again.

"Whoa whoa whoa," I said, putting my hands up. "Hear me out. I have a peace offering." I dumped the cash onto the table. Ricky's eyes bulged.

"How much is that?" he asked cautiously.

"Five or six large," I said. "At least. But this is just the tip of the iceberg. Read the note." Charlie and I backed away from the table as Ricky nosed his way over. He flipped through a stack of bills, then found the key. He unfolded the note and his lips moved while he read it, and they slowly curved into a malicious smile when he got to the end.

"Bring the van around," he announced. "We're going to the bank." Then he thrust a stubby finger at me. "I'm not done with you yet."

"Fair enough, Ricky," I said. "See you around."

ꝏꝏ

"And that's how Charlie Cushman accidentally saved your life," I told Jack Nealon, across a card table behind his grocery store on the Hill.

"Never liked Pickett," he muttered, and I couldn't help but notice his hand shook a little as he took a sip from his comically tiny espresso cup. "You want one of these? Not bad, for a grocery store."

"Thanks, but I'm late to get back to work," I stood up and anxiously stuffed my hands in my pockets. "So Jack... we good?"

"Yeah, kid. We're good."

I never did get a chance to have lunch, but I was feeling pretty fantastic nonetheless as I headed across town and back to work. I had cut the list of people in Portland who wanted to murder me from three down to one, in under an hour. I was feeling lucky, and I thought I might be able to clear the table by the time I had to buy that beer for Black Friday.

If only I could remember who the third person was.

There's definitely a third one.

I think?

Dammit.

Travis Kennedy lives in Scarborough, Maine, with his wife Liv and their daughter, Ella. He invented the term "No shoes, no shirt, no problem." His work has been featured in the Haunted Waters Press literary journal "From the Depths," the humor website "The Rotting Post," and Panoply Zine. His first novel, *Booty*, an adventure comedy, is available on Amazon.

TOTALLY MISUNDERSTOOD
by Lorraine Sharma Nelson

His mouth was open in a big O, his eyes wide and glassy. Even in death, the look of surprise on the man's face couldn't be misconstrued.

Detective Isha Naidu's dark brows drew together, as her gaze once again zeroed in on the gaping wound in his chest, most probably delivered by a shotgun at close range. The bullet had torn through the chest, scattering bits of bone and flesh in its trajectory through the heart.

Isha shook her head as she turned and headed back to her car, hunching down in her coat. The medical examiner caught up with her as she walked.

"So, what do you think, Detective? Someone caught him by surprise, right?"

She grimaced. "Looks that way, doesn't it?"

Dr. Reddy nodded, glancing back at the body, still in the driver's side of the Prius. "We'll finish up here and head back. I'll have a report for the chief just as soon as the body is I.D.'d."

Isha slid into her car, deep in thought. No I.D., and no credit cards to identify the victim, but his empty wallet was still in his pants pocket. And there was a sizeable amount of cash tucked in a manila envelope, hidden under the front seat. A thousand dollars. Considering his car, which had clearly seen better days, and his ill-fitting cheap suit, it didn't make sense.

She glanced back at the grey Prius, now covered with mud splatters from the puddles left over from yesterday's downpour, before the rain turned to snow and froze everything. The energy-efficient car looked so out-of-place in this rural area of northern Maine, where most people drove pickups and vans. And of course, the ubiquitous Subaru.

Her lips twisted as she pulled onto the snow-covered dirt road. She was one to talk about being out-of-place. Here she was, a little Indian woman, in a town where practically everyone was of Irish extraction. The medical examiner, who was also Indian, an elderly couple from Chengdu, China, who ran the Chinese restaurant, and a few people of English descent, were all the diversity that existed in this small rural community.

What she should have done, when she got her degree in Criminal Justice from Harvard, was head down to New York City, where people of all races and ethnicities co-existed. Instead, she found herself accepting a position in law enforcement in the little town of Misunderstood, in as rural a section of Maine as one could get.

Misunderstood. Population: 221. By next week, it'll be 223, after Shannon Murphy has her twins.

When she phoned her parents back in India to tell them of her new job offer, they thought she was crazy for even considering it. "Isha, you'll be an oddity," her father said. "Those people have probably never even seen an Indian person before. The only Indians they know of are Native Americans. You won't be accepted. You'll be miserable. An outsider."

But Isha saw it differently. This was an opportunity to spread her wings. Explore new places. It was a whole new adventure. Besides, she loved the name of the town. It called to her. Picking up the phone right after her call to her folks, Isha accepted the position of detective for the Misunderstood Police Force.

Even now, two years later, Isha still had a hard time keeping a straight face whenever she had to explain that she was from the Misunderstood Police Department.

She turned up the heat as she headed back to the station. The cold for the past two weeks had been almost unbearable. And it was only November. It didn't bode well for the long winter ahead.

By the time she pulled into the parking lot of the Misunderstood Police Station, the air had changed, become charged. Dark clouds gathered overhead, and the threat of snow hung over the rural community. Isha pulled the edges of her coat tighter together as she headed inside. Of course, this was the one thing she hated about living here. This miserable, infernal cold that held the entire state of Maine captive for six months every year.

Inside the warmth of the station, she shed her heavy coat, making a beeline for the office of the chief of police. She knocked politely, then popped her head in. "Chief?"

Aidan O'Connor glanced up from his computer screen and glared at her. "Did I say you could come in?"

She ignored his comment and strode right up to his desk, leaning over it so she could meet him eye-to-eye. "Chief, we have a homicide on our hands."

"I know."

"Right here in Misunderstood."

"I know that too."

"Well, then. Surely you see my point?"

O'Connor scowled at her. "What point? You haven't made any sense yet."

Isha refrained from rolling her eyes, knowing from experience how much the gesture annoyed him. "Come on, Chief. You know we can't wait until the body is identified. If we're going to solve this thing, we need to follow the trail before it gets too cold."

O'Connor stared at her. "What trail? There's a trail?"

"Well, place has been established. We just need time-of-death. And motive. We need motive." She leaned closer. "Which is why we need to have the body examined *now*."

O'Connor sat back and crossed his arms. "Absolutely not. We're not...*you're* not breaking the law just because you can't follow protocol."

This time Isha did roll her eyes. "Oh, come on, Chief. This is a murder we're talking about here."

O'Connor leaned forward so fast, Isha jerked back in surprise. "I know that, Naidu. I'm the Chief of Police. People who work here generally fill me in on what's happening. Especially if there's a murder involved."

Isha glared at him. "A man is dead, his I.D. is missing, and you're making jokes."

O'Connor sat back with a sigh. "Look, he'll be identified soon. Then your fellow countryman can proceed with his autopsy."

Isha clamped her mouth shut. The chief knew that Dr. Reddy was American born, and that, despite being Indian, he'd never been to India. He also knew it was one of the few things that could really annoy Isha, so he referred to the doctor as her 'fellow countryman' whenever he wanted to get a rise out of her. Like now.

Well, too bad, because this time she wasn't taking the bait.

She looked at her boss for a long moment. "How often have I been wrong on a case?"

He shifted in his chair, his eyes darting away from her. "Now, Detective—"

"How often, Chief?"

He sighed, his gaze shifting back to her. "Never."

"Out of how many?"

"I don't remember. A lot." He cleared his throat. "I think you've made your, point, Nai—"

"Twelve. I've been the lead detective on twelve cases, and I've solved every one." She grinned at him. "And there's one more thing."

"Which is?"

"This will be my thirteenth case. And you may not know this, but thirteen is my lucky number."

"Oh. Well, that's different, Naidu. You'll solve this case because it's your lucky number."

Isha scowled. "Sarcasm doesn't become you, Chief."

O'Connor sighed, and leaned forward. "Exactly how did you expect me to react to a cockamamie statement like that, Naidu?"

Isha's eyebrows shot up. "Cockamamie? I didn't know people still use that word."

"It's a perfectly serviceable word," O'Connor snapped.

"If you're ninety."

"Okay, we're done here. Go away and let me get some real work done."

"Come on, Chief? What harm is there in me snooping around while we're waiting? I mean, it's not like he's going anywhere."

Chief O'Connor opened his mouth, presumably to argue with her, or quote rules, or say something sarcastic, but then his shoulders slumped forward in what Isha knew was defeat. "Fine. Go. I don't want to see you back here for the rest of the day, understand?"

Isha briefly considered hugging the man. "Thanks, Chief. I won't let you down." She whirled toward the door.

Behind her, she heard his muttered "I need an aspirin," but wisely chose to ignore it, shutting the door softly behind her.

The hunt was on.

ϱϱϱ

Isha, and the two officers she worked best with, Dillon Walsh and Liam Kelly, returned to the scene of the crime. The car had been impounded, and the only thing left in its wake were the frozen tracks made by the wheels.

By the time the trio had searched the entire vicinity for clues, the sun was sinking behind the mountains.

"This place has already been swept for clues, Detective," Walsh said. "What were you hoping to find that hasn't already been found?"

Isha shook her head, staring at the spot where the car had been. "I don't know, but there has to be something. There's always something." She bit her lip, frowning as she scanned the surrounding area. "Who did you say the land belonged to?"

"Andy Miller," Walsh said. "He owns that big dairy farm about two miles down."

"Anything else down this way?"

Kelly cut in. "There's a few homes past the farm, but that's about it. Nothing else."

Isha stared down the road for a moment longer, then turned back to the others. "Let's go over every square inch again, before we lose any more light."

Walsh groaned. "Not again. I can barely feel my fingers. It's colder than a witch's—"

Kelly cleared his throat.

"—toes out here." Walsh threw Kelly an amused look.

Kelly scowled at him. "Yeah, well that's why they pay us the big bucks. Let's just do this and get outta here."

After a further half hour of combing the entire area, Isha finally straightened. "Okay, guys. We're done here. Let's go."

"May I ask what the point of all this was, Detective?" Kelly asked, as they headed back to the station.

Isha shrugged, blowing on her fingers. "I just needed to be certain that the evidence crew hadn't overlooked anything."

"I think it's more like you think you can do a better job than them finding clues," Walsh muttered, staring out the backseat window.

"I'm going to pretend I didn't hear that," Isha said mildly.

"Appreciate it," Walsh replied, and Isha could hear the laugher in his voice.

ϱϱϱ

Isha was at her desk when her boss popped his head out the door and called her into his office.

"I understand you took Walsh and Kelly away from the case they're working on, just so you could go digging around in the dirt at the scene of the crime?"

Isha bristled. "Did they tell you that?"

"Of course not. They'd never snitch on you. For reasons unbeknownst to me, they actually like you."

"'Unbeknownst'? Another new word. Have you been brushing up on your vocabulary, Chief?"

"Now listen, Naidu—"

A sharp rap at the door interrupted him. "Oh hell, now what? Come in."

The door opened, and Dr. Reddy, the medical examiner strode in, a big smile on his face, and a file clutched in his hands. He nodded at Naidu, then turned to the chief. "Did you tell her that the body's been I.D.'d?"

"What?!!" Isha glared at her boss.

Nonplussed, he shook his head. "She hasn't given me a chance yet. What do you have for me?"

"I emailed you the report on our victim, but here's a hard copy as well." He handed the file over, and smiled at Isha. "Seems our John Doe is one Peter Bailey, an investigative reporter for a small newspaper somewhere in New York."

She frowned. "The city or the state?

"The state."

Her frown deepened. "What's he doing all the way up here, in the middle of the boonies?"

"Hey?" O'Connor said, glancing up from his perusal of the report. "I resent that."

Isha snorted. "Oh, come on. We live in the middle of the boonies. You know it. I know it. Get over it."

The chief scowled at her, something she was so used to, it hardly registered anymore. "What I meant was, there are a lot of small towns in New York state as well, Detective, as you should know. Maine is not the only state that has rural communities far from everything."

"Yeah, so?"

"So…never mind. I forget what I was saying. Now shut up and let me read the report. Or better yet, go away and let me read in peace."

Isha turned to Dr. Reddy. "Jai, can you summarize it?"

"Hey? Am I talking to myself?"

Isha turned quickly to her boss. "Sorry, Chief. I just thought the good doctor could give us a quick rundown."

"Well, let's see," Dr. Reddy said, scratching his chin. "Not much to tell. You've already surmised that Mr. Bailey died from the bullet to the chest. Time-of-death was around 2 a.m., so he was dead for about five hours before someone found him and called it in. Since the bullet was lodged in the back of the driver's seat, it's safe to say he was shot where we found him—in the car, hunched over the wheel." Reddy looked up, his gaze shifting from Isha to the police chief. "That's about it."

"Except for who shot him and why?" O'Connor muttered. He turned to Isha, scowling again. "Well, don't just stand there gaping at me, go do your job. Find Mr. Bailey's killer."

ꝏ

"I see. Thank you so much, Mr. Cross. I just got the email. Really appreciate it." Isha closed her eyes and nodded as she listened to the voice on the other end of the phone. "Yes, sir. You may rest assured that I will find the suspect. They won't get away with it."

She hung up the phone and noticed Liam Kelly watching her with a quizzical expression on his face. She gave him a brief smile, then turned her attention to the email.

"So? What's the story?" He rolled his chair over to her, leaning in to read her email.

"Stop breathing down my neck and I'll tell you," she said, elbowing him away. She scanned the email then glanced up at him. "That was the editor of the *Edenville Times*, a small newspaper in a town about an hour outside of Buffalo. Seems our Mr. Bailey was pursuing a tip concerning Andy Miller's dairy farm."

Kelly's eyebrows lifted. "What about it?"

"Someone—I don't know who yet—found out that Bailey had written an article about an organic farm that used pesticides, and decided that he would be the perfect man to expose Andy Miller's nefarious practices."

Kelly's brows snapped together, and his eyes lit up. "What nefarious practices would those be?"

"According to Bailey's source, Andy's touting his dairy products as organic, when in reality he's using growth hormones in his cows."

"Holy shit. No kidding?" Kelly rubbed his chin. "Man, if that's true, and that news got out…"

"He stands to lose everything. All the big name grocery chains that carry his brand." She swiveled her chair around and leveled a gaze at Kelly. "He couldn't let that happen, could he?"

"No," Kelly said. "Should we—?"

"Pay a visit to Andy?" Isha rose to her feet and reached for her down coat. "Let's go."

ꝏ

Andy Miller's eyes narrowed as he stared first at Isha, then at Kelly. "So you think I murdered that loser?"

Isha gazed coolly back at Andy. "That *loser* as you so eloquently put it, Andy, is now dead." She leaned forward, lowering her voice. "Did I mention he was shot through the heart at close range?"

Andy Miller winced, shifting in his chair. "Wasn't me," he mumbled. "I got nuthin' against him."

"Except for the fact that he could have ruined you." Isha watched him closely, noting the nervous twitch of his fingers against his thighs.

"It's all lies is what it is. I run a respectable business." Andy rose suddenly and started pacing. "Damn outsiders think they can come up here and start pokin' around. They don't know nuthin.'"

Isha watched him for a minute more, knowing that it unnerved him, before she spoke again. "I understand your son works for you."

Andy stopped. Turned to her. "Yeah. So?"

"I'd like to talk to him."

"I don't think so. He's busy."

Isha smiled. "That wasn't a request, Andy. I can either talk to him here, in the comfort of your lovely kitchen, or he can come down to the station for questioning? Which'll it be?"

ꝏꝏ

"My pa says you got some questions?" Steve Miller sat across the table from Isha, glaring at her with open hostility.

Isha dove right in. "So, Steve, where were you between the hours of, say 1:00 and 3:00 a.m. this morning?"

The boy shrugged. It didn't escape Isha's notice that here was a strong, strapping young man who would have no problem overpowering most men much older than his twenty years.

"In bed, where most good little boys are at that time," he said, a smirk on his clean-shaven face. "Why? Where were you?"

She smiled, resisting the urge to reach across the table and slap that smug smile off his face. "Don't play games with me, Stevie. You're way out of your league." She leaned across the table, splaying her hands out on either side of her. "Now, I'm going to ask you again, where were you between the hours of 1:00 and 3:00 this morning?"

Undeterred, Steve leaned over the table, meeting her halfway. "And I just told you, I was in bed."

ꝏꝏ

"So, which one did it, do you think? Father or son?" Kelly shot her a quick glance before focusing his attention back on the road.

Isha sighed, staring out at the rolling fields that disappeared into the distance. All Miller land. All prime property. "They both had motive. The story would ruin Andy's business sure enough, and Steve would stand to lose his sizeable inheritance." She turned to Kelly. "How did the interviews with the farmhands go?"

Kelly shook his head. "No go. I interviewed all eight of Andy's workers. All of them had alibis. Besides," he shot Isha a quizzical glance, "what would any of them gain from exposing the farm's shady practices? They'd all be out of jobs."

Isha nodded, biting her lower lip. "How about any disgruntled ex-employees of Andy's wanting to get even for being fired?"

"I had Walsh check on that. Andy's had the same people working for him for years. Sounds like he treats them pretty decently."

Isha nodded. "Of course. If he is misrepresenting his products, he'd have to pay his people pretty well to keep their mouths shut. Wouldn't you?"

They drove in silence for a while before Isha spoke again. "Okay. Well, who's left on the suspect list?"

"Just Andy's ex, Fiona."

ooo

"State your full name, please."

The woman raised her perfectly-groomed, platinum-blonde brows as she stared back at Isha. "You already know my name, Detective."

Isha smiled. "Yes, ma'am. Just state it for the record, please."

The woman sighed as if Isha was asking her for a monumental favor. "Fiona Flannery Miller."

"Thank you, Mrs. Miller. Now, if you don't mind, could you—"

"Fiona, please."

"Fiona, then. Forgive me, but I have to ask. Where were you between the hours of 1:00 and 3:00 a.m. this morning?"

Fiona's brows pulled together. "I was in Madawaska with Frank, my boyfriend. He's from Boston. We stayed at a charming little Bed and Breakfast called…ummm…The Wildwood Inn. Very romantic place. Although I did imbibe way too much." She smiled at Isha, her cheeks pinking ever so slightly.

"I've been introducing Frank to the charms of country life. Although we both still prefer the Back Bay to the country. I have a condo there, you know."

"No," Isha said. "I didn't know. I'm sure it's beautiful." *And I bet it costs your ex a pretty penny to maintain.*

"Oh, it is." Fiona cocked her head to the side, smiling at Isha. "There's nothing like the culture and sophistication of city life, is there?"

"No ma'am, although I must say I prefer life out here in the country."

The older woman looked at Isha in mock horror. "Oh, you poor thing. You've forgotten what it's like in civilized society, haven't you?"

"I think I've got all I need," Isha said, wondering if she'd get into trouble if she called Fiona Miller a pompous, pretentious bitch. She stood quickly, before the impulse got too strong.

"Are you quite sure I can't offer you some coffee, Detective? I'm afraid I don't have any appetizing hors d'oeuvres around these days to serve with it. Frank is on a special healthy-eating plan. He won't allow me to have cookies or cake or anything like that in the house anymore. Only organic and sugar-free stuff now, as you can see." She gestured toward the bowl of snacks on the coffee table.

Fiona beamed. "He's an actor, you know. He has to keep himself in good shape. That's why he eats all this tasteless crap. You can't buy it in stores either. I have to special order the food for him from a company in California.

Fabulously expensive, but I don't mind. He says he has to be in the best possible shape at all times, because one never knows when opportunity will come knocking." She looked at Isha expectantly. Waiting.

"Really?" Isha said. "How interesting. Has he done anything I may have seen?"

"He did a diarrhea commercial a few years ago for Full Stop. You know it, right? That brand that plugs you up right away? Maybe you saw him in that? He was the man holding his stomach and rushing into the men's room."

"Uh…no. I must have missed that," Isha said, quickening her steps. "If you'll excuse me, I need to get back to work."

Back at the police station, she sat at her desk, her hands wrapped around a cup of steaming, milky chai, just like her mom used to make back in India. It was Isha's go-to comfort food. And right now she needed some comfort. She stared at her computer screen, re-reading her reports on Andy, Steve and Fiona Miller.

One of these three suspects killed Peter Bailey, of this Isha had no doubt.

The question was, whodunit?

Andy? He certainly had motive. And Bailey's Prius *was* found on the road leading to Miller's Farm. He stood to lose all his lucrative accounts if the story broke.

Then there was Fiona, the ex-wife. She stood to lose her healthy alimony, plus all the perks, like her condo in Boston's tony Back Bay, and her big house in Misunderstood. Isha frowned as she stared at her notes. The problem was that Fiona and her Bostonian boyfriend were at the Wildwood Inn in Madawaska at the time of the murder. Although that was just an hour away. Technically, she could easily have driven back to Misunderstood once the boyfriend was asleep, shot Bailey, and gone back to the inn before she was even missed.

And finally, there was Steve, Andy's twenty-year-old son. Heir to the entire Miller business and fortune. He stood to lose everything if Bailey's story went public.

Whoever killed the reporter would have made contact with him at some point, arranging to meet him on that quiet stretch of road leading to Andy's farm. Maybe on the pretext of showing him evidence of Andy's nefarious practices, while everyone was still asleep.

Misunderstood was a small town. Word would have gotten around that a reporter was snooping around, asking questions about Andy and his dairy farm. It wouldn't have taken much to contact the man, and convince him that they wanted Andy exposed, for a price. Maybe that was why there was so much cash on him when he was found.

Isha groaned, sitting up and stretching the kinks out of her back. This was all mere speculation, she knew. But her instincts usually proved her right. She trusted them. And they told her that she was on the right track.

Yet, she was missing something. Something so obvious she could almost taste it. *But what?* On a whim, she retrieved the bag from the evidence room that contained the one meager clue found at the scene of the crime.

A shiny, end piece of a candy bar wrapper. Isha stared at the glossy green item, turning it this way and that. She'd seen this wrapping before, but where? What would the entire bar look like encased in this shiny, neon green…?

Suddenly, everything clicked into place.

"Walsh? Kelly? Up and at 'em. Let's go." Isha grabbed her bag and coat, and practically sprinted for the door, the two men close behind her.

"Where are we going?" Kelly asked, as Isha pulled the car out of the station parking lot.

"You'll see," she said, and refused to say anymore, despite the repeated attempts of her colleagues to yank more information out of her.

ᘓᘓᘓ

"Hey? I recognize this swanky place," Walsh said from the backseat, as they pulled into the driveway of a large wood-framed house, set beside a picturesque stream. "Wow, what wouldn't I give to live in a place like this."

"The only way we could afford something like this is in our dreams, bro," Kelly said, sliding out of the car and walking over to Isha. "What gives, Detective? What are we doing here?"

"You're about to find out," Isha said, striding up the path to the front door. Out of the corner of her eye, she saw Kelly shake his head as he fell into step beside her. He hated it when she got all mysterious and dramatic about a case, but she couldn't help it. She loved the unveiling. That sense of satisfaction—like nothing else on earth—when she uncovered the motive, and solved the case. When the perpetrator could finally be brought to justice.

Those were the moments that made her decision to follow her heart and go into law enforcement worthwhile.

She rapped on the door—three sharp knocks—and waited.

Fiona Flannery Miller opened the door and gaped at Isha, her mouth hanging open. "What on earth are you doing here?" she said when she found her voice. "What's going on?"

"Detective Naidu, and officers Kelly and Walsh, Misunderstood Police Force," Isha said, holding up her badge.

Fiona glared at her. "Is this a fucking joke?" she snapped. "Like I don't know who you are. You just interviewed me."

"Yes, ma'am. May we come in? This won't take long."

Fiona hesitated, glancing behind her, then looked back at Isha. "Is something wrong? Steve—"

"Your son is fine, Mrs. Miller," Isha said quietly. "Now, please…"

Fiona hesitated a moment more, then sighed and stood back. She led them to a cheerful room at the back of the house, with floor to ceiling windows all around.

"The conservatory," she said, gesturing for the officers to sit. "My favorite room." Fiona sat down on the edge of an oversized sofa, and clasped her hands tightly in her lap. "Now, what's this all about?"

"Mrs. Miller, I have to ask you where your boyfriend, Mr. Parker is."

Fiona blinked. "Frank? Why?"

"Just answer the question, please."

Fiona's brows drew together for a moment, then she barked out a laugh. "Is this about the murder? Don't be ridiculous, Detective. You know he was with me in Madawaska when the…uh…incident occurred."

"Yes, ma'am. Your alibi checks out, but we still need to talk to him. Is he here?"

Fiona folded her arms. "I don't have to tell you anything. He has nothing to do with that messy business."

"And you know this how?"

Fiona rose and stepped toward her, lowering her head so that she was eye-level with Isha. And bellowed in her face. "He's. My. Boyfriend. That's how I know."

Fish for dinner, Isha thought, resisting the urge to take a step back. "Mrs. Miller, I'm going to ask you one more time—"

"What's going on down there?"

Isha turned toward the voice. A man who looked much younger than Fiona Miller descended the stairs, buttoning a denim shirt over skinny white jeans. "Frank Parker, I presume?"

"You presume right." His gaze flickered over the two men standing behind Isha before coming to rest on her. "And you must be the detective handling that murder case everyone's talking about in town."

"Yes, sir. I must be." Isha took a step toward him. "Frank Parker, I'm arresting you on suspicion of murder."

"No." A choked sob rose from Fiona.

Isha turned to the stricken woman. "I'm sorry, Fiona, but it's true. Mr. Parker knew that once Bailey exposed Andy, the Miller empire would come tumbling down and you would lose your generous alimony. He couldn't let that happen."

ooo

As they walked toward the front door, Isha glanced at the bowl of granola bars sitting on the coffee table, their garish, neon-green wrappers winking in the light of the chandelier above.

Lorraine's story, "Totally Misunderstood," is her second story to be published by Level Best Books and she couldn't be happier. She is a New England UNICEF USA Board member and a school volunteer. Lorraine’s short stories have been published in horror, fantasy and crime anthologies, and have also won two sci-fi awards.

She can be found at her website:
www.lorrainesharmanelson.com
Goodreads: https://www.goodreads.com/LorraineSharmaNelson/
on Twitter at: twitter.com/loneriter and on Pinterest
at: www.pinterest.com/lloneriter/

THE ANONYMOUS DONOR
by David Steven Rappoport

As Beauregard "Otter" Frenchette walked into the Horeb Country Store in Maine a few days before Halloween, Cassandra Ouellette, the owner, was taping paper goblins and witches to the front window. She placed these carefully, so as not to take attention away from a "Nixon for President" sign she had also placed in the window.

"How are you today, Mrs. Ouellette?" Otter asked.

"Special on canned peas. Two for a dollar. Aisle one."

"I wanted to ask your advice." Otter said.

Cassandra scowled slightly. Life did not require advice; it required endurance.

"This is our first Halloween here," he continued. "We don't know how many trick or treaters to expect."

"Can't tell you. Alice doesn't trick or treat any more," Cassandra replied, referring to her teenage daughter. "Teenagers go out on Halloween now just to smash pumpkins and get pregnant. Candy is on aisle two."

Otter noticed an elegant older woman he'd seen around the village. She wore a flannel skirt and simple blouse, which reflected Horeb's lack of fashion consciousness, but her neat bun, pearls, and regal posture suggested somewhere fancier—Cape Elizabeth, a tony suburb of Portland, or Beacon Hill in Boston.

Otter picked up several bags of candy. He intentionally selected varieties he didn't like. This was in deference to his tendency towards ovoid pudginess. Though he made consistent efforts to fight it, it seemed resistant to all variants of starvation and exercise—particularly as his age had crept well above 40.

Otter turned towards the cash register—there was only one in the store—and found the elegant woman standing in front of him.

"I think you'll need more candy than that," she said in a cadenced New England voice. Her articulation suggested brains and money. "You'd be surprised how many children there are in Horeb. God, in a masterstroke of irony, made New Englanders as fertile as they are frosty. You're Otter Frenchette, aren't you?"

"Yes. How did you know that?"

"Because of your striking impression," she replied.

He did make an impression. Otter was out of place in Maine, but in truth he was out of place everywhere. It was mostly the way he presented himself: tall and portly, with wild red hair and a straggly and long red beard. In winter, he wore overalls, a raccoon coat, a coonskin cap, and motorcycle boots. In summer, he wore shorts, sandals and the coonskin cap. It wasn't that he was affected; it was that he liked what he liked and was disinterested in trivialities such as the visual impact he had on others.

“I'm Petrovna Ball,” she continued. “I don't believe we've met. I live around the corner from you in the yellow Federal house. I understand you've recently relocated to Horeb. Welcome."

"I believe I've heard your name," Otter said.

"Have you?" She said. "Not everything they say about me is true. I can declaim Longfellow's *Hiawatha* in its entirety from memory, but only because it was one of my maternal grandmother's three requirements for staying in her will. The other two were learning to espalier pear trees and voting Republican. Anything else you've heard about me is probably a tall tale. This is serendipity—meeting like this. I was going to stop by your house. Becky Rameau speaks highly of you. She was impressed that you found her husband.”

“He was more drunk than lost.”

“That is what all men discovered with their mistresses would like us to believe.”

"How do you know Mrs. Rameau?”

“Christ Episcopal. We sing together in the choir. I thought you might be kind enough to assist me. There's a situation."

"What kind of situation?"

"The kind that one wouldn’t want to take to the police—no crime seems to have been committed—but the circumstances are odd. Very odd. Let me explain. I'm the President of the Greasepaint Players, Horeb’s community theater group."

"I didn't know Horeb had one."

"Oh yes! We meet in the community building attached to the town hall. It's a modest facility, but it does provide us with a small theater, as well as rehearsal and office space.

"We present four plays each year for four performances each. To raise money for our productions, we sell tickets, we hold bake sales, and have an annual dinner dance. We also pass around a bucket at the end of every performance. Our latest production was last weekend. Usually, we find around $100 in the bucket. Last weekend, there was more than $10,000. All cash."

"Really?" Otter asked, surprised. "If someone wished to make such a substantial contribution, you'd think they'd send a check so they could take the tax deduction. In any case, there couldn't be too many people around here with such financial means."

"With the capacity, one or two. With the capacity and the inclination? That number would be zero." Petrovna said. "So there it is: I can think of no one likely to have tossed ten grand into the bucket but someone did. We’re terribly curious. Would you be willing to look into it?”

 QQQ

“I’ve been asked to investigate.” Otter said to his wife, Baibin. She was an ample woman in a simple house dress. Her waist-length flaming red hair was speckled with gray. As she frequently did in the early evening, she played sea shanties on her harp with a martini placed invitingly beside her.

"Investigate what? Has someone been murdered?" She asked between plucks.

"No, but there's a very odd situation. Someone has made a large anonymous donation."

"Why does that require an investigation?"

"Ten thousand dollars was discovered in a bucket."

"I see. Will you be very late?"

"I don't believe so."

She nodded. "Two TV dinners are warming in the oven," she said. Then she took a sip of her drink, and continued to play "Rolling Down to Old Maui."

ƍƍƍ

Otter asked Petrovna for a copy of the play's program. He also asked to see the performance space, and to speak to whoever had collected the money.

The facilities were as Otter imagined. There was a large room they used for rehearsals that was actually a basketball court. The auditorium proper, which was primarily used for school assemblies, had a small stage at one end. Off of it, there was a former storage closet that now served as the Greasepaint Players' office.

After this brief tour, Petrovna introduced Otter to Melody York and Bob Wells.

"Did anything unusual occur during this production? Let's start with the rehearsals." Otter asked.

"I don't remember anything," Bob said.

"Our male lead missed the technical rehearsal. That's when we run all the lighting and sound cues," Melody said. "That threw us off, though God knows that sort of thing has happened before."

"Who was that?"

"Carl Walker."

"And what about the performances themselves?" Otter asked.

"The usual—a few missed lighting cues and some forgotten lines. But nothing worse."

"Were you two in the cast?"

"No, no." Bob explained. "Melody runs the lights and I pull the curtain. Then, after the performance is over, each of us takes one of two old metal buckets..."

"Those buckets are a Horeb tradition. They say the Greasepaint Players has been using them since the 1930s," Melody added.

"Right," Bob continued. "So each of us takes a bucket and Melody collects from the right side of the audience and I collect from the left."

"Did this $10,000 come in one payment or several?"

"One payment. In thousand dollar bills. On the last performance," Melody said.

"Correct," Bob added. "It was in my bucket, but I didn't notice who dropped it in. People usually contribute singles, so somebody putting in ten bills wouldn't be that unusual. I was too busy passing the bucket to notice the denominations."

"Did you notice anything unusual while you were collecting contributions?" Otter asked. "Someone taking an envelope out of a coat pocket? Someone there who wouldn't normally attend? Anything unusual at all?"

"Again, not really," Bob said. "There were some unfamiliar faces, but that's common—relatives and friends of the actors who don't live in Horeb."

"Did any of these unfamiliar people catch your attention for any reason?"

"No," Bob said.

"I was surprised to see a few teenagers," Melody added. "That doesn't always happen. You know how they are—interested in being with their friends, not in community activities."

"Presumably they didn't have anything to do with the contribution, but maybe they saw something," Otter said.

"Teens do have some money," Petrovna interjected. "It's a rare young man who can't somehow manage to come up with the cash for a second-hand car."

"That's not the same as throwing money into a bucket," Otter responded. Then he asked Melody: "Do you remember which teenagers you saw?"

 QQQ

Otter spoke to the teens Melody mentioned—Becky Ramsey, Phil Purington, Heidi Bolduc, and Jason Connors.

 QQQ

"Why did you decide to go to the play, Becky?"

"I dunno."

"Could you be more specific?"

QQQ

"My mother likes us to be there," Phil reported. "She was in the play. She always likes me and my brother and my Dad to go when she's in the play. So we went to the play."

"Did you enjoy it?"

"It was okay."

"Did you notice anyone put a lot of money into the collection bucket?"

"No."

"Did you notice anything unusual?"

"No."

ଢଢଢ

"I was going to go to the movies in Gethsemane," Heidi said. "But my boyfriend's father's Pontiac broke down. So, I didn't have anything else to do."

ଢଢଢ

"Becky told me at school she was going to go," Jason said.

"So you and Becky were on a date?"

"No. She doesn't like me that way."

"But you like her that way?"

Jason, who was a tall and skinny young man just past puberty, shrugged and blushed.

"Did you notice anything odd during the play?"

"What do you mean?"

"Anything unusual."

"I guess not."

"You guess not?"

"It was just boring."

As Otter was leaving Jason's house, he noticed a late model Ford Thunderbird convertible in the driveway.

"That's a nice car," Otter said. "Is that your dad's?"

"No, it's mine," Jason said.

"Really?"

"Yeah," Jason confirmed.

"Do you have a job after school?"

"I bag groceries."

"Where?"

"Carlisle's in Gethsemane." Carlisle's was the local supermarket. Everyone shopped there, including Otter.

"Do you like working there?"

"Yeah. It's great," Jason replied enthusiastically. "And they're going to pay my college tuition."

"Really?"

ଢଢଢ

Otter discreetly asked around. Jason's family was far from wealthy; Maine families usually were. There was nothing unusual about a 17-year-old with wheels, but teens in rural Maine bought affordable and practical transportation. They didn't buy new convertibles.

Thus, Jason's car seemed a bit odd, though perhaps Jason was simply a hard worker who'd taken extra shifts to make the car payments. It wasn't much of a lead but Otter hadn't a better one. He kept an eye on Jason for a few days, but observed nothing suspicious. Jason went to school, he went to work, and he went home.

On Sunday, Otter followed Jason to the Horeb Methodist Church. Curiously, Jason went there alone, while the rest of his family went to the Catholic church down the street.

In the pews, Otter recognized faces from the village. Petrovna was there. She waved at him when he walked in. Ernestine Cutter, a neighbor he knew slightly, was there too. She also waved. But one face surprised him: Eben Carlisle, who was sitting down the pew from Jason. Otter recognized him from a blown-up photograph over the cash registers at his store, displayed just above his nobody-beats-our-prices-double-your-money-back guarantee.

The church service was pleasant: a few hymns, an uninspiring sermon, the passing of collection plates.

Otter noticed there was something waxy on the surface of the plate. Perhaps it needed a good cleaning. He tossed in a few dollars and passed it along.

After church, Otter caught up with Petrovna.

“I’m surprised to see you here. Didn’t you say you attended Christ Episcopal?” He asked.

“God is everywhere, don’t you think?” She replied.

"I didn't know Eben Carlisle lived in Horeb."

"Yes," Petrovna said. "He owns that big farm on Merrymeeting Bay as you drive into town from Gethsemane. That man is no end of surprises. He's an atheist, you know."

“No, I didn’t. How do you happen to know that?”

“I’ve known Eben all my life.”

"So he doesn't attend church regularly?"

"I don't know what Eben Carlisle does or does not do," Petrovna said. "I don't pay any attention."

"Nonetheless, he owns a chain of successful grocery stores. Perhaps he's your mystery contributor."

"I very much doubt it," Petrovna said. "Eben isn’t generous. Did you know his brother sued him last year? Eben was cooking the books to keep him from getting his share of the profits from the family business. Also, there's a personal reason he isn’t our man. Years ago, we were engaged. I gave him his ring back. He would never contribute to something in which I was involved.”

"You mentioned others in the Village with the capacity to give $10,000 if not the inclination. Tell me who you were referring to besides Eben Carlisle."

"Ernestine Cutter. But she's never shown any interest in the Greasepaint Players. And Lucy Rockland. She's never shown any interest either."

ꝏꝏ

Otter went to speak to Ernestine Cutter about the contribution. She said she hadn't attended a Community Players presentation in decades. She made charitable contributions at the end of the year, and only to hospitals and universities.

"And what about Eben Carlisle?" Otter asked her.

"Petrovna's right that he's not a good man. But I don't know why he'd have a grudge against her."

"She broke off their engagement."

"That's not true, dear—Eben broke it off with her. He fell in love with another girl. I'm sure he handled it like a louse – he never did have any tact. I'm not surprised Petrovna lied about it. She must have felt wicked humiliated."

Later, Otter knocked on Lucy Rockland's door. It was answered by one of her daughters, who was clearing the house prior to putting it on the market. Lucy, it seemed, had been moved to a nursing home some months earlier; clearly, she hadn't attended the play.

ℓℓℓ

"Are you sure there's no one else in Horeb with the capacity to make a large contribution?" Otter asked Petrovna when they next spoke.

"No."

"Has anyone been rumored to have come into money lately?"

"No."

"Have you heard any other instances of such large, anonymous contributions in the Village?"

"No."

ℓℓℓ

Otter was out of ideas. As he and Baibin handed candy to trick-or-treaters on Halloween night, he pondered his next move in the donation matter. Then an inspiration appeared on his doorstep.

"Twick or tweat," a tiny girl in a pink cardboard rectangle said, thrusting a pail in his direction. She was with a slightly older boy, dressed in a yellow construction paper cylinder.

"What are you?" Otter asked, handing the girl a fistful of candy.

"An eraser," she said.

"I'm her pencil," the boy said.

A pencil and an eraser. Otter considered it. It was possible, just possible.

ℓℓℓ

The following Sunday, Otter returned to the Horeb Methodist Church. He took a seat in the back and surveyed the congregation. Most of the same faces were present – including Eben and Jason.

At the opportune time, Otter made his move. He approached the pew where Jason and Eben were both seated though not next to each other. A collection plate was passed. Otter saw Eben surreptitiously write something on the plate with a small black pencil before dropping in a one-dollar bill and an unmarked white envelope.

Otter hurriedly pushed past parishioners and sat between Eben and Jason just in time to receive the plate.

Otter studied it. Under the coins and bills the following had been written with a wax pencil: "ABR 367."

Otter tossed in some money and passed the plate along. When it reached Jason, Otter saw him discreetly move the money aside and glance down at the code. After studying it for a moment, Jason subtly moved his finger onto the spot and rubbed the markings away. Then he slipped the white envelope into his pocket.

Otter's hunch was correct. Eben and Jason weren't there for spiritual uplift; they were passing information.

But what did "ABR 367" mean?

Was it a biblical passage, perhaps the basis of a cipher? Otter doubted it. It wasn't a standard biblical reference—such as "1 Chr" for "1 Chronicles" or "Lk" for "Luke."

Were Eben and Jason engaged in trading, such as passing information on stocks? This also seemed unlikely. New York Stock Exchange abbreviations were typically all letters, usually three or four, sometimes with a hyphen, such as TAP or PGEM or AES-C. American Stock Exchange and NASDAQ abbreviations were similar.

What about account numbers, inventory numbers, passwords, references, formulas, or registrations? It could be any of these. Yet, Otter knew the likeliest answer was, as Occam's Razor suggested, the simplest. He considered the apparent points of intersection between Eben and Jason. There seemed to be only two: the Horeb Methodist Church and Carlisle's Supermarket.

Eben Carlisle might be low enough to rob the collection plate—but the gains to be ill-gotten were very small. "ABR 367," whatever it was, probably had something to do with bigger spoils.

ooo

Otter monitored Jason's comings and goings more closely, particularly from work.

One evening, when the store closed at its usual nine o'clock, Otter observed that Jason didn't emerge with the other employees.

Otter peered into the store's glass front wall. The lights had been dimmed from their open-for-business brightness. Yet, Otter managed to see a shape—presumably Jason—walking in a crouched position towards the back of the store. When he reached it, Otter saw a door open, then quickly close again.

Suddenly, someone lunged at Otter and he was on the ground.

"Where's your identification?" A voice said.

"You've made a mistake," Otter explained. "I'm not involved in this."

"Involved in what?"

"How should I know? That's why I'm here."

ℓℓℓ

The conversation did not grow more cordial, and Otter spent the rest of the night in jail. However, as looking in a store window isn't a crime, and as there was no evidence he'd done anything worse, the police let him go in the morning. He did receive a stern lecture to keep out of police business—certainly not the first time that had happened.

Otter called Baibin to explain, then had a quick breakfast at a local diner. While waiting for his eggs, he made a call to Carlisle's and had a chat with one of the employees. Then he phoned Petrovna.

"Can we meet?" He asked.

ℓℓℓ

"You look like you slept in a ditch," Petrovna said, as she ushered Otter into her office at the Greasepaint Players.

"Jail."

"What did you do?"

"Nothing and no charges have been filed. I do, however, have an explanation for you about your mystery contributor. In fact, I have two explanations. Perhaps you'll help to clarify which one is correct."

"I'll do my best," she responded.

"You were right about Eben Carlisle. He is greedy; so greedy that he's been skimming cash off the top in his largest supermarket. My guess is that he's still trying to screw his brother out of profits so he can pocket them himself - and, of course, whatever you steal from your own company you don't have to pay taxes on."

"That sounds like Eben."

"It gets worse. Eben's using a teenage boy, Jason Connors, to help him do it."

"Why would Jason participate?"

"Money. He bought a new Ford. Also, I think Eben promised to pay his way through college. Jason said something to me about the store paying his college tuition, but I checked and Carlisle's doesn't offer that as an employee benefit. Jason's family isn't well off. Teenagers don't always think about consequences and that kind of money is hard to turn down.

"There's a lot of cash in a supermarket. Do you see where I'm heading with this?"

"No, I don't."

"Eben's been laundering the money in church. The Horeb Methodist Church is small; it has one center aisle, and two side aisles. There are two collection plates. Their weekly journey is always the same, from the center aisle at the rear to the front on the side. One plate moves west to east, is passed to the next pew where it moves east to west, then is passed to the next pew where it moves west to east again, and so on through all the pews. The other plate follows the same path but in reverse. Eben knew the plates always moved the same way. By arranging himself and Jason in the same pew but alternating who was on the right and who was on the left, they could pass information and money back and forth in the plates.

"Presumably, Carlisle's safe has a sophisticated mechanism. Let us suppose that because they deal in cash they change the combination frequently, perhaps twice a month. Eben writes each new combination in wax pencil on the collection plate. Jason reads the information, memorizes it, and erases the markings. Jason, of course, works at the store bagging groceries. Once a week, he hides when the store closes, then takes cash from the safe—always a different amount—always small enough to look like shrinkage or a bookkeeping error—though that's still a lot of money in a supermarket—and enough to add up to a substantial sum over time. The following Sunday, Jason passes the cash to Eben in an unmarked envelope in the collection plate. The Sunday after that, Eben passes Jason's cut to him, also in an unmarked envelope."

"That's ingenious."

"But something went wrong. I don't know exactly what. Perhaps Eben's greed demanded larger and larger amounts. Perhaps Jason just made a mistake and took out too much cash. In any case, a store manager must have become suspicious, called the police and, of course, notified senior management—which is to say, Eben.

"At that juncture, presumably Eben told Jason to lay off—and to be damn sure he didn't expand the evidence trail by spending any more money. I'm sure Eben did his best to scare Jason. He probably told him that if he screwed up, they'd both end up in jail. Jason was probably terrified. Jason knew that you collected donations. He'd been to your performances. He decided to dump whatever cash he had laying around into your bucket—where it couldn't be easily traced back to him."

"Does this mean they're both going to be arrested?" Petrovna asked.

"Based on the police surveillance of the store, it appears so. Who knows? Eben and Jason may have been arrested already."

"But you said there were two explanations."

"Yes, I did. The second explanation is a variation of the first. Everything I've just told you remains the same except for one thing—Jason didn't put the money in the bucket."

"Who did?"

"You."

"Don't be absurd!" Petrovna protested.

"You don't like Eben Carlisle. You don't like him a bit. Why should you? I understand he treated you very badly. You're also very well off and had access to the buckets."

"So what?"

"Bear with me. Carl Walker—the cast member that missed the technical rehearsal—works as a store manager at the Carlisle's in Gethsemane. I just spoke to him. He told me that he missed that rehearsal because of an emergency at work. When I asked what kind of emergency, he said 'irregularities.' If he offered that explanation to me, he likely said the same to you. That led you to think Eben might be up to something—and since it was Eben, whatever it was, it wasn't good.

"Next, there's Jason's car. You noticed it was awfully fancy for a Maine teenager. In fact, you made a number of observations. Why was Eben in church? He's an atheist. Why was Jason there? His family is Catholic. Why were Jason and Eben always seated near each other? You're a smart woman. You put all this information together.

"Of course, suspicions aren't facts. Further, you're a woman with far too much dignity to get your hands dirty. So, you tossed that money into the bucket yourself so that you could ask me to investigate. You hoped I'd end up discovering incriminating evidence—which, of course, I have."

Petrovna was taken aback, but after a few moments of reflection, she said, "Well done. There's no point in denying any of that. After all, I haven't done anything illegal."

"No, you haven't. Getting Eben Carlisle locked up is a service to the community. So is your contribution to the Greasepaint Players. Your generosity will be appreciated—if you tell them about it."

"I think not. Let's just say that I prefer to remain an anonymous donor."

David Steven Rappoport's first mystery, *Husbands and Lap Dogs Breathe Their Last*, was published by Mainly Murder Press in 2016. *Mystery Scene Magazine* said it was "as riotous as mystery novels get" and "a delightful journey into the weird." His short story "Leftovers" was a winner of the *Mystery Times* 2015 competition, and is featured in an anthology from Buddhapuss Ink. www.davidstevenrappoport.com.

THOSE AMBER EYES
(The Continuing Adventures of Mylo and Myla)
by Verena Rose

"Myla, look, look. Don't those eyes remind you of someone?" asked Mylo of his sister who was lying nearby, basking in the sun.

Interrupted while taking her afternoon nap, Myla answers with annoyance. "WHAT. IS. IT. Mylo, can't you see I'm relaxing?"

"Look. Outside there are two kittens. They both have eyes like Octavia," Mylo said with wonder.

"What are you telling me? You think the kittens are part owl?" asked Myla sarcastically.

"Gosh, Sissy, why do you always treat me like I'm stupid? I know they're not owls, but they have those amber eyes."

"Alright, let me see what you're talking about," said Myla in a very put-upon tone of voice.

०००

"Mylo, Myla, where are you?" called Lydia Morgan.

Lydia was on vacation at her friend Brenda Newcastle's home in Bar Harbor, Maine, trying to recover from the near tragedy that happened at the Solstice in the Hills Cat Show in Pigeon Forge, Tennessee, that Fall. Her Ragdoll cats Mylo and Myla had been "catnapped." Since the experience she was finding it very hard to let them out of her sight.

"There you are, my precious darlings. I see you've found a nice sunny place to nap," said Lydia, discovering them in the great room.

Looking down, she realized Mylo was circling around her legs, moving her further into the room, aiming her toward the sliding glass doors. Stooping, she picked up her handsome boy and walked with him over to the door to see what was out there. Snow had been falling all day and at first everything looked white. Then she saw them, two sets of amber eyes.

"Brenda, come quick! Outside, in the snow, there are two small kittens," Lydia yelled to her friend.

"Two kittens? What are you talking about?" said Brenda, running into the room.

"There, outside, under that bush at the corner of the patio. It looks like one is gray and white and the other is black and white."

"Those look like old Mr. Trundy's kittens," said Brenda. "His female, Bathsheba, had kittens a few weeks ago and he decided to keep these two. I think their names are Biggie and Bitty."

०००

"Biggie and Bitty. What kind of names are those for cats?" scoffed Myla while rolling her eyes. "I do see what you mean about their eyes. They are the same

color as Octavia's. Speaking of Octavia – look there. An owl is circling outside."

"Myla, we have to do something! That owl is going to grab the kittens," said Mylo excitedly.

"What do you think we can do?"

"We have to get Momma or her friend to open the door. Then I can run out and try to communicate with the owl.

"Are you nuts? That owl will scoop you up first – you're a bigger morsel."

"Maybe he's related to Octavia and I can reason with him. I'll tell him we have an owl friend in Tennessee," said Mylo with confidence.

०००

At that same moment, Lydia noticed the owl circling over the area where the kittens were hiding. She knew she had to get out there and get them to safety. "Oh, no! There's an owl circling. I'm going out to get those babies inside out of the cold and harm's way." Grabbing her coat, Lydia opened the glass door to the patio and, as she stepped out, Mylo darted by her, heading toward the kittens.

०००

Whoosh! In an instant Mylo was in the grip of two powerful talons carrying him away.

"MYLO!" yelled Myla from the open door. "Mylo, you silly boy, what have you done?"

"It's okay, Sissy, I'll be back soon. Help Momma take care of the kittens," shouted Mylo as he was carried off over the treetops.

"How is Momma ever going to get over this?"

०००

Outside Lydia was heading toward the kittens when she saw, from the corner of her eye, the owl swoop down and grab something behind her. She turned in time to see the owl scooping up . . .

"MYLO, no!" she screamed as she ran, trying to grab him from the owl's talons. Not being fast enough, she was left standing there helplessly watching as Mylo was carried away. All of a sudden, things started to get dark and she felt herself falling.

"Lydia, it's me, Brenda. Can you hear me? Wake up."

As Lydia started to come to, she began sobbing. "An owl took Mylo. Please we have to go after him."

"We will, Lydia, we will," said Brenda encouragingly. They could hear the pathetic mewling of the two kittens. "Let's get these two inside, then you and I will get dressed properly to go hunt for Mylo. I think we should check on

Mr. Trundy, too. There is no way he would have let these kittens outside, especially in this kind of weather. Which way did the owl fly?"

Lydia, trying to compose herself, said through free-flowing tears, "Over that way, over the treetops."

"That's towards Mr. Trundy's house. We can check on him while we're looking for Mylo."

"Please, we've got to hurry, otherwise Mylo will be that owl's dinner," said a terrified Lydia.

The two women grabbed the little kittens who were too cold and frightened to resist and ran back into the house. They quickly fixed a basket with a warm towel and placed them in it close to the fireplace.

Holding Myla in her arms, whispering into her fur, Lydia said, "Myla, look after these little ones while we go hunt for your brother."

ƍƍƍ

"Now isn't this too special. My silly brother goes on tour with an owl and I get left here with two infants," grumbled Myla.

"Hello, owl, my name is Mylo. Do you know an owl named Octavia? She lives in Tennessee and she saved my life a few months ago."

"Octavia? Do you mean the Great Horned Owl Octavia who lives in Pigeon Forge, Tennessee?" asked the owl, staring down into a pair of striking blue eyes.

"Yes, that's her! She was very kind to me and my sister. Some really bad guys kidnapped us and she helped us escape and get back to our Momma. She even helped us to get the bad guys arrested," said Mylo proudly.

"I heard about this through the owl network. In fact, Octavia is my sister and we were told to look out for you and your sister. The network spread the word that you'd be visiting Bangor sometime this winter. My name is Octavian. I apologize for not recognizing you sooner."

"That's okay. I'm very glad to meet you, Octavian, and I'm always up for an owl ride. Your sister gives really good ones!"

"I need to make a stop first to check on my wife and owlets. Then I'll get you home."

ƍƍƍ

All dressed in warm coats, gloves, hats, scarves, and wearing snowshoes, Lydia and Brenda headed over to Mr. Trundy's house. It wasn't a far distance but in the snow it took them over 15 minutes to get there. When they arrived, they noticed that the inside front door was open. Brenda pushed on the glass door and called, "Mr. Trundy are you home?" No one answered. She did hear loud meowing coming from the back of the house. She tried again. "Yoo hoo, Mr. Trundy, it's Brenda Newcastle from next door. Are you here?" Growing concerned, she and Lydia stepped into the house, only to find chaos. Furniture was overturned and drawers were hanging open and the contents strewn about the floor. Turning to Lydia, Brenda said, "We've got to get out of here and call the police. I know Chief Lewis personally and he's got an all-terrain vehicle. He'll be here in no time."

She dialed the police. "Hi, this is Brenda Newcastle out on Sand Dune Road. May I speak with Chief Lewis please?"

"Hello, Ms. Newcastle, let me see if he's in his office," said the dispatcher politely.

"Hello, Brenda, what can I do for you?"

"I'm over at Mr. Trundy's house and he's not answering my call. I stepped into the foyer and I can see that the living room has been disturbed. The furniture is toppled and drawers from the desk have been emptied onto the floor. And I can hear the cat in the back of the house. It's probably locked in a room because otherwise it would have come to the door when I came in. I'm really worried about him. Can you come over here now?"

"Yes, of course. Don't go any further into the house and don't touch anything. I'll be there in less than 30 minutes," said the Chief.

"Is it okay if we leave for a bit? My friend's Ragdoll cat ran out of the house and we think it was scooped up by an owl. It's a long story."

"Okay, go ahead, I *will* need you to come back as soon as possible though. Your friend does realize that her cat is in grave danger, right?"

"I know but I have to help her. She's already had one traumatic experience with her cats and if she doesn't at least try to find him, I worry for her."

ععع

Back at the Newcastle house—

"Well, well, well. What have we here. Two frozen kittens. What on earth were you thinking, going out in the snow like that?" asked Myla of the two kittens who were cowering under the towel. "And what are your names again?"

"Hi, I'm Bitty," said the little black and white kitten. "And this is my brother, Biggie. We need help getting back home to our Momma. Some brute came into the house and was yelling at the man who cares for us. He locked Momma in the bathroom and picked us up and threw us outside."

"That explains one piece of craziness. What about your names? Biggie, Bitty???? Who gave you such ridiculous names?" Myla asked, shaking her head and rolling her eyes.

"You know, you're not very nice," said Bitty defensively. "The man who cares for us and our Momma gave us those names. They're actually short for Little Big Ears, because Biggie has big ears, and Bitty is short for Little Bitty Bit because I'm very tiny."

"I may not be nice, but I'm the one here taking care of you for now. And you better hope my Momma and her friend are able to find my brother because it's all your fault he's gone. He's too kind-hearted and he couldn't stand to see you outside in the cold. Then what does he do? He runs to the rescue and gets swooped away by an owl."

"We're very sorry, we didn't know what else to do. We know the lady who lives here is very nice because she comes to visit the man. We thought she'd take us in until we can go home," explained Bitty.

"Does your brother ever talk? It sounds like you run the show, a little like me."

"Yes, he talks but not to strangers. Once he gets comfortable with you, you'll be sorry you asked. He will talk your ears off."

ϱϱϱ

Lydia and Brenda left Mr. Trundy's house and started searching for Mylo. They hadn't been out long when they saw the Chief's vehicle turning into the drive of the old man's house. Brenda was torn between going back to find out where Mr. Trundy was and continuing the search for Mylo. She knew she had to support her friend. There was time enough to get the story from the Chief.

ϱϱϱ

Mylo loved to fly. He'd fallen in love with it when Octavia took him for a flight in Tennessee and it was even better this time. Flying over the treetops looking down at all of the snow on the ground was breathtaking. As they were flying, he noticed an SUV speeding down the road, away from the house next door to Brenda.

"Octavian, where does that road go? That car is going much too fast in this weather, don't you think?

"You're right, it is, and that road leads directly to the dock. Well, here we are," said Octavian, landing on a large branch of a very tall tree. He put Mylo down and nudged him into the hollow of the tree. Inside it was warm and cozy and Mylo came face-to-face with another Great Horned Owl and her two little owlets.

"Hi there," he said, a little breathless from the flight. "My name is Mylo. You must be Mrs. Octavian."

The owl looked at him rather quizzically and answered, "Yes, my name is Ariadne and these are my children, Leah and Louis."

"Pleased to meet you, Ariadne. And of course, Leah and Louis, too," he said.

"My dear, I must apologize for not bringing home dinner yet this evening. As you can see, what I thought would be dinner turns out to be a friend of my sister Octavia. Remember we heard that ~~the~~ two blue-eyed cats would be visiting Bangor and that we should watch out for them," explained Octavian.

"We do have some leftovers from yesterday. We'll be fine for another day," said Ariadne.

Mylo remembered the car and waited for the owls to finish their discussion before he said, "Octavian, I think something is amiss back home. Before you scooped me up, we discovered two little kittens crouching under a bush by the patio at Miss Brenda's house. I heard her say they belonged to the man next door and that he would never have put them outdoors. I think something happened at his house and that car is the key."

"What do you suggest we do?" asked Octavian.

ǫǫǫ

It was getting dark. Totally discouraged, Lydia and Brenda made their way back to Mr. Trundy's house to check in with the Chief. They arrived back to find not only his vehicle but two others parked in the drive.

Climbing the steps to the door they were stopped by Sgt. Morse. "What can I do for you ladies?"

"We're here to check in with Chief Lewis. We're the ones who found the house in disarray and called him. He gave us permission to leave to look for my friend's cat," said Brenda.

"Okay, wait here. I'll go get the Chief."

Chief Lewis said gently, "Brenda, thank you for coming back quickly. Unfortunately, I have some very disturbing news for you. Mr. Trundy is dead. He's been murdered. He was lying on the floor in the kitchen."

"Chief, that's awful. Who could have done such a thing and why? He was such a nice old man and, as far as I know, didn't have much that anyone could want to steal," said Brenda, shaking her head.

"Apparently, he did have something of value in this house. I called his niece in Portland to notify her of his death. When I told her his house had been ransacked, she asked about his scrimshaw collection. It seems Mr. Trundy owned a very valuable collection of antique scrimshaw pieces. She told me he had received many offers to buy but that he always refused. He insisted that they would remain in the family. She's on her way here now," said the Chief.

ǫǫǫ

Mylo thought for a while and then said, "I think you should take me back to the house and maybe I can find out what is going on. If you don't mind, can you stay nearby in case I need you?"

"I can do that," said Octavian. "Let's go."

As they flew back to the house where Mylo was staying, they saw several vehicles in the drive of the house next door. He called up to Octavian, "I think my Momma and Brenda are in that house. Can you drop me down and I'll check?"

"You got it – going down."

Octavian dropped Mylo at the back of the house out of sight of the big man standing on the front steps. Mylo went up the back steps and started scratching at the door and calling out with his loudest "MEOW." He could hear footsteps and suddenly the door flew open and standing there was none other than his very own Momma. Before she could scoop him into her arms, he yelled out to Octavian, "Don't leave until I find out what's going on."

ǫǫǫ

Lydia gave a loud scream and grabbed up a most wonderful sight – her Mylo. "My precious boy, are you alright? Look, Brenda, it's Mylo, safe and sound right here on Mr. Trundy's back porch."

"Thank heavens. At least one tragedy has been averted," said Brenda to her friend.

"Brenda, why don't you take Mrs. Morgan and go on back home. I will come over later to take your statements. Also, would you take Mr. Trundy's cat with you?" asked the Chief. "It probably needs to be fed and the niece won't be here for several hours."

"Of course, we'll take Bathsheba with us. I'm sure she's missing her babies, too."

The two women, each one carrying a cat and bags of additional cat food, snowshoed their way back home.

ooo

Before they left Mr. Trundy's house, Mylo got the story of what had happened from Bathsheba. While he was being cuddled and carried home by Momma, he called out to Octavian, "The old man has been murdered and whoever did it stole something really valuable from him. I think that car we saw contained the murderer and he was heading to the dock to get away. Do you think you can get there and delay him?"

"I'll head there now. Do you have any idea how to get the police there?" asked Octavian.

"I'm not sure yet. They probably will put out an APB and, in this weather, it's going to be hard for the murderer to get away too fast," answered Mylo.

"I see you survived another flight with an owl," sneered Myla. "And in the process, I got left here alone with these pesky kittens."

"Will you shut up, Myla. You're always complaining. Can't you be nice for once?"

"Well, I never! How dare you speak to me that way? I'm your sister and I think I deserve some respect."

"You get respect if you give respect, Sissy. I love you dearly but you've got to stop treating me like I'm beneath you," he said firmly and lovingly. Turning away from Myla, he walked over to the basket where the kittens were resting. "Hi, little ones, I'm Mylo."

ooo

The two friends were glad to be back in the warmth of Brenda's cottage. Brenda ~~stooped to~~ put Bathsheba down to go check on her kittens.

"Thank you, Brenda, for going out with me to find Mylo. I think I've come to the conclusion that I cannot travel with these cats ever again." Lydia said, shaking her head. "Especially Mylo, he can't seem to stay out of trouble and I love him too much to lose him."

Brenda hugged her friend and said, "I'm very glad he wasn't hurt and we were able to bring him home safely even though he found us instead of us finding him."

There was a knock at the door and Brenda went to the foyer to let in Chief Lewis.

"Ladies, do you feel like you can answer some questions now? The crime scene crew will be at Mr. Trundy's for a while yet. We've determined that someone broke into his house, attacked him, and either forced him to tell them where the scrimshaw collection was or killed him first and then ransacked the house until they found it."

"That's horrible. He was such a nice old man. I'll never forget how kind he was to me after my divorce," said Brenda, starting to tear up. "I can't believe he's gone."

"We're waiting for his niece to get here. I need to get more information from her about the scrimshaw collection and a list of those who wanted to buy it. It's possible one of those potential buyers didn't want to take no for an answer. In fact, she believes it was an ex-boyfriend."

ϱϱϱ

Bathsheba ran into the great room to check on her kittens. She found them being groomed by a gorgeous cat with brilliant blue eyes. Giving a soft meow, she walked over and introduced herself. "I'm Bathsheba and these are my babies."

"I'm glad you're here now. My name is Myla and that cat over there that you've already met is my brother Mylo. I think Biggie and Bitty are fine but I know they've been missing their Momma. We haven't told them anything about the old man. We thought that should come from you."

"I appreciate that. They were very fond of the old man and will be very sad to hear he is dead. Thank you for caring for them. When that bad man threw them out the door, I feared they would die in the snow before anyone found them."

Myla nodded and said, "You have my brother to thank for their rescue. He's the one who saw them outside under the bush and managed to maneuver our Momma over to the window to see them and bring them in. Of course, then he also got snatched by an owl. Fortunately, the owl is the brother of a friend of ours and he brought Mylo back safely."

"You and your brother are friends with an owl?" said Bathsheba disbelievingly.

"Yes, that's a story for another time. Now we have to figure out how to help the humans get the bad guy. Mylo says he and Octavian, that's the owl, saw a car speeding away from the old man's house going toward the dock. We think that's the guy who killed the old man. Mylo has sent Octavian to the dock to keep an eye on the guy."

"Wow, you and your brother are regular detectives. What can I do to help?"

ɷɷɷ

As he was finishing up his questioning of Brenda and Lydia, Chief Lewis received the message that Mr. Trundy's niece was waiting at the station. He left, telling the ladies that he'd let them know if there were any new developments.

At the Police Station, Chief Lewis found Amanda Trundy waiting in his office. "Ms. Trundy, I'm heading up the investigation into your uncle's murder. I need to get information relating to the scrimshaw collection and the people who had been making offers to buy it. Especially anyone who kept trying to get your uncle to sell."

"Of course, Chief Lewis. I'll do everything I can to help. I can't believe Uncle Raymond is dead. He is, was my Great-Uncle and the only family I had left. As I told you, I think I know who did this. His name is Rupert Butler and he's my ex-boyfriend. We broke up about a month ago, mostly because I wouldn't try to strong-arm my uncle into selling the collection to him." She began to cry.

"Do you know where he is now?" asked the Chief.

"No, I don't. He does have a boat that he mostly lives on which means he might be anywhere. I would suggest you check the dock. With this snow coming down like it is, if he did come here by boat he might not be able to cast off."

"Thank you, Ms. Trundy. Can I request that you stay in Bar Harbor tonight? I might need to ask you some more questions or have you identify the scrimshaw should we pick Butler up and recover the collection."

"I'm happy to stay. I'm going to call Ms. Newcastle to see if she'll put me up tonight. I know she has Bathsheba and the kittens and I'm going to have to find homes for them now that Uncle Raymond is gone. Unfortunately, as much as I'd like to, I can't take them home with me."

ɷɷɷ

After seeing Mylo safely back home, Octavian flew off to check at the dock. When he got there, he saw a man all in black climbing onto a cabin cruiser carrying a large box and furtively looking around to see if he had been seen by anyone. Octavian was sure this was the bad guy but he wasn't quite sure what to do. While he was considering what to do next, he heard the sirens and decided to take cover up in a tall tree. A few seconds later, two police cars pulled up to the dock. From a microphone he heard, "You, on the boat, stop, put your hands in the air and turn around."

Cornered, the guy in black had no choice but to surrender. The police took him into custody and drove him away. Octavian knew his job was done and hoped he would be able to let his new friend Mylo know.

 QQQ

The phone rang and Brenda answered to find Chief Lewis on the line asking to speak to Amanda Trundy. She hadn't been there long and was relaxing with a cup of hot tea. "Of course, let me get her for you."

"Ms. Trundy, this is Chief Lewis. We've apprehended Rupert Burke at the dock. He thought he could get away before anyone was the wiser. And we did find a case with some antique scrimshaw in his possession. We'll need you to come down to the station and verify that the scrimshaw is your uncle's collection."

QQQ

Octavian flew back to the house where Mylo was staying and landed in the tree outside the patio glass door. Through the window he could see three full-grown cats laying by the fire and two little ones in a basket. All sound asleep. Not knowing whether it would work or not, he let out a very loud "HOOT HOOT." Nothing. Then another "HOOT HOOT." Inside he saw one head lift up and over to the door came Mylo.

Even through the glass Octavian could hear the "MEOW and thank you, my friend. Tell Ariadne it was lovely meeting her," said Mylo who flicked his tail goodbye and went back to his place by the fire.

QQQ

The next morning Amanda went to the police station. When she came back, Brenda and Lydia could tell something was bothering her, something more than the recent events. Amanda said, "Brenda, I need your help. I live in Portland in a very small apartment."

"Let me stop you right there. You're worried about Bathsheba and the kittens. Correct? Well, you can stop worrying. Lydia and I have been talking and Bathsheba can stay here with me and Lydia is going to adopt Biggy and Bitty. Mylo has bonded with the little ones and Lydia has plenty of room for them where she lives."

"How can I ever thank you? I know Uncle Raymond would be pleased to know that his beloved Bathsheba and her kittens have found good homes," she said, jumping up to hug first Brenda then Lydia.

QQQ

Overhearing the conversation about Biggy and Bitty going home with them, Myla took a swipe at her brother. "Now you've done it! Those two are going home with us and it's all your fault. You have to be Mr. Fun and Games. Always getting into trouble and coming out without a scratch and I have to clean up the messes after you."

"Aw, Sissy, lighten up. I bet even you can't resist those amber eyes!"

Verena Rose is the Agatha Award nominated co-editor of *Not Everyone's Cup of Tea, An Interesting and Entertaining History of Malice Domestic's First 25 Years* and the Managing Editor of the upcoming anthology *Malice Domestic 13: Mystery Most Geographical*, due out in time for Malice Domestic 30 from Widside Press. Verena serves as the Chair of Malice Domestic, is one of the founding members of the Dames of Detection, and co-owner/editor/publisher at Level Best Books. When not indulging her passion for mysteries Verena works as a tax accountant. She lives in Olney, Maryland, with her four cats: Jasper, Alice, Matty & Missy.

A.K.A. BOB JONES
by Michael Bracken

At seven-fifteen every morning for twenty-three years, Bob Jones had taken breakfast at Ricky's Diner in Holyoke, Massachusetts, a city trapped between the Connecticut River and the Mount Tom Range. He sat at the counter, ate two scrambled eggs and two slices of buttered toast, watched the morning news on a television mounted to the wall at the far end of the counter, and drank two cups of decaffeinated coffee while flirting with Maria Sanchez, a wide-hipped waitress who, at thirty-three the morning he first walked into Ricky's, was young enough to be his daughter.

One Monday morning in mid-July Bob walked in precisely at seven-fifteen and faced an empty diner and a blank television screen. Carmelita Moreno, a girl barely out of high school, pushed a cup of decaf across the counter as he settled onto his favorite stool two down from the cash register.

He asked, "How about some news?"

"Not this morning, Mr. Bob," she said.

"Why's that?"

"Nobody wants to watch this morning."

Bob looked around. "Where's Maria?"

"She's—she's—" Carmelita appeared on the verge of tears as she ran into the back.

Ricardo Cortez Junior, only son of Ricky and known by most as R.J., stepped out from the kitchen. He wore a sweat-stained white T-shirt stretched tight around his ample girth and a food-splattered white apron tied low beneath his overhanging belly.

"What the hell was that all about?" Bob asked.

"Maria was murdered yesterday," R.J. said. "Stabbed to death. I'm surprised you didn't know. It's all over the news. Every channel."

Bob did not own a television and only watched the news during breakfast at Ricky's. "How'd it happen?"

"Two *pendejos* jumped her on the way to noon Mass at St. Mary's. That's what the cops said. They were all over this place yesterday afternoon."

"What were they looking for?"

R.J. shrugged. "Whatever it was, they didn't find it."

"They ask about me?"

"No." R.J.'s eyes narrowed. "Why would they do that?"

"Known associates," Bob said. "They always ask about known associates."

"They wanted to know was she married, did anybody have a beef with her, stuff like that."

"What'd you tell them?"

"Everybody loved Maria. There isn't a soul in the world would want to hurt her."

"The two guys. They say anything about the two guys?"

R.J. shook his head.

"How'd they know there were two?"

"The man who found her, he said she was still—" A hitch in R.J.'s voice caused him to pause for a moment. He dabbed one corner of the dirty apron to the corners of his eyes before continuing. "He said she was still alive. He said she told him two men attacked her. He called the 9-1-1, but she was gone before the EMTs arrived."

"This guy, he have a name?"

"The cops never said."

The bell above the front door tinkled and they both turned to see an older couple walk in and settle into the first booth. Carmelita hurried from the back to fill their coffee cups.

"We thought about closing today, Mr. Bob," R.J. said, "but Maria wouldn't have liked that. We are closing for the funeral."

"When's that?"

"Wednesday afternoon. We're closing Wednesday afternoon." R.J. hitched up his apron. "I'll get your breakfast."

"Not this morning," Bob said. "I'm not hungry."

He left a two-dollar bill next to his untouched cup of decaf and returned to his second-floor, two-bedroom apartment several blocks away.

ooo

Harvey Knost, the retired Holyoke police officer who lived in the apartment next to Bob's, stood in his open doorway nursing a tumbler of Jack Daniel's, watching the early morning traffic, and scratching his belly as Bob ascended the steps. He saw the look on Bob's face when he reached the head of the stairs and asked, "What cat ate your canary?"

After learning about Maria, whom he also knew from his many visits to Ricky's, Harvey invited Bob into his apartment.

"If anybody needed a reason to drink," Harvey said, "it's you."

They sat at the chrome and yellow Formica kitchen table. Harvey poured three fingers of Jack into a tumbler for Bob and then added three more to his own.

"You ever think about your days as a cop when you hear about things like this?" Bob asked. "About what you did? About what you failed to do?"

Harvey shook his head and tapped his glass. "This helps."

"Is it enough?"

"The past is never far away," Harvey said as he lifted his glass. "If you stop moving, it'll catch up."

"You think we've stopped moving?"

"I sure as hell have," Harvey said. Six years Bob's junior, they had been neighbors ever since Harvey's wife kicked him out of their home eleven years earlier. "So, I drink to forget shit like this. People die for no good reason and there's nothing we can do about it."

"Some people deserve to die."

"Maybe they do," Harvey said, "but not Maria."

"No," Bob said. He downed his drink. "Not Maria."

Harvey refilled Bob's glass and again topped off his own. They drank in silence for several minutes.

Finally, Bob broke the silence. "I wish I knew who they were—the punks who did this."

"What could you do if you did?"

Bob shrugged.

"I know a few guys still on the force," Harvey said. "I could find out what they know, maybe get a line on the witness."

"Do that," Bob said. He finished his drink, thanked Harvey for his concern, and returned to his own apartment.

ϘϘϘ

The second bedroom had been converted into a library. Bookshelves lined all four walls, and in the center Bob had placed an overstuffed chair with a floor lamp on one side and a small table on the other.

He settled into the chair, a little woozy after breakfasting on Jack Daniel's, and let his past catch up to him. Because he freelanced for much of his career, moving from place to place as assignments dictated, he had acquired little of value until he finally settled in Holyoke and began building his book collection one careful purchase at a time. He owned several first-edition hardbacks, some of them autographed, and many well-thumbed paperbacks purchased at garage sales and used bookstores. He retained the tools of his trade, but had not opened the lock box in which he had packed everything since tucking it on the top shelf of the library closet.

Only a few minutes earlier Harvey had offered to learn what he could about Maria's killers, or the man who found her after the attack, but Bob had not immediately considered what he might do with the information. Though he only saw Maria for a short time each morning, their twenty-three-year relationship was the longest he'd ever had with a woman. He wondered if he owed the waitress anything for her friendship.

ϘϘϘ

Carmelita served Bob's breakfast the next morning and again on Wednesday morning. Wednesday afternoon, Harvey drove him to St. Mary's for Maria's Funeral Mass because Bob lost his license several years earlier when night blindness made driving difficult. The two men arrived late and were lucky to slip into the last pew before Mass began. Though neither man was Catholic, they prayed, sang, and genuflected along with everyone else.

They did not follow the hearse to the cemetery. Instead, Harvey drove the opposite direction.

"Did you see how many people were there?" he asked. Maria had never married, had no children, and had been loved by everyone. "All those people were her family. Family isn't blood. Family is choice."

"Where are you taking me?" Bob asked.

"Hold your horses, cowboy," Harvey said. "We're meeting a guy I know, says he can help us out."

Half an hour later, Harvey pulled his Impala to a halt in the gravel parking lot of the Dive Inn, a hole-in-the-wall bar with a nautical theme nowhere near any body of water larger than a mud puddle. Inside, Harvey introduced Bob to John O'Neil, a Holyoke homicide detective nearing retirement who had caught the Maria Sanchez case.

After exchanging pleasantries, Harvey bought a round of beer. Then he asked about the witness.

"His name's Ira Goldstein. We had him look at the mug book, but what good could that do? The perps were long gone before he found Ms. Sanchez." John leaned forward to emphasize what he said next. "That's what Goldstein says, anyhow. He says the vic was alive when he found her, but the coroner's report suggests otherwise. Seems obvious Goldstein saw something and doesn't want to cop to it. He may have seen the entire thing, and he's afraid the mooks'll come back for him if he fingers them."

"Any idea what they were after?"

"Not a clue," John said. "Looks random, but it could have been an initiation. Both La Familia and the Latin Kings are openly recruiting. Far as we can tell, the perps didn't take anything, and we can't find anybody who had a beef with the vic. The most unusual thing we found was the wad of two-dollar bills in the vic's wallet. Seven of them. Who the hell uses two-dollar bills?"

The three men finished their beer in silence.

"What can I tell you boys that you don't already know?" The homicide cop removed from his pocket a scrap of paper with Ira Goldstein's address on. He slid it across the table to the two men. "We got nothing to work with and more pressing cases. Shit happens, and it was her day to land in it."

 QQQ

A short, pudgy man in his early forties opened the apartment door. He wore Ben Franklin half-glasses, and he looked over the top of them at the two elderly men standing in the hallway outside his apartment.

"Mr. Goldstein?" Bob said.

"Who are you?" Ira Goldstein asked. "What do you want?"

"We need to talk to you about Maria Sanchez. She was buried this afternoon."

Ira tried to slam the door but Bob's size-eleven wingtip prevented its closure.

"You wouldn't tell the police what you saw," Harvey said. "We're hoping you'll tell us."

"I didn't see anything."

Harvey pushed the door open and Bob followed him into Ira's apartment as the younger man backed away.

"I have a wife. I have a daughter," Ira said.

"Are they home now?"

Ira shook his head. "I don't want any part of this."

"You became part of this when you dialed 9-1-1," Harvey said. "You didn't have to do that, you know."

"I—I couldn't just leave her there."

"She didn't tell you anything," Bob said. "She was already dead when you called for help."

"No, I—"

"You saw the men who killed her, didn't you?" Harvey said.

"No—"

"We know you did," Bob said. "So do the police. They just don't care enough to force it out of you."

"And you do?"

"Somebody has to care," Bob continued. "You certainly did. You didn't do anything to prevent her death, but you just told us you couldn't leave her there."

"So, what did you see?" Harvey asked.

Ira took off his glasses and pinched his nose. "My wife and daughter will be home soon. Will you leave if I tell you?"

When his two unwanted visitors nodded, Ira told them of two Hispanic men in their early twenties, one tall and thin, the other short and round.

"A Mutt and Jeff team," Harvey said, but Ira didn't understand the reference.

Bob did.

"They stabbed her. Several times."

"Both of them?"

Ira hesitated. "No. The short one held her. The tall one stabbed her."

"Did they say anything?"

"I couldn't hear."

"Did they take anything?"

"Not that I saw."

Bob and Harvey asked a few more questions, learned that the killers had worn black wife-beater undershirts, that the taller one had tattoo sleeves on both arms and that the shorter one had a scar on his left cheek.

Bob and Harvey left before Ira's wife and daughter returned, stopped at a liquor store long enough for Bob to buy a fifth of Jack Daniel's, and they cracked the bottle open once they reached Harvey's apartment. Bob only downed three fingers, and he returned to his own apartment long before Harvey finished the bottle and passed out in his lounge chair.

ععع

Thursday morning, Bob walked to Ricky's Diner. He arrived at seven-fifteen, ate two scrambled eggs and two slices of buttered toast, watched the morning news, and drank two cups of decaffeinated coffee. He did not flirt with

Carmelita.

From there he walked to St. Mary's, following the most direct route and the one he thought Maria most likely to have taken each Sunday on her way from the diner to Mass. Several businesses—many of which closed on Sunday—and an equal number of empty storefronts lined the boulevard much of the way to the church before giving way to apartment buildings and public housing. He passed the alley in which Maria's body had been found, not entering it until the return trip.

Bob stood and stared at the bloodstained concrete where Maria had taken her last breath. He looked up and down the alley at windowless brick walls, secure steel doors, and overflowing Dumpsters. He examined the buildings across the street from the mouth of the alley and located only one window with a direct view into the alley, a second floor window belonging to an accounting firm that offered tax preparation services. He could see Ira Goldstein watching him from inside the office. Neither man acknowledged the other.

Starting with the businesses flanking the alley's mouth, Bob visited each one on both sides of the street going all the way back to Ricky's Diner. He asked the owners, the employees, and the customers if they had known Maria, if they had been open on Sunday, if they had seen anything, and if they knew anyone matching the description of the Hispanic Mutt-and-Jeff duo Ira Goldstein had described.

The people he spoke with were a near-equal assortment of Caucasians and Hispanics, the two largest ethnicities represented in the city's population. Many knew Maria and all had heard of her murder. No one had seen anything. No one knew anything. No one recognized the two men Bob described. Several of the people with whom Bob spoke told him the police had already questioned them, and a few wanted to know why an old *gringo* was asking so many questions. He only said, "Someone has to."

By the time Bob dragged himself up the stairs of his apartment building, he knew little more than he had known that morning. When he passed Harvey's apartment, the retired cop jerked open the door and said, "Where the hell have you been all day?"

Bob told him.

"You should have told me," Harvey said. "I would have gone with you."

"Even retired, you stink of cop," Bob said. "I wanted people to talk to me. Fat lot of good it did. They were all happy enough to tell me about Maria, but they clammed up the moment I asked about Mutt and Jeff."

Harvey invited him inside. "I'll open a can of Dinty Moore, call the liquor store, and have them deliver a couple bottles of Jack Black."

Bob stepped into his neighbor's apartment, settled at the kitchen table, and waited while Harvey placed his liquor order. When the call ended, Bob asked, "What are they hiding? What are they afraid of?"

"I've seen this before," Harvey said as he dug through the cabinet looking for the beef stew he'd promised. "They're thinking any one of them might be next."

Before Bob could respond, a delivery boy knocked on the door.

"I'll get it," Bob said.

He had seen the young man in the liquor store earlier that day when he was retracing Maria's steps and asking questions, but they had not spoken.

"You live here?" the young man asked.

"Yeah," Bob said, not thinking there was much of a difference between one apartment and the next. He paid the delivery boy and tipped him a two-dollar bill.

ooo

A few hours later, Bob left Harvey asleep in his lounge chair and returned to his own apartment. He had not consumed nearly as much liquor as his neighbor and he wasn't ready for bed. He took a bottle of water from the fridge and settled into the overstuffed chair in his library with a paperback mystery he'd purchased two weeks earlier. Halfway through the third chapter, he fell asleep.

Bob woke to the sound of an apartment door being kicked open. He bolted from his chair with only the paperback for a weapon, and rushed from the well-lit library down the short hall into a pitch-black living room before he realized the noise he heard wasn't coming from within his apartment, but from the apartment next to his.

Without hesitation, he dropped the book, jerked open his apartment door, and ran the dozen steps to Harvey's apartment. The door stood open, the jamb splintered. No lights were on inside, but the streetlamp behind him cast enough light over his shoulder for Bob to see his neighbor curled into a fetal ball on the floor, his arms protecting his head as two men kicked him repeatedly.

As he ran inside, Bob grabbed the first thing that looked like a weapon, a half-empty bottle of Jack Daniel's. He swung it one-handed, smashing it into the side of the shorter man's head.

"¡Mierda!"

Both of Harvey's assailants turned, the shorter man with one hand pressed to the side of his head as blood leaked between his stubby fingers. Bob swung the bottle a second time, but the taller man caught it in mid-swing and wrenched it from Bob's grasp. He followed with a roundhouse right that caught Bob's jaw and collapsed him on top of his neighbor.

Bob struggled to right himself to continue the fight, but he need not have bothered. The two men were gone before he reached his feet. He stumbled to the door in time to see a black SUV racing from the parking lot.

He turned on the light and knelt at Harvey's side. His neighbor had been badly beaten but was still conscious.

As he patted Harvey's pockets in search of his cellphone, Bob asked, "What were they after?"

"They came to the wrong place," Harvey said. "One old white guy looks like another. They thought I was you. They wanted to know why I was asking so many questions and who I was working for."

"What did you tell them?"

Harvey tried to smile. "I couldn't get a word in edgewise."

Bob located Harvey's cellphone and prepared to dial 9-1-1.

Harvey stopped him and took the cellphone from his hand. "No. Don't. That's more trouble than it's worth. Those two won't be back. They did what they set out to do: scare a defenseless old man."

Bob helped Harvey to his feet, righted the lounge chair, and settled the retired cop into it.

"Give me that." Harvey pointed at the Jack Daniel's bottle on the floor. "I think I need a drink."

While Harvey medicated himself directly from the bottle, Bob soaked a washcloth in warm water, and used it and a towel to wipe away his neighbor's blood.

"I'll be okay," Harvey insisted. "They weren't professionals. I'll look like shit for a few days, but they didn't do any serious damage."

"You certain?"

"Hell, yes, I'm certain. My ex-wife did more damage with a frying pan when she found out I was banging her cousin."

As Bob cleaned the blood from his neighbor's wounds, Harvey used his cellphone to call a guy who cleaned up and secured crime scenes. When Harvey finished, he said, "He'll have a new, better door in place before daylight."

Bob finished wiping the blood from his neighbor's wound and headed toward the bathroom. He kicked something he had not previously noticed and looked down to see an open switchblade half under the end table. He realized Harvey's assailants had lost the knife in the darkness before they'd had a chance to use it.

Harvey heard the clatter of the knife when Bob kicked it, and he followed Bob's gaze. "That's likely the knife they used on Maria," he said. "Those two asshats probably weren't smart enough to clean it."

Bob collected a plastic grocery bag from the kitchen and nudged the switchblade into it. Then he sat with Harvey until the new door, with two deadbolts and a set of keys for each of them, was successfully installed.

As Bob prepared to leave, Harvey tapped the bagged switchblade. "I'll get this to John on the Q.T. He'll know what to do with it."

ooo

At seven-fifteen Friday morning, after realizing he had inadvertently led Maria's killers directly to Harvey's apartment and uncertain whether he should continue his search for Mutt and Jeff, Bob walked into Ricky's Diner, settled onto his favorite stool two down from the cash register, ate two scrambled eggs and two slices of buttered toast, watched the morning news, and drank two cups of decaffeinated coffee. When he finished, he slipped a two-dollar bill under the corner of his coffee cup.

Before Bob could rise from his stool, Carmelita gathered into her hand the single bill he'd left as a tip. "Every day you leave a tip, Mr. Bob," she said. "Maria she saved them."

Carmelita revealed that each Sunday Maria used the seven two-dollar bills Bob left her that week to light seven votive candles before Mass. "She said she did this for you," the young waitress said. "She said you were a troubled soul and needed God to watch over you every day of the week."

Bob stared at the young waitress. He had not known that Maria prayed for him.

"Do you know the kid who delivers for the liquor store?"

"Ernesto?" Carmelita asked. "He's bad news. He wants to be a gangbanger like his big brother."

"Where does he live?"

ꝏꝏ

Even though he no longer possessed a valid driver's license, Bob borrowed Harvey's Impala and cruised the neighborhood around Ernesto's home. The fourth time past the little bungalow with the black SUV parked in front, he saw a short, round man with a bandage on the side of his head exit the house, walk to the bungalow next door, and be greeted by a taller, thinner man with tattoo sleeves.

He returned the Impala to the parking lot behind their apartment building, returned Harvey's car keys, and poured out all the Jack Daniel's in Harvey's apartment. "Don't call the liquor store. I need you sober tonight."

Once inside his own apartment, Bob retrieved the lock box from the top shelf of the library closet and sat in the overstuffed chair in the middle of the room. Harvey had been right a few days earlier when he'd said that the past is never far away, and Bob let all the memories he had suppressed flood back.

Though he had retired twenty-three years earlier with no public recognition of his accomplishments, Bob had been quite good in his chosen occupation, and he vividly remembered each successful assignment. When he finished his silent stroll down memory lane, Bob pulled on a pair of cotton gloves, opened the lock box, and retrieved a .22 automatic, a suppressor, and a box of ammunition.

He spent the afternoon disassembling, cleaning, and reassembling the automatic, ensuring that he left no fingerprints on any part of the weapon. Then he cleaned the cartridges before loading the magazine.

After the sun disappeared behind the horizon, Bob dressed in black running shoes, black pants, black T-shirt, black jacket, and thin black leather gloves. He slipped the .22 into one jacket pocket and the suppressor into the other.

Then he walked next door and let himself into Harvey's apartment. The retired cop sat at the kitchen table nursing a cup of coffee and nervously tapping his fingers. Recently showered and freshly shaved, he still looked like the punching bag he'd been less than twenty-four hours earlier. But he was sober.

"I need you to drive and not ask questions."

The two men stared at one another for a moment before Harvey nodded and finished his coffee.

Soon, they were cruising the neighborhood Bob had cruised earlier. They watched both bungalows before determining that the men they sought were alone in the second bungalow watching soccer on a big screen television. Bob slipped out of the Impala, told Harvey where to wait, and made his way carefully through the back alley to the house. He removed the suppressor from his jacket pocket and attached it to the .22 he removed from the other pocket. Then, surprised to find the back door unlocked, he let himself in, eased through the kitchen, and stepped into the living room behind the taller man.

Less than five minutes later, he returned to the Impala where Harvey was waiting, and they returned home.

ჲჲჲ

Saturday morning Bob Jones settled onto his favorite stool at Ricky's Diner. Carmelita slid a cup of decaf across the counter to him, but her attention was on the television at the far end of the counter. The other customers were also watching the television, as was R.J. who had stepped out of the kitchen and stood with his arms crossed.

"Have you seen the news, Mr. Bob?" Carmelita asked.

He had not, so he watched with everyone else as a local newscaster described the organized crime-style killing of two young Hispanic males who had been wanted in connection with the recent murder of a local waitress. They had been linked to her murder through blood and fingerprints on a switchblade retrieved by police during routine investigation.

"Each was shot twice in the back of the head," reported the young woman covering the event live at the scene. "The bodies were discovered shortly after midnight by the younger brother of one of the victims. According to an unnamed source, this was no drive-by shooting, but a professional hit identical to a long string of still-unsolved organized-crime-related killings that ended abruptly twenty-three years ago."

Her image cut away for a brief pre-taped statement from the chief of police.

The young reporter returned to the screen and said, "At this time police are searching for suspects."

When the reporter threw it back to the newscaster in the studio, everyone turned away from the television and began talking animatedly about what they'd just seen.

"Those *pendejos* got what they deserved," R.J. said, loud enough for everyone to hear. No one disagreed.

Carmelita turned to Bob. "The usual, Mr. Bob?"

He sat at the counter, ate two scrambled eggs and two slices of buttered toast, and drank two cups of decaffeinated coffee. He did not flirt with Carmelita, but he left her a two-dollar bill tucked under his coffee cup and hoped no one felt the need to light candles for him at Mass.

Michael Bracken, recipient of the Edward D. Hoch Memorial Golden Derringer Award for lifetime achievement, is author of several books, including *All White Girls,* and more than 1,200 short stories published in *Alfred Hitchcock's Mystery Magazine, Ellery Queen's Mystery Magazine, Espionage Magazine, Mike Shayne Mystery Magazine,* and many other anthologies and periodicals. He lives and writes in Texas.

UNSTRUNG QUARTET
by Patricia Dusenbury

Hank closed his eyes and let the glorious sound wash over him. Whether or not the first violin, married to the viola, was having an affair with the cello, the quartet played in perfect harmony. Whether or not the second violin was gay and in love with the first or straight and enamored of the viola, nothing detracted from the music. One critic had famously described Windsong as four musicians making love to their instruments. Hank wished he could have seen them live.

The trouble began halfway through the second movement, an allegretto. The viola lagged, then sped up and lagged again. The others struggled to adjust to her erratic tempo. Hank paused the video and zoomed in on her face. A perfect oval, delicate features—she would have been pretty if her expression weren't anguished. He panned back out and hit resume.

The performance became increasingly ragged until the violist lay down her instrument and, one hand covering her mouth, rushed off stage. The second violin hurried after her. The first violin apologized to the audience, and the curtain came down.

Why hadn't her husband gone to help her? Why not the cello, the other woman in the quartet?

Hank reran the video, this time focusing on the others. The first violin played with drama, his eyes closed and his torso moving in concert with his bow. Longish dark hair framed strong features. Women would find him attractive. The second violin's eyes were also closed and his lips slightly parted. High cheekbones and fair coloring gave him a Slavic look. His movements were more restrained, a slight crouch on the low notes and a straightening on the higher ranges. Only the cello, feet firmly planted and eyes on her music stand, seemed earthbound—and earthy. Auburn curls resisted a restraining headband, and ample breasts strained to escape her blouse. A man looking at the instrument between her legs could wish to take its place.

When the viola wandered off tempo, the first violin opened his eyes and cut a quick glance in her direction. She continued to falter, and his expression morphed from annoyance to concern. Initially, the second violin frowned and the cello looked puzzled. As the viola grew increasingly erratic, their expressions also became concerned. Hank watched until the curtain came down then turned the video off.

Natalie Patroni had spent that night being violently ill. Victor, her husband, wanted her to see a doctor, but she'd refused, insisting it was just a bout of food poisoning. The lobster salad she'd eaten for dinner must have been a little off. They were miles from the ocean; she should have known better. The next morning, Natalie felt better—at least she'd stopped vomiting. Although still unable to keep food down, she sipped ice water to ward off dehydration and sent Victor to rehearse with the others.

Hank checked his notes. Victor had told the sheriff that the rehearsal was necessary because they were playing one of Haydn's early quartets, and the first violin played a dominant role. They would miss Natalie, but practice without him would have been pointless. The other members of the quartet had confirmed this, and Hank, the music lover, knew it to be true.

When Victor returned, Natalie was on the sofa watching television. She seemed tired, which was understandable given her sleepless night, and still had no appetite. They'd discussed the upcoming performance, and she expressed determination to be at rehearsal in the morning. Instead, she'd awakened early and, once again, was violently ill. Victor called the desk and asked for a doctor. The doctor called an ambulance.

Two days later, Natalie Stein Patroni died in the hospital, the victim of amanita poisoning. If she had gone to the emergency room sooner or received treatment earlier, if they could have arranged an immediate liver transplant, she might have survived.

Natalie's death stunned the music world and cast a pall over the festival. The Berkshire County Sheriff's Department ascertained that the deceased had eaten Mushroom Lorraine for lunch approximately eight hours before becoming ill, a timeframe consistent with amanita poisoning. They concluded that a poisonous mushroom had somehow gotten into the Mushroom Lorraine, essentially a quiche Lorraine plus mushrooms, that she'd ordered from room service. It wouldn't be the first time someone had confused *Amanita phalloides,* aka the death cap, with an edible mushroom.

Management at the Inn where Windsong was staying vehemently disagreed. They sourced their food locally and carefully from reputable providers. Natalie Patroni had indeed ordered a Mushroom Lorraine, but her slice had been one piece among eight from the same pie, and no one else got sick.

Jason and Amy Stein, Natalie's parents, also disagreed, which was why private investigator Henry Witherspoon had just watched a video of Natalie's last performance. Tomorrow night, he would be sleeping in a room at the Inn where all four members of Windsong had stayed and where the remaining three would be staying next weekend. They had chosen to honor their commitment to perform at the festival's closing weekend—albeit without Natalie. The Inn wasn't cheap, and Hank hoped his stay wouldn't be a waste of the Stein's money, but he feared otherwise.

"Random accidental death. Shit happens," Sheriff Tyler had said when Hank called him.

"Could it have been intentional?"

"Maybe, but we couldn't find anything. And we looked."

After talking to the sheriff, Hank met again with the Steins and offered to return their money. If someone had murdered their daughter, he or she was going to get away with it. Any proof was long gone before anyone started to look for it, and more time had passed. "I'm a private investigator not a magician," he said, "not Sherlock Holmes."

"I know who you are. I checked you out before contacting you. You're a damned good investigator, and you've just demonstrated that you're an honest man." Hank had shaken his head, but Jason Stein would not be dissuaded. "If you won't take the job, we'll have to find someone else."

At that, Hank had acquiesced. He liked the Steins, they were nice people and vulnerable in their sorrow. A less ethical investigator could take advantage.

The Colonial Inn fronted on the green in the center of a lovely Berkshire town that would look like a picture postcard if it weren't for the traffic that jammed the roads on all four sides of the green and leading up to it. Happily the Inn provided parking for its guests. After checking in and unpacking, Hank walked down the street to the county offices and introduced himself to the deputy working the desk.

"I spoke to Sheriff Tyler last week. About the Natalie Patroni death."

"He's gone for the day, but I'll let him know you're in town."

"Are you familiar with the case?" Getting a nod, Hank continued. "The victim's parents said there was no autopsy. Her husband claimed the body, and she was cremated the next day." The Steins had been stunned by the speed with which this occurred.

"She died in a hospital. There was no question about the cause of death." The deputy shrugged, but he sounded dissatisfied. Tyler had, too.

Sensing a trend, Hank asked, "What didn't you like?"

A tight smile broke through the deputy's careful neutrality. "I never mentioned not liking anything, but if you find something you don't like, we'd appreciate being informed."

"Count on it. And here's my card in case anyone wants to talk to me."

He returned to the Inn and chatted up the woman at the front desk. "This is my first time here. It's a pretty little town. Pretty crowded, too."

"Our music festival draws people from all over the world. For two months every summer, we're practically a city. You were lucky to get a room."

"You had a cancellation."

Her smile faded. "More than one. A musician died—you must have heard about it. She was staying here, and some people blame the Inn."

"I saw it on the news. It didn't sound to me as if the Inn was at fault. Whoever sold you those mushrooms, that's who I'd blame."

"I guess." She looked over his shoulder and frowned. "I'm sorry, sir, but I have another guest."

"One quick question," he said. "Where should I go for dinner?"

She handed him a brochure about the Inn and one about local restaurants. "Our guests often choose to eat with us, but the others are good too. If you decide to go elsewhere, it wouldn't hurt to call ahead and make sure they can take you."

He left her with what he hoped was a charming smile, found a comfortable chair in one of the side parlors, and settled in to read the Inn's brochure.

From its 1793 beginning as a six-room stagecoach stop, the Inn had grown into a resort hotel that occupied an entire block. Older sections faced the main street, while more recent wings extended along both side streets. A brick wall with one marked gate enclosed the back of the property. The sizable interior space was given over to gardens and a swimming pool, a croquet lawn, a badminton court, and a cluster of cottages. It was accessible from most first floor rooms, the restaurant terrace, and the bar. Hank opted for the bar and stopped to buy a cold beer and say hello to the bartender before walking outside and finding a quiet place to sit and think.

Birds sang, bees buzzed lazily from flower to flower, and rabbits grazed on a lawn so lush it looked like carpet. The breeze carried sounds of children playing in the swimming pool. Marco Polo, Hank remembered that game. The cottages—there were six of them—gleamed white in the afternoon sun. Victor and Natalie Patroni had stayed in number five. It was occupied, so as much as he'd like a look inside, that wasn't going to happen.

He finished his beer, returned to his room, and called room service. "I'd like the Mushroom Lorraine."

"I'm sorry sir, that's no longer on the menu, but we have an asparagus quiche."

He settled for steak, baked potato, and salad. When it came, he gave the young man who brought it up a generous tip. "Have you worked here long?" He squinted at the nametag. "Caleb."

"Since the beginning of June, but I worked here last summer, too."

"So, it's a pretty good summer job."

"The best money you can make round here." Caleb patted the pocket where he'd stuck Hank's tip.

"I'll be staying through the weekend performances. Probably see more of you unless someone else brings my dinner."

"I'm the only one does room service at dinner—seven days a week."

Hank laid his cards on the table. Might as well—he was meeting with the manager tomorrow morning, and word would get out. "I'm a private investigator," he said. "Natalie Patroni's parents hired me to look into her death."

Caleb took a step backward, and Hank hastened to reassure him. "I don't care how much weed you smoke." He'd caught a telltale whiff when Caleb walked in. "My job is to figure out how a poisonous mushroom got into her quiche. My question to you is when and where can someone mess with food being brought to a customer's room."

"They can't."

"Don't you leave your cart outside the door, unattended, when you deliver an order?"

"At breakfast, yeah, but people go out for lunch and dinner. We're not so rushed. Besides, she was staying in one of the cottages. Everything on the tray went to that cottage. They opened the door, and I wheeled it in."

Hank thanked Lady Luck for sending him the right waiter. It wasn't often that she smiled. "Straight from the kitchen to the cottage?" he said.

"If you don't believe me, you can look at the security video."

"She and her husband stayed in a cottage." Hank raised his eyebrows. "Separate bedrooms?" The Steins suspected there'd been trouble in their daughter's marriage. Nothing anyone could put a finger on, but her mother said Natalie had appeared preoccupied the last several times they'd talked.

"All four of them stayed in one of the three-bedrooms," Caleb said.

"They work together and they live together." Hank remembered the program notes about four musicians functioning as one. "That much togetherness would get on my nerves."

"All they care about is music—at least that's all I ever heard them talk about except for 'thank you, please put the tray here'"

"They're coming back in a couple days."

"Staying here again," Caleb's brow knitted. "That's kind of weird."

"Yeah."

Hank had been taken aback when the Steins told him Windsong would play the closing weekend as scheduled, albeit as a trio. He'd said something about Natalie's husband being in mourning, and Amy Stein had jumped to her feet. "Mourn her? He's—" She never finished the sentence. Jason had put a restraining hand on her arm and reminded her that they didn't know what happened. "We're hiring Hank to find out."

ℓℓℓ

Negotiations between the Inn and the Stein's lawyer had smoothed the way for Hank's investigation. The manager, a tall balding man, thin except for a small belly, showed him around the kitchen and expanded upon the Inn's position. The recipe for the quiche Natalie had eaten called for mushrooms cut into quarter-inch slices. The quiche was cut into eight pieces.

"How good is your math?" he said.

"Passable," Hank said. It hadn't been his best subject, but it hadn't been his worst.

"Try this," the manager said. "One bad mushroom would mean at least six bad slices. So the first bad slice goes into the quiche. What were the odds the second bad slice ended up in the same piece? The third, the fourth, the fifth, and the sixth bad slices?" He slapped the table to emphasize each number. "I talked to a statistics professor over at the University. The chance of that happening is one in 32,768."

Hank had to agree those were long odds.

"Bill Kenyon has a farm twenty minutes out of town. He sold us those mushrooms. He'll tell you the odds of him accidently including a death cap with the shitakes are zero."

"I'd like to talk to him, see his operation."

"Don't expect a friendly welcome. Bill believes he's been treated unfairly, and he has a point. Look at us. We're not buying his mushrooms. We used to make seven Mushroom Lorraine every weekday, ten or twelve on weekends, but people stopped ordering them."

Hank refrained from saying he'd tried and was told they were off the menu. It was probably one of those chicken and egg things. He thanked the manager for his cooperation and left with the address of the Kenyon farm.

ℚℚℚ

Thick low walls made from stones that had been dug to clear the fields edged the highway and marked property lines. Hank wondered if he would have had what it took to carve a farm out of this rocky soil, to weather the long cold winter. What would those early settlers—they must have been a tough lot—think of their descendants hosting a music festival?

"Your destination is on the left," his phone announced.

What would those settlers think of a smart phone?

He parked in the shade and approached the house. A big man stood on the porch, his thumbs hooked in his belt. "If you're here to buy mushrooms, sorry, I only sell wholesale."

"I'm looking into Natalie Patroni's death."

"Sheriff's already been here. He and the county agent poked around without finding any trace of an amanita—death cap or otherwise, but I still got the blame. 'The likeliest explanation,' he says, and now I can't give my shitakes away. The last flush went in the compost."

"Innocent until proven guilty didn't apply to you. Huh?" Hank shook his head sympathetically.

"Nothing proven because it didn't happen."

"Is there any way it could have happened?"

"If amanita spores got in with the shitakes, they wouldn't become mushrooms. The conditions aren't right. But say an amanita miraculously develops, I would have seen it fifty feet away. They are different goddamn colors."

"Where do your mushrooms grow?' Hank said.

"Are you a reporter?"

"I'm a private investigator working for Mrs. Patroni's parents."

"If you're looking for some reason they can sue me." Bill came down the steps.

Hank raised his arms in surrender. "No, no. They aren't after you. They're not convinced it was an accident. Is there a way someone could have snuck a bad mushroom in with the good ones?"

"I've thought about that a lot, and I haven't come up with anything."

"Maybe a pair of fresh eyes. Could you show me around? I've never seen a mushroom growing operation."

"What the hell. I've got nothing better to do." Bill started walking toward the barn. "We got rid of the cows and put in mushrooms—more money for less work until the sheriff told people we were poisoning our customers."

They entered the barn, and the smell hit Hank's nostrils—dampness, soil, and something more pungent, perhaps left over from the cows. His eyes adjusted to the low light, and he saw racks of shelves lining the walls. A few held what looked like brown cinder blocks dotted with tan mushrooms, but most were empty. Black cylinders the size of trashcan liners hung from the ceiling. Clumps of long-stemmed white mushrooms protruded from holes in their sides.

"I grow shitakes and oysters, shitakes in those blocks." Bill pointed to the shelves. Demand is down for reasons already discussed, so I've cut back production. The cylinders are for the oysters. People are still eating oysters."

Hank walked over to examine the shitakes. The blocks were made of pressed sawdust.

"Did you hear about the guy who divorced his wife because she treated him like a mushroom?" Hank shook his head and Bill snickered. "She kept him in the dark and fed him bullshit."

The joke confirmed Hank's suspicions about the odor. "I think I've seen enough."

Before leaving, Bill picked three shitakes. "There's something I want to show you. I've got books back at the house."

The books were all about mushrooms. Bill opened a coffee table size one to the section on amanitas and laid the shitakes he'd picked next to pictures of death caps. Here we've got three stages of development. Can you tell the difference?"

"The shitakes are darker, browner."

"Right, and the death caps have a green cast. Now compare the shapes. The edges of the mature death cap might turn down, but shitakes roll under. Both have veils and they're both gilled mushrooms, but the details are totally different. If I had a death cap here, you'd see that they smell different and they feel different."

"I see it when you show me, but…" Hank studied the pictures. "I want to remember what death caps look like in case I ever run across one."

"Never eat a wild mushroom with gills and a veil that is growing in dirt. Anything looks like a puffball, cut it open to be sure. Immature amanitas can be mistaken for edible puffballs, young ones for meadow mushrooms, but I never heard of anyone confusing an amanita with a shitake."

"Would it make a quiche taste funny?"

Bill smiled. "People who've survived a death cap say it tasted delicious." He picked up another book. "Here are your edible mushrooms and their poisonous look-alikes."

"All of these can kill you?"

"Only a couple of the amanitas and it doesn't take much." He measured a scant inch with his thumb and forefinger.

Hank nodded. He'd researched amanita poisoning before coming and discovered that Natalie Patroni was in good company: a Pope, a Tsarina, and Holy Roman Emperor Charles VI were among the notable victims.

"The others cause what docs call NADIVO." Bill chuckled. "Nausea, diarrhea, and vomiting."

"Think I'll stick with store-bought mushrooms."

"You can find my mushrooms in supermarkets."

"Where could I find a death cap?" Hank said

Bill pointed out the window. "The fungus is among us. You got time for a little 'shrooming?"

"You bet."

At first Bill had to point them out, but Hank soon developed an eye. Mushrooms really were everywhere. In twenty minutes, they found a dozen different varieties. Bill gleefully picked several that looked like thick yellow flowers.

"Chanterelles fried in butter and served over toast—a meal fit for a king. You wanna stay for lunch?"

"No thanks." Hell would freeze over before he ate a wild mushroom. Bill might find NADIVO amusing; he didn't. "I have work to do."

He left the farm with dirty knees, a bag containing three death caps in various stages of development, and an idea. Back at the Inn, he stopped by the manager's office to ask if the gardeners wore uniforms. Getting a yes, he asked if he could borrow one. Four backbreaking hours later, he returned the uniform and told the manager what he'd found.

"Do you still have surveillance videos for the night before Natalie became sick?"

"Yes, but the area in question is neither well-covered nor well lit after dark."

"Time for plan B," Hank said. Not that he had one—not yet.

ooo

Dimitri Sokolov was the violin player who'd run to Natalile Patroni's assistance. According to Caleb, Dmitri liked his vodka and most evenings stopped by the bar for a drink before dinner. Which was why Hank, dressed in clean clothes and the dirt scrubbed from under his fingernails, sat nursing a beer at a table by the bar's garden entrance.

Right on schedule, Dimitri appeared. He walked across the lawn head down and hands in his pockets, lost in thought. As soon as he cleared the door, Hank stood, blocking his progress. "Excuse me, Mr. Sokolov. Can I buy you a drink? My name is Hank Witherspoon, and I'm a big fan of yours."

Dimitri looked up, surprised. "Thank you, but—"

Hank tried his most winning smile. "Just a quick drink. I'd be honored."

Left with the choice of pushing past or accepting a free drink, Dimitri accepted.

Hank signaled, and the bartender brought over a bottle of vodka in ice, two tall shot glasses, and a platter of dark bread. Dimitri raised his eyebrows.

"I was hoping you'd say yes," Hank said. "So I asked the bartender what you liked."

"This is very kind of you, but I cannot stay long. As you must know, we're performing this weekend. Tomorrow rehearsals begin early."

"The show must go on." He paused. "I don't know how you do it."

"For us, the music offers comfort." Dimitri sipped the vodka then took a bite of buttered bread. "It is life."

"You're Russian."

"I'm Russian by way of Estonia, Katrina is from Denmark, and Victor is Italian. Natalie was American. Music is international."

"The program says you'll be playing viola."

"A trio does not require a second violin; it requires a viola."

"And you can make the switch?" Hank snapped his fingers. "Just like that?"

"I was trained on both." Dimitri refilled his shot glass. "I will be playing Natalie's viola. A part of her will still be with us."

"So Windsong will become a trio?"

"Only temporarily. A new viola will join us, and I will return to my violin."

"I saw the concert when Natalie became ill," Hank said. Not a lie—he'd watched the video four times. "You rushed to help her. That's why I wanted to buy you a drink. Consider it a thank you from her parents."

"You know Natalie's parents?"

"I'm a private investigator, working for them."

"What are you investigating?"

"They want to know where that poisonous mushroom came from. I visited the farm where the Inn buys its mushrooms." He shook his head. "It didn't come from there."

"You are sure?"

"Positive, but I'm still trying to find out where it did come from." His grenade tossed, Hank stood. He gestured toward the ice-encased bottle. "Have as much as you want. It's on Natalie's parents." He went up to the bar to sign the tab.

Dimitri's reflection in the bar mirror knocked back another shot of vodka—no sipping this time. He'd tell the others about this investigator working for Natalie's parents, repeat what he's said about the mushroom. The killer would recognize the risk and, with any luck, take action.

Hank returned to the privacy of his room and called Sheriff Tyler to tell him that he'd found the probable source of the poisonous mushroom and, he believed, had narrowed the suspect list down to the surviving members of Windsong.

"I'm not surprised," Tyler said, "but can you prove anything?"

"A few minutes ago I had a drink with Dimitri Sokolov. I'm hoping I said just enough to flush the killer out. Time will tell, but nothing's going to happen until dark. Too many people around now."

Hank selected a restaurant from the brochure the receptionist had given him and made a dinner reservation. He would be eating elsewhere until the person who'd killed Natalie Patroni was safely in jail.

ΩΩΩ

Hank, the sheriff, and a deputy took turns watching from the window of a first floor room whose lucky occupants had been "upgraded" to a suite. The vantage gave them a clear view of the area where Hank had found what looked the top of a hen's egg poking through the moss beneath a large oak. Odds were the mushroom that poisoned Natalie came from there or somewhere close. Bill, who was a good guy despite his warped sense of humor, had assured him that death caps grew in clusters, and they grew back in the same place they'd been. Hank had spent the afternoon crawling around under trees. If there was another cluster on the Inn's property, he'd missed it.

The watching proved tedious—no lights, no TV, and not much to talk about—but it paid off. Shortly before midnight, the door of Windsong's cabin opened. The security lights shone copper on curly hair belonging to Katrina Hansen. Hank sighed. He'd been hoping it wasn't her, even thinking about asking her out when it was all over.

She walked casually toward the main building then cut over to the big oak and knelt on the ground. The sheriff and his deputy gave her time to start digging.

ووو

The next morning, Hank stopped by the Sheriff's Department. "I'm leaving today, but I wanted to check in, see how it was going."

"Ms. Hansen confessed," Sheriff Tyler said. "Turns out we had it all wrong."

"What do you mean?" Hank thought he'd nailed it.

"It wasn't the quiche. She sprinkled a chopped up death cap on the victim's salad. And her motive? You're not going to believe it."

"Not sex?"

"Nope, music. Victor Patroni had been offered a job in New York, and Natalie was bugging him to take it. She wanted to settle down and start a family."

"So?" Hank said.

"According to Ms. Hansen, that would be a disaster. Natalie could be replaced, but not Victor. He's a musical genius, and without him, Windsong would be just another string quartet. She couldn't let that happen because." Tyler made quote marks with his fingers. "The music is more important than one silly woman's desire to reproduce."

"Wow."

"Her only regret is getting caught."

NorCal SinC member **Patricia Dusenbury**'s first novel, A Perfect Victim, won the 2015 Eppie for best mystery. Secrets, Lies & Homicide (2016) and A House of Her Own (2017) were finalists. Her short stories have been e-published by Mystery Tribune and Flash Bang Mysteries and included in the noir anthology, Black Coffee. Raised in Connecticut, Patricia lives in San Francisco.

THE EXPLORER
by Maurissa Guibord

Boston, 1924

Ellen Langford sat by the window and gazed at the snow as it whipped and eddied along Mt. Vernon Street. She enjoyed watching a storm like this, though she felt guilty to be enjoying it from such a comfortable perch. Here she was, in the warm and spacious parlor of their Beacon Hill home while Arthur …

That was just the trouble. Ellen twisted the gold wedding band around and around on her slim finger. She had no idea *where* her husband was, or what he might be facing. His most recent letter lay on the table beside her and she picked it up once more.

12th September 1924
Matto Grosso, Brazil

Dearest Ellen,

Slow progress. Rain and biting insects incessant. We are losing our photographer, Mr. Shepherd. He scratched at a wound on his neck from a *Sututu,* one of those infernal burrowing larvae and it's become septic. He'll go to the lumbering camp in Juarana where there's a crude infirmary. I'll send this letter along.

Jungle here as dense as we've ever experienced. We're close to the location where the Briggs expedition turned back. So, six weeks from our targeted location to search for the lost city. We strive for speed because we've had word of another team, financed by a Russian that set out one month ago from La Paz. But I have confidence in our superior resources and experience, especially our superb native guide, Benicio. My Portuguese has improved-- so much that he and I are able to understand each other with no difficulty. Or so he pretends. Ha!

Tell Max his father has bagged another jaguar, a beautiful, sleek female that stalked our camp for several nights. She came into my tent, lured by the smell of a fresh monkey carcass I'd left at the foot of my cot. The new Winchester performed admirably!

Dr. Erickson complains everyday about the conditions and already suggests turning back. I knew he wouldn't be fit for this trip. I only hope he doesn't slow us down too much.

Each night I think of you, my goddess, my beautiful Ellen and thank God for my blessings at home. Thank you for the package, especially glad to have the tobacco and tea. The shortbread cookies suffered an attack of meal worms, but everything else I will enjoy.

Your devoted husband,

Arthur

Ellen sighed and folded the letter. She was a lovely woman with long auburn hair, luminous gray eyes and an air of quiet composure. Although recently, when they dined together her mother remarked that Ellen had 'lost some of her shine'. It was true. Fine lines now pulled at the corners of her mouth and deeper ones marked latitudes of worry across her previously smooth brow.

But what of it? Arthur wouldn't notice such things when he came home. He always declared her 'his goddess'. He thought her steadfast, unchanging and perfect. Silly of course, but he always made her feel as if she *were* those things.

And Arthur? She'd known from the moment she met him that he was extraordinary. Arthur Langford possessed more drive, more enthusiasm and more sheer *life* than anyone she'd ever known.

His current expedition, supported by Harvard's Natural History Society, trekked in the deepest regions of the Amazonian rainforest, searching for a fabled 'lost city of gold'. The letter she held was written in September. It was nearly Christmas now; anything could have happened.

She rubbed at her temple. If only she could be there with him. But, as Arthur had told her numerous times, that was impossible.

A shriek and the pounding of feet heralded the entrance of four-year old Bonnie. She was trailed by her older brother Max who held his toy rifle in the crook of one arm, muzzle down, as he'd been taught.

"You're dead, Bonnie. I shot you."

"I'm not. You missed!" said Bonnie with breathless defiance. She stopped abruptly in front of the claw-footed display cabinet. She tucked her chin down and pressed her tummy against the glass door. "I want to hold the pretty necklace."

Ellen quickly rose and guided her away from the case. "We can't touch any of Daddy's things sweetheart, they're just to look at."

Arthur always kept the cabinet locked. It housed the most precious items he'd collected from his travels which ranged from the exquisite, to the grotesque, to the simply macabre. The necklace Bonnie coveted was a gift from a tribal chief; it was strung with hundreds of opalescent snail shells, each one carved into a tiny bird or fish. Spearheads, small stone axes, and shards of pottery each bore a tag indicating their origin. Two huge crystal points, one of amethyst and one of tourmaline were displayed alongside a vial of gold nuggets panned from the Tipuani river. On the upper shelf lay a tightly wrapped leather pouch containing poisoned darts made by Pacaguara warriors, the tiniest scratch from which could kill a man in moments. Beside the pouch, and as big as a dog's head, lay the dried skull of a monstrous bushmaster snake with its curved double fangs. Arthur had killed the twenty-foot long viper with a machete on his first expedition. The skull still gave off a faint, foul odor of rot that would always evoke *jungle* to Ellen. It made her ill just to look at it.

"There's a letter!" Max's excited cry came from the foyer.

Ellen felt the familiar, nearly painful leap of her heart at seeing the yellowed envelope with Arthur's sprawling script.

October 3rd, 1924
The River Xingu

Dearest Ellen,

The land here is an endless wonder. But the rivers! Yesterday I learned of a fish, only an inch or two long and shaped like a tiny eel. *Canduru.* It wriggles into any human orifice it has access to and cannot be removed except with the most excruciating pain because of its backward facing barbs. Some local had to have one cut from his-- well you can imagine.

We lost Caufman, our mule and horse man. He slipped from the raft and was taken down by a crocodile. Very quick. I'm told they wedge their victims under a ledge or a dead log and eat them after the flesh has putrefied. You'd be surprised how quickly the group shrugs it off when a man dies, even telling jokes about it. It reminds me of the war.

We all suffer with blood blisters from the stinging insects. Even when it's quiet I hear the flies buzzing in my ears. I can't tell if it's real or an effect of this low fever which I've had for a few days now. It's not the 'Yellow Jack' because Dr. Erickson assures me I would be dead by now. Ha! He's dosing me with quinine and some other horrible tasting stuff. I have no doubt it will soon clear up.

Passed a settlement yesterday of the Maricoxis- a tribe well known in this region as cannibals. They gave us no sign of aggression but it caused several of the natives we hired as bearers to abandon us. So, we will all carry more from here on. I don't mind. Fewer men travel faster anyway.

Tell Max we killed an anaconda several weeks ago that had curled itself around the waist of one of the men as he slept. It would have crushed him to death had McCrawley not clubbed its head with the butt of his rifle. 18 feet long, but I'm told they can grow much bigger. I used Shepherd's photographic equipment and (hopefully) captured an image of the brute.

The dangers are many, but for the chance to discover a lost city of Amazonia, an advanced civilization that predates the Incas, what would we not sacrifice? I know you share my conviction and I'll have so many tales to tell you and the children upon my return. Triumphant return!

Yours,

Arthur

"I want to see Daddy's anaconda." This from Max after Ellen had read a few (very selected) parts of the letter aloud.

"When he comes back, he'll show you the picture," said Ellen quietly.

"When I'm older I can go to the jungle with him."

Ellen turned and stared into her son's blue eyes, eyes that were so much like Arthur's. She felt suddenly breathless, as if she'd been lifted to some great elevation.

"Well," she heard herself say at last. "That will be very exciting, won't it?"

Max seemed satisfied by this and wandered away. Ellen began to read the letter once more, but her hands shook so much she had to stop.

It was simply too much. How could Arthur carry on as if nothing was wrong?

Why did he seem to take such delight in describing the horrific conditions, the dangers and accidents that occurred almost daily? Arthur loved her. He couldn't purposefully mean to be this cruel. It was as if he wanted her to keep a running tally of his ever-increasing wager against mortality.

Perhaps he really didn't fear death. As Ellen sat and thought of this she rubbed her thumb along the delicate knuckles of her left hand. Back and forth, over and over, as though praying a rosary over four tender, whitened beads.

ૡૡૡ

When they'd, met Arthur was studying archeology at Harvard. Her first impression, as she recalled, was foolishly girlish and took in little beyond the vivid blue of his eyes and the sinewy form of his arms under rolled-up shirtsleeves. But he was full of imagination and a cheerful sort of energy that Ellen found irresistible. They shared a love of history and art and conversation about the world. Together they read about the exploits of men like Roosevelt and Percy Fawcett as well as the discovery of Machu Picchu by Hiram Bingham.

When Arthur told her that he wanted to accomplish great things too, Ellen simply took it for granted that he would.

America entered the Great War four months after they were married and Arthur enlisted immediately. Their first child, a son, was born while he was fighting in Northern France. After hearing the news, Arthur wrote and told her that he would carve the name of their son into the wall in one of the limestone caves there. It was his name too, for their firstborn was Arthur Langford Jr.

The baby died of meningitis when he was 6 months old.

Even now, years later, Ellen had the dream sometimes. She wandered in a dark place under the ground, running her fingers over cold walls, searching for her son's name in the stone.

After the war it seemed a miracle that Arthur returned, that he'd survived when so many had not and it was with a fierce, almost animal passion that she loved him for it. She rejoiced to feel his skin, warm and smooth against her own in the night. And afterwards, as they shared quiet talk against the darkness, it seemed to her that her own wounds, invisible and unspoken though they were, began to heal.

But something in Arthur had changed and soon he was gone on his first expedition to South America.

Each time he came home their meeting was as loving as ever. Arthur would be lean as a whippet, his nose sunburned, his skin hardened with new scars. At first he would delight in each luxury of home: the hot tap water, the extravagances of steaks and newspapers and a soft bed. And her.

But soon he was restless. "You know, I've been thinking of a curious thing that Rollins pointed out about those markings ..." and he would be off, his excitement growing as he planned his next trip to a new location, where no one had ever thought to look before for a lost city.

They'd been married for twelve years now. Arthur had been far away from home for eight of them.

December 12th, 1924
11° 43' S
54° 35' W

Dearest Ellen,

Our hardship continues. Of the original ten expedition members we've lost five. Barrows was killed by an arrow in an attack from the river-bank by a band of Guarayos. Leonards and St. Croix both contracted yellow fever and passed very quickly. I told you about Shepherd and Caufman already.

The food is running low as we have found little fresh game to eat. Hunger makes the party bad-tempered. Accusations of thievery are flung back and forth. These men would seem to tolerate anything, even murder, over the theft of a cup of rice or a squib of tobacco!

That fool Erickson now tries to cast doubt on my every decision. He's too soft to be out here and his poor attitude only depresses the others. He's begun to drink. He shoots off his revolver into the trees at the slightest noise. His nerves are shot.

Only McCrawley and Jeffords remain strong and steady of spirit, as well as Benicio. I'd give up the rest and gone on with just those three if I could!

I remain confident that we are close to finding the lost city. Tomorrow we climb to the top of a nearby hill. There have been stories of carved monolithic figures seen in the distance from that spot. I will have more news very soon!

We'll send a group back to Riberalta to replenish our supplies. I will send this letter by way of that station.

I remain your ever-faithful husband and hope to soon make wonderful discoveries!

Arthur

P.S. You'll be pleased to hear that my fever is gone. Erickson of course takes all the credit. Insists I keep taking his foul medicine.

Ellen dropped the letter and sprang from her chair. She paced the floor of the parlor, twisting and rubbing her hands. It was unbearable. Arthur was out there, depending on men too drunk or too sick to even take care of themselves.

She unrolled one of the numerous survey maps from a previous trip. She found the location he'd indicated and pressed her fingernail hard into the paper to mark the spot. Whole expeditions had disappeared into that region, never to be seen or heard from again. Perhaps this mark was the last she would ever know of her husband's fate.

And that would be the worst pain of all. How could she go on like this? To be left never knowing, never being certain of what happened. To wait and imagine and fear, for months or years. Possibly forever.

She wasn't strong enough. She couldn't bear it.

After she put the children to bed, she prepared a small parcel with Arthur's usual favorite items. She took a long time with her own letter, trying to find the right words, trying to explain how very proud she was of him.

She finished by writing:

I wish I could be stronger. Please forgive me.

Forever yours,

Ellen

April 7th, 1925

Dearest Ellen,

I can only write a short note as we've met a passing group of Echoca Indians who say they will carry this letter to the next village.

We've had trouble finding the landmarks that should mark our current position, though our calculations have been checked over and over. Many of the written reports from past expeditions are misleading, and the so-called government maps are rubbish!

Your package was waiting for me at Riberalta and one of the bearers brought it back with him. How good to have some fresh pipe tobacco, chocolates and a tin of my favorite black pekoe!

Thank you for your loving words, but forgive? Nonsense. I will think of you tonight my goddess.

Yours always,

Arthur

When the news of the expedition finally did come, it was by telegram. A clean and colorless, single sheet of paper was delivered to Mrs. Ellen Langford.

Arthur Langford had died suddenly, of apparent heart failure in his tent. The remote nature of the camp, the conditions and temperature had necessitated that his body be cremated. His remains would be shipped by steamer to Boston.

When she saw the news grief rolled into Ellen like a tide that had been held back for a long time. She let herself be swept away. She'd held this sadness inside her for so long. For years, it had been tightly compressed in the knotted muscles of her neck, in the throbbing pulse at her temple, in the bitter bile at the back of her throat. It was a relief to finally let it out.

Her mother came to look after the children. They told Max and Bonnie that their father had gotten sick in the jungle and had gone to sleep. He was in heaven now.

Funeral preparations were made, memorials and receptions planned. When they spoke of it everyone agreed: Arthur Langford had died as he would have wished, in the jungle. At the edge of a great discovery. A hero.

Eight weeks later Dr. Carl Erickson, one of the senior members of the expedition, arrived in Boston and came immediately to call on Ellen.

It was obvious the past year had taken a toll on his health. He was a large man yet his flesh seemed to droop from his bones. His clean, but wrinkled trousers looked as though they were inches too large in the waist and were held up only by his tight belt. His mild, slightly bulging brown eyes had a yellow tinge.

"Mrs. Langford," he said, taking her hand in his own which was marked by scores of small scratches and bites. "I had to come to you, to express my deep regret at the passing of your husband. It was," he took a deep breath and stepped back from her, shaking his head, "A terrible day. The worst of many terrible days. If any of us were to make it through, I thought it would be Arthur. He seemed…invincible."

"No one is invincible," said Ellen quietly.

"No." Erickson rubbed a hand over his grizzled chin, looked as if he was going to say something and then changed his mind. "No," he repeated.

She indicated a chair for him and poured him a drink. After they were both seated she leaned forward. "Dr. Erickson please tell me. What happened? I must know. Was Arthur alone? Was he in pain?"

Erickson took a swallow of his sherry, coughed, shook his head. "No pain Mrs. Langford. At least, we saw no evidence of it."

"Thank God."

"It was Benicio who found him," said Erickson. "He thought it was strange that Arthur hadn't risen. He was always the first one up, organizing the packs, checking the maps, planning our course." Erickson cleared his throat. "Though we butted heads more than once, I respected Langford very much. He was a remarkable man."

Ellen made no reply to this and he continued:

"At first it seemed Arthur was just asleep. Except he lay on his back with his hands gripped tight. Like so." Erickson clutched at his shirt, his fingers drawn into rigid claws over his heart. "He was pale but there was no sign of injury. The contents of a small table and his cook stove had been knocked over. An aluminum cup, his pipe, some food and a tin of loose tea were on the ground. Some maps and papers scattered."

"Benicio raised the camp with his shouting," he said. "Unfortunately, I couldn't understand much of it." Erickson gave her a rueful look. "Don't speak the Portuguese lingo like Arthur could. At one point Benicio kicked at the dirt and I did manage to catch something he said. It was '*Taya*,'"

Ellen inclined her head sharply. "What was that?"

"He said '*Taya'*," repeated Erickson. "That's the nickname the natives have for a particularly nasty snake. A small, but deadly one. The fer-de-lance."

"He was bitten by this snake?" Ellen asked with a frown. "Is that what caused his heart to…"

"No," the doctor interrupted. "No, my dear, we didn't find a snake bite. But we were all of us covered with so many sores and scabs from the damned flies, never mind the dirt, we, er, *I* could have missed it. But there would have been some discoloration, blackening of the skin. No sign of that." Erickson shifted in his chair. "Some of the native workers mumbled about a curse." He stared down into his glass and swirled the contents. "Nothing but foolish chatter."

Erickson tossed off the rest of his drink in a gulp, set down the glass and looked at Ellen squarely. "Arthur died of heart failure. It happens you know, with the stress, the heat, the poor nutrition."

Ellen leaned back into her chair and nodded slowly. "Thank you, Dr. Erickson. It's a relief. To know for certain."

Erickson nodded. "The rest of us decided to pack it in after that. By some miracle we all came back safely."

"I am glad to hear it," said Ellen, almost absently. It had come as no surprise to her that without the force of Arthur's authority, his sheer will, the expedition had ended. "Will the society send another group?" she asked. "To look for the lost city?"

Dr. Erickson spoke distinctly, "Madam, I cannot speak for the rest, but I will never step foot in South America again."

After Erickson departed Ellen felt grateful for his visit. What a blessing to know that Arthur had died peacefully.

Death would have come as a surprise to him, she thought. But she wondered, in those last moments had he felt any fear, any regrets? Had he thought of the family he'd left behind so often and for so long?

She closed her eyes and let herself imagine it. She was there in the tent with Arthur, just as she'd always longed to be.

It was evening. The air was heavy with the smell of wet and decay. A pot of water bubbled over the small kerosene cook stove. Arthur opened the small tin of loose tea and spooned a portion into the strainer. He poured hot water over the leaves and then after a few minutes, drank from the dark, fragrant brew.

His eyes widened. He staggered and knocked over the flimsy camp table. He gasped a last breath as the paralysis set in. The poison would have acted rapidly.

Ellen opened her eyes and let out a long, slow breath. Her beloved Arthur, the celebrated explorer, had died while on a scientific expedition in the jungle. It was over. She could let go of the constant fear. She could set down the burden of his great destiny.

Benicio must have suspected the truth somehow, she thought. Perhaps he had seen such a case before or smelled something unusual in what remained in the tin or the drinking cup. If so, he would have been frightened to touch the stuff himself. He wasn't kicking the ground, searching for a poisonous *Taya*, as Professor Erickson thought. He'd been trying to tell them that something was wrong with the *tea*.

Because before sending that last package to her husband, Ellen Langford had unlocked the display cabinet and taken the poisonous darts from their leather pouch. Then, at the kitchen table, and with infinite care, she'd used a paring knife to scrape their coating of shiny black resin into Arthur's tin of black pekoe.

There had been no choice really. The uncertainty of how and when Arthur would meet his end had become unbearable. She loved her husband far too much to wait for him to die.

There had only been one solution.

She'd had to kill him.

Maurissa Guibord is the author of two novels for young adults and numerous mystery short stories. She has been a finalist for the Agatha and RITA awards. She lives on the coast of Maine.

ALL THAT SPARKLES
by L.D. Masterson

Yeah, all right. I killed her. I admit it. But it's not like I robbed her of a lot of years. Hell, the old girl must have been a hundred and ten. And I didn't mean to. I kinda liked Madeline. But she was like bait in a trap. Every afternoon her nurse wheeled her into the sunroom and left her napping…all dressed up like she was going to some fancy to-do, with her hair done and wearing some pieces of really fine jewelry. I'm talking the good stuff. Worth a nice chunk of change. The nurse said it made her feel good to get all dolled up but I figured I could put those gems to a lot better use than being worn by some old lady sitting in a sunroom.

But I'm getting ahead of myself here. My name's Baxter. I'm the transportation coordinator for Wellesley Manor, which is this really posh nursing home in Wellesley, Mass, just outside Boston. It's a small place, just for these rich old broads who can't live in their fancy mansions anymore because they're too sick or too old or sometimes because someone in the younger generation forced them out. But don't feel sorry for them. Not for being in this place.

Now don't let my fancy title fool you, I'm basically just a chauffeur. I drive the ladies—the ones that can leave the grounds—wherever they want to go…shopping or church or to their doctors (I get a lot of those) or maybe to a show. And cemeteries. I take a lot of them to visit their dear departeds.

For most of them, the only time they ever leave the Manor is when I take them out in that fancy van. Goes for me, too. The job comes with a room on site, so I'm on call twenty-four seven, and I don't have my own wheels so even on my day off I'm pretty much stuck here. But I never planned to stay long. When I saw the ad, I figured what the hell…if I couldn't come up with some way to score living with a bunch of old dames with more money than teeth, I should just hang it up.

So anyway, I've been here a few months and I've got a nice little stash going. A lot of these dames don't have anyone so I play nice with them when I take them out and some of them like to show their appreciation with a tip or a little gift. I'm careful to keep it under the radar. The people who run this place are real picky about stuff like that. And every week or so, when I'm waiting for someone to get done doing whatever they're doing, I swing by this gym over in Natick where I've got a locker rented, and I add my latest to the stash.

But it was getting old. Bits and pieces are fine but I'm not staying in the place forever. I wanted one hefty score and then I could get outta here. So I decided on Madeline's brooch.

Here's the set up. Miss Madeline—we call all the old girls "miss"—had a private nurse. Kind of a combination nurse-lady's maid-companion, who lived in a room next to hers. Which, if you knew what the rooms here cost, would tell you the lady had some serious dough. So every day, this nurse would get Miss Madeline dressed and put a couple pieces of jewelry on her. Now, I know my jewelry. I've had some experience along those lines…but we won't go into that. I decided that fancy brooch, the one that looked like flowers with a bunch of diamonds and sapphires and other stones, was my best bet. Especially since the nurse put it on her most Saturdays and that was the nurse's day off. After she got Madeline ready for the day, she turned her over to the house nurse till bedtime. That house nurse is a cute chick named Cindy. She's a good kid but taking care of a bunch of old ladies isn't exactly her dream job, so I figure she's not so likely to notice if the brooch ain't there when she puts her ladies to bed.

Plus, on Saturdays they bring in some speaker or entertainment of some sort and invite all the ladies to the community room to see it. "Invite" means everybody goes…unless you're still feisty enough or loud enough or maybe rich enough to say no. Then you get to be wherever you want. For Miss Madeline, that's the sunroom, only now it's winter so you're looking at more snow than sun. Most Saturdays, Miss Madeline's the only one in the sunroom.

So I picked my day and a week ago I handed in my two-weeks' notice. That way my leaving is already on the books and it won't look suspicious when they figure out the brooch is missing. And on Saturday morning, I made my move.

Everything went like it was supposed to. Madeline was wearing the brooch. Her regular nurse was gone. Cindy wheeled her into the sunroom right on schedule. And there was no one else there. I headed down to the lounge and mingled with the ladies, doing little things for them so they'd remember seeing me there…as much as some of them remember anything. I offered to get a couple, Miss Hazel and Miss Agnes, some lemonade from the kitchen. Then I slipped back to the sunroom.

By the time I got there, Miss Madeline was sound asleep, her chin resting on her chest, oxygen tube running under her nose, over her ears, and to the tank on her chair, like it should be. I walked over nice and quiet and started to unpin the brooch.

Her hand came up and closed over mine. I looked up and her eyes were wide open, staring at me and I could tell she knew exactly what was going on. She opened her mouth and took a deep breath. I covered her mouth with my hand to smother the scream, trying to figure out what to do. I could try to tell her I saw her brooch thing was undone and I was trying to fix it. Nah. That would fly with some of these girls but not this one. She struggled against my hand and I squeezed harder, just to keep her quiet while I came up with a way out. Then she wasn't struggling so hard. I guess I knew what I was doing but I didn't have a choice, see? I just stayed like that till she went all limp then I let go and eased her chin back onto her chest like it was when I came in. I tucked the brooch in my pocket, put her hands back into her lap and covered them with that little blanket. Then I grabbed a couple lemonades from the kitchen and went back to the others.

So here we are. Saturday night. Cindy might not have noticed the missing brooch but she sure as hell noticed the old lady was dead. The doctor came, and the cops. I'm not so stupid that I hoped they'd think she just died, all natural like. I watch the cop shows. They can always tell. By early evening the word was out. Miss Madeline was dead and her brooch was missing. They're calling it a robbery-murder.

The cops have got this place locked up tight. Which ain't hard since security is pretty tight here all the time. The grounds are walled all the way around with just the one entrance at the end of the driveway and it's gated with a guard. Not much chance they'll blame this on some stray intruder.

Of course, the staff get questioned first. I'm ready for it. I've stashed the broach in this little spot I found in the furnace room so I have no trouble with the cops searching my things. Hell, I don't have that much.

The detective's name is D'Angelo and he's got some miles on him. That old hangdog look that might lead some guys to write him off, but I see the shrewdness in those bloodshot eyes. I've got to be careful with this one.

We go over my work history and my duties.

"You handed in your notice last week."

"Yes sir."

"Why is that?"

"Antsy," I admit with my best lopsided grin. "These ladies are nice enough and all that but just waiting around till one needs me to drive her to church or to the doctor or whatever isn't enough for me. I need to be doing something more…I don't know, more active. I get bored sitting around." Actually, they keep me pretty busy, especially in good weather, running them here and there all day but D'Angelo seems to accept my excuse.

"Uh huh. And where were you this afternoon?"

"Well, no one had called for the van—they don't much on Saturday because of the entertainment—so I was helping out in the community room."

"Helping out how?"

"Um, I helped set up the chairs. Got the ladies all settled. Stuff like that."

"And people will confirm that? They'll remember you being there?"

I screw up my face like I'm trying to remember. "Miss Agnes and Miss Hazel will. I got them some lemonade." I'd picked Agnes and Hazel specifically. They were best friends, a couple dotty old birds who would remember me serving them but would have no idea exactly when or how long it took. Even better, they would likely argue about it…how long it took me; was the lemonade cold enough; was it pink or yellow? Let the detective sort through that alibi.

He makes some notes on his little pad.

"About the victim…"

"Miss Madeline. Now that's a shame. She was one nice old lady."

"You remember this brooch of hers?"

I blow out a long breath. "I think so. Maybe. Thing is, she was always dressed real nice with her hair just so and her jewelry on. To be honest, I figured it was fake stuff. I mean, who'd wear real jewelry in this place?"

I think he bought it.

Later, after D'Angelo left and the ladies were all tucked away for the night, I slip downstairs to retrieve the brooch. There are still a couple uniform cops hanging around but I have no trouble getting past them. Tomorrow's Sunday and I'll have a van full of ladies to drop at various churches. And while they're listening to the good word, I'll nip over to Natick and add Miss Madeline's brooch to my stash. Then I finish out my week and I'm outta here.

I only forgot one thing. I didn't check the weather.

Early Sunday morning, I wake up and look out the window at a gray sky dumping thick fat flakes on top of a heavy blanket of fresh snow. The garden gnomes I use to judge the depth of a new snow are completely buried. The snow has to be over two feet. That means at least eight inches of new stuff fell overnight.

Okay. No problem. A little snow isn't going to change anyone's plans. The ladies will still want to go to church. This is Massachusetts, for cripes sake. We know how to handle snow.

I get dressed—Miss Madeline's brooch wrapped in my white handkerchief tucked deep in my front pants pocket—and head down to the office to pick up my list of passengers. Of course, I fully expected to be searched when we leave but if I can't plant a piece of jewelry on one of these old birds till we get outside…well, I need to find a new line of work.

The Sunday day manager catches me in the hall.

"Mr. Baxter. I'm to tell you the van will not be going out today. The roads are just too dangerous and we're holding a special service in the chapel for dear Miss Madeline. You'll want to attend, of course."

Crap. I'm standing there with the stolen brooch burning a hole in my pocket as the manager stares at me, waiting for me to turn toward the chapel.

"Oh, yeah. Of course."

The service drags on forever. Some of the ladies are weeping, some nodding off. Madeline's private nurse is there, crying up a storm. I try to look like I'm fighting back tears. If I don't get out of there with the brooch, I will be. Finally there's a closing hymn, sung by a gathering of squalling cats, and we're free to go.

But where? Detective D'Angelo is back, with a couple other detectives and some new uniform cops. They're pretty much all over the place now… the detectives asking questions and the uniforms searching everyplace they can. Which isn't *every*place because some lawyers have shown up, too—guess they came by dogsled—and I overhear them arguing about "privacy" and "search warrants".

I'm walking the halls, trying to decide what to do, and I pass the sunroom door, all crisscrossed with yellow crime scene tape. *Damn it, Madeline. Why couldn't you have stayed asleep like you were supposed to? You really screwed things up for me.*

The TV is on in the community room, even though there's no one in there. I wonder if the cops are keeping everyone in their rooms so they can't compare stories. Like I said, I watch all the cop shows. That blond weather girl who always wears the nice tight tops is saying something about twelve to sixteen inches. There'll be no Sunday cemetery runs this afternoon. I slip my hand into my pocket and finger Madeline's brooch. Should I hide it in my room?

Or maybe back in the basement? No, I'll just keep it with me. I'm not likely to get searched just walking around, as long as I don't try to leave. It's just for today.

Monday morning I'm ready to go again. The schedule shows three ladies have doctor appointments, which are pretty much a sure thing. I pull on my boots and cut across the lawn to the garage to make sure I've got a shovel and a bag of sand in case I have to clear a walkway. All part of the service, and this morning I'm more than willing to provide it.

The snow is still coming down, making everything weirdly quiet. There's no wind and the cold air feels good after being cooped up yesterday. But as I come around from the back of the garage, I see the driveway hasn't been plowed from the garage to the main drive. What the…?

I storm back to the lobby, or try to. It's hard to work up much speed in snow up to your thighs. At the front entrance, I pull up short. The cops are there, setting up one of those metal scanner things that you have to walk through. Crap.

I ease in the door and work my way around the cops. No one pays any attention. I figure they're going to be checking people going out, not in. One of our managers is there, watching the cops, and looking really pissed off. Stuff like this isn't supposed to happen at Wellesley Manor. I walk over to her, eyeing the cops with a sneer to let her know I'm on her side.

"Mrs. Curtis."

"Mr. Baxter."

"Do the police really have to do this? It's going to be upsetting for the ladies."

"As I have told them. Repeatedly. To be searched and scanned like common criminals. It's not like any of our residents could have harmed Miss Madeline. The very idea is absurd."

"Well, someone killed her."

I whirl around at the unexpected voice behind us. Detective D'Angelo walks on very silent feet. Something I'd have to remember. Before Mrs. Curtis can speculate on the murderer, I change the subject.

"Mrs. Curtis, I have to take several ladies to doctors appointments this morning but the drive in front of the garage hasn't been plowed."

"I'm sorry, Mr. Baxter. You should have been told. The van won't be going out today. Travel conditions are not safe enough for our residents. All appointments are being re-scheduled."

I want to argue but I can feel D'Angelo's eyes on me. And I feel the weight of the dead woman's brooch in my pocket. "Oh, okay. That's good. I was a little worried about taking them out in this." I give the detective a half-nod without meeting his eyes and head down the hall like I have someplace to be. His last words hang in the air... "Well, someone killed her."

The snow stops sometime during the night, although the Tuesday morning sky is still heavy and gray. This time I check in the office before getting my pants soaked. No, the van isn't to go out today. Many roads are still snow covered and sidewalks have been buried by the plows.

I make a point of wandering around looking bored and restless where I might be seen by D'Angelo, trying to re-enforce the excuse I gave him for handing in my notice. But I'm anything but bored. Several of our ladies' family members are showing up—most with lawyers in tow—to take dear old whoever out of this "unacceptable situation." Some temporary, some permanent. Management is wringing their hands and blaming the police. I'm more interested in how the cops are handling the search of everything that goes out the door, and which of the ladies are leaving. Several of my regulars are already gone.

By Wednesday morning, skies are clearing and the sun on the snow looks like a field of diamonds. My kind of sparkle. I dress for duty and present myself at the front office. Mrs. Curtis is busy trying to convince some guy in a really expensive suit that his aunt is perfectly safe and all this unfortunate business will be over in a matter of days. Well, it sure will be for me. Friday is my last day on the job.

I give Curtis a wide berth and slip into the office. Roberta is manning the welcome desk.

"Hey, Robbie. What have you got for me today?"

She shakes her head. "Nothing."

Not again. "Aw, come on, the roads can't be that bad. Everybody and their brother has been in and out of here the last couple days. And I know the drive to the garage was cleared yesterday."

"No, the van's been cleared to go out, but for appointments only. Just scheduled stuff."

"Okay. So…?" I could think of a couple regular Wednesday trips.

"Well, when the storm hit, a lot of things got re-scheduled." She picks up a piece of paper I can see is the transportation schedule. I reach across the desk and take it from her.

"What about Miss Eleanora? She always gets her hair done on Wednesday. She wouldn't put that off." I scan the list. Every item on Wednesday had been crossed off.

"Her grandson picked her up yesterday. For a 'visit' until this police matter is settled."

I hadn't seen her go.

"Help me out here, Robbie. There's got to be something. Some errand I can run."

"You got a problem, Baxter?"

D'Angelo.

I turn to face him. "Yeah. I haven't been out of this place for five days and I'm getting stir crazy."

He gives me a long stare and I try not to squirm. My hand wants to slide into my pocket and cover the brooch.

"Oh, five days isn't so long. I know lots of guys stuck inside for twenty, thirty years. Or longer."

He holds the stare for another minute then walks away. I swallow twice and hand the sheet back to Roberta. "Never mind. I'll just hang around here today."

Thursday morning is a repeat of Wednesday. I'm cleared to take the van but no one's going anywhere. There are fewer cops around, mostly just at the exits to make sure everyone goes out the front door. But D'Angelo is still there and I can tell he's got his eye on me.

That afternoon, I catch a break. My pair of dotty birds, Agnes and Hazel, decide they want to go to a show. The roads *and* sidewalks are deemed safe enough, and I bring the van around to the front door.

They're waiting in the lobby, all twittery about going through the metal detector. Being a gentleman, I offer to hold their coats. It's a piece of cake to lift one of Hazel's fine kidskin gloves from the pocket and slide the brooch inside. While everyone's attention is on the ladies, I let the glove drop to the floor just to the outside of the arch and give it a little kick toward the door. Then I hand our coats to a cop for inspection and step through the detector.

D'Angelo appears out of nowhere and I wait, one eyebrow cocked in silent question. Does he want to search me? He looks like he's considering it then turns away. I take Hazel's coat from the cop and help her into it. He follows suit with Agnes. As I shrug into my own coat, I "notice" Miss Hazel's glove on the floor and pick it up for her before herding them outside.

At the van door, I slide the brooch out of the glove to restore it to my pocket.

And drop it.

It makes the tiniest ping as it hits the pavement. I bend over and scoop it up but not before it catches Hazel's eye.

"Mr. Baxter, what is that?"

I pretend not to understand. "Your glove, Miss Hazel. It fell out of your pocket. You really should put them on. It's quite chilly today."

She takes the glove but makes no move to put it on.

"I don't mean my glove. I mean what was that you dropped? It looked like jewelry. I think it's mine."

"Oh, that. No, that's just a little gift I picked up for my mother. You remember, I'm going to be leaving this week. Tomorrow's my last day. I'm going to stay with my mother, to take care of her...she's not been well." *Come on, you old bat. You love to talk about people's ailments. Forget the brooch. Ask about my mother.*

"No, I want to see what's in your pocket. I think it's mine."

I see D'Angelo through the glass doors, watching us.

"No, it's not, dear," Agnes chimes in. "I saw it, too, and it definitely wasn't yours. It's just a trinket nice Mr. Baxter bought for his mother. Now let us go or we'll be late."

She might have not trusted me, but Hazel had complete faith in her dear friend.

"If you say so, Aggie." She stepped to the van door and allowed me to help her in.

"Any problem out here?" D'Angelo crossed the short distance from the door to the van.

"Nope. We're all good." I offered Miss Agnes my hand to help her up the van step.

But she turned to the detective. "It was nothing, Officer. Hazel thought Mr. Baxter had picked up something of hers but she was mistaken."

I held out my hand again, trying to turn her toward the door. *Okay. Fine. Now shut up and get in the van.*

"You see, I know all of dear Hazel's jewelry and she'd never wear anything that gaudy."

I stood there, frozen, as she drove the final nail into my coffin.

"In fact, the only lady here who wore pieces like that was...God rest her soul...dear Madeline."

L.D. Masterson lived on both coasts before becoming landlocked in Ohio. After twenty years managing computers for the American Red Cross, she now divides her time between writing and enjoying her grandchildren. Her short stories have been published in numerous anthologies and magazines and she's currently working on her second novel. Catch her at: http://ldmasterson-author.blogspot.com or http://ldmasterson.com.

A VERY LUCKY BOY
by Emilya Naymark

Eddie Barrie liked a good scotch. He also liked languid evenings in cigar bars, a tumbler of Macallan glowing amber in his hand, a perfectly aged Cohiba at his lips. He owned three Prada suits, a Porsche, Louis Vuitton shoes (two pairs of loafers and one of sneakers), and a Piaget watch in the warmest, sweetest rose gold.

Actually, to say he owned those things would be to mangle the truth. Eddie no more owned them than he owned his name, which was not Eddie Barrie at all, but Cosmos Dimitrios Papadopoulos. At twelve he had rebelled, violently and irrevocably, against the name his father bestowed, and with it, against the rules of his father's house. Well, no, the rules he could have swallowed. But not the fists, no, those were difficult. Worse, his father's fists were grimy, stinking with the day's labor, because, he'd said once after smashing Eddie's head into the kitchen table, the dirt and grime were honest, gotten through hard work, and worthy of respect.

Eddie knelt at the rear door of a beachfront bungalow and shone a slim flashlight at the lock. Coming to Dennis Port had been half emergency, half inspiration. Cape Cod was nearly deserted on a Tuesday night in January, the bungalows and beach cottages buttoned up for the winter and the year-round residents cozy and quiet behind drawn shades where the knife-sharp wind couldn't get them.

A quick shimmy with his pick, and Eddie slipped into the dark, cold house. More than anything, more than a drink, or food, or even revenge, Eddie craved a bath. The house's owners were clearly snowbirds, probably sunning their retired (judging by the AARP magnets on the fridge) asses on a Florida sundeck. He found the thermostat and turned the dial to eighty, located the bathroom (olive green tiles, seashell motif on the curtains and soap dish), and ran himself a scalding, steamy, fragrant bath.

And only when his skin flushed pink, and the tension in his back unknotted, and the bruises on his chest and ribs stopped complaining, he covered his eyes with his hand and allowed himself a moment of despondency.

He had nothing. Had jumped out of his apartment window (and good thing he lived on the first floor) wearing only a pair of jeans, a white oxford shirt, charcoal cardigan, and the utterly inadequate-for-the-weather Vuitton loafers. It was pure luck he still had his wallet and the lock pick and flashlight. Plain old luck. He always knew he had a guardian angel, and the presence of wallet with its fake IDs (well how else would he have gotten into the cigar bars?), pick, and flashlight in his otherwise empty hands was proof. He'd escaped, his eighteen-year-old body strong enough to endure and overcome the violence visited upon it by Anton's thugs, and his legs fleet enough to outrun them.

Now that he was warm again, with four walls between his flesh and the icy gusts buffeting the cottage, not to mention the miles between him and Anton, he tucked the despair away and explored the kitchen.

The snowbirds left little. An almost empty box of Wheaties, six cans of clam chowder, one of creamed corn, and, of all things, two tins of smoked oysters. He was luckier with the booze. Mixed in with dusty rosé and Merlot bottles, Eddie found a barely touched fifth of Glenfiddich.

By the time he warmed a bowl of chowder in the dark (no need to advertise his presence to the neighborhood) arranged the oysters on a plate, and sipped his way through a couple splashes of whisky, he believed fortune was with him in force. An optimism burbled through him, and he made a mental list of people to call in the morning. He'd have to buy a phone first, since Anton had crushed his under a boot heel. Damn Anton. Eddie forked an oyster and chewed thoughtfully. Luck was a malleable thing - mutating when examined from different angles. It was bad luck he had sold Anton's drugs (quite a bit of drugs, felony level) to an undercover (and how was he to know the tattooed, goateed, long-haired biker was a cop? How?), but very good luck he had escaped both the detectives and, eventually, Anton. Bad luck he was now a hunted man, but good that he could really, truly, start over. New everything - new name, new clothes, new location. He'd go to California. To hell with Boston winters.

He was so preoccupied that when the black cat jumped on the kitchen counter, its presence took a few seconds to filter through. He swallowed and rose from his chair, all senses at attention. If there was a cat, the homeowners were near. Maybe they'd gone to stay with friends or a grown child and would return soon.

But no, something was off. He hadn't seen cat food or a litter box. Dust begrimed all rooms. There'd been thick swaths of it on the tables, the oaken floorboards, the toilet even. Whoever lived here had not been around for months.

The cat stared from the gloom, illuminated by moonlight flooding through the patio doors. Its fur was black, but strangely shiny, almost gleaming. Perhaps it had gotten in through a basement window, seeking warmth and food — much like himself.

Eddie offered his half-eaten oysters to the cat, placed the plate gently on the counter.

The cat didn't move. Didn't turn to sniff the sharp aroma, didn't dart away from him, didn't hiss, didn't purr. It was as inert as if it'd been stuffed, and for a second Eddie wondered if it was a bit of taxidermy he'd missed on his first inspection of the kitchen. But who would miss a thing like that?

"Hey there," Eddie whispered and extended his hand, fingers inches from the creature's leathery nose.

The cat's eyes glimmered, as if an emerald crystal inside swiveled and lit, and it stood up, jumped to the floor and sauntered into the hallway. Eddie followed.

In a universe more kindly disposed toward him, he'd have let the creature go. He was tired, sore, still hungry. But he was also a boy alone, and he liked cats, and the prospect of sharing this lonely night with another living being was comforting.

The animal ran into a bedroom, hopped onto the window seat, balanced on its hind paws, reached with the left forepaw, and unlocked the latch.

Eddie froze. The chowder turned cold and unpleasant in his stomach and his heart thudded once, hard, against his ribs so his breath caught.

The cat used both front paws to slide the window up, did the same with the screen.

Then Eddie lost his mind. Only lunacy explained what he saw next. The cat's forepaws rotated two-hundred-seventy degrees at the shoulder, so that they were sticking up over the creature's back. Like wings. Into which they then expanded. Its hind legs folded under its belly like the landing gear of an airplane, and the cat, which was no longer a cat, flew off into the moonlight.

Eddie stumbled to the open window and watched the not-cat fly down the sandy, starlit path toward the black ocean until it blended into the blacker sky.

Eventually he closed the screen and the window and grabbed the rest of the Glenfiddich. He crept under dusty blankets, hugging the whisky to his chest and, against all expectation, fell asleep. He dreamed of a furry creature sitting on his chest, pressing on his ribs, on his bruises. In the dream, Eddie asked the creature to move, his bruises hurt too much, and the beast obliged, sliding down to warmly, wetly, snugly straddle his hips.

The morning dawned with a begrudging slowness as if it too wanted to remain warm and sleepy under the covers. Cloudy, dim, with a fierce, keening wind, the day promised to be disgusting, but he had to face it. Eddie couldn't stay in this house forever. If nothing else, he needed food. He was starving. He refused to think of last night's nightmarish incident. He'd been exhausted, had drunk superb scotch on an empty stomach. Who wouldn't hallucinate!

But as he searched the house for clothes, money, anything useful, he avoided that window and did not enter the kitchen.

The snowbirds were thrifty. They'd taken most of their warm clothing with them, or at least the man had. If Eddie did not want to freeze to death, or stick out like the stranger up to no good that he was, he needed to dress the part. With a sigh, he unfolded a mulberry-pink quilted jacket from the closet. He was a slim boy and the woman's jacket fit him fine (or as fine as a cheap knockoff could fit anyone). He'd stick out, all right, but more like someone's hipster-ish nephew staying the week rather than a failed gangster wannabe.

When he fled yesterday, he'd taken the bus on an inspired whim, and the bus brought him to Dennis Port. He then walked to the beach, working under the assumption that the cottages closer to the shore were more likely to be shut for the season. Now he backtracked, taking thirty minutes to walk into town, the wet wind smacking his face, and his fingers painfully cold in his pockets. At the 7-Eleven he bought a pay-as-you-go phone. He had a bad moment when a dark-blue Mustang cruised past him (it didn't mean it was Anton's guys, surely more than one person in Massachusetts owned a dark-blue Mustang), and he turned his face away, counting on the pink jacket as camouflage. Anyone who knew him knew he'd never wear something so dumb. In any case, the car kept going.

As he walked to the house, the wind turned sleety, his toes growing numb inside the ruined Vuitton loafers.

He arranged the phone, a loaf of bread, a pound of sliced Gouda, a half-pound of salami, and three tins of tuna on the coffee table (he refused to enter that kitchen). He wasn't clear on why he bought the tuna, since he didn't like it much, but a tiny voice he pretended to ignore suggested cats liked tuna.

The daylight, already anemic, gave up shortly after noon, casting the living room into a dreary dimness. It would have been nice to turn on lights or the TV, but Eddie didn't. He knew how to keep a low profile.

He assembled a salami and cheese sandwich and made his first phone call. Two calls later Eddie was no closer to regaining his life.

His friend Alec, an occasional freelancer for Anton, had shushed him, making Eddie wait while he sequestered himself somewhere more private. No, Eddie couldn't stay with him. No, he didn't have extra money for Eddie. No, he shouldn't come back and try to talk it out with Anton, and definitely a big, fat NO to Alec negotiating on Eddie's behalf. In fact, and Alec only told Eddie because he liked him, Anton had an idea where Eddie was. Eddie'd been seen taking the bus, and he better leave. Soon. Now.

Sound advice if you had a bank account. Or a cash stash. Or friends you could count on. Eddie poured himself a finger of scotch and let it sit in his mouth. On his walk today he'd scoped five more houses he could pilfer. He didn't like being a petty thief - it's not how he thought of himself. But what choice did he have?

The second person he called was his brother, Stavros, who at twenty-one hadn't ever felt the need to change into a Steve or a Stan, lived at home while pursuing an electrician's license, and was the parental favorite. Stavros offered Eddie a loan of six hundred dollars if Eddie returned home and enrolled in an apprenticeship program.

Eddie thanked his brother, hung up, and threw his phone across the room. He would never go back home. He'd rather walk into the freezing ocean. It'd be a cleaner death than being pummeled nightly until either his kidneys ruptured or his skull shattered.

He had two more fingers of scotch before calling the next person - his last hope. Danielle was not his girlfriend. Neither did she qualify as a friend, but he'd kept her supplied with Oxy (easy enough to hide a few pills when delivering bags of them) in exchange for whatever she was in the mood to dispense - hand jobs, blowjobs, kisses, lap dances, sex (twice), and, amazingly, conversations lasting long into the night. Danielle did not seem surprised to hear from him. Nor worried. Nor happy. She asked him where he was staying and he said never mind, but she asked again, and he said why, do you wanna visit, and she said maybe honey, and he told her where (because damn that would be good), and she said later honey and hung up.

It took Eddie a full five minutes to sort out why this call disturbed him. Danielle never called him honey, never spoke to him in that high, sugary, fake-y, girlfriend (which she wasn't) voice. He pictured Anton looming over her, fisting his favorite filleting knife in one hand, a pillbox full of Oxy in the other.

Sleet turned to snow, but not a fluffy, quiet snow - a hard-driven, icy, savage onslaught that shook the house and rapped a discordant tattoo on the roof.

Eddie fingered the small gold cross resting against his sternum. He'd had the cross since childhood, deep-seated superstition forbidding its removal.

So when the cat stepped into the living room, exuding its own faint glow, Eddie jumped, startled to an electrified hyper-awareness. Touching the cross had been a prayer of sorts, as much as he allowed himself. Under happier circumstances, in daylight, warm and with a pocket full of cash, Eddie usually felt both too lucky and too imperfect to qualify for prayer. But today was far from happy. He'd been pining for a companion, was cracking with loneliness, and the cat came.

"Hey!" he said. "Hey, come here." He crouched on the wood floor and extended his arms, willing the cat to run to him. "I got you something. You like tuna fish? Yes?"

The cat examined him with its emerald eyes, then disappeared into the dark hallway.

"Wait, wait!" Eddie rushed after it, his eyesight so acclimated to the gloom he saw it right away, sitting by the kitchen door. "You don't want to go into that storm, do you?" he asked, because that's what people do - they talk to animals as if an answer can be imminent. They never expect the animal to reply. Expecting a reply is for crazies.

"The storm doesn't bother me," said the cat.

Eddie gasped and stepped back, but a part of him, the part that rejected his father and the stupid, ugly, cheap, and violent life he represented; the part of him that sought beauty and fine things and believed those things were attainable just by coveting them enough, that part of him swooned with excitement.

The cat rose to its hind legs and used a forepaw to turn the doorknob, then opened the door, the storm a white veil. Looking back at him once, it vanished into the blizzard.

Without thinking, without hesitation, Eddie followed. The cat was a black smudge ahead of him and he ran after it, uncaring of his feet sinking into thick drifts, his cardigan growing heavy and wet. They emerged onto the snow-covered beach, the heaps and hollows of white like an inverse photograph of the vast ocean beyond.

The cat padded to the water's edge, paused, then jumped. Mid-jump, its front legs hinged along its torso, its hind legs pressed together and fused into a tail, and by the time it hit the water, it no more resembled a cat than it did a lamp.

Eddie staggered into the surf up to his knees. He barely noticed the pounding waves.

And then he heard it. A faint music. Someone laughed. Glass breaking and more laughter. He squinted into the chaos of snowflakes and wind. There.

Not far from shore, a ship. Its lights winked through the storm like stars, bobbing and weaving on the swells.

Enthralled, he listened, his entire being stretching toward that siren ship until a large wave knocked him down and he had no choice but slog up the frozen path to shelter.

He was definitely losing his mind.

At the house, sleep seized him and pulled him under as soon as he lay down, but the respite was temporary. He surfaced to consciousness in the dark, the storm quieter, a soft, cottony swishing beyond the windows, and the bedside clock's numbers glowing four-twenty.

The bad weather continued into the next day - unpleasant, blustery, sleety. He hoped the storm meant no one was out and about, but to his dismay he saw the blue Mustang parked resolutely across the road when he opened the front door. He banged the door shut and pressed against it, his breaths coming fast and ragged. He was neither calm nor steady when he crept out the back patio doors and clambered over the fence into the neighboring yard.

The first three houses he burgled didn't have what he needed. Even their stashes of food left him unmoved. He hit the jackpot in the fourth house. His stomach clenching with fear and adrenaline, he dragged the inflatable dinghy through iced backyards and over splintered fences, avoiding the roads and that damned Mustang. The weather worked in his favor -- nobody, not even vengeful thugs -- wanted to be outside.

He was a lucky boy, and luck was with him still. He felt it -- the special magic, the thrilling anticipation of something just around the bend, delicious and fantastic.

When the cat appeared this time, he was ready. In addition to the dinghy, he'd filched a pair of knock-off UGGs, a horrendous udder-colored (but warm) fleece sweater, wool socks, and leather gloves so salt-stiffened, they had greeted him from their shelf like cockscombs.

The cat nodded with approval when he showed it the little boat, then led him to the beach, stopping and turning, waiting for him whenever he got stuck or, once, sank into a snowed-over dune. It was only seven, but seemed like deepest night, the stars and moon blotted by the ceaseless storm and the streetlights dark with a power outage.

With all the lights out along the shore, the ship was easy to spot—a fairy boat suspended in the blackness.

Eddie pushed the dinghy to the shoreline and hopped in. The cat jumped and perched on the rounded rim. The tide was with him—he'd looked that up—and the current lifted him, plummeted him downwards, filled the bottom with ice water, flooded his ludicrous UGGs, but carried him. Outward, outward, throwing him into the air, then the breathless comedown, over and over, his face glossed with salt-water, everything anesthetized except for his heart and lungs, which beat and expanded with his yearning.

He lost all sense of direction, of time. He tried to row, but a furious swell ripped the oar from his frozen hands and overturned the dinghy. He held on somehow, then climbed on top of it, riding it upside down, which he never thought was possible, but there you go. Amazingly, the cat also persevered, a solid, shining, black presence, its glossy head pointed at the yacht, and the dinghy seemed to obey its unspoken command, slowly, slowly bridging the vast distance between it and the fairy ship.

He'd transitioned from being cold to almost warm. He wondered if this was dangerous. If it was a sign he was about to die. It would be sad to die like this, though - so close to the pleasure boat. He would have liked to step on board, see the people who had sounded so happy when he listened from the icebound shore.

Up, down, up, down, almost like a cradle. He smiled at the stars, wondered why he was seeing stars all of a sudden, the clouds must have cleared, but why was sleet still pelting him? Then he felt a tightness around his chest, the cat's paws tying a harness, except they weren't paws anymore but metal grips, and he was lifted into the air, weightless, as if flying, dreaming, then hands on him and a hard deck under him. The relief flooding him was so overwhelming it was almost sexual, and he laughed, though it came out a cough and then he had to spit lots and lots of seawater.

"You made it, sweetheart," someone said.

"He's yummy," someone else said.

When his senses returned, he lay naked and lusciously warm, buried under silky sheets and thick duvets in a cabin just large enough for the wooden bed and a dresser. The dresser had a deep well carved into the top and a thermos waited there. He sat and reached for it—mulled cider spiced to perfection with cinnamon, cloves, and orange zest. He drank all of it, then climbed out of the bed and looked for his clothes, but whoever undressed him had taken them. He wrapped the sheet around himself like a toga and draped a blanket over his shoulders.

The dimly lit corridor was all shellacked wood walls, floor, and doors. Brass fittings, delicately etched glass light fixtures - this, this now was his kind of place. He heard murmurs and low music up ahead, strings, deep and rich, a cello and a viola tugging at him, beckoning.

The next room was as dim as the corridor—a burnished beauty of thick, wine-red carpet, dark walls interrupted by vast, emotional paintings, leather couches and chairs, a bar. Waiters in black tank-tops carried trays of drinks and food. Eddie's attention snagged on two girls he would have sworn were thirteen or fourteen—in heels and black hotpants. They moved with languor, as if dreaming on their feet, and their skin seemed colorless, unhealthy.

In the middle of all this stood an intricately carved wooden chair, and in this chair sat a person. Twenty or so men and women gathered around, blocking Eddie's view, but he saw a black suit and white shirt, a pale hand with an ornate ring. A pretty blonde bowed and kissed the ring, said something to the seated person, then raised her head and looked straight into Eddie's eyes.

He retreated and clutched the ridiculous blanket tighter to his chest. The blonde smiled and called out, "Oh, you're awake! Come here, come on!"

And then everyone was staring at him, and he was in the most commonplace nightmare of all—naked before a well-dressed crowd. Well.

Eddie was not common. The situation was suboptimal, but he had gambled a winter squall to be here, and he would not be daunted. He let the blanket drop to the floor and, as regal in his sheet as an emperor, marched into the room.

The crowd, their eyes dancing, their teeth white and lustrous, parted, and in a few strides he faced the carved chair and the person within.

She nodded to him and extended her hand, and he knelt on one knee as if proposing, and kissed the ruby-encrusted ring.

"Welcome aboard, Cosmos," she said. She wore her hair short, an apricot-hued crewcut, her lips a dark, cool red. The suit, he saw right away, was a man's suit, cut and tailored to fit her small figure—as costly as everything else he'd seen on this ship. He didn't wonder how she knew his name. Money bought information, and this woman had buckets of it.

The only question was why were they interested enough in him to accumulate information? Just then the cat wove between his legs and jumped onto the woman's lap. She drew an expensively manicured hand over its head.

"You've met Roy, haven't you?" she asked.

Eddie nodded, said, "He's a beautiful cat. He..." But the words withered in his mouth because the woman twisted Roy's head and removed it, as easily as opening a soda bottle. Metal gleamed inside, a snarl of wiring. She peered in and frowned. "Needs a cleaning," she said, and a waiter appeared and scooped the cat's body and head from her lap.

She looked at him again, eyes as green and artificial as the cat's.

"Roy's reports didn't do you justice, Cosmos."

"Eddie," he said, wondering how the cat presented its reports. Typed them? Downloaded them directly from its glossy head? Roy's nature comforted him - it's easier to accept high tech than one's insanity. Or magic.

"I like Cosmos better," she said. "It's limitless and vast."

"Okay," he said. She could call him anything as long as she let him stay.

She touched his wrist, turned his forearm to the flickering lights, traced the firm flesh with its faint marbling of vein in the elbow crook.

"Young skin," she said, "repairs so quickly. You were near dangerous levels of hypothermia when we pulled you aboard. And now..."—she smiled—"...perfect again."

"Thank you," he said, meaning thank you for the compliment, for drying and warming and welcoming me.

She cocked her head. "Tell me what you want from us," she said.

And as strange as that question was, with its implication of a conversation already started, he knew exactly how to answer.

"I want to work for you," he said. "As anything. Whatever you need. I have experience and skills."

"I know," she said. "I know all about you."

He didn't ask. He'd ask later. About that, about Roy. But now he held his breath and waited.

"But of course," she said, and following some gesture he didn't catch, the pretty blonde approached and placed a warm little hand on his nude shoulder.

"Come along," she said. "I'll show you around."

She led him to a white-walled cabin furnished with medical equipment and indicated he sit in a chair.

"You'll be working with us?" she asked, pulling blue latex gloves over her hands. "I'm glad to hear it." She sat facing him on a stool and placed his forearm on the armrest. "You're lovely, you know that?"

His face warmed, her closeness, her frank appraisal going straight to his groin. He smiled. "So are you," he said, pitching his voice low.

She grinned and winked. "Here's what I need to do," she said. "I'm going to draw blood from you. Only a little more than if you were donating at a blood drive. Are you okay with that?" She leaned toward him, her breasts perky and perfumed against his arm, and he was so hard his hips twitched. He licked his lips.

"Okay," he croaked.

"Good! We'll do a quick analysis and then you're all set. Once you're approved, you will make a blood donation once every five days. In between donation days you'll perform light service duty—help with the meals, drive us to appointments once we're ashore. A few hours a day. How does that sound?"

It sounded fantastic. "So you need me to be a blood donor?" he asked as she tied a rubber strip around his arm.

"How old do you think I am?" she asked.

He knew better than to answer honestly, so he squinted at her poreless skin, the faint crow's feet around her eyes, the negligible jowls. Then subtracted six years.

"Twenty-four!" he said.

She giggled and kissed him—a luxurious tangle of lips and tongue, her fingers massaging his thighs. When she withdrew, she said, "Fifty-two, sweetheart."

"What?" He was dizzy from the kiss, desperate to grab her and press her onto his lap, get his hands under that ridiculously short dress. What was she talking about?

"That's where you come in," she said, and looked at his tented crotch, gave him a self-satisfied smile. "We are a club. A very exclusive club with very expensive membership dues. We are in the life-span extension business. There are many therapies that don't have full FDA approval. But we know they work. We do our own research. One of the therapies we practice is the infusion of young blood plasma. It does wonders for everything from memory to skin's resilience. Resistance to disease."

She drew a needle from a drawer. "This is the cubital fossa," she said, tapping at the crook of his elbow. "Nobody ever knows what to call it, but that's the name." She inserted the needle and dark-red blood flowed through a tube and into the containers she'd prepared.

"So..."—his mind was getting foggy again—"...you're like vampires or something?"

"Something," she said.

"You're not fifty-two," he said. "That's crazy."

She shrugged, her breasts almost exposed now and he couldn't take his eyes off her. The blood flowed and flowed out of him.

Well, a life like this in exchange for giving his young blood to a bunch of rich old vampires, it wasn't so bad. It was wonderful. He was fortunate and he always had been.

After she removed the needle and covered the tiny hole with a Band-Aid, she took him to his cabin, fed him wine, caviar on toast points, and steak tips. Then, when he was woozy, sated, and adequately refueled, she straddled him and let him do everything he wished.

Eddie fell asleep that night happier than any other time in his life.

He was yet to see the mansion on the mainland where young boys and girls (who'd chosen the life he chose this evening) lived behind locked doors. Or the operating rooms where they went upon reaching a certain age, or the medicine cabinets full of experimental drugs.

All that was in the future.

Tonight he slept a very lucky boy.

Emilya Naymark has had stories published in Zouch and 1+30, THE BEST OF MYSTORY. She loves science, technology, and crime fiction and believes the best stories can happen at the intersection of all three. She lives and writes in New York's Hudson Valley.

RULE NUMBER ONE

by Alan Orloff

"You look like crap, Pen."

Pendleton Rozier, my longtime mentor, opened the door wide, then coughed into the crook of his elbow. "If only I felt that good."

I stepped into the entryway of his shotgun shack in Revere, the dump he'd been living in since I met him, and handed over a brown take-out bag. "Here. This'll help."

He shuffled over to a beat-up recliner and plopped down, while I sat on a folding bridge chair across from him. He set the bag on a metal TV tray and fished inside. Removed a container of soup and a plastic spoon. "Chicken noodle?"

"They were out. I got lentil barley." I shrugged. "All they had."

Pen snapped off the flimsy lid and took a spoonful. Blew on it for fifteen seconds, hand shaking as he did.

I'd known Pen for almost thirty years and had pulled dozens of jobs with him, from the small hold-ups when I'd just been starting out to an all-out blitz at a UPS warehouse two years ago. He'd shown me the ropes, given me advice. Saved my life a couple of times, too. Now, my teacher—my friend—looked older than his sixty-four years. He'd been heading downhill for a while.

He slurped his soup, then made a gagging noise as he dropped the spoon onto the tray. "Blech. Who would ruin good soup with lentils, anyway?"

"Sorry."

He tried to fit the lid back on the container but after a moment of fumbling around, he gave up and leaned back in his chair. "Kane, as much as it hurts me to say, I'm losing my edge. Afraid I'm going to make a mistake that'll cost me—or someone else. Feh. I'm gonna hang it up. Retire." His voice caught. "Right after this one last gig."

"Didn't you say you were going to do this until the day you died?" He'd been squawking about retiring for the past ten years, but this time, his stone-cold eyes told me he was serious.

"Can't a guy change his mind? I'm going to relax for as long as I've got left. Move to a trailer park in Boca and enjoy some early bird specials." Pen sputtered off into a coughing jag. When he finished, he wiped some spittle from his ashen face. "So, how's the job coming along? Ready for me yet? The ride is gassed up and rarin' to go."

I needed some clean wheels for when I dumped the van we were using, and Pen had always delivered. Despite his age—or maybe because of it, no one suspected a geezer waiting in an idling car—he was a damn good driver. At least he used to be. "You sure you're up to it?"

He waved his hand. "Don't let the coughing and wheezing deceive you. I've never failed on a job yet, and you know it. I got enough left in the tank for this. Wouldn't do it if I didn't."

"Sure, sure." The truth was, I didn't need Pen—what I had planned didn't require a fast getaway, and I didn't anticipate any problems. But I owed him for all he'd done for me, and it seemed fitting to throw a bone his way and send him off to sunny Florida with a few bucks in his pocket—fifty thousand of them. Call it a token of appreciation for showing me the ropes, watching out for me.

Pen squeezed my arm. "Thanks, Kane, for giving an old guy one last thrill."

ℴℴℴ

The late-afternoon Allston Diner crowd had thinned, and the servers were stealing some downtime before the dinner rush began. *If* there was a dinner rush. I'd only eaten there once before, a few months ago, and that was at eight a.m. after an especially profitable office burglary two exits down the Mass Pike.

Of course, compared to the latest haul, that job was chump change. Penny ante. A paltry piss in a deep lake.

Across from me, my unseasoned partners in crime—both in their thirties, younger than me by two decades—finished up their meals. Jimmy Fitzpatrick, the Irish thug wannabe from Southie with the non-stop mouth and the pasty skin, devoured anything as long as it was fried and doused with ketchup. Nagelman, who always looked like he'd just been released from solitary, gaunt and pallid, was vegan. Or some such crap. I couldn't keep up with all the latest diet fads, and frankly, I didn't trust a guy who wouldn't eat red meat. It didn't help that all the leftover slimy green gunk in the bottom of Nagelman's bowl made me queasy.

I balled up my napkin, tossed it onto my empty plate, and stretched an arm across the back of the vinyl booth.

"They got good pie here." Fitzpatrick wiped a ketchup smear off his chin.

"Maybe we should discuss what we came here to discuss." Nagelman glanced around, then leaned forward and adjusted his thick-lensed glasses.

"We can multitask," Fitzpatrick said. "We ain't idiots."

"I didn't say we were idiots. I just think we should get down to—"

"And who the eff put you in charge, anyway?"

I held up my hand. "Girls, girls. Relax. Why don't we talk business first, then those that want pie can get pie. Okay?"

"Yeah, yeah." Fitzpatrick glared at Nagelman. "Whatever."

"Fine," Nagelman said, glaring right back at Fitzpatrick.

I cleared my throat. Broke out a fresh smile. It was always much more enjoyable to deliver good news than bad, although I sometimes *did* look forward to dumping bad news on those I despised. "Our interested party is ready. Finally."

It had taken a few weeks before my fence had lined up customers for the unique—and highly identifiable—treasures we'd stolen from a truck bound for a chichi Back Bay museum. About a dozen bejeweled pieces from some twelfth-century Russian dynasty.

"Wa-damn-hoo," Fitzpatrick said. "'Bout time. First stop, Vegas, baby!" He tapped out a drum solo on the edge of the table with his fat fingers.

Next to him, Nagelman issued an audible sigh, and the expression on his face screamed relief more than happiness. "Thank God."

Did Nagelman ever smile? "He wants to meet tomorrow afternoon at three. That work in your schedule?"

Fitzpatrick nodded. "You bet."

"We'll all go to the meet, right? As planned?" Nagelman chewed on the inside of his cheek while his pupils jittered.

"That's right, boys. Tomorrow at about this time, we'll be one million bucks richer. Each of us." I'd planned the entire operation, but to keep peace—and because that honor-among-thieves notion was complete horse manure—we'd worked out an arrangement. Fitzpatrick and Nagelman would hold onto the goods in a secret location, and I wouldn't divulge the name of the fence until the deal was ready. As for Pen, I'd pay him fifty thou out of my share, but I hadn't mentioned his involvement at all, not wanting to get into any arguments about bringing in another guy.

After the exchange, we'd split the proceeds and go on our merry ways, off to spend our loot.

At least that was the plan we'd all agreed upon.

Sometimes plans changed.

Nagelman wanted to run through the specifics again—what time to meet and where, who would take the lead during the meeting, contingencies if things went south—and we spent about thirty minutes hashing it all out. When we finished going through it all yet a third time, he seemed satisfied.

"So, we're good?" I asked.

Two nods.

"Now, can I order some pie?" Fitzpatrick said.

"Knock yourself out."

"I gotta take a leak first." Fitzpatrick got up. "If she comes while I'm gone, I want a big slice of Boston Cream, got it? Maybe some extra whipped cream on top. And ask for a cherry, too. I'm in the mood to celebrate, and nothing says celebration like a plump, red cherry."

When Fitzpatrick was out of earshot, I leaned across the table. "You gonna be okay? We talked about this, right? Three mil divided in half is a lot more dough than it is split three ways."

Nagelman dabbed his sweaty forehead with his napkin. "I know. But…you don't think he's got a clue, do you?"

"Him? He wouldn't know a clue if it burst out of his chest like that monster in *Alien*. Trust me, he's a dolt." I glanced over my shoulder toward the rest rooms. "But I don't trust *him*, so you need to keep an eye out. Make sure he doesn't get the idea that he can rip us off and sell the goods on his own."

"He couldn't."

"I know he couldn't; my guy's the only one around who will touch our stuff. But he might *think* he can. So watch him, okay?"

"I will, I will. Don't worry."

"I'm not worried in the least." I smiled. "You want some pie, too?"

"No thanks. They probably use lard in the crust."

"Isn't that the best part?"

ϱϱϱ

My phone rang. *Fitzpatrick.*

"What's up?" I said.

"Just checking in. We got the van," Fitzpatrick said. "Everything on track with the meet?"

"Yep. Where are you?"

"Gas station. Nagelman's in the can."

"How's he seem?" I asked.

"Like a mouse in a snake's cage. He could use a Xanax or three."

"Do you think he suspects anything?" I asked.

"Hard to tell, he's always so twitchy. I asked him a few questions to feel him out, and he got all sweaty, like he does when he's stressed. Best guess? I think he's afraid I know about him and you planning to double-cross me, although I suppose he might sense we're about to screw him. But so what? If he figures it out, I can snap him in half. His physique is certainly an argument for eating meat, huh?"

"Don't hurt him, Fitzpatrick. There's no need." I didn't have a problem stealing stuff from people—things can always be replaced. I drew the line at physical harm, unless absolutely necessary. I was an artful thief, not a two-bit goon. Not hurting people was one of Pen's top ten rules. Right below his numero uno directive: *never trust anyone*. "Just be cool."

"Whatever you say. You're the bossman."

My other line beeped. *Nagelman.* "Got another call. Listen, the last thing we need is you getting all macho and screwing this thing up. Remember, three mil divided by two is a lot more than if we have to divide it by three. See you in a little while."

I clicked over to the other line. "Yeah?"

"It's Nagelman. I think he might be on to us. Christ, he was—"

"Slow down, slow down. Take a deep breath. Now, where are you? Can you talk?"

I heard a slew of inhalations and exhalations, followed by Nagelman's only-slightly-less-frantic answer. "Exxon restroom. Fitzpatrick's waiting for me in the van."

"Okay. Now tell me why you think he might be on to us."

"He was asking all kinds of questions. He suggested that me and him double-cross you, but the way he said it made me think he knew what we were up to. I'm pretty sure he was toying with me, Kane."

Goddamn Fitzpatrick, always looking for ways to mess with people. I hoped he hadn't somehow spooked Nagelman. Unpredictability made me nervous. "You're overthinking things here. I'm sure he honestly wants to screw me. He doesn't like me, and he sure doesn't respect me. What better way than to cut me out of my own job and steal my share of the take?"

"You didn't see his eyes, Kane. He's a psycho. And I'm afraid he knows about us crossing him. He'll probably kill us both and smile while he's doing it."

"Trust me, he doesn't know squat about our plan. This time tomorrow, we'll be a hell of a lot richer, and we won't be worrying about Fitzpatrick. Or anybody else, for that matter."

"I'll feel so much better when this is over."

I wouldn't bet on that. "Sure you will. Now, just try to take it easy. And don't get into it with him. I know how much of an a-hole he can be, but do your best to play nice. Can you do that?"

"I'll try."

"Remember, kid, it's just you and me on this."

ǫǫǫ

Nagelman drove the van; I rode shotgun and Fitzpatrick sat in the back. I hadn't known where they'd stored our haul until Nagelman brought the van to a stop right before the barricade arm leading into the Jiffy-Stor site. He rolled down the window, punched the code into the security pad, and the red-and-white arm rose with a jerk.

A few snowflakes from a developing storm blew in through the window.

Fitzpatrick leaned forward from the back, poking his head between the two front seats. "Some security. Hell, you could just drive right through that ridiculous arm and nobody would even notice for a week. This place is deserted."

Nagelman rolled through the entrance and wound his way up a slight hill to the storage facility. Like a thousand similar places, Jiffy-Stor comprised a series of sprawling warehouses, subdivided into hundreds of tiny units, each with a rollup door and cheap-ass lock.

I didn't know why anyone would store anything truly valuable here; it was mostly surplus furniture and sentimental keepsakes and junk that people thought they'd use again but never would—like exercise equipment and sewing machines.

"Well, I got to hand it to you. You guys picked a safe place to stash the stuff," I said. "No self-respecting crook would be caught dead prowling around here."

"It was my idea," Fitzpatrick said.

"Actually, I think it was my idea," Nagelman said.

"Whoever's idea it was, good job," I said, cutting off further argument.

Nagelman drove to the back of the place, past five rows of units, and hooked a right to follow the asphalt circuit.

"I can almost taste our dough," Fitzpatrick said, opening his door before the van had even come to a stop in front of the unit they'd rented.

He was out and fiddling with the lock as Nagelman and I came up behind him.

"*Aaaand* here we are." Fitzpatrick snapped the lock open and removed it from the hasp. Rolled the door up. Flicked the light switch. Off to one side were six boxes. "Just to be safe, we marked them, 'Old clothes.'"

"Brilliant," I said. "Let's load them up and get going."

Fitzpatrick turned toward the boxes. Nagelman winked at me and said, "So Fitzpatrick, how are you going to spend your share?"

Fitzpatrick hoisted a box, smiled. "Hookers. Craps. Booze. The usual." He walked past me toward the van, flashed me a conspiratorial look, and called out over his shoulder. "How about you, Nagelman? Big plans?"

"Gonna move to San Francisco. Buy into a buddy's smoothie shop." Nagelman picked up a box and followed Fitzpatrick. I grabbed a box, too, and we loaded them into the van. Then we each made another trip, and we were done. Three million dollars in antique treasures weren't very bulky.

I thought about Pen lying on the beach in Florida in a few weeks. Nice.

We climbed into the van, and Nagelman started it up.

"What about you, boss?" Fitzpatrick said. "What are you going to do with your dough?"

I thought about Pen, living in squalor, too broke to go to the doctor. "Mutual funds. I'm saving for retirement."

ააა

"We're almost there," I said.

"You sure this is the right way?" Nagelman asked, voice nasal, as he steered the van down a winding road three miles past the middle of nowhere. The snow swirled in the wind, mini white tornadoes. The forecasters were predicting somewhere between six and ten inches; so far, about an inch had accumulated on the roads. Maybe I'd copy Pen's idea and move to a warmer climate.

"Yep. GPS don't lie."

Nagelman jerked the wheel to avoid a pothole, then overcorrected, causing our precious cargo to shift abruptly.

"Hey numskull, try not to land us in a ditch, okay?" Fitzpatrick barked from the back of the van.

"You wanna drive?" Nagelman said. "Be my guest."

"I could drive better than you with my eyes closed, that's for sure."

"Will you two just cut it out?" After spending the last month immersed in this job with these two chuckleheads—planning it, executing it, waiting for a buyer to materialize—I now knew what it would have been like to have squabbling children. I pointed up ahead. "Hang a left here."

We bumped along for another three minutes down an ever-narrowing driveway until we came to a house. “This is the place.”

“Here?” Nagelman looked around.

There wasn’t another structure within sight.

“Right here.”

“I don’t like this,” Nagelman said.

“You don’t like anything,” Fitzpatrick said. “Don’t worry, it will all be over soon.”

“Look, my guy likes privacy when he conducts business. He needs to control the scene. In fact,” I said, pointing up into some nearby trees, “he’s probably watching us right now, so don’t do anything stupid.” *Stupider than normal, anyway.*

Both Nagelman and Fitzpatrick craned their heads, trying to catch a glimpse of the security cameras through the van’s windows.

“Let’s go,” I said.

We got out of the van and huddled near the driver’s door as I issued the orders. “When we get inside, let me do the talking—all the talking. After I make sure he’s got the money on hand, we’ll bring the merchandise inside and wait for him to do an appraisal. Then we’ll get our money and be off. No fuss, no muss. Okay?”

“Sure, boss,” Fitzpatrick said.

Nagelman nodded. “I won’t say a word.”

“Good. Now, who wants to stay in the van with the stuff?” I asked.

Nagelman looked at Fitzpatrick.

Fitzpatrick looked at Nagelman.

Neither said a word. I knew each was trying to figure out if staying with the goods or going inside with me was the best way not to get squeezed out of the deal.

“Well?” I asked. “Who’s it going to be?”

“Why don’t you stay,” Fitzpatrick said to Nagelman, “and I’ll go in? Just in case there’s trouble, I can handle it better. No offense, of course.”

“What if someone tries to hijack the van while you’re inside?” Nagelman countered.

“I’m sensing some distrust here,” I said. “Forget it. You can both come in with me. No one’s going to hijack the van while we’re inside. I trust my guy completely. Come on.”

I led the other two up a scuffed path toward the front door. Two shutters hung crookedly on ground-floor windows, and one upstairs window had been boarded up. A few optimistic wisps of grass poked through the snow on the front lawn.

When we got to the porch, I stopped, took a few steps backward, and pulled a gun from the waistband at the small of my back. “So here we are.”

“I’ll pat him down, boss.” Fitzpatrick started toward Nagelman, sneer in place. “You idiot. You had no idea we were cutting you out, did you?”

“Hold it right there, Fitzpatrick,” I said.

Fitzpatrick glanced at me, saw my gun pointed at him, and stopped, jaw clenched.

"Now who's the idiot?" Nagelman said, advancing on Fitzpatrick. "How does it feel to be the one getting—"

"You stop too, Nagelman," I said.

"What?" He examined my face, realized I wasn't joking around, and froze.

Fitzpatrick shook his head slowly. "Crap. I knew it. Triple-crossed."

Nagelman didn't say anything, but he looked as if he might puke.

"Very slowly, I want you to remove your guns and toss them on the ground, toward me. Flinch, and I shoot. Fitzpatrick, you first."

"I'm not armed. You said we wouldn't need it," Fitzpatrick said.

"Me neither," Nagelman said.

"Sure, you're not. Look, if it's easier for you, I can take them off your dead bodies. It doesn't matter much to me."

Fitzpatrick slowly removed a gun from the pocket of his coat and tossed it on the snowy ground a yard from my feet.

"Thanks. Your turn, Nagelman."

"It's on my ankle. Don't shoot me while I take it out." He bent down and removed his piece from the holster and tossed it near Fitzpatrick's gun.

"Now your phones," I said.

They tossed their phones next to their guns.

"I didn't trust you a bit," Fitzpatrick said. "Bastard."

"Well, someone very wise once told me you should never trust anybody. Good advice, don't you think?"

I picked up the phones and retrieved their weapons while keeping mine trained on my partners—my *ex*-partners. "Now, please get down on your knees."

They hesitated a moment, then Fitzpatrick dropped down at once, while Nagelman eased down one knee at a time.

"Please don't shoot us. Please," Nagelman whined.

"I'm not going to shoot you," I said. "Unless you get up before I drive off. Then I'll use you both for target practice."

"Bastard," Fitzpatrick said again.

"Nice doing business with you. And remember, don't trust anyone." I smiled. "Adios, amigos."

"Bastard," Fitzpatrick said a third time.

I trotted to the van, started it up, and roared off.

Three mil, not divided by anything, was best of all.

ΩΩΩ

I pulled up next to a Volvo station wagon behind a grocery store about ten miles from where I'd left Fitzpatrick and Nagelman. Pen leaned against the Volvo's hood, smoking a cigarette. A white crown of snow topped his knit cap. When I hopped out and tracked around the back of the van, Pen had exchanged the butt in his hand for a Beretta, and it was aimed at my chest.

"What the hell?"

"Sorry, bud." Pen stood straighter and seemed to have more zest than yesterday. More color in his face, too.

"Feeling better, I take it?" I asked.

"Amazing recovery, don't you think? I owe it all to clean living. Wanna toss me the keys to the van?"

I flipped them up in a graceful arc, and Pen snatched them cleanly out of the air. "No hard feelings, right?"

"No, Pen. I still love you."

"You remember all those times we talked about our dreams, how we couldn't wait to hit the big score so we could retire on some tropical island somewhere? Well, now I can, thanks to you. I really appreciate your effort."

"Don't mention it."

"I must say, though, I'm a little disappointed in you, Kane. Your failure to master rule number one—never trust anyone—reflects poorly on me as a teacher." He clicked his tongue against the roof of his mouth. "I guess that's how we learn, by making mistakes. Next time, you'll remember."

I watched Pen drive off. He'd turned on me, and part of me stung from my old friend's betrayal. I'd been his prize pupil. I liked to think he'd really cared about me.

But another part of me was content, happy even, as I pictured the proud look on my teacher's face when he opened those boxes and found a jumble of old clothes. I *had* mastered the most basic lesson, and now I'd passed the final exam.

I'd stashed the merchandise in a safe place before I met up with Pen—an insurance policy against a cagey old pro. If he hadn't double-crossed me, we would have picked up the goods on the way to our buyer, and we'd have gone through with the deal, smooth sailing. Then I'd have given Pen his dough, and we would have parted ways with a smile and firm handshake—teacher and pupil, partners in crime, dear old friends.

Sad to see, Pen losing his edge. He hadn't even bothered to check the boxes before taking off.

Thankfully, he'd left the keys to the Volvo in the ignition. I hopped in and started it up, hoping the future would be kind to Pen.

Without the big score, I didn't think he would ever make it to his tropical island. Maybe one day I'd visit him in that run-down trailer park in Boca, and we could laugh about how things had transpired.

Or maybe not.

Alan Orloff's debut mystery, DIAMONDS FOR THE DEAD, was an Agatha Award finalist. His seventh novel, RUNNING FROM THE PAST, was a winner in Amazon's Kindle Scout program. His short fiction has appeared in JEWISH NOIR, *Alfred Hitchcock Mystery Magazine*, CHESAPEAKE CRIMES: STORM WARNING, *Mystery Weekly*, 50 SHADES OF CABERNET, and WINDWARD: BEST NEW ENGLAND CRIME STORIES 2016. www.alanorloff.com

GOOD TO BE HOME
by Trish Perrault

The town's streets were quiet as Gino Fiori drove the police cruiser down the main drag. Even though it was nearly ninety degrees, a group of elderly men was playing cards in front of the barbershop. Passing the ballroom dance studio, Gino stared at the poster that filled the window: a smiling couple twirling beneath a spinning disco ball. Before they separated, Rita had begged him to take lessons, but he refused because he had two left feet.

The radio under his dashboard beeped, and he heard Ana Lewis, the new police chief, shout his name. Gino's shoulders tensed. He picked up the receiver and pressed the button on the side. "Yeah?"

"Did you hand out those flyers?"

On the papers scattered on the passenger seat, a middle-aged man with a broken nose stared up at Gino. Above the picture, a notice in red ink said, "Community Alert."

"Not yet. I'm getting a late start." Gino spat out the side window. He didn't remind Ana that he'd been busy with a traffic accident all morning.

"Your cousin's getting released early—you need to get them out," she said, irritated.

Gino replaced the receiver and rubbed a hand against his wet forehead.

Beneath a maple tree, a toddler splashed in a blue plastic pool. Gino remembered Angela at that age. She'd run to him, her arms outstretched as if he were a superhero. Those days were long gone. Angela was heading into her sophomore year of high school. She'd taken a summer job at an overnight camp. They texted back and forth a couple of times a week, mostly jokes or pictures of the kids at camp. Gino was relieved that Rita hadn't said anything to Angela about their temporary separation.

The radio popped. Ana's voice came through again.

"Hey, did you talk to Sal yet?"

Gino grabbed the receiver and pressed the button down. Hard. "I plan on it." In his mind, he counted out the years before he'd retire. Nine more and he'd be fifty-five. Sometimes he wished he'd taken the promotion, but he hadn't wanted to deal with all the town politics. Besides, he didn't join the police department to sit behind a desk. Gino liked seeing people around town and knowing he was responsible for keeping them safe.

"Get over there," Ana said, her voice sharp. "Dammit, those are your neighbors. There are kids on that street!"

Shoving the receiver back under the dashboard, Gino swore. He wished his old supervisor hadn't retired. The former chief was friends with his uncle Sal and knew he had suffered three heart attacks. The first heart attack had occurred after Sal shot and killed his brother-in-law Eddie in a hunting accident. Gino was about twelve and his cousin Lenny had been ten.

Instead of turning around and heading directly for Suffield Street, Gino took the longer route, the one he used to follow on family vacations when they drove to the Cape. He turned down Farm Road and hit the gas, past the new homes going up in fields that once had cows and sheep.

Beside him, the flyers rattled in the wind. Some slid off the seat and onto the floor. At a stop sign, he bent forward and threw the papers back onto the passenger seat. No one, not even Sal, had talked to Lenny in seven years. Sal once asked Gino to search the police databases, but Gino hadn't bothered, telling Sal there was no trace of Lenny. He hated deceiving his uncle, but he had no interest in knowing what had happened to his cousin. Gino told people, when they asked, that no one had heard from Lenny in years—which was the truth—and that his uncle was heartbroken—which was also the truth.

Gino didn't miss Lenny, the man, but sometimes he wondered what had happened to Lenny—the boy he grew up with. Sweat trickled down the side of his face as he thought about what Lenny had tried to do to Angela. Swearing, Gino pressed the gas pedal.

At the end of Farm Road, River Street headed east or west. East led towards the shore. He sat there until a Chevy came up behind him, and then he spun the steering wheel and drove in the direction of Main Street.

The fan in the cruiser rattled along with the engine. Tired from the heat, Gino radioed in that he was taking a fifteen-minute break and pulled the car into an empty parking space in front of the store. The barometer on the bank next door read nearly eighty-percent humidity. He grabbed a couple of flyers and got out of the car.

ꝏꝏ

Inside the market, the air was a bit cooler. Fans rattled in the window frames along both sides of Duncan's Grocery Store. Gino took a handkerchief from his back pocket and mopped his face. It felt good to be inside.

At the front of the store, a sign advertising homemade Italian ices leaned against the cash register. Gino ordered a lemon ice and listened to the flies stuck to the sticky paper above the counter. The boy behind the counter moved as if he had all day. Gino watched a moment, then repeated his order, pulled a thumbtack out of the corkboard, and stuck a copy of Lenny's flyer on the wall. Behind him, Gino heard Mrs. Duncan, the store owner. He used to pick up Mrs. Duncan's husband when he was too wasted to drive home. As a thank you for helping her family, Gino was offered free coffee whenever he came in during the morning.

He glanced over at the Mrs. Duncan but could only see the top of her gray head behind the deli case. She was waiting on a blond woman. Gino noticed the younger woman's soft curves, wondered who she was, and then picked up the morning newspaper. He bet that by the end of the week his cousin's picture would be on the front page.

The blonde laughed, and Gino froze.

Mrs. Duncan lifted a chunk of blue cheese and laid it down on the scale. "I haven't seen you look this good in years, Rita."

"I feel a bit like Marilyn Monroe," Rita said, swinging her thick hair so it skimmed the back of her red blouse. Gino folded his arms across his chest. He liked his wife better as a brunette.

"Gino's sure to notice." Mrs. Duncan winked. "Spiffing yourself up—good for you!"

"Just trying something new." Rita's voice sounded flat.

"Well, I bet Gino will notice!"

Gino stepped closer. He hadn't talked to his wife in weeks and was tired of waiting to be forgiven. He'd been living at a hole-in-the-wall efficiency while she calmed down—not that he blamed her for being upset.

He barely made out his wife's voice over the loud fans. "I doubt that will happen."

"He's a good father and has a good job, Rita." Mrs. Duncan yanked on a roll of plastic wrap. Her voice was loud. "Men aren't perfect, you know."

"I know." Rita reached for the package of cheese.

"Women aren't perfect either."

Rita bent over to get a bag of rolls. Mrs. Duncan turned to face him and gave Gino a quick wink. He winked back. Gino knew he wasn't perfect, but he was glad there were people still on his side.

Before Rita could spot him, he paid for his ice and went outside to wait. Maybe today would be the day Rita would talk to him.

ola

Whatever hope Gino might have had of talking to Rita alone vanished when a white BMW pulled in next to his cruiser.

Karen smiled at him behind her dark sunglasses. She wore her blond hair pulled back like she had in high school.

"Fancy meeting you here, Stranger," she said, her tone playful.

Gino glanced over his shoulder to see if Rita was coming out of the market. He didn't know how she'd react if she saw him with Karen.

He and Karen had dated in high school, but Karen had flirted with all of his buddies. Gino had broken it off and started seeing Rita. Rita made him feel comfortable. Over the years, whenever he ran into Karen, they would flirt, nothing serious, just in good fun. They were both married and had kids.

Karen got out of the car. He looked away but noticed her short skirt. "I hear your cousin is coming home."

Gino rubbed the back of his neck and watched the front of the store. "Who told you that?"

"Oh, a reliable source." She stood in front of him now. He could smell her perfume.

Gino recalled a few months back when Karen sat on his lap the night of their 30th high school reunion. Rita hadn't gone with him; they'd had a fight.

He had plenty of excuses for why he cheated that night after he left the house. The biggest one being that Ana had told him earlier that day that his cousin Lenny was in a California state prison because he had raped some little girl. His sentence was reduced because he provided key information in a drug investigation, and now he was being paroled. Lenny was coming home.

When Gino had told Rita the news, she flipped out. She didn't want Lenny to come back and demanded that Gino fix the situation. He had stormed out of the house and then headed over to the hotel where the reunion was going on.

Gino glanced at the front of the store then over at Karen. She'd removed the rubber band at the back of her head. Karen's long hair fell against her shoulders. Gino remembered how smooth the strands felt in his hands. Looking down at the lemon ice melting in the cup, he took a scoop and shoved it into his mouth. The ice tasted sour against his tongue.

"I heard Dave's leaving town." He lifted the spoon and tasted the ice again. His lips puckered.

"Yeah." She looked down at her manicured fingernails. "What about you and Rita?"

The street was quiet. Too hot for anyone to take a stroll. He noticed Rita's old yellow VW bug. He'd told Rita that the thing with Karen happened only once, which was the truth, but Rita told him it was one time too many. "Nothing new."

Karen took out a cigarette and lit the tip. "Ana stopped by my office last week to tell me about Lenny."

He crushed the cup of ice and shot it towards the trash bucket. "Why'd Ana tell you?"

"I'm the school principal," she said, immediately defensive.

"Of course." School would be starting in a couple of weeks. Gino's heart pounded.

"Lenny was always a little weird," she said, blowing out a stream of smoke.

Gino's eye burned. "Can't always tell. Even if you see them every day." He noticed a pebble in his front tire.

"Maybe." Karen crushed the cigarette beneath her sandal. "Remember he used to babysit kids in town? Didn't you think that was odd?"

He opened his mouth to tell her no but instead kicked the tire. The pebble remained stuck in the rubber tread.

Gino didn't tell her that Lenny used to babysit Angela when she was little. Rita had been taking night classes, and Gino had been on night shift.

Karen waited for Gino to answer, and, when he didn't, she said, "Let me know if you want to get together."

As she headed across the street, the door to the market opened.

Rita stepped outside, her hand raised to shield her eyes from the sun. Gino knew the exact moment when she saw him because she lost her grip on the paper bag she was holding.

Rita stayed on the top step as if debating whether to walk down the steps or go back inside. She repositioned the brown bag and clutched it against her chest.

"Rita?"

Her gaze was directed towards the post office across the street.

"Rita."

"What do you want from me?"

"To talk."

The paper bag settled against her waist. "I'm done talking."

He glanced over his shoulder and then back at Rita. "I just ran into her."

"Really? You think I care?" Her blue eyes flickered over the contents of her paper bag. A stalk of celery poked out the top.

"I told you that was nothing."

"Gino—I. Don't. Care!" Her face tightened with each word she spoke.

Gino took a deep breath, trying to slow his thoughts. He hated when Rita talked to him that way. She was usually easygoing and soft spoken.

He went to reach for her but let his hand fall to his side. "Can we go someplace and talk?"

Her fake blond hair glistened in the sunlight. Gino wanted to tell her she didn't need to change her hair, but he knew it wouldn't matter.

"There's nothing more I want to hear from you."

Taking a flyer from his pocket, he held it out towards Rita. She recoiled when she saw Lenny's picture. "He's coming back," he said.

"When?"

"Today on a bus—he's staying with Sal."

She lifted her chin as their eyes met. "No, Gino. That can't happen."

"I need to hand out these flyers, and then I'm going over to talk to Sal."

Behind Rita, in the store window, Mrs. Duncan watched them. She held a piece of paper in her hands and shook her head.

Rita got into her car and started the engine. "I'll be at the house."

ǫǫǫ

As he drove towards the house that he and Rita owned, memories of the day he had found Lenny in the bathroom with his daughter flooded his mind. Angela had been seven at the time. Gino had gotten out of work early, picked up Rita after her night class, and headed home. Gino was the one who found Lenny naked in the tub. Angela stood next to the tub, her hands covered with bubbles, in her bathrobe. Lenny started yelling that he wasn't doing anything and stood up, bubbles sliding down his naked body. Gino roared, but, before he could do anything, Rita ran in from the kitchen with a steak knife. Gino restrained her in the hallway as Lenny escaped through the kitchen door. They found their daughter crying and scared in her bedroom closet. In the hallway, he'd strained to hear every word as Rita gently questioned Angela; she told Rita that Lenny had said she was dirty. From Angela's answers and what they witnessed, they believed Angela hadn't been fondled. Later, when he located his cousin hiding in a car, Lenny pleaded with Gino to believe that it was all a horrible misunderstanding. Gino remembered how he'd hesitated. Then he punched his cousin in the face. When Gino went home that night and told Rita that Lenny was gone and wouldn't be back, Rita had been furious with Gino for not arresting his cousin.

For several weeks after that night, Angela refused to take baths and started crying and wetting her bed. Privately, Gino wondered if Lenny had done something to Angela but he didn't have the courage to talk to his wife about his fears. Instead, he watched Angela closely and over time, he began to relax.

Flexing his fingers, Gino thought about the girl in California. His gut hurt. He wished he'd arrested Lenny and told his uncle Sal what Lenny had done. Clinching his fists around the steering wheel, Gino wished he had the power to go back in time to do things the right way.

ooo

Gino parked in front of the two-story house that he and Rita purchased twenty years ago. Gino had bought the house because it was near his uncle's.

Rita's VW sat behind the house under the basketball hoop. The door to the house across the street opened, and an elderly man wearing suspenders and a long-sleeved shirt bent down and picked up the afternoon paper.

"Sal!"

"Gino!" the old man yelled back. "You going over to talk to Rita?"

Gino ignored his uncle's question and grabbed a flyer. He rolled it up as he crossed the street. "What'd the doctor say?"

"They upped my meds. Nothing new." Sal's face was the color of a sardine. "He wants me to stop driving."

"Maybe you should."

"I tried calling you today," Sal said. "I've got great news—Lenny's coming home." Gino's uncle slapped his back. "Can you believe it, after all this time?"

A girl, about five years old, rode by on a bright pink bicycle. She smiled at Gino.

"When's he coming in?"

"About six." His words came out in small gasps as he climbed the steps one at a time. Gino thought about calling Ana with this information, but instead he reached over his uncle's shoulder and held the front door. "He's taking a taxi from the bus station."

Gino followed the older man down the dimly lit front hall. Pictures of Sal, Gino's father, and their families lined the walls.

"Did he say how long he plans to stay?"

"Permanently." Sal pulled a chair out from the table and sat down. His face folded into a wrinkly grin. "Seven years without a word, and then all of a sudden he calls to say he'll be home around dinnertime."

"Did he tell you where he's been?"

Sal started shaking some pills out of a medicine bottle. His eyes focused on the opening. "I went to the market and picked up some steaks and potatoes. You and Rita are welcome to come over."

Gino sat down across from him. Above their heads, a shotgun hung on the wall. When they were teens, Lenny told Gino that it was the gun his uncle Sal used to shoot his brother-in-law Eddie.

"Doctors keep making me take these damn pills. Like that's going to make a bit of difference."

"Sal, about Lenny…"

"Sometimes, I say to myself, what's the point?"

"About Lenny—there's something you need to know."

His uncle's dark eyes were wet. "Dammit, Gino, can't you just be happy your cousin's coming home? Haven't you missed him?"

Gino rested a hand on his holster. "Sal, Lenny's been in prison."

Sal's head was shiny under the florescent light. "What are you saying?"

Gino unrolled the flyer he'd been holding and slid the paper across the table. "He raped a girl."

"No!" Sal shook his head and flung the paper away from him. "No, that's bullshit. My son wouldn't do that."

"Sal, read it." Gino held the paper out to his uncle. "I'm handing this flyer out to everyone on the street. Lenny's picture is going to be in the newspaper."

The old man hit the table with his fist. "I don't believe it. My boy wouldn't do something like that."

Gino pushed the flyer back across the table. Outside, an ice cream truck's music played.

Sal picked up the paper and flung it under Gino's nose. "You believe this crap?" His voice was hoarse.

Gino's throat hurt. "Yeah. I do."

Sal crushed the paper into a ball and threw it across the room. "He's your family!"

"He was given twenty years."

The faucet in the sink dripped against the porcelain.

"Why would they let him out if he did that?" His uncle's voice shook, as did his hands. "They wouldn't let him out."

Gino stood up and went across the room to pick up the balled-up notice. His fingers shook as he smoothed out the wrinkles. "The system—the government—they do this all the time." He tried not to see the kid he once knew. "They let the sick ones out even though the government knows they're going to hurt more people."

Gino heard the scrape of the front door. Footsteps echoed down the hall. Sal looked up at the ceiling above the table.

"I'll keep an eye on him," Sal whispered. "He won't do anything again."

Gino stared at the rifle on the wall. "People like Lenny don't stop, Sal. You can count on it."

Sal's body rocked back and forth. "Remember how, as a boy, Lenny used to help your Aunt Bea in the kitchen?"

The sound of footsteps moved closer to the kitchen. Gino's holster felt heavy against his side as he rested a hand on his belt.

"I couldn't figure it out. Why he all of a sudden wouldn't leave his mother alone." Sal softly rubbed the sides of his stiff index finger. "Then I caught Eddie, Bea's brother—the man I welcomed into my home—with his hand down Lenny's pants."

He felt sick thinking of Lenny being molested as a little boy. "Lenny never told me."

Sal's irises dilated. "I wanted to kill Eddie. Right then and there."

Gino remembered how he struggled to keep himself from pounding Lenny's face into the pavement after he'd found him trying to get Angela into the bathtub with him.

Sal pulled out a cloth handkerchief and blew his nose. "Those types like Eddie, they don't change." The old man cleared his throat. "I took Eddie out deer hunting."

"What happened?" Gino said, his eyes shifting from his uncle to the doorway. Rita, her face strained, stood in the doorway.

Sal didn't reply to Gino's question; he just drummed his fingers on the table.

"Eddie deserved that bullet, Sal," Rita said, finally stepping into the room. Her footsteps were light as she crossed the linoleum to stand beside his uncle.

A slight smile crossed Sal's thin face when he saw her.

"I never told Bea," he said, absently patting her hand. "The police chief came, but he didn't ask too many questions. We were friends."

Rita ran a hand over Sal's shoulders. "Lenny hurt a girl," she told him. "He raped her. She was only six."

Sal hung his head over the flyer. "Why would he do that?" His arthritic fingers pressed the flyer against the table. "He's my son," his voice cracked. "He couldn't have done that stuff." His head lifted, and his wet eyes went back and forth between Rita and Gino. "Why would he do that?"

"I don't know, Sal. I don't."

Sal's fist banged the table and knocked the sugar bowl on its side. Gino wished for the hundredth time he'd understood earlier what Lenny had grown up to be.

His uncle's fist hit the table again.

"Were there others?" His uncle asked, his voice hoarse as he lifted his head and met Gino's gaze.

Gino crossed his arms in front of his chest. The muscles in his throat closed.

"Were there?" his uncle asked, this time louder.

Gino gave a curt nod, then looked away, as he sucked air into his empty lungs. A harsh sob from Rita drew his eyes to her. Tears ran down her face as she flung an arm across her face.

"Oh, God." Sal's voice cracked. "Not Angela. Not her."

His heart pounding, Gino wiped his stinging eyes as he thought of his daughter and the little girl in California. His mind shied away from the questions: How many other girls had Lenny hurt? How many had he let Lenny hurt by not arresting him that day?

He looked at Rita when she spoke.

"People like Eddie and Lenny…don't change." Rita sat down beside Sal at the kitchen table. "I don't want him near her," she said, her hand nervously stroking his arm.

"I'm sorry, Rita," Sal whispered.

Rita shot Gino a look. "Lenny will do it again, Sal. He will, I know it."

A shudder went through Sal's body. He squeezed Rita's hand.

"He needs to be stopped," Rita said.

Sal's shoulders fell. His voice was soft when he said, "I'll handle Lenny. I'll handle him."

Gino took a step towards Sal and Rita but knew he wasn't wanted.

Rita murmured something into Sal's ear.

"What are you going to do?" Gino demanded, his heart racing.

Ignoring Gino, Sal patted Rita's hand in a fatherly manner and gazed into her eyes. "Take your husband home and work this thing out."

Rita stiffened. She jerked her hand away, but Sal held her fingers. "Work things out." Then he regarded Gino for a moment, shook his head, and said, "Don't be a fool and lose what you've worked so hard to get."

"Tell me how you're going to handle Lenny. I need to know…I need to tell Ana."

"Let's go, Gino." Rita walked in the direction of the front hall. When he didn't move, Rita grabbed his hand. His thumb touched her wrist, and he felt her pulse flutter. Gino looked into his wife's face; her expression was guarded, but she met his eyes. He followed her down the hall.

When they stood in front of their house, Gino said, "We should go back."

"We can't go back, Gino."

He looked over at Sal's modest house. "You sure this is what you want?" His chest felt tight beneath his uniform.

"Angela will be home in a couple of days."

Gino considered the houses that lined the street. He thought of how Angela liked to read books under the oak tree in their front yard and how she dressed up as a wizard every Halloween. "I need to hand out Lenny's flyers."

A yellow taxicab rounded the corner.

"It's hot out here," Rita said, pulling on his hand. Her eyes were slightly puffy as if she'd had trouble sleeping. The taxi slowed down as it neared Sal's house. "Let's go for a swim."

Gino thought about handing out the flyers, but instead he followed Rita into the house. He ignored the sound of the man's voice calling his name.

ƍƍƍ

Gino was in the swimming pool when he heard what sounded like thunder nearby. Thick clouds covered the once blue sky, and he wondered how soon the rain would follow. Rita had been reading him an email from Angela. She stopped, put the iPad down on the table, and stood.

There was a second blast. This time closer. A jagged bolt of lightning lit the distant mountains.

A siren sounded in the distance.

Rita shook her head as Gino reached for the pool ladder. "Stay."

The water felt cold against his hot skin as Rita untied the knot at her waist and slipped out of her cover up. In her swimsuit, he could see that she'd lost weight. His tongue suddenly thick, Gino swallowed. He suddenly wanted to make love to his wife.

Rita stepped onto the diving board and dove into the pool. She surfaced a few feet away from him.

Another siren sounded. This time louder than the first.

Gino noticed the tears that ran down Rita's already damp face.

He let go of the ladder and pulled his wife against his thick chest. He looked up at the darkening sky and felt her body tremble against his as the thunder rolled over the valley.

Trish Perrault writes stories about life-altering moments in the lives of her characters that offer greater insight and understanding. She earned her MFA in creative writing from Lesley University (January 2017) and is an adjunct professor at a community college. Trish lives in upstate New York with her family.

THE BANSHEE OF ADAMS, MASSACHUSETTS
by Keenan Powell

Summer, 1896
Adams, Massachusetts

A crow swooped, talons open, screaming, screaming. Liam flailed his arms overhead, shielding his head and face. The crow vanished, then swooped again, screeching his name. "Liam, Liam."

"Liam," his mother whispered, shaking him awake. "Can you not hear that?"

Her hand on his shoulder was cold. Crinkly white hair sprang away from her mouse-colored braid. She looked mad, as certainly she was.

"It's the banshee," Mary Barrett said, her voice hushed.

To the Irish-born like his mother who still believed in fairies and spirits, the banshee's scream heralded death. Mixed up in her madness was some recognition that her son, Liam, was a policeman. And when the banshee screamed, her son, the police officer, would leave home to quiet the spirit and prevent a tragedy.

But it was not a banshee, Liam knew. It was Mrs. Maguire, a woman old enough to have grandchildren but who had none. She roamed the streets of Adams late at night, banged on windows and doors, cursed and yelled about imagined injustices. Lies, secrets, and complicities. Moldy bread sold by the baker. Sour milk delivered by the dairyman. A flock of women on the street who whispered amongst themselves about her, she was sure.

The last bit was probably true. The people of Adams long ago had agreed upon the case of Mrs. Maguire. They had given up reasoning with her.

Occasionally someone would suggest she should go to the asylum. But the women were against it. Who amongst them did not have problems? Who amongst them would gladly be singled out and sent away? Mrs. Maguire, like his mother, was simply "away with the fairies."

No, it was best to steer clear of her if one could. When Mrs. Maguire broke something, a door or a window, the men of Adams would fix it the next day. The women of Adams made sure of it. They made sure she had enough to eat and coal for her fire. They made sure castaway clothing was left on her doorstep.

Because they felt sorry for her. She'd lost her husband and her only child, a son. There was no family left to care for her, or for her to care for. It could happen to any of them. Each of them was just one war, one epidemic, one famine away from childless widowhood.

Another scream, venomous and hateful.

"Sure, it's the banshee, Liam," Mary Barrett said. "Someone will die."

Liam usually found Mrs. Maguire on the Hoosic River bridge in the middle of Adams town, drawn by her sobbing. She would be exhausted from her rampage, face slick with tears and snot, oily hair hanging in limp ropes from her head, her clothes crusted with dirt and filth. He'd guide her home, talking with her quietly until she became drowsy enough to sleep. Even though he was a generation younger than her, she had confided in him. She talked about her dead son, James, and the father who was responsible, the father who wasn't home the night James died. She knew, she said, James was murdered and that the people of Adams were hiding the truth from her. Sitting on her stoop, she'd hang on Liam's arm, begging him to help. Her head would loll and she would mutter, "the father, the father." She was always very drunk.

At thirty-four-years old, Liam didn't feel equal to the task of consoling a mourning mother, but it fell to him as a police officer. Only last year, Chief Curran in his stiff double-breasted uniform had hired Liam for the newly-formed Adams police force after witnessing Liam settle a barroom argument before it turned into a brawl. The Chief had observed, he said, something special in Liam: an ability to calm people. And Liam had been happy to serve as a keeper of the peace, having seen brutality and violence in his youth.

Kate, Liam's sister older by just one year, entered his bedroom. She clutched a woolen shawl around herself which she took off and wrapped around her mother's shoulders. "Back to bed, Ma."

A shriek. Not a scream this time, but a shriek.

The night sounds stopped. Birds outside went silent. The old cow and the chickens in the yard, a moment ago fluttering and moving with agitation, stilled. The three people in Liam's bedroom frozen into a tableau, holding their breaths. Liam in his bed, up on one elbow. His mother gripping his arm. Kate with her gentle hands on Mary's shoulder.

"You go, Liam," Kate said as she drew their mother away.

ǫǫǫ

He dressed in the work clothes and boots he had cast off after he finished farm chores that evening and began trotting towards the bridge. After the last shriek, there had been no more sounds from Mrs. Maguire. It wasn't unusual for her to wear herself out, but Liam had never heard a shriek like that before from her. He was running now, passing homes with candles flickering inside. The residents, wakened by the screams, waited to see if they were needed.

Silvery streaks of moonlight rippled across the river's surface as Liam staggered to a halt. There was no one on the bridge. In the shadows along the riverbank, there was no movement. This place was as quiet as a graveyard save the gurgle of water.

Liam's attention paused on flotsam beneath a fallen tree. When his eyes adjusted to the gloom, he saw.

He lunged into the cold water, leaning against the current. He sunk his fingers into a mass wedged beneath the tree, Mrs. Maguire's woolen dress. He pulled but she didn't move. She seemed rooted to the place. Her face was hidden by hair tangled in the branches.

There may have been a chance she was still alive. Until the doctor said otherwise, Liam would believe that she could be saved. That was his job.

He pulled harder. His boots sunk in the muck. His pants, soaked now, tangled around his legs. The heavy weight of his own sodden clothes pulled him down into the stench and slime of rotting things.

He pulled again, harder this time, and felt the tree give way with a snap of wood and shredding of cloth. As she broke free, the current lifted her and tried to drag her away. He held on, slipping in the mud, sliding into the water waist-deep. He felt one boot, then another pulled from his feet, as he pistoned his legs toward land, pulling her along. Mud turned to dirt beneath his feet and he fell to his knees, her weight straining his arms. She could still be alive. Crawling, he dragged her onto the dry land.

His lungs burned. His arms and legs were stiff from cold. His shoulders and elbows ached.

He put his ear to her mouth. There was no sound. No warm, misty breath.

A man stumbled upon him, a drunk, coming from the direction of Adam's only brothel.

"Fetch Doctor McPherson," Liam ordered, his voice choked from exertion.

"Maybe the priest?" the little man suggested, face widened in an effort to appear earnestly sober.

"The doctor, now! Tell him to hurry." Liam scrubbed Mrs. Maguire's limp hands to warm them. He patted her cheeks, called her name.

He carefully pulled her hair away from her face. She reeked of whiskey. Moonlight made her pale skin look even more ghostly. But she seemed at peace, so much so that he hardly recognized her without that tight mask of anger she always wore.

Liam's face stung. With his fingers, he probed and found a long thin welt across his forehead and cheek, probably from a branch that had struck him in the struggle. He had no memory of it.

०००

As Liam waited for the doctor, he scrubbed Mrs. Maguire's arms and called her name, even as he heard movement begin again around him. A bat flew overhead, leathery wings beating. Grass rustled as a fox stalked a rabbit. A fish broke the water's surface. At the edge of the narrow valley, Mount Greylock, a charcoal lump against the night sky, sometimes disappeared when clouds scudded overhead, then reappeared again.

Liam squeezed her hand. "The doctor will be here soon," he said but he suspected it may be too late. With each wash of moonlight, her bluing face glowed.

Dr. McPherson, an old Scottish man who still spoke with an accent, trotted up with his black bag and knelt beside the body. He looked the body over, touched a wrist, pulled open an eyelid. "I'm sorry, Liam," he said. "There's nothing to be done."

"Are you sure?"

Dr. McPherson put a hand on Liam's arm. Grizzled with white whiskers, he smelled of cigars. "I'm sorry, son."

A few men had gathered. Dr. McPherson instructed two of the watchers to bring his wagon around. They were to take the body to the surgery until the undertaker could claim her in the morning.

Just as the men were dispatched, old Father O'Brien limped up the road, his large, soft body wobbling with each step. Liam was unable to make out the features of his face in the murky night but recognized the painful gait, the cane upon which he leant, and the violet stole draped upon an arm. The drunk must have gone for the priest after all, Liam guessed. At least he had sent the doctor first. The priest stood over the body, kissed the stole, hung it round his neck and then began murmuring Latin prayers.

Liam drew the doctor aside while the priest prayed. "Don't release her to the undertaker just yet," Liam interrupted. "There will be an investigation."

"Are you serious?" Dr. McPherson asked, the acrid burst of his tobacco breath stinging Liam's eyes. "It's not murder. I know how you Catholics feel about these things, but the fact is that she committed suicide. She threw herself over the bridge. A deeply disturbed woman. Everyone knows that, even the coroner." Dr. McPherson himself had been accused by Mrs. Maguire of lying about James' death. His windows had been broken by rocks she had thrown more than once. But he had never complained.

Father O'Brien finished the ritual with the sign of the cross and wobbled back home without speaking to anyone.

The doctor may have been right this time. Nevertheless, Liam persisted. In the case of an unnatural death, the coroner would conduct an inquest. That was the law. Liam was sworn to uphold that law. Mrs. Maguire, the victim of so much tragedy, deserved as much.

"With all due respect, Doctor," Liam said, "the coroner will decide."

ೞೞೞ

The sky was turning pink as Liam walked home, soggy boots in hand, wet clothes clinging to him. With each breeze, his skin prickled. The gardens he passed were rich in color: green grass, red roses, purple lilacs. But to Liam, today, the color had drained away from pretty, little Adams town.

When he squelched into the Barrett's sitting room, Kate put her mending down in her lap. "Your face," she said.

Their mother was sitting in her rocker, her head drooped to her chest, eyes closed. He stepped closer to make sure she was breathing and saw her chest softly rise and fall. A vein in her neck pulsed with her heartbeat. Spittle oozed from the side of her mouth. With a forefinger, he caught the strand before it dropped onto her dress.

"It's nothing," he said, wiping his hand on his pants.

ooo

After he changed into his wool police tunic and trousers, he sat at the kitchen table watching as Kate stoked the cooker's fire and then stood watch over the warming porridge. Steam filled the room with the aroma of cooking oats. They spoke quietly so as not to disturb their sleeping mother.

"Mrs. Maguire, the banshee herself?" Kate asked.

"Gone to meet her maker, I'm afraid," Liam said. "Drowned near the bridge."

Kate crossed herself. Liam felt he knew what she was thinking. Bad things happened on that bridge. Not only had the Maguire boy met his end there, but their father had too. He'd lost his footing coming home from the pub during a rainstorm. That was the night when Liam's world changed. He gave up his plans for law school and took his father's place at the mill because his family needed the money. That was the night his mother slipped even further away.

Their father's death had been the end of their mother's sanity, fragile as she was before. Surely, the death of an only child would be enough to destroy Mrs. Maguire's mind.

"You don't think she…?" Kate left the question unsaid. Suicide was a mortal sin.

"Probably," Liam answered. "But, it's up to the coroner. Whether she did it herself or it was an accident or something else."

"Something else? Surely not, Liam. Who would kill that old lady? She was mean, sure, but she never really hurt anyone, did she?"

"The coroner will want information. There was the boy who died. And, there was the husband, but I don't remember what happened to him. What have you heard from the church ladies?"

"As if I have time for gossip," she scoffed. Kate ran the house and the farm now that their father was dead, Liam was a police officer and their mother was away with the fairies. After work, Liam did what he could to help but often as not by the time he came home, the chores were already done.

Kate sipped her tea. "Try Sadie Monaghan," she whispered. "She knows all that is worth knowing."

ooo

Sadie waddled before Liam, her potato-shaped body rolling like a sailor from foot to foot, as she led him to her sitting room. "I've not much time for you, Officer Barrett," she said when she stopped to face him, drying her hands on her apron. "With Mrs. Maguire's passing, I'm after making the arrangements, don't you know."

Sadie Monaghan was the owner of Adam's only boarding house and a formidable person. The other women deferred to her authority in all matters open to discussion due to the sheer force of her personality. She was one of the few women who did not work in the mill or attend to a brood of children. Instead, she owned her own business. She was also said to possess the second sight, but Liam wondered if she merely paid better attention than most. At any rate, she was central to the community and, as Kate said, she knew everything worth knowing.

She pointed him to a horse-hair sofa and took a seat opposite.

"Thank you, Mrs. Monaghan," Liam said from his perch on the sofa's edge. "I was wondering what you can tell me about Mrs. Maguire."

"I figured as much," she said. She tapped the wooden armrest with a chubby forefinger as she gathered her thoughts. "Mary Elizabeth Maguire arrived in Adams with her husband, Felix, and their boy, James, some thirty year ago. They lived on a farm, a nice small piece of land near your own. I don't like to speak ill of the dead, but even in those days, Betty and Felix both were fond of the drink. She blamed him for the boy's death and drove him away. Since then, the other ladies and I would give her some mending to do now and then, a fine hand she had when she wasn't in her cups, to help her get by. She did some cleaning as well for those who could afford her."

"The husband, Felix, is he still alive?"

"He lives down in Pittsfield, managing a farm for some rich fella, don't you know."

"And the boy, James? Drowned, I understand."

"Indeed," Sadie crossed herself. "Fell off the bridge, right there in the same place where you found poor Betty. He was just twelve, maybe thirteen. You know how reckless they are at that age. So hard keeping them from killing themselves. Horseplay, they say. The boys liked to climb on the bridge railings. He must have fallen off and hit his head. It was late at night and there was no one with him at the time. His parents being drinkers and all, he wandered about freely. Not that he was bad, no, not at all. He was a good boy, an altar boy even. Now, if you're not needing anything more, there's baking to be done. Go to the doctor's now, have him see to that face of yours."

ბბბ

The alcohol Dr. McPherson daubed on Liam's face burned so much his eyes watered.

"That's a nasty scratch you got there, son," he said. "Not surprised given the state of Mrs. Maguire."

"Other than the drowning you mean?"

"Take a look for yourself," the doctor said.

Dr. McPherson knew how he hated viewing bodies but it was a part of his job. Liam suspected that the old doctor was making a show of it, punishing him for pursuing what he believed was a waste of time. He led Liam through the house to the sickroom and pulled the sheet off the corpse. Liam fixed his eyes on her face only. It wasn't right looking at her body and he would not be made to unless it was necessary.

Shock made his spine buzz. "Her face!"

The hair had been combed away. Again, as at the riverside, she seemed peaceful. But there were scratches all over her face and a large purple and blue mark on her left cheek.

"Scratches like your own," the doctor said. "And she probably got that bruise when she hit a rock. Just as I told you, son. It was an accident. She fell, or jumped for all we know, into the river, then hit her head and drowned."

ஒஒஒ

After a short train-ride south, Liam found the Pittsfield estate where Felix Maguire was employed. When Maguire came to the kitchen door, he took his cap off and then hesitated, eyes shifting about the room until he landed on Liam seated alone at the kitchen table. The cook, a formidable woman who no doubt guarded her territory like a terrier, had absented herself upon Liam's request.

Maguire was as small and thin as a starved cat but the lay of his clothes suggested a sinewy, strong body. His face and hands were darkened by the sun, his thinning hair the color of the earth. A fine web of broken blood vessels across his cheeks were from the drink, but the whites of his eyes were blazing, nearly blue. He had been sober a long time.

"Officer," Felix said as he stepped inside and closed the door.

"Liam Barrett from Adams, Mr. Maguire."

Felix waited, edging his fingers around the brim of his cap.

"I have some bad news for you, Mr. Maguire. Perhaps you would prefer to sit down."

"I'd prefer to stand, if it's just the same to you, Officer."

"It's about Mrs. Maguire, sir. She's passed on."

Maguire nodded. He seemed to have anticipated the reason for the visit, even before they had concluded their greetings.

"God rest her soul," Maguire said. "She blamed me, you know, for the boy's death."

Maguire leaned against a wall, his mettle drained away. He nodded again. "And right she was. I should have been there. I could have been a better father." He looked Liam in the eye. "I wasn't at home that night. I was somewhere else, a place a married man did not belong. If only I had been home with the mother and the boy. I quit the drink and the women, but it did no good. She couldn't forgive me. So, I left."

"Was she a devout woman?" Liam asked.

"You're asking me if she done this to herself," Maguire said. "Could have. She didn't give a tinker's damn about mortal sins or what those men in black dresses preach. Aye, her mind was a dark place. If she had drink taken, she could surely have..." his voice cracked. "She could have done what you said."

"One last question, sir. Where were you last night?"

"Sleeping in the barn with a foaling mare," Maguire said. "You can ask anyone."

The father, the father. Liam could see Felix Maguire had nothing to do with his son's death. He was guilt-ridden, certainly, for being a poor family man, but he wasn't carrying the kind of guilt that comes from murdering your own son. That kind of guilt was easy to see; it made a brittle shell around a person. This man was vulnerable in his mourning. He didn't kill anyone.

Not that Mrs. Maguire had ever accused him of murder after all, only of being responsible for the boy's death. She needed someone to blame. He was convenient.

After Maguire returned to his work, Liam confirmed his alibi with the cook. Liam hadn't suspected him, but for the sake of thoroughness, the question had to be asked. Maguire indeed had spent the night in the barn.

ΩΩΩ

Trees whisked by as the train to Adams gained speed. Liam had never known James Maguire. He was just a year or two old when the boy drowned. It could have just as easily happened to any boy, to Liam himself. James hadn't done anything bad. He was a good boy, an altar boy.

When Liam was twelve, about the same age James was when he died, old Father O'Brien had asked him to serve as an altar boy. Liam's mother said no. She claimed that she needed him at home for farm chores because his father worked in the mill, but that wasn't true. There was just the one cow and some chickens. Liam could have easily done his chores and served as well. Liam had never known his mother to lie, much less to a priest. When he asked his father about it, his father said to mind his mother and speak of it no more.

The train's rocking lulled Liam to sleep. He dreamt of priests and screaming crows and a boy, Liam himself sometimes, drowning in the river, then suddenly standing on the bridge, fighting the crow. It screeched louder and louder until the train halted and Liam woke.

The father, the father.

ΩΩΩ

It was early evening when Liam left the train station on his way to the priest's home and nearly twenty hours since Mrs. Maguire had died.

Old Father O'Brien opened the door just as Liam raised his hand to knock. "Oh," he said, startled by the sight of someone on his stoop.

"A word, if I may, Father?" Liam asked.

"Not now," the priest said. "I must catch the last train." One suitcase was stacked by the door. Another was in his hand.

"Are you leaving us?"

"I need a rest, son," the priest said. "The bishop will be sending a new priest to take my place."

"It's all rather sudden," Liam said. He had always remembered the priest as a tall, robust man until age and arthritis had bent him. But tonight he seemed even more shrunken.

The priest put down the suitcase and limped toward a nearby chair. He sat, a process which took longer than Liam thought it should, with a show of gripping an armrest, turning himself about and easing down with grimaces and groans.

"Last night, Father. What happened?"

"I tried to ease her suffering," the priest said. "You saw how the woman was, confused, angry, constantly accusing. Suffering, she was. Her screams woke me. I went to her, offered her solace. Nothing I said calmed her. She became angrier and angrier, and even more confused. Ugly things she said. Then, she struck out at me. I merely held my hand up in defense. She must have lost her balance."

The left side of the priest's face was swollen with a darkened splotch like the mark on Mrs. Maguire's face. In the dark of the early morning when Liam had last seen the priest, he had not noticed the bruise. He realized that the priest had kept his face down during the Last Rites and left the scene without speaking to anyone.

"Did she do that to you?" Liam gestured to the priest's face.

The priest examined his face with papery fingers. He winced and dropped his hand to his lap, his fingers trembling like disembodied spider legs.

Liam waited.

"I'm sorry, what was it?" the priest said.

"That bruise on your face. How did you get that?"

The priest's eyes cast about as if he was searching. For the truth, perhaps, or for a plausible lie? "She struck me," his voice barely a whisper. "That poor, suffering woman."

"And you struck her back?"

"It was an accident, you must understand. I put out my hand only to protect myself. It was dark. I couldn't see well."

"You pushed her."

"It was an accident, I'm telling you. Aren't you listening? I put out my hand, to stop her, she struck me and lost her balance and fell."

"And why was she so angry with you, Father?"

"The boy," the old priest said. Liam noticed then how his red-rimmed lower lids fell away from his piss-colored eyes. "She accused me," he seemed to choke, "of indecencies. How dare she? He was such a beautiful boy."

"James Maguire?"

The priest nodded. "Lovely brown curls, bright blue eyes, merry all the time, rosy cheeks like apples." The priest seemed to smile at an imaginary boy. "Skin like silk."

"Was his death an accident too?" Liam asked.

The old priest snapped out of his reverie and gathered himself into a pious glare. "He took his own life. Hung himself from the bridge and I found him. I cut him down. I didn't want the family to suffer, so I said I'd found him floating there on my morning walk. It was better for everyone."

A clock somewhere in the depth of the house struck the hour.

"Oh, dear," the priest said. "I've missed my train."

ǫǫǫ

The sun had set by the time Liam made it to the coroner's office. Before his election, the coroner, a grave bearded man dressed as undertaker, had been a barber. He agreed with Liam that if the boy had hung himself, then old Doc McPherson was sure to have known about it. He would have seen the rope burns. But the doctor had lied, saying the boy had fallen and drowned, confirming the priest's story.

"The old lady was right," the coroner said. "They lied to her, doctor and priest. Be that as it may, the inquest will find that Mrs. Maguire died by accident."

"But Father O'Brien killed her! He admitted as much."

"He admitted to self-defense and nothing else. A jury would not convict him, a priest, and a crippled old man at that. And who am I to take on the Church? Adams is a Catholic town. My constituents are Catholic. I dare not. I'd lose my job."

And then he would be a barber again.

"And what about the boy? He was driven to suicide by the priest."

"There's no evidence to suggest Father did anything to that boy. Only the ramblings of an old crazy, and now dead, woman. No eye witnesses to say the priest bothered the boy. No one to say the boy told them such stories. And you cannot make the priest testify against himself. Even I, a mere coroner, knows that. It seems you have no real evidence, do you, Officer?"

The coroner put on a stovepipe hat as he led Liam out of his office and onto the street. "Let them rest in peace, Officer Barrett, both mother and son."

ǫǫǫ

When Liam entered the Barrett home, his mother was rocking, crooning a Gaelic lullaby to the doll in her arms.

Liam squatted beside her rocker. "I've some bad news, Ma," he said. "It's Mrs. Maguire, God rest her soul."

His mother frowned. "She's followed the boy, has she? 'Twas the father, she always said. 'Twas the father." She raised the doll to her shoulder and patted its back. Then her stare turned out the window where she had sat every night since Liam's father died, still waiting for him to come home. There was no talking to her anymore. She was gone again, away with the faeries.

Keenan Powell illustrated *Dungeons and Dragons* in high school, then ditched art for law school and moved to Alaska. A past recipient of the William F. Deeck-Malice Domestic grant, her credits include short stories published in *Mystery Most Historical* (Wildside Press, 2017) and *Busted! Arresting Stories from the Beat* (Level Best Books, 2017).

Visit her at www.keenanpowellauthor.com.

POISONING PENELOPE
by Suzanne Berube Rorhus

The rental car screeched to a stop under the hotel's awning and the bellman took an involuntary step backwards. Two women, mindless of the driving rain, burst from its front seats and jerked their suitcases from the rear before the bellman could cover them with his umbrella. "Welcome to the Intercontinental Boston…" he said, his voice fading away as the women pushed through the revolving door into the hotel's lobby.

"Now, Penelope, don't you worry about a thing," the older woman said, setting down her suitcase and removing her drenched overcoat. "I'll park the car after I check in and then I'll come straight to your seminar. You can check in afterward. Do you have everything you need?"

Penelope patted her satchel. "My presentation and samples are in here," she said. "I'm just nervous, I guess." She pulled her wet blonde hair into a ponytail, using a hair tie from her wrist. Her outfit, blue jeans with high heels and a light green jacket over a white t-shirt, made her look even more young and vulnerable than usual. "I wish our plane hadn't been late. I could have used an hour alone in my room to get ready for this."

"Nonsense, you'll be fine. Remember, you're the expert, and everyone in the room paid big bucks to hear you speak." She hugged the younger woman with the hand that didn't clench her briefcase. "Do you want me to take your suitcase and have it held for you at the front desk?"

"I need some things from it, including the display cover of my book. I'll just take it with me, but thanks anyway. You're the best agent ever, Joyce."

"Remember what I always say, I might be a shark, but at least I'm *your* shark. Now go knock 'em dead, tiger!"

Joyce Redstone, founder of Redstone Reads Literary Agency, picked up her suitcase and strode to the reception area.

"Are you here for the Slash and Slay conference?" the ridiculously young and perky woman behind the counter asked, swiping her credit card.

"Yes. Could I send my bag up to the room with the bellman? I don't have time to go up right now."

"Certainly. Etienne, our bellman, will take it right up. Here's your room key, and if you'd like to park in our covered garage, you have in-and-out privileges. Enjoy your stay!"

After she handed her coat and suitcase to Etienne and parked her car, Joyce stopped by the concierge desk to finalize the details for the two parties she had to host at the conference that weekend. The first, for her cash cow client Annika Lyngblom, author of a bestselling series about a hairdresser who solved murders between perms, would be held that night. Annika decided to launch her latest book, *Trimmed to Death*, at the Slash and Slay conference so more of her fans could attend. At the reception, Joyce planned to serve foods prepared according to the recipes in Annika's books. Not that Annika wrote the recipes herself, of course. She hired a chef to devise fancy appetizers on behalf of her protagonist, who cooked when she wasn't sleuthing or coloring hair.

Tomorrow night's party would be better. Penelope Baird, author of *Poisonous Penelope's Pocketbook of Potions*, had been nominated for an Slayed award by the attendees. If she won, and Joyce was sure she would, the party would last well into the night.

By the time she registered for the conference, Penelope's session had begun. Joyce flipped through her conference guide until she found the "Poisonous Penelope" lecture, held in the Hamilton room from 9 to 10 a.m. She slipped into the back of the crowded room.

As far as she could tell, the seminar was going fine. The room was packed with mystery writers eager to learn about the various potions and poisons displayed on the table in front of Penelope. Joyce anticipated that her agency would soon receive a slew of murder mysteries based on obscure poisons.

On the overhead screen, a slide listed all the common household products that contained acetaminophen. When combined with alcohol, acetaminophen was a refreshingly easy way to inflict a painful liver death on a loved one. Around the room, writers wrote furiously.

One gentleman, apparently laboring under the belief that the entire session had been scheduled for his personal consultation, asked Penelope an endless series of detailed questions about his work-in-progress, prefacing each question with long explanations of his plot.

At his insistence, Penelope passed around a small vial containing extract of wolfsbane. "Also known as monks hood or aconitum, the wolfsbane plant has been used as both medicine and poison around the world since prehistoric times. Arrows were tipped in it. Wolfsbane root can easily be mistaken for horseradish, though when applied to the lips it causes intense tingling sensations followed by numbness. A lethal dose causes the respiration to become depressed and the heart eventually stops in diastole. Small amounts were used internally in medicines to fortify the body. I guess that's a case of 'what doesn't kill you makes you stronger.'"

Joyce smiled when the crowd chuckled at Penelope's joke. She was a shoo-in for the Slayed, and frankly it couldn't happen to a nicer gal.

"Now," Penelope continued, placing the wolfsbane on the table and picking up another bottle. "Let me tell you how to make a healthy person die of a heart attack and have it be attributed to natural causes. It just takes foxglove," here she waved the vial "and patience."

After the lecture, Joyce repacked Penelope's bags while her client answered questions and signed copies of her book for her fans. With each signature, Joyce heard a cash register "cha-ching" in her head.

Joyce carried her briefcase and Penelope's satchel while the younger woman pulled her suitcase and toted her still-wet coat. They took the elevator down to the lobby level and walked towards the reception area, chatting excitedly about the warm reception Penelope had received.

A blast of cold wind struck Joyce in the face and she turned towards the front doors. She shivered, and not just from the cold. The cash cow herself, Annika Lyngblom, had just arrived. Joyce forced a smile onto her face.

"Annika, darling, so good to see you," she said, air kissing her client's cheeks.

Annika, flanked by Etienne and a cartload of matching luggage, said, "Oh, Joyce, I'm so glad to run into you. You wouldn't believe the time I've had. The weather in Boston is simply beastly today." She launched into a list of complaints that incorporated not only the weather, but also the city traffic, the hotel location, and the early hour. Etienne stood patiently next to the luggage cart, but Joyce saw Penelope edge away from the group and head to the reception desk. The girl was no fool.

"So if you could hurry back with that, that would be wonderful," Annika said.

"Pardon?" Joyce must have missed something in the tirade.

"My shampoo. You know I can't look my best if I have to use the hotel shampoo. I'd have to cut my hair off to let it recover. I've found a salon that sells it less than ten miles from here, so that should be okay. Just send it up to my room when you return, please."

"Just a minute! You and I are supposed to go over your contract this morning. I've got a major studio wanting to option your first book and you can't keep putting them off. I don't have time to hare all over the city looking for shampoo."

Annika's predatory eyes sharpened. "Did you get all the changes made to the contract I wanted?"

"I got more money for you," *and for me*, Joyce added mentally. "I also arranged for you to write the screenplay on spec. You have a non-speaking role in one scene, but there is no way they are going to make you a producer on this movie. You're not putting up the money and you have no experience in film. This is a good contract."

"Really, Joyce, I could have negotiated better myself. Tell you what, why don't you hurry back with the shampoo and I'll check into my suite. I'll meet you in the lobby bar in half an hour and we can look at this contract then. Deal?"

Annika and Etienne headed for the reception area, leaving Joyce with her briefcase, Penelope's satchel, and no coat. She sighed. Sometimes she really did hate being an agent.

ϱϱϱ

Annika tapped the bell on the reception desk, though the clerk was only three feet away. "Annika Lyngblom," she said and waited for the flash of recognition. None came. Really, people were so illiterate these days. "The author? I want to check in."

The clerk tapped her long manicured nails against the keys. "I'm sorry, Ms. Lyngblom, but the plumbing in your suite flooded last night. That room is unavailable. I've taken the liberty of booking you a suite at the Ritz Carlton, which we will pay for. Tomorrow night, we welcome you back to the Intercontinental. I'm so sorry for the inconvenience."

Annika stared in disbelief. Did this woman expect her to trek around in this weather? "Don't be ridiculous. Find me another room in this hotel for tonight, then tomorrow night I'll move into my suite. Which you will comp for me."

"I'm afraid we are completely booked tonight, ma'am," the clerk said. "It's this conference. Every room is full."

"I *am* the conference! I'm the headlining author; they can hardly hold the conference without me. You'll need to put someone else at the other hotel." Annika glanced around the lobby, spying Penelope.

"You there! There's been a mistake with your room. You're booked at the Ritz Carlton."

Penelope stuffed her room key into her pocket as if afraid Annika would wrestle it from her. "I'm already checked in, and I have no intention of switching hotels." Her voice barely squeaked.

"Well, I suppose I could share the room with you," Annika allowed. "I certainly hope you don't snore. What's our room number?"

Penelope could only shake her head vigorously. Her wide, frightened eyes sought help from the reception clerk, but no assistance came.

Annika studied her face closely. "We have the same agent, do we not? I'd hate to tell Joyce that you forced me to stay at another hotel, thus rendering me incapacitated for my many public appearances this weekend. That would unfortunately cost dear Joyce a great deal of money. Besides, think how helpful it could be for you to have an author of my stature guiding your career. Or how unhelpful it could be to have me as an enemy?"

After a few more minutes of negotiation, Penelope agreed to share her room for one night. The clerk removed the room charge from Penelope's bill and fawned over her in gratitude.

With Etienne and the luggage cart leading the way, they set out for the elevators.

ꝏꝏ

After Penelope ushered Etienne out the door with a generous tip, she returned to her room to find Annika's suitcases strewn across one bed. Her coat draped over the single chair and her toiletries bag blocked the bathroom entrance. Annika herself lay on the other bed, one arm over her eyes.

"Honestly, this room is so small! I don't know how you manage without a suite. Still, at least I'll be in my suite tomorrow, thank God."

Penelope hoisted a bag off the bed, hoping to find enough space to sit.

"Gentle with those bags, please," Annika reprimanded her. "I don't want my clothes to get wrinkled. While I'm thinking about it, I know we're 'roommates,', as it were, but I'd prefer if you didn't use my things, especially my toiletries. So unhygienic, you know, plus they are quite expensive. I need to look my best for this evening."

She picked up the phone. "That reminds me." She dialed the front desk, arranging for a half hour massage in the room. Penelope wondered if the fee would appear on her hotel bill at check out. She made a mental note to inquire at the front desk.

"You won't mind giving me a bit of privacy during my massage, will you? So much more relaxing to be alone, don't you think? Tell you what I'll do, though. Tonight is the launch party for my newest book, *Trimmed to Death.* Why don't you come as my guest? I'm sure you can meet people who could help your career. You *have* written a book, I assume?"

ϘϘϘ

Joyce shook her drenched hair and stepped to the bellman's station, smiling at the young man behind the desk. "Could you please run this up to Penelope Baird's room? I don't know her room number." She handed him Penelope's satchel.

That done, Joyce took her briefcase and the bag containing Annika's shampoo to the lobby bar. With a groan, she plopped into a booth and caught the server's eye. "Irish coffee," she said, "very hot and very strong."

"Excuse me, aren't you Joyce Redstone?"

Joyce glanced up at the middle aged man who stood next to her booth. She debated whether to admit her identity, but the man apparently needed no confirmation. He slid into the seat opposite Joyce and opened his notebook. With a quick push on the bridge of his spectacles, he launched into a lengthy pitch for his nearly completed 'fiction novel'. As if novels came in other flavors.

Joyce tried twice to interrupt to tell him she didn't represent science fiction, but the writer was dauntless. His voice washed over Joyce, eventually soothing her into a trance-like state. When her coffee arrived, she slurped it eagerly, ordered another, and planned what she would say to Annika when the woman eventually showed up.

The Hollywood contract was an excellent opportunity for Annika, and of course, for Joyce. The option fee was generous, an A list actress was already interested, and Annika could write the screenplay despite her lack of experience in film. Most writers couldn't even score tickets to the film's premiere. Annika was crazy if she thought the studio would make her a producer.

After drinking her second Irish coffee to its dregs, Joyce realized Annika had no intention of showing up to discuss the contract. She swore, startling the writer in the middle of describing the miraculous arrival of space aliens in chapter forty one.

Joyce tossed her card onto the table. "Sounds fascinating. Send me the manuscript." She gathered her things and rushed out.

At the bellman's stand, she handed Etienne the bag with Annika's shampoo. "Please send this up to Annika Lyngblom's room," she said. She checked her watch. If she hurried, she could chat with her fellow agents for a few moments before their two pm panel discussion.

ℚℚℚ

Penelope opened the door. Etienne the bellman and an older woman stood in the doorway. Etienne handed her a small paper bag.

"This is for Ms. Annika Lyngblom," he said, "and Mrs. Eggleston is here for her massage appointment." Penelope tipped him again, ushered the woman into the room where Annika lay sprawled on her bed, then peered into the bag. Shampoo, obviously one of the 'expensive toiletries' Annika had warned her not to touch. Penelope took the bag into the bathroom, leaving precious Annika alone with her masseuse.

After disrobing, Penelope drew a hot bath and rummaged through Annika's toiletries bag. She selected conditioner, a loofah, and body lotion, lining them up along the edge of the bathtub next to the shampoo.

She sank into the tub, basking in its warm embrace. Pouring a generous amount of Annika's shampoo into the palm of her hand, she scrubbed her hair. The shampoo tingled on her skin and she felt a rush of heat on her scalp. "Quality stuff," she murmured, relaxing as the shampoo soaked in.

"I can't believe Queen Annika travels without bubble bath," she grumbled. She reached again for the shampoo, this time frothing it into the bathwater. The bubbles didn't last long, but the tingling sensation spread to her entire body.

She tilted her head back and closed her eyes.

ℚℚℚ

After her session, Joyce slipped into the restroom. The agents panel had actually been rather amusing. The moderator had asked the panelists to describe the worst query letters they'd ever received, and the resulting conversation had been entertaining.

Alone in her bathroom stall, Joyce enjoyed a moment of peace. The problem with these conferences was that all the wannabe writers in attendance wanted her to represent their books. Everyone wanted a piece of her. She'd been here all day, and still hadn't even seen her hotel room.

"Ms. Redstone? I saw you come in here," a woman's voice said from the other side of the stall door. Joyce jerked and passed gas in surprise. She tried to peer through the gap in the door, but could only see a flash of violet from the woman's suit.

"I wanted to give you my manuscript," the woman continued. A thick envelope slid under the door, bumping against Joyce's stilettos. "That's just the first ten chapters. You can download the rest from my website."

Joyce rolled the envelope and stuffed it into the sanitary napkin wastebasket mounted on the stall wall. Just another couple of hours and she'd be able to relax in her room. She would skip the conference banquet and evening entertainment for sure.

ƍƍƍ

In the hospitality room, Joyce made a meal of canapés and bourbon. The food was actually pretty good. Annika's chef consultant must really know her stuff.

She cringed when the guest of honor spied her from across the room and headed toward her. Annika trapped Joyce and launched into a litany of complaints.

"Can you believe the nerve of this hotel?" she demanded. "Denying me my suite and forcing me to bunk with that dreadful woman!"

Joyce struggled to keep up. "You're sharing a room with someone?" *Poor soul*, she thought. "Who? Why?"

Annika was only too happy to bring her up to speed. "And not only does Penelope insist on moving my things around, she also used all my expensive toiletries! She used my nice shampoo, then left it on its side and let it flow down the drain. I swear, I'm going to kill that woman when I get my hands on her." Nearby guests edged away from Annika and her fury.

"Penelope used your shampoo?" Joyce asked, horrified. Annika seemed pleased by her shocked expression.

"Exactly!"

The woman in question chose that moment to enter the hospitality suite. Annika stomped over to her and began a heated discussion in forced whispers. Joyce turned back to the bar and demanded another bourbon. "Hold the ice this time."

She finally caught up with Penelope at the canapés table. The younger woman had selected a plateful of goodies and was determinedly chomping her way through them.

"Are you all right?" Joyce asked. The young woman looked shaky and glassy eyed. Penelope's forehead glistened with sweat and her normally bouncy hair hung in limp curls around her face.

"I'm not feeling very well," Penelope said. "It's so warm in here. Must be all the hot air coming out of the royal windbag." She turned her back to Annika and popped a stuffed mushroom in her mouth.

"Why don't you lie down?" Joyce asked. She placed her hand against Penelope's temple. Her pulse raced and the skin felt clammy.

"Annika's stuff is everywhere. I'd have to pack her suitcase just to sit down in my own room."

Less than an hour later, Penelope collapsed. Joyce could hear a woman shrieking but did not recognize her own voice until a paramedic gave her a sedative injection and the shrill screams faded.

ƍƍƍ

The next day, Joyce sat in a small conference room with a homicide detective from the Boston police department.

"Are you feeling better, Ms. Redstone?" he asked, pouring her a mug of coffee from a hotel urn. He was perhaps a few years older than Joyce and quite handsome in an uptight way. His hairline had retreated to mid-skull, however.

"Yes, thank you, though of course this has been a terrible shock. Simply terrible. Penelope was one of my favorite clients and her career was just about to take off. I can't believe she's dead. How did she die?" She chewed the tip of her manicured fingernail, then forced herself to appear calm. No need to arouse suspicions in the good detective.

"We're still waiting on the results of the tests from her autopsy, but it appears she died of asphyxia. Basically, she just stopped breathing and her blood pressure hit rock bottom. There were no obstructions in her airways, though, so the cause of asphyxia is undetermined.

"We've gone through the papers and samples in her room. She carried a huge quantity of poisons with her, enough to wipe out the whole conference. It's possible she came into contact with something unintentionally."

After thirty minutes of questions about Penelope's movements on the day of her death, the detective asked if the late Ms. Baird had had any enemies.

"No, of course not!" Joyce said. "Everyone loved her."

"We've learned she'd been in an argument with a Ms. Annika Lyngblom before her death. Know anything about that?"

Joyce considered the possibilities. If Annika were in jail, there'd be no question of her producing a film. She'd probably sign the Hollywood contract immediately just for the cash to pay her lawyers.

On the other hand, it'd be just Joyce's luck to learn the contract had a morality clause.

"Oh, that was nothing," she said at last. "The two women were sharing a room. You know how difficult that can be." She chuckled.

"Do keep me informed of your investigation please, Detective. As Penelope's agent, I am responsible for her literary estate. I'd like to deal with opportunities as they come up. Penelope's widower back in New York is going to be too devastated to settle her affairs."

She reached into her purse for a business card. As she withdrew the card, a receipt from a local beauty salon fell to the floor. The detective picked it up and whistled.

"Fifty bucks for a bottle of shampoo," he said. "Thank God I'm going bald."

"Beauty has its price," Joyce said, stuffing the receipt back into the depths of her bag.

ooo

Joyce and Annika checked out the next morning. Joyce stopped by the concierge desk to ship Penelope's suitcase home to her husband, but she'd tucked the satchel with Penelope's potions into her own luggage.

Annika clung to Joyce's arm. "You have no idea how dreadful it's been," she whimpered. "That ridiculous detective asked *so* many intrusive questions."

"Don't worry about it, darling," Joyce said. "He's just doing his job and we're free to go now. Let me tell you what I've arranged for you." She signaled the bellman to load Annika's luggage into her rental car.

"You and I are heading to the Catskills to a fabulous spa I know up there. I've scheduled the works – massages, facials, pampering, everything. We'll go over this contract and relax."

She helped her client into the car.

"But first, we'll stop by the salon and get another bottle of your favorite shampoo."

Suzanne Berube Rorhus attended the Squaw Valley Community of Writers and is an active member of Mystery Writers of America and International Thriller Writers. Her published short fiction has appeared in *Ellery Queen Mystery Magazine* and in various anthologies. In addition to writing, she is now in her first semester of law school.

GEORGE SAYS
by Steve Roy

The gun's muzzle was as dark as a bad girl's dream. It made Leo Rosen think of the Callahan Tunnel on the north-end and that, of course, made him queasy. In truth, many things made Leo Rosen queasy; airplanes, long car trips, dog drool, the smell of gasoline, magnolia trees, women with tattoos on their ankles, green onions and of course, Katie Couric. He hadn't lived in Boston since he was a teenager, but his dad had always taken the Callahan when they'd go to Salisbury on hot days in the summers and Leo had always hated it. Maybe he was just claustrophobic, but even now, the thought of that damned tunnel turned his stomach sour.

"Who the hell are you?" said a hoarse voice from behind the desk. Despite the deeply shadowed office, Leo could see that the owner of that voice held an unsteady grip on a very large revolver.

The guy with the gun reached over to a bankers lamp on the desk and a dull glow of yellow sprinkled across the room. Leo could see more clearly now. Before him, sat a man with a once athletic build, blonde hair receding from a patrician forehead, watery blue eyes with red splotches, dark circles beneath those eyes and a pair of ears which seemed much too small for his head.

He had a store-bought tan, wore a shocking-pink polo shirt, and sported a Rolex the size of a softball on his right wrist. It was a Submariner and though only the stainless version, it still must have set him back six-grand at Sidney Thomas on Boylston. So the guy was flashy, but all in all, he was presentable enough. The gun though, that was the real issue, what with it having a barrel large enough to garage a Mini Cooper and the fact that it was pointing directly at Leo's teeth.

Leo was not an expert on such matters, but he guessed that gun to be a .357 or maybe even a .44. He'd seen both on TV cop shows and felt confident it was one or the other. One thing was absolutely certain though, if the guy pulled the trigger it would leave a hell of a hole.

"You're not really gonna shoot me, are you?" Leo said. "I mean I'm not a burglar or anything like that."

He felt he should look around the office to be sure it was just the two of them, but he seemed unable to pull his eyes from the blue steel of the revolver.

"I won't say it again. Who are you and what do you want?" Leo detected a soft edge in the blond guy's words, which almost certainly came from the dwindling bottle of Glenlivet on his desk.

In his head Leo heard himself say, "Things must be pretty bad my friend, if you're getting drunk at 10:30 in the morning." Wisely though, he kept that little thought to himself and instead replied, "I'm sorry. My name is Leo, Leo Rosen."

Despite his precarious situation, Leo's voice held steady. He knew George would be proud.

"I was just looking for suite 410. The lady at the leasing office said it was available for rent. She thought it would make a good place for an accounting office."

"This is Suite 400, flash," the blond guy said. "410's down the hall, near the rest rooms." He'd lowered the gun some. It now pointed at Leo's stomach instead of his face, not much of an improvement, but at least a start. "So, you're an accountant, huh?"

Acid bubbled away in Leo's stomach but he thought it unwise at the moment to reach for his TUMS, so he suffered in silence. Now his indigestion could have come from the smell of scotch in the air, he'd never been partial to scotch. It could have been the Spanish omelet he'd eaten earlier at the Sunrise Café off of Salem Street. The proprietor, a Mr. Vartibidian, had promised to hold the green onions, but he was Armenian and Leo wasn't sure he trusted Armenians all that much. Most likely though, it was due to the thought of developing a second belly button, courtesy of the shaky hand holding the large gun. Such things had a tendency to cause agita. George called it a cost of the trade.

"This your place, then?" Leo asked, always the agreeable conversationalist.

"Yeah, that's right. Name's Carl, Carl Marshall," he replied. "Marshall and Pickering Investment Management." Marshall waved his gun at the words stenciled across the frosted glass then returned his aim to Leo's midsection. "Like it says on the door."

"Sorry, I didn't notice." Leo cracked a sheepish grin as he retrieved his glasses from his jacket pocket. "Guess I should have used these."

Marshall tensed in response, narrowing his eyes and extending his arm directly at Leo's stomach. "Easy friend," he said.

It was a stupid mistake, one he never should have made, and for a brief moment, Leo felt sure everything might just spin away and Marshall would indeed pull that trigger.

"Oh my," he said, placing a pair of well-used, wire frames on his nose. They hung slightly to the left and had a small wrap of scotch tape which steadied one arm of the frame where a screw had gone missing last year. The tape itched but he decided against scratching. He liked the current configuration of his belly button just fine, thank you very much, but he did make a mental note, once again, to fix those frames.

After giving Leo the once over again, head to waist and back again, Carl smiled, shook his head sadly and lowered the gun to his desk. The gesture wasn't overtly dismissive, yet the message was clear. Marshall felt no danger from the little accountant.

"Sorry about the gun. I guess I'm just jumpy," Marshall said. "Have a seat, Mr. Rosen. Let me offer you a drink by way of apology?"

Marshall raised the cut glass tumbler in his hand and contemplated the amber liquid there. It only came a third of the way to the glass's rim now.

"No, thank you, Mr. Marshall. I don't drink," Leo said without taking the proffered chair. "Listen, I don't mean to pry, but my friend, George, said I should inquire about the building security before I sign a lease and now, well that seems like particularly good advice. How safe is this area? Do the other tenants on your floor arm themselves? Does Mr. Pickering feel the need to go around with a gun as well?"

"Relax, Leo. There's nothing to worry about and there are no other tenants on the floor. Both 410 and 420 are empty, have been for at least six months. Damn economy is killing everyone, I guess, and there never was a Pickering. I made the name up 'cause I liked the way it sounded. As for the building, well you're as safe here as in your own mama's womb."

"Then, why?" Leo gestured toward the pistol.

"Oh, this?" he said, wiggling his wrist and the gun in a dismissive turn. "Just a short-term misunderstanding, that's all. See, I've developed a bit of a cash flow problem recently and I'm being cautious while I work it out."

"I understand, Mr. Marshall. I guess I'm not always as cautious as I should be, and my friend, George, has suggested repeatedly, that I try to be more careful. Still, guns do make me nervous." Again, Leo gestured to the pistol on the desk.

"Oh, I get you," Marshall said and slid the revolver into the open drawer to his right. He returned his attention to his dwindling drink, finished it and filled the glass again, pouring almost all of the remaining scotch and skipping the ice.

A sudden spray of lights erupted from a video poker site on Marshall's computer. They danced across Marshall's face, green blinking to red and then to blue and back again. It was followed by a flurry of bells and whistles, which startled Leo.

"Look at that. I drew a fucking inside straight," he said, staring at the screen in disbelief. "Can you believe that shit? I just won two hundred dollars on a hand and I wasn't even trying to play. Where the hell was that luck last Tuesday?"

He hit six or seven key strokes then turned back to his visitor, who asked, "What happened Tuesday, if you don't mind my asking?"

Leo was like that. Always asking questions that probably weren't his business. No one ever seemed to mind, though. He was easy to talk to, easy to like. George often said it was his face, friendly and non-threatening. Leo disagreed. He'd never cared for his own appearance, thought of his own face as bland and nondescript, much like the rest of him. He barely topped the chart at five-foot six, had a lean, pale face with wispy hair and watery green eyes. Still, he did have a nice smile, an easy smile, the kind of smile you could trust. That's what George said and at least on that point Leo had to agree.

Marshall took a deep breath then smiled at Leo Rosen again. "Don't know why I'm telling you this, Leo, but you seem like a good listener and I gotta tell someone, I guess. You see, I gamble a little. On occasion, I lose a little. On some occasions, I lose a lot."

Leo nodded and smiled, more of a grin, actually, one nearly as bent as his eyeglass frames. Still, the friendly tilt of his head encouraged Marshall to continue. Leo was indeed a good listener.

"In general, I'm pretty good at it though, and it gives me what I can't find anywhere else. That rush is better than sex and it don't nag you about mowing the lawn the next day."

Again, Leo nodded and again he smiled his crooked grin. He understood all about rushes and needs, though he'd never played poker himself.

"Thing is, I hit a cold spell a couple of months back. Happens to even the best of us, am I right? I was into a couple of different guys, nothing too large, three or four grand apiece. I always spread the risk around so even if I ran into a bad streak, I'd never owe any one book enough to make them take much notice. Still, I'd started to feel itchy lately, like maybe I'd used up my luck here and what I needed was to get out from under. You know, clear the slate. When you're running cold, sometimes you gotta shake things up. You ever hear that?"

Leo shook his head slowly as his smile softened further.

Marshall stared briefly at his now empty glass. It no longer seemed to offer what he needed, maybe because it was empty or maybe because someone was actually listening for a change.

"Anyway, I heard about this game they run on Tuesday nights, up in the penthouse of the Battery Wharf Hotel. It belongs to a guy, name of Angelo Carrano. You ever hear of him?"

"No, can't say that I have," Leo said as he stepped a bit closer. Marshall didn't seem to notice. He was intent on finishing his story.

"Carrano's a made guy and he doesn't let just anyone into his game. You need a rock-solid recommendation from someone with real juice and there's a minimum twenty-five large to buy in. Sounded like just the thing to change my luck, right? So, I moved some money here and some money there and I called a guy who knew another guy and long story short, I'm sitting at the table with some real high rollers. Nothing like what I'm used to, I can tell you that. There were even a couple of guys from high up in the Patriarca family there that night, at least that's what someone told me. Anyway, it was a sweet deal, kind of like you see in the movies, high class all the way, food, broads, top shelf booze."

Marshall trailed off and his gaze returned to the empty glass in his hand. After a long and painful pause, Leo broke in, "I take it things didn't work out the way you expected?"

"Amazing grasp of the obvious, my friend," Marshall said. "Let's just say I can't count on not being noticed anymore. Mr. Carrano was kind enough to give me a week to come up with the money. Like I got a hundred and thirty-eight thousand bones just lying around. Well, the week's up and I don't have the money, so I expect some of Carrano's boys will be stopping by any time now."

"That's why the gun?"

"Yeah, that's why the gun. You know the thing is, if I could just get a little space, I might still be able to raise the dough. It would mean selling the house and liquidating what I got left in my accounts. It'd also mean starting over somewhere, but I could do it. I'm still pretty young, you know? I still got the gift. All I need is a little space and a little time."

Leo Rosen removed his glasses and returned them to his jacket pocket.

"Carrano's not known for his patience but maybe I can talk him into giving me a few more weeks." Marshall eyes blazed with false hope, despite an emerging glimmer of tears. "Maybe he'll listen. You think that's possible, Leo?"

"Who knows, Mr. Marshall?" Leo said. "Anything's possible. I've become something of an optimist myself in recent years. It's like my friend George always tells me, no matter how bad things may look at the moment, you get a fresh start every morning."

Marshall glanced back over his left shoulder toward the windows, where Leo had wandered, then returned his attention to that terribly empty glass on his desk. All he could do was shrug.

"No offense friend, but who the hell is this George, anyway? You been yacking about him since you got here." Marshall's words were noticeably sloppier now, a heavy dose of scotch and despair will do that.

"He's just a friend of mine, a good friend. He helped me turn my life around when I hit a rough spot myself a while back. Helped me start a new career. Help me recognize some other things about myself, things I'd always struggled with. I'm a much happier person, now. I'd have to say George is the best friend I've ever had."

"Must be nice, having a friend like that," Marshall muttered to himself.

"Yes, it is. Say, is this your wife, Mr. Marshall?" Leo Rosen asked, inching closer to the desk and pointing toward a framed picture there. "She's quite pretty."

"Yeah, Emily's a peach. I guess I'll have to tell her everything soon enough. I haven't had the heart yet. But I know she'll understand."

"Don't worry about that, Mr. Marshall. She understands."

The .22 coughed once as the slug entered the soft apex of flesh behind the blonde man's temporomandibular joint, the spot where the lower jaw meets the cranium, just below Carl Marshall's left ear. A .22 was good for close work, like around the temporomandibular joint. Small and easy to handle, it fit snuggly into Leo's jacket pocket and the sound it made would have gone unnoticed, even had the other offices on the floor been occupied.

This was one area where Leo and George differed. George liked larger armament and an appropriate distance from his marks, while Leo, on the other hand, was a proponent of close work. He also favored the Remington .22 caliber hollow point in such situations. George had shown him how to cut thin slits across the bullet's indentation to make it mushroom even more upon impact. That way, it would bounce around in the brain pan for a while and it almost never left an exit wound, which saved a good deal on dry cleaning expenses. Carl Marshall was dead before his head hit the desk.

Killing people was Leo Rosen's chosen profession now, just as it had always been George's. It turned out that killing people for money was far more lucrative than the accounting profession and in some strange, hard to define way, more emotionally rewarding as well. Who knew?

In an interesting turn of events though, Leo's current assignment had come not from Angelo Carrano, to whom Carl Marshall owed such a large sum of money, but rather from the lovely Emily. Yes, Emily was a peach. She'd been fully capable of accepting Carl's snoring, his occasional infidelities, the fact that he left his dirty underwear wherever it happened to fall. She'd even been willing to put up with his gambling, as long as it didn't impact her own lifestyle too greatly, but the thought of losing her home at the unfortunate age of forty-three proved a bit more than she could bear.

She'd found Carl's marker Wednesday morning, after retrieving his well-used socks and boxer briefs from beneath the bed and hanging up his gabardine slacks in the closet. The amount of the marker was clearly more than he could hope to repay. So, she made the decision right there to clear the slate and collect a tidy insurance benefit in the offing. Emily was nothing, if not practical and she had grown up in the north end, after all. George was not Boston based, but his work was well respected in the community. Calls had been made to people, who knew people, who knew people and somewhere along the line someone knew of George and that in turn had led to Leo.

"Yes, a friend like George is one of life's greatest comforts, Mr. Marshall," Leo whispered to the rapidly cooling body of Carl Marshall. "He's taught me so much. In retrospect, some of those things might have proven valuable to you, as well."

Leo Rosen reached over and pulled the chain on the banker's lamp, blanketing the newly silent Carl Marshall in shadows once again.

"First, never point a gun at a man, unless you intend to shoot him."

Leo pocketed his .22.

"Second, never shoot a man, unless you intend to kill him."

Leo closed the office door behind him.

"And finally, never eat green onions in the morning."

Leo belched deeply then popped a couple of cherry TUMS from the roll in his pocket, chewing them with vigor. He now felt certain Mr. Vartibidian had lied to him earlier. There had indeed been green onions in his omelet. It was true, you really couldn't trust an Armenian. Leo made a mental note to speak to Mr. Vartibidian on the matter before he left town.

Steve Roy lives in Atlanta, Georgia. He is an attorney by training, a business owner of necessity, but a writer by choice, with stories published in *Read by Dawn*, *Shadow Regions*, *Futures Mystery Magazine*, *Deathlehem Revisited*, *Crooked Holster* and *Busted! Arresting Tales from the Beat*. He is seeking an outlet for his second novel, *Wednesday's Child.*

EMILY
by Harriette Sackler

Detective Sally Metcalfe sat at her desk, sipping coffee and browsing the morning's paper. She'd arrived at the station a half hour before to allow for some pre-shift quiet time. When her desk phone rang, she grabbed the receiver right away.

"Oakmont P. D., Detective Metcalfe."

"Detective, Ed Fogel here. Donny White and I are over at the cemetery. Responded to a 911. Got a body over here."

"Bet there are plenty of them where you are," Sally couldn't help but see the humor in the situation.

"Yeah, you're right, Detective, but this one's above ground. Young woman. Looks like a fatal head injury. Reported by an older woman walking her dog."

"Too bad. Silvio and I will be there in ten."

When Sally disconnected from the call, she stood and put on the jacket that was hung over the back of the chair."

"Dom," she called to a guy several desks over, "we got a case."

ୡୡୡ

By the time they pulled up to the entrance to Liberty Cemetery, the sun had begun brightening the sky. They could see the two patrol officers, talking to the woman who had reported the body. She held a tiny dog in her arms.

"Hello Ma'am," Sally said. I'm Detective Metcalfe and this is my partner, Detective Silvio. Can you tell us what happened?"

"Well, I was taking Ginger for her early morning walk and found this poor girl right here at the entrance to the cemetery. Since George, my husband, always makes me take a cellphone with me when I take Ginger on walks, I called 911 right away.

"Thank you for doing that, Mrs....."

"Waldron, Susan Waldron."

"Thank you, Mrs. Waldron. Is there anything else you can tell me? Did you see anyone else nearby? Hear anything?" See anything suspicious?"

"No, I'm sorry, Detective. There was nothing. Just that poor girl."

"If you happen to remember anything, here's my card. You can contact me day or night. We have your contact information also. Now, I'd like these two officers to drop you off at your home. Best not to be walking around alone right now."

ୡୡୡ

The young woman looked to be in her early thirties. She was stylishly dressed in a tailored pantsuit and wore earrings, a watch, and bracelet, which indicated that robbery wasn't a motive. Her handbag lay nearby. Her wallet appeared intact, with cash and credit cards in place. A driver's license identified her as Molly Stern, with a San Francisco address. They learned from a supply of business cards that she was a clinical psychologist. Sally would place a call to the practice as soon as business opened at 9:00 a.m. California time. She couldn't find a local number anywhere. There was no cell phone in her purse.

When the coroner arrived on scene, a preliminary exam placed time of death between 9:00 p.m. and midnight the night before. It didn't appear that the victim had been sexually assaulted, but after the autopsy, more definitive info would be available. No robbery. No sexual assault. So far, this case was a puzzlement.

ooo

Sally was able to speak to the secretary at Community Psychology Associates a little after nine in the morning, their time. The woman was extremely distraught to learn of Dr. Stern's death, but couldn't think of one person who had ill feelings toward her. She reported that Dr. Stern was spending the summer back East researching a book she was completing on the subject of creativity and depression. She had cited a number of prominent writers and artists who had suffered from this mental disorder and Emily Dickinson was the focus of her research. Since Amherst and its surroundings housed Dickinson's diaries and original works, Stern intended to spend her summer in the area, examining original materials and conferring with academics who were experts on the prominent poet's life and work.

She also was able to get contact information for Dr. Stern's parents who had retired to Arizona. She dreaded making the heartbreaking call to them about their daughter's death.

Sally learned that Dr. Stern was staying with a close college friend who was now on the faculty of Oakmont College. The secretary provided her with the address and phone number of Vanessa Howard and after disconnecting from the San Francisco call, Sally wasted no time in contacting Dr. Howard. Her phone went straight to voicemail, so Sally left a message asking her to call as soon as possible regarding an urgent matter.

ooo

Just as Sally was about to run down the block to pick-up some lunch, her phone rang.

"Metcalfe speaking."

"Detective Metcalfe, this is Vanessa Howard returning your call. I apologize for not getting back to you sooner. I was teaching and just got your message. What can I do for you?"

"Dr. Howard, I was told that Molly Stern was staying at your home this summer. Is that correct?"

"Yes it is," Dr. Howard responded. "Is something wrong?"

"Can you tell me when you last saw her?"

"Let me see. It was Tuesday morning. We were both leaving the house at the same time. I didn't see her Tuesday evening or this morning, but that's not unusual. Molly spends a great deal of time at the college library and comes and goes as she pleases. I assumed that she got home late last night and left early this morning. Detective Metcalfe, is something wrong?"

"I'm so sorry to tell you this. Molly Stern's body was found early this morning in Liberty Cemetery. We're trying to piece together her movements and gather as much information about her as we can."

Dr. Howard's gasp, followed by her expression of grief, came over the phone line loud and clear.

"Dr. Howard, I know this is a terrible shock," Sally said, "but it would be very helpful to us if I could meet with you to help gather details about your friend and her work here in Oakmont."

"Yes, of course," Howard sniffed. "I'm going to head home now. I couldn't possibly teach the rest of my classes today. My teaching assistant can cover for me. Would you like to meet me at my home in, say, forty minutes?"

"That would be fine."

ꝏꝏ

Vanessa Howard lived in a lovely cottage on a quiet street in Oakmont, several blocks from the entrance to the cemetery. Its exterior was well maintained and the front yard was beautifully landscaped and filled with a profusion of roses, daisies, and other colorful flowers. A Honda SUV and a Toyota Prius were parked in the driveway.

Sally's knock on the front door was answered momentarily by a teary-eyed woman who clutched a swath of tissues in her hand.

"Detective Metcalfe?"

At Sally's nod, the distraught woman stepped aside to allow her to enter the house.

"Please forgive me. Molly was my best friend. We met in our freshman year at UCLA and have been close ever since. It was so good having her with me this summer. We can talk in the living room. Can I get you something to drink?"

When they were settled into comfortable chairs in a nicely furnished sitting area in the small living room, Sally addressed Dr. Howard.

"Again, I want to extend my sincere condolences to you. We've notified Dr. Stern's parents, who are on the way from Arizona, and her secretary will make co-workers aware of the death. But now, we need to know as much about her as we can. Any bit of information can be helpful in identifying the person or persons who are responsible. For that reason, you can be of tremendous assistance and your permission to go through Dr. Stern's possessions is of utmost importance."

"I'll be of any help I can," Dr. Howard wiped her eyes. "And, of course, you have my permission to check anywhere in my home for anything that can help you in your investigation.

Molly was using my guest room as home base and her rented Prius is in the driveway. Oh, and please, call me Vanessa."

"Thank you, Vanessa. Now, can we begin with anything you can tell me about Dr. Stern?"

"Well, Molly and I attended UCLA and became friends when we enrolled in several of the same classes. She was very bright and maintained good grades without having to exert much effort. But she had a thirst for knowledge and a great deal of energy. She participated in a number of campus activities, often assuming a leadership role. I, on the other hand, had to work a little harder and spent most of my time studying. But our relationship just clicked, and we became close confidantes and provided support for each other."

Vanessa had to stop for a moment when tears overwhelmed her. When she recovered, she continued.

After graduation, I went East to pursue graduate studies in literature at Columbia, while Molly entered Berkeley's graduate program in clinical psychology. It was during graduate school that she met Ron Ellis, her future husband, who was an adjunct faculty member in the engineering department. Their marriage lasted about four years. But, when Ron felt it was time for them to settle down and start a family, Molly balked. She just wasn't ready, and the strain of the different expectations they held for their marriage caused too much of a rift for them to remain together."

Sally looked up from the notes she was taking.

"Did the marriage end badly?" she asked.

"No, as a matter of fact it didn't. Molly left the marriage with a sense of relief, and Ron remarried about two years after the divorce and now has a family and a happy life."

"Then, what road did Dr. Stern travel?"

"Well, she joined a mental health group of psychiatrists and psychologists in San Francisco. She was pleased with her choice and developed a large, busy practice. And, since she was always an avid reader and possessed an interest in the lives of the writers and poets she admired, she began to explore the possible links between creativity and mental health. Over time, she focused on the life of Emily Dickinson, her favorite poet. Molly was working on a manuscript about Dickinson's secluded life, symptoms of depression, and their effect on her writing. She came to Massachusetts to consult with professors who were expert on the famous poet and to do research at both U-Mass Amherst and Oakmont College."

"Do you happen to know the names of those she consulted?" Molly asked.

"As a matter of fact, I do. I'd be glad to make a list while you check around the guest room. Unfortunately, I don't have a key to Molly's car. She kept that in her purse.

QQQ

Sally went through the contents of the room Molly was using. Neither her laptop nor her manuscript were in the room, and Sally assumed that Dr. Stern kept them with her. Her cell phone, which hadn't been found in her purse or at the crime scene, was also missing.

Sally would request that a crime scene investigator come out to check the Prius while she began interviews with the professors Molly had contacted. Hopefully, something or someone would turn up shedding some light on the case.

QQQ

When Sally returned to the station, she wasted no time checking out the faculty bios for both Oakmont College and U-Mass Amherst. There were five names on the list that Vanessa Howard had prepared for her. Two of the professors taught at Amherst and three at Oakmont. All five were faculty in the literature departments of their respective institutions. One, Dr. Harrison Manning, was the chair of the department at Oakmont. After reviewing their impressive credentials, Sally could well understand why Dr. Stern had sought their input.

After placing phone calls to all of them, emphasizing the necessity of meeting as soon as possible, Sally was able to set up appointments with all but Dr. Manning for the next day. A call to the CSI unit resulted in a negative response regarding possible evidence in Dr. Stern's car. With no cell phone and no laptop available, it would be much harder to close the case.

QQQ

The next morning, Sally arrived at the Amherst campus of the University of Massachusetts at nine. With assistance from students on their way to class, she made her way to the Literature Department's faculty offices. Professors Thomas Leland and Beatrice Smithson greeted her and expressed distress at Molly Stern's death. They both reported that they had found the young woman to be enthusiastic and committed to completing her manuscript. She had consulted them regarding their research of the latter years of Dickinson's life. They had been looking forward to reading the text, which promised to be a unique clinical analysis of the famous poet's life. They had not read her work-in-progress, but were happy to share their research and perspectives with Dr. Stern. Neither could imagine who would wish to harm her or why.

Molly's next back-to-back appointments were with Professor Jan McQueen and Adjunct Professor Linda Wilson at Oakmont College. She would have been happy to meet with them jointly, but their schedules didn't permit that.

Dr. McQueen was a delightful grandmotherly woman. She exuded a warmth that no doubt made her a favorite with students. But it was almost immediately apparent to Molly that this woman was an expert in her field and would be a fair, but demanding, instructor.

"Dr. McQueen, is there anything you can tell me about your meeting with Molly Stern that might help us in our investigation?"

The professor considered the question for a moment before responding.

"No, there was nothing about my meeting with Dr. Stern that could help. However, my colleague, Linda Wilson, will undoubtedly have some information that might be of interest to you."

Sally wanted to hear more.

"Can you tell me what that might be?"

"Well, I'd prefer she spoke to you directly, Detective. I wouldn't want to pass along secondhand information that might not be accurate."

"I understand, Professor. I'll be meeting with Dr. Wilson in about an hour. Thank you for the heads up."

Both women rose, signaling the end of their conversation.

"It was a pleasure meeting you, Professor. Thank you for your help."

"Good luck, Detective. That lovely girl's murderer needs to be punished."

ooo

Linda Wilson was a skeletal, high energy young woman. Sally guessed that she probably expended every calorie she ate just keeping herself in gear. Sally liked her immediately.

"Detective, I must say, that after spending all my days researching and lecturing about dead authors and poets, a murder investigation is quite an interesting change of pace. How can I help?"

Sally couldn't help but laugh at the irreverence of the statement.

"I met with Dr. McQueen this morning, and she mentioned that you might have some information that could impact our investigation. Can you tell me about it?"

"Yes, of course. Just something I overheard. Whether it's important or not is for you to determine."

Dr. Wilson sat back in her chair, appearing to consider what she was about to say.

"Detective, Harrison Manning is the chair of our department. His office is next door to mine. To be perfectly honest, he no longer enjoys the high esteem of his colleagues as he once did. He hasn't published in years and seems to have lost interest in his position at the college, Word in the pipeline is that if he doesn't take retirement very soon, he'll be replaced as chair."

"I see," said Sally. "That would be quite a blow to him, I'm sure. You know, I've left several messages for him but haven't gotten any reply. I was informed that he was one of the professors that met with Dr. Stern."

"I know he did," Linda Wilson replied. "And I also know that he had a heated argument with her."

"Please, tell me whatever you know about it."

"I was returning to my office after class when I met Dr. Stern. She was about to enter Harrison's office and didn't look terribly happy. We greeted each other, and I continued on to my office. Several minutes later I heard raised voices from next door. Although I couldn't hear most of the exchange, I did hear Dr. Stern accuse Harrison of plagiarism and threaten to destroy his career. Needless to say, that would be an extremely serious charge to make against any academic, no less a department head. Shortly thereafter, I heard Harrison's door slam and I assumed Dr. Stern had left. Several hours later, Harrison left his office and didn't return for the rest of the day. I know this since I hold student conferences on Tuesdays and don't leave here until after nine."

"Dr. Wilson, you've been extremely helpful. If you think of anything else please contact me at any time," Sally said, as she handed the professor her card.

"Good luck, Detective. Dr. Stern was a lovely woman and would have made a significant contribution to the research done on one of this country's foremost poets."

ଉଉଉ

At seven o'clock that evening Detectives Sally Metcalfe and Dominick Reggio stood at the front door of the Manning home. It was a modest, but well-kept colonial on a large tract of property. A small middle-aged woman in tailored slacks and sweater answered their knock. After introducing themselves, they asked to speak to Dr. Manning.

"My husband is in his study. Please come in and I'll tell him you're here. She led them to a comfortable living room that exuded warmth and welcome.

She returned in a moment, followed by a tall, stooped man who looked like he was carrying the weight of the world on his shoulders. His clothing was disheveled and his graying hair appeared uncombed. His skin was pasty and dark shadows circled his eyes. Sally's impression was that she was looking at a man who was unwell.

"Detectives, I'm Harrison Manning. How can I be of help?"

Sally explained the purpose of their visit, and the professor's faced paled even more.

"I am sorry to say that I made an inexcusable mistake that I'll regret for the rest of my life. It was an act of desperation to save my flagging career. But there is no excuse. None whatsoever."

"Dr. Manning, before you say anything more, I think it would be best for us to head down to our headquarters and continue our discussion there," Sally said.

"Whatever you think best, Detective. I would like my wife to accompany me. I think she can be helpful also."

ଉଉଉ

After settling Dr. Manning in an interrogation room with a cup of tea, Sally read him his rights, turned on the video recorder, and asked him to tell her about his interactions with Dr. Stern.

"She came to me to consult about the book she's writing. I'm considered a noted scholar on Emily Dickinson and her poetry, for all the good it's doing me now," he replied.

"Can you tell me what you mean by that?"

Dr. Manning looked down at his hands as though carefully considering his response.

"My professional career has been on the decline of late. To be perfectly honest, for some time now, I've had difficulty keeping up with the responsibilities of both my office as department chair and as an academician. I haven't published at all over the past year and find my attention lapsing at the oddest moments. My memory is no longer as sharp as it once was, and I've been concerned that something is very much wrong."

Sally could feel the man's anguish. His frustration was palpable.

"Have you consulted a physician, Doctor?"

"Yes, I did, Detective and the results were not encouraging. I have been diagnosed with the onset of Alzheimer's and the prognosis is poor. My condition will progress rather rapidly until I will be nothing but a shadow of my old self."

"Doctor, I'm very sorry to hear that," Sally said. "Did your condition impact your interaction with Dr. Stern?"

"I'm sorry to say it did." The professor's voice broke, and it took a moment for him to collect himself.

"Dr. Stern requested that I read her manuscript and offer my professional opinion on the accuracy of its content. She wrote beautifully, and Emily Dickinson came alive on the pages of the manuscript. The depression she suffered and the tragedy of her reclusive life were linked to the creative mind and the toll that mental illness has taken on so many of our most prominent writers, poets, and, artists. Her book promised to be a brilliant addition to both academia and mental health research."

The professor paused to sip some tea from the cup in front of him and then continued in a halting voice.

"It was then that I did something reprehensible, a shameful act that I never would have accepted by any of my faculty or students. I plagiarized portions of Dr. Stern's manuscript in order to write an article for a preeminent literary journal. I don't know what possessed me, but I believe I wanted to publish once more before resigning my position. I wanted to prove myself worthy in the eyes of my colleagues. Just one more time."

Dr. Manning broke down and cried as Sally waited patiently for this broken man to collect himself. It was heartbreaking to watch, and Sally had to remind herself that she was conducting a homicide investigation and the man sitting across from her could very well be a murderer.

When the professor continued, it was in a voice barely above a whisper.

"One day, Dr. Stern visited me in my office to pick up the manuscript she had left with me, along with my comments and observations. When she gathered the packet I had prepared for her, she inadvertently took the draft of the article I had written. The following day, Dr. Stern stormed into my office, accusing me of plagiarism and threatening to expose me to the academic community. I would leave my position in shame, with my legacy destroyed. Before I could respond, Dr. Stern left."

"Professor, did you murder Dr. Stern in order to prevent her from going public with her accusations?"

"Detective, I swear to you on all that is holy, I did not."

ꝍꝍꝍ

Sally questioned Dr. Manning for an additional hour. He told her that after Dr. Stern left his office, he sat at his desk, unable to move. About fifteen minutes later, he was surprised by the arrival of his son, Peter. The young man was a student at U- Mass. in Amherst, and occasionally stopped by his father's office when he came to the Oakmont campus to visit friends.

"Peter told me he had stopped by my office a little earlier, but when he realized I had someone with me, he went down to have a cup of coffee, before returning to see if I was free. I told him about the book Dr. Stern was writing and that she had come to Oakmont to do additional research. We talked for about half an hour, then we both left my office, Peter to head back to Amherst and me to go home."

"What happened when you arrived home?" Sally asked.

"I was very upset and I told my wife what had transpired. She urged me to call Dr. Stern and make the situation right. I did. Dr. Stern accepted my apologies, expressed compassion for my health diagnosis, and told me that as long as I didn't publish my article, she wouldn't take further action. My terrible lapse in judgment would cause neither of us additional pain."

ꝍꝍꝍ

Before sending the Manning's on their way, Sally checked with Dom, who had interviewed Mrs. Manning and didn't believe that she was complicit in Dr. Stern's death. While she was fiercely devoted to and protective of her husband, she felt that bridges had been mended and Dr. Manning could retire without the taint of plagiarism diminishing his long career.

"I also think that Dr. Manning didn't commit the murder, but let's get a warrant for their house, cars, and his office. I also want to have a talk with their son."

ꝍꝍꝍ

After a quick stop at the Amherst's registrar's office to pick up Peter Manning's class schedule and dorm and room number, Sally was able to intercept him as he left a class in the math building.

"Peter, I'm Detective Sally Metcalfe, Oakmont P.D. I'd like to speak to you few moments about a case I'm working on. I know you don't have a class until this afternoon, so is there a quiet place we can talk now?"

Um, I guess so. We can sit outside on the quad, although I don't know how I can help you," Peter replied, looking uncomfortable and confused.

As they settled on a bench on the manicured lawn that served as a relaxing space for both students and faculty, Sally lost no time in asking Peter about his visit to his father's office several days before.

"Peter, Dr. Manning told me that you had stopped by his office at the time Dr. Stern was with him. Did you notice raised voices at the time? Did it appear they were engaged in an argument?"

"No, I didn't hear raised voices coming from my Dad's office." Sally noted that Peter looked like he was ready to bolt.

"Did you know that your father had plagiarized Dr. Stern's work to write a journal article?

Peter's face turned white and his eyes teared. Sally was surprised at his response to her question.

"Detective, I think I need to talk to a lawyer."

ɷɷɷ

Peter had indeed heard Dr. Stern arguing with his father and threatening to ruin his career. He couldn't believe his dad was guilty of plagiarism and wanted to tell Dr. Stern what a terrific guy his dad was and how she must surely be mistaken. He had followed her home and, thus, set in motion a plan to meet with her.

The next night he parked his car near her house and waited for her to return from the college. When she drove into the driveway and gathered her things to enter the house, he intercepted her.

"Excuse me Dr. Stern I wonder if I can have a word with you. My name is Peter Manning."

"Ah, Dr. Manning's son. Would you like to come inside? I'm staying here at my friend's house, and I'm sure she wouldn't mind making some tea for us."

"If you don't mind," Peter said, "I'd prefer to speak to you privately. Would you mind if we took a short drive? There's a diner a few minutes away where we can grab a bite. My treat."

"That sounds fine, Mr. Manning. Although, I can't imagine what you want to talk to me about. My business with your father is completed."

"Peter. Please call me Peter. I just want to tell you some things about my father that you don't know. It's important to me."

"Well, let's go," Dr. Stern responded. "I really could use a hamburger and fries about now."

They drove a few blocks before Peter parked his car at the entrance to Liberty Cemetery.

"Have you ever been here before?" Peter asked his passenger. "Ever since I was a kid, I would come here whenever I wanted to be alone. It's an historic site, you know. Dates back to the Revolutionary War. Some pretty famous people are buried here. If you haven't already, you might want to spend some time looking around when you have the time. Some of Emily Dickinson's relatives were laid to rest in this cemetery. There's one family plot right near the entrance. I know you're writing about her."

"Now that's really interesting," Dr. Stern said. "I haven't visited here before. Listen, wait here a moment so I can take a quick look at that family plot and then we can head for something to eat.

Dr. Stern grabbed her purse and left the car before Peter could accompany her. He turned off the engine and sat back, thinking about the conversation they would have at the diner.

All of a sudden he heard a scream. Jumping out of the car, he ran into the cemetery. Dr. Stern was laying on the ground, her head surrounded by a pool of blood. She must have tripped on the pebbled path and hit her head on a grave marker. He tried to check for life, but it was clear that she was dead.

Peter panicked. Who would believe that he didn't harm her? How could he explain why they were at the cemetery at this time of night? Her conflict with his father would become public. Not thinking clearly, Peter ran to his car and drove away. It wasn't until he reached his dorm that he realized Dr. Stern's lap top and cell phone remained in his car.

ɷɷɷ

When the investigation was completed, Molly Stern's death was ruled accidental. There was no reason to bring Peter Manning to trial. True, he'd failed to report the death, but the D.A. declined to file charges. Why ruin a young man's life for a decision that resulted from shock and fright. Detective Sally Metcalfe had done her job. Molly Stern's tragic death was put to rest, but certainly not to those who loved her. As far as Sally knew, Dr. Stern's book was never published.

Harriette Sackler serves as Grants Chair of the Malice Domestic Board of Directors. She is a multi-published, two-time Agatha Award nominee for Best Short Story. As principal of the Dames of Detection, Harriette is co-publisher and editor at Level Best Books. She is a member of Mystery Writers of America, Sisters in Crime, Sisters in Crime-Chesapeake Chapter, the Guppies, and the Crime Writers' Association. Harriette is the proud mom of two fabulous daughters and Nana to four grandbabies. She lives with her husband and two little Yorkies in the D.C. suburbs. Visit Harriette at www.harriettesackler.com

THE NUT JOB
by Lida Sideris

"A nut job just walked in. Don't give him more than five minutes, Lyndrea. Understand?" Sergeant Low grabbed his steaming coffee mug off my desk and headed back to his office.

I turned toward the three people in the station lobby. Which one did he mean? The man wearing finger puppets on one hand? Or the guy pacing the floor and pretend-playing his saxophone? Either one of these two could be the sergeant's nut job. Or maybe it was the elderly man in the big, bad shades walking toward me. They made him look like an invader from outer space.

"Can I help you, sir?" I asked.

"Yes," he said.

He stood straight despite the fact he was pushing sixty or more. Large, gnarled hands curled on top of his wooden cane, gripping a carved pelican head. It was cold out, but he wore shorts, a plaid button-up, and white Nikes with double Velcro straps. Possibly ex-military if his crew-cut meant anything. His eyes were hidden behind blacked-out lenses.

"Could you remove your sunglasses, sir? We don't permit them inside the station."

"You're younger than I thought," he said.

I could barely hear him above the chorus of ringing phones and chatter. He made no move toward his glasses.

"I'm a cadet," I said. It was only my second week at the front desk, but I didn't tell him that.

His head scanned the room. "Your shift is almost over."

My eyes dropped to my wristwatch. It was ten past four. Twenty minutes to go. How did he know? I cleared my throat and spoke louder. "Sir, please remove your sunglasses." My knee bounced up and down. I'd watched shoplifters, thieves, and Level 3 sex offenders come through the station, but this guy rattled my nerves more than any of them. "I'll go get the sergeant." I stood.

"I'll wait for you outside," he said. He turned away and ambled out of the precinct.

Why would he wait for me? I debated telling the sergeant. What would I say? An old guy who could hardly walk wouldn't take off his shades when I asked him to? The guy didn't break any laws. Yet.

I stayed a few minutes past my shift to help an older lady fill out a stolen purse report.

"You're doing good, Lyndrea," Sergeant Low said. "We're proud of you. Now go home."

"Yes, sir," I said and filed out to the locker room.

I traded in my white shirt, black trousers, and leather shoes for my jeans and sweatshirt. I slipped my backpack over my shoulders and headed out. At twenty, I was on the younger side of the cadet program, but I had me a ton of experience. Real life experience that came from growing up in Compton,

California, home to gangsta rap, Serena Williams, and the only bullet proof, drive-thru funeral home. I'd left that life behind when I turned fifteen and moved to Boston to live with Gran.

The October sun shone weakly when I stepped outside. I waited a few minutes. No sign of the old guy. He wasn't dumb enough to hang around a police station. No reason to. I swung a right and headed home. I got to the Greenway and surveyed the benches. No trace of anyone wearing big, black shades. Hardly any benches were occupied at all. Most folks were on their way home. Like me.

Home was a condo in a brick and stone building at the edge of the North End, where the streets were clean and quiet and safe. People went for walks without nasty name calling or fear of bullets flying. Our building had a bright, eight-story high atrium, a library, and a gym room I could use any time. Bunnies played in the bushes outside. Boston harbor gleamed behind us. It was a slice of heaven.

I was so busy picturing home I didn't see him sitting on a bench outside Faneuil Hall until I was a few feet away. One arm slung casually across the back. A hand curled around the pelican head on his cane. His black sunglasses pointed in my direction. I marched up to him.

"You following me?" I asked.

"It seems to me I was here first. Are you following me?"

I clicked my tongue. "You know that's not right."

"Sit down and I'll explain."

Tourists and office workers crisscrossed the Marketplace. It was a hub of activity…and a good place to be if something sketchy went down. Was something sketchy going to go down? Maybe this guy was in trouble and just needed to talk. People like him came into the station all the time. I sat on the far end of the bench.

"Congratulations on your commendation," he said. "Your keen observations led to an important arrest."

"Oh, is that what this is about?" He'd read about me spotting a robbery suspect and calling in the detectives the other day. "Thank you, but I was just doing my job. Why couldn't you congratulate me in the station?"

"Because that's not all I wanted to say."

He shifted around on the bench. I did the same. I thought of texting Gran to tell her I'd be late, but I didn't want to seem rude. Plus, she'd still be at the Boys & Girls Club. She wouldn't be home until later.

"What else you got?" I asked when he went all "silence is golden" on me. I was getting fidgety.

"You're going to help the detectives make another arrest," he said.

"Now how would you know that? Are you a psychic or something?"

"This isn't about predicting the future. It's about following a lead."

"What do you know about leads?" I asked.

"I worked in law enforcement most of my life. You know from your short time in the station that we deal in facts. And a little bit of intuition. Not fortune telling, Lyndrea."

"How do you know my name? Right. You read about me in the paper. Look, what's this about? I gotta get going."

"Like you, I lived in Los Angeles," he said.

Wait a minute, was that in the paper?

"I'm retired, but my connections keep me informed."

"L.A. connections in Boston?"

"I was based in Los Angeles. My job took me around the country."

A couple stopped near us. He clamped his lips together until they moved out of earshot.

"What's your name?" I asked. He seemed to know a lot about me, and all I knew was that he was an ex-cop or something.

"Simon."

"That's it? What kind of law enforcement were you in, Simon?"

"U.S. Department of Justice."

"For real? Like a special agent or something?" I asked.

He turned his head away.

"How do I know you're not playing with me?"

"You don't," he said.

He got that right. "And now you're retired and living in Boston. How long you been here?"

"A year or more."

He might be legit. "You probably already know how long I've been here," I joked.

"Since you were fifteen. After your mother died of a drug overdose."

I shot up. That was not in the paper. "Okay, that's enough. You using government files to get personal information on me? 'Cause I'm not down with you violating my privacy." I walked away and stopped. I re-traced my steps and peered down at Simon. "You gonna be straight with me? Why are we even talking?"

"Lyndrea, do you know how to beat a lie detector test?"

"There's only one surefire way. Tell the truth."

"That's what I'm going to do, to the extent I can. Sit."

I did as I was told, keeping to my end of the bench. I turned to look at him. "Why didn't you take off those funky glasses when I asked?"

"Photophobia. I suffer from extreme light sensitivity. Indoors and out."

"Is that why you retired?"

"No. I retired before my eye problem," he said. "The sensitivity started when I turned seventy."

"How old are you now?"

"I'll be eighty in a few months."

"Whoa. That's a lot of years to be around. I mean, in Compton, you would be real old. Now that you're retired, are you on some kind of neighborhood watch?"

"In a way, I am. I spend most of my days sitting outdoors. In the Common, the Public Garden, and here. I people-watch." He shifted against the hard bench and passed the cane to his other hand. "But I'm not very good at following persons of interest. I'm a little slower than I'd like."

"Persons of what? Oh wait." I clicked my tongue. "I get it. That's where I fit in. You watch and I follow. Is that what you want? Why would I do something like that? Following people is not my thing."

He slumped a little and his weathered face cracked a grin that took me by surprise. It made him look vulnerable and sweet...almost. Gran got the same look when she was talkin' to the kids she helped. My best guess was this guy was used to having a job, but his body parts weren't working so good any more. He was having trouble completing some assignment he was on.

"You want me to do your legwork, don't you? I mean, literally." I slid closer to him.

"There's been illegal movement of drugs in and out of Boston over the past six months," he said.

"You sure are good at being vague."

"Heroin mostly."

I pulled back and stiffened. Now he'd hit a nerve. Heroin killed Mama.

"The players change, so do the places," he said. "Like you, I have keen observation skills. I've been watching. For the past month, every Wednesday between five and six, an exchange takes place. Right here, in the Marketplace."

"Shouldn't you be telling this to the police? You know I'm just a cadet."

"The police would take my report, file it somewhere, and forget about it."

I couldn't argue with that. This guy had no specifics. He was a nobody with less than enough facts. My next question was one I knew Sergeant Low would ask. "Why don't your old bosses help you out?"

"To my former agency…" He let out a deep breath. "I'm persona non grata."

"What's that mean?"

"I'm not welcome anymore."

"Because you're not supposed to be doing this kind of surveillance?"

"Because when you reach a certain age, people don't take you seriously anymore."

"You don't have much to go on from what I'm hearing."

"And you don't have much to lose by humoring an old man. Especially since you have a vested interest in what I'm saying. Because of what happened to your mother."

"No." I stood again. "I don't do anything that could get me into trouble. I'm just starting out. I want be a police officer. A good one. I'm willing to work hard to do that. But I'm not willing to take a risk on playing with a puzzle that's missing most of the pieces."

I quick-stepped away, aiming for Washington Street. A few more blocks and I'd be home. Five years ago I never thought I'd be living clear across the country, without Mama. When she was high, Mama didn't care about anything or anyone. Including me. I was a persona non whatever to her.

I turned around and wound my way back to the bench. It was empty. I pushed out a sigh and wandered through the Marketplace.

I'd walked about ten yards when I spotted him, standing on the cobblestones, hunched forward, hands resting on the pelican head. His back was to a noisy bar, his attention fixed on the vendor carts across the way. I moved in closer.

"What are you looking at?" I asked.

"Watch the last cart."

Fifteen minutes ticked by while we watched. My legs were aching. I wanted to complain until I remembered Simon had six decades on me. The waiting had to be harder on him. Any time the cart vendor's head turned in our direction, Simon looked away or dropped his chin and fiddled with something inside his jacket. I took his lead and did the same. I was officially sucked into his craziness.

"Here's your chance, Lyndrea," he said. "To cut off a dealer."

The vendor didn't look like any drug dealer I'd ever seen. He was an average Joe in his thirties, wearing a polo shirt and jeans. He handed out hotdogs, pretzels and small bags of nuts to anyone who paid him. Nothing suspicious about that.

The sun dipped downward as we continued our watch. Soon, the only person wearing sunglasses was Simon. And a woman standing near the cart. Her reddish hair was tucked under a bucket hat. A bomber jacket swallowed her upper body. The vendor reached behind his cart and slid open a compartment. He pulled out a brown cloth bag by the handles, big enough to fit Gran's old Bible. He zipped up the top and handed it to her. The bag bulged at the sides. Far as I could tell, no money was paid. The lady cradled the bag against her chest and took off toward Faneuil Hall.

"Follow her, Lyndrea."

"I'm not following anybody."

The woman weaved her way through the Marketplace.

"Use your observation skills," Simon said. "You're good at being invisible."

Now I knew he was a nut job. Either that or he was going blind. "Are you kidding? I'm big, I'm black, and I stick out like a giraffe in a herd of sheep."

"Giraffes know when and how to blend in. So do you. You're even-minded and you're capable of making split-second decisions. You've got what it takes."

"How could you know any of that?"

"Go after her. You'll know when to call it in."

He gave me a little shove. I dragged my feet.

"What are you expecting me to do?" I asked.

"Watch the bag," Simon said, ambling behind me. "She'll head past City Hall and get on Tremont. That's as far as I've gotten."

We were surrounded by tourists. I didn't look like one, except for my backpack and plain looking clothes. My hair was still pulled back in a bun. No one seemed to give me a second glance.

"Lyndrea," he said. "We're losing time."

Right then, I knew I was going to cave in. If this had to do with a drug deal, I needed to know. Plus, he was an old man, maybe suffering from dementia or something, who was asking me for help. Was this what happened to some folks after a long career in law enforcement? They imagine everyone's a crook. I'd give it thirty minutes, tops.

I picked up speed and hustled toward City Hall. No sign of the lady. My head hurt, but more than that, my heart felt bruised. Thinking about Mama did that to me.

I spied a bench on my left. It wasn't like I needed to sit or anything, but I sure could use a bench right now. In two quick moves, I stood on it and peered over the heads in motion along the City Hall sidewalk. I spotted the bucket hat at the end of the line. I hopped down and pushed through the foot traffic.

The woman was crossing Court Street about ten yards ahead. I caught up with her on Tremont and slowed my pace. Fifty feet back seemed a reasonable distance between us. When she stopped at a light, I disappeared into a doorway, but it didn't seem like I needed to. She never once looked behind her. It was fair to say she wasn't expecting trouble. Maybe because all she carried were hotdogs and pretzels for dinner.

I kept it up until she hung a right into the Common. I followed, but stayed on the outskirts, keeping her in view. I pulled out a baseball cap from my backpack and put it on, my steps moved parallel to hers. She strolled past the Bandstand and made a left toward Boylston. Toward me. I stopped in my tracks.

A scraggly man in sweats loitered beneath a lamppost by the tennis courts. He said something to her, but she kept her head down and went right on walking. I picked up my feet.

We crossed paths where the brick walk ended and the asphalt began. I paused and gave her the lead before hustling again, keeping back a good distance. She continued toward Boylston.

Was I crazy to be shadowing someone because an old guy claiming to be ex law enforcement asked me to? Yep. I'd give it five more minutes and head back. The five minutes were on account of I figured she'd be at her destination soon. That bag had to be heavy. Then I'd prove to myself that Simon was just another senior citizen whose brain cells weren't working so good these days.

I reached the street and looked both ways. She'd disappeared. I hurried to the corner of Charles Street. No sign of her. If she wasn't on either road, where would she be? She could have gone into any of the tall buildings lining the streets. Or...she might have gone back in the park. I'd take a quick lap around the Common before heading home.

I never made it to Tremont. I put on the brakes when I saw a head bobbing in the Central Burying Ground. She was crouching behind a tree. No one else was in the cemetery. I padded inside. It was getting dark, which made the place look spooky. The grass was dying out. And the headstones were either sinking or leaning sideways like they were trying to escape.

She knelt behind a grave marker. I could see the top of the brown bag sitting next to her. She dug the ground with a small shovel. I switched direction and called the station.

"This is Cadet Lyndrea Watson," I spoke real low. "Calling in a malicious property damage in progress at Central Burying. Can you send in an officer?"

An officer was always on patrol at the Common. And I had a Taser inside my backpack if I needed one. I disconnected and moved in for a closer look.

She stopped digging to stare up at me. I turned my back to her and inched around the grave markers, making like a tourist. Kneeling down, I wiped the face of a headstone with my fingers. I could see her from my side view, digging faster, deeper, with both hands. I moved to another headstone. She grabbed the bag.

"Come on," I whispered. Where was the uniform?

She was pushing down hard on something. Then she scooped up bunches of leaves and dropped them in front of her until she had a pile nearly a foot high. She could be tampering with evidence. I straightened and edged in her direction.

She stood, a scowl planted on her face.

"Ma'am," I said. "Mind if I ask—"

"Step away from behind the marker, miss," a voice said behind me.

I turned. It was Officer Hassan. He wasn't much older than me, but the uniform gave him the credibility I lacked. And I knew he carried more than just a Taser.

The woman shuffled sideways a few feet.

"I don't want any trouble, Officer," she said, removing her sunglasses. "All I was doing was paying my respects to my great granddad. May he rest in peace. Is that against the law?"

"I'll need to see ID."

I peered over the headstone. The brown bag was missing. The pile of leaves rested between her and the grave marker.

"She was burying something." I pointed to the pile. "Under there."

"Officer, this girl was harassing me. Using language I can't repeat."

"I don't use that kind of language, ma'am," I said. "And this is the first time I'm addressing you." My heart thumped hard against my chest.

"Your ID, miss. Do you have a driver's license?" Officer Hassan asked her.

She nodded and reached into a pocket, beady blues glaring my way. She handed him the small card.

I moved toward the pile of leaves and toed around with my sneaker. The dirt underneath had been newly turned.

"Why were you digging here?" Officer Hassan came around to face the headstone.

"It's a custom in my family to leave food for our departed, instead of flowers," she said. "Food to nourish our ancestors."

"Your ancestor was Wing-Kai Hong?" I read the name on the marker.

"Yes," she replied sharply. "It's an old Chinese custom to leave food on graves."

I did a quick Google search on my smartphone. "She's right," I said. "In the Asian culture food is left for the dead." My cheeks burned. Sweat gathered in my armpits. "But you buried it and hid it under leaves."

She did an eye roll. "That's because of the squirrels, honey. If I left it out, they'd eat it. How would that help my ancestor?"

"Sorry to trouble you, Miss." Officer Hassan passed the license back to her.

"Wait," I said. Squirrels are real good diggers. I stood in front of the marker, blocking it from her view. "What was your relative's name again?"

"Wing," she replied.

"And the rest of it?" I asked.

"I don't have to answer that."

"One more thing," I said and turned to Officer Hassan. "I want to look a little deeper."

"We're done here," he said and whispered to me. "We do not want a lawsuit on our heads."

"Just humor me, please? I have…reason to believe her story requires confirmation."

"It'll be your head," he said and stepped back.

I bent over and stuck my fingernails in the cool, damp earth. I dug like a hungry dog unburying a favorite bone. I uncovered the bag. I lifted it up by the handles, shook off the dirt, and unzipped the top.

"I tried to tell you." She threw me a sour look.

The bag was filled to the brim with walnuts.

"I'll be filing a complaint with your superior. Give that to me." She grabbed the bag, spilling a few on the ground.

"I am so sorry." I'd made a big mistake. "I really am." I reached down to gather the nuts and accidentally stepped on one, smashing it under my sneaker. I sucked in my breath.

The shell cracked in pieces, revealing a fine white powder. The woman bolted. In three seconds Officer Hassan was in pursuit. He tackled her twenty yards out. I called the station.

०००

"How many pounds of heroin did you say?" Gran asked.

"Fifteen," I said. It was good to be home. It took less time than expected to get the woman booked and ratting out her partners. The police had scoured the Marketplace, but the vendor had disappeared. A special agent was posted at the Burial Ground awaiting the pick-up of the drug-filled walnuts. The operation had started a little over a month ago, just like Simon said, and was due to shut down by the end of this week. She was caught in the nick of time.

I'd gone back to Faneuil Hall Marketplace, but couldn't find Simon. I told the station about my informant. They didn't seem all that interested. I'd complete a full report tomorrow.

"You'll get more than a commendation for this one," Sergeant Low had said to me.

I took my place at the dinner table.

"Hold on, don't start eating yet," Gran said. She set three more plates out. "We're expecting company."

"Who?"

"A few volunteers from the Boys' and Girls' Club. I've told everyone there about you. We're all so proud. Me especially." She stroked my cheek and disappeared into the kitchen.

The doorbell rang moments later. I greeted the guests with Gran. They'd barely made it through the door before Gran started gushing about my tracking down a drug smuggler. I'd stopped listening. My attention was fixed on the last guest who'd ambled through the doorway. He'd changed into trousers and a tie, but his gnarled hands still gripped the cane with the pelican's head.

"Lyndrea baby, have you met Simon?" Gran asked. "He's one of our new volunteers. He's an excellent listener. You get acquainted while I check in on dinner." Gran breezed away.

"I looked for you at the Marketplace," I told him.

"It went well?" Simon said, eyes hiding behind the black shades.

"Yes. Because of you. Thank you, a lot." I slipped my arm through his and led him to the table. "Which agency were you with again?"

"DEA, special agent."

"No foolin'? That's where I'd like to work someday."

"I told you. You've got what it takes."

Lida Sideris is the author of *Murder and Other Unnatural Disasters,* a light-hearted mystery set in Southern California. Like her heroine, Lida worked as an entertainment attorney for a film studio. Unlike her heroine, she wasn't blackmailed into solving a murder. Lida was the recipient of the Helen McCloy/Mystery Writers of America scholarship award. To learn more, please visit www.LidaSideris.com.

CORWYN'S HOLLOW
by Shelagh M. Smith

"Mummy, may I go out and play?"

Eight year old Devon Curtin fidgeted in his chair, his spoon making an ungodly clanking against his empty cereal bowl. His mother, Emily, ran a hand through unkempt red hair and muttered, "No, Devvy. Not this morning."

"But why not?"

"It's too cold and raw." Her mouth turned down at the corners as she added, "And we have Mr. Dunning coming by."

Devon stared at his misshapen reflection in the spoon. "I don't like him much."

Emily chewed her lip, already ragged. She felt the same. "It's important to be polite to your elders."

"He's not polite to me."

"He's an adult."

"Why do adults get to be rude?" Emily had to admit she didn't have the answer to that one herself.

"Just be polite, love."

"I'll be very extra polite if you let me go out and play."

"You know I don't like you out there all alone."

"I won't be alone! I'll be with Gilly."

Emily gnawed on a nail. The landlord was coming round again, the cupboards were bare, and here was Devvy going on again about his stupid friend Gilly. Sometimes she wanted to scream at him that there was no Gilly, no Queen of the Faerie Mists, as he called her. It was all a silly child's game, something she was sure he'd drummed up to help manage the loss of his dad, now eight months gone and no return in sight. Even she missed him sometimes, the way he would hunker down with her, wrapping her in his arms, his red and black checked work shirt smelling of smoke and a hard day's labor, though nowadays she was just as happy to have him gone, especially when she remembered how those homey smells turned to whiskey and tobacco.

"Please, mummy," he whined and Emily felt her insides fray.

"Fine," she said. He was out of his chair in a flash, heading for the door. "Don't forget your slicker!"

A splash of yellow raincoat was the last she saw as the door rattled shut behind him.

"Don't be long," she called, but her voice faded away around her. Maybe being gone was the best she could hope for.

ɷɷɷ

Mr. Dunning was right on time, all six foot six of him, toothy and gray haired and oily. Even though it misted outside, Emily saw the sheen of sweat on his broad forehead.

"Good afternoon, Emily," he said, hat in hand. He stepped inside, casting his eyes about and rocking on his tiptoes. She wondered how he avoided knocking his head on the ceiling.

"Mr. Dunning," she said, and awaited his response, the one he always gave.

"Call me Leonard, dear. Lenny, if you like."

She didn't like it, not one bit, but she did it anyway. "Cup of tea, Leonard – Lenny?"

"That would be lovely."

Emily moved to the kitchen and felt his eyes on her backside. "Just a tick." She'd hoped he would stay put in the living room, but knew better. The chair scraped out from the kitchen table, creaking as he sat. She busied herself with the kettle, and waited for him to begin, as he always did, like an old clock that was stuck.

"It's the first of the month," he started.

"So it is."

"And the rent is due again."

"So it is."

"Do you have it?"

She let the silence sit between them. Of course she didn't—he knew she didn't—but she hated saying the words. She hated being a failure as a mum. Was that why Evan left her? Maybe, she supposed. Just had enough one day and vanished into the mists. Why couldn't that happen to dear old Lenny?

"I'm a bit short."

"Speaking of a bit short, where's my boy Devvy this afternoon?"

The phrase grated on her nerves. She wanted to scream that he wasn't *his* boy; he was *her* boy, just as he'd always been. Devvy had never hurt her, never raised a fist, or called her vile names fueled by alcohol and failure as her husband had.

"He's playing," she said and as soon as the words left her lips, he was out of his chair. She felt the warmth of him behind her and tried not to jump when his hands came to rest on her shoulders.

"Shame," he whispered. "I brought him his favorite candies. The lemon drops."

The thought of them made her gag, how he would clumsily press them into her son's hand as he shooed him outside. And Devvy—poor sweet Devvy—would go gleefully. She supposed they reminded him of his father. He always had one in his mouth, working at it and gnawing away, the hard candies making such terrible cracking sounds as they turned to mush.

She turned off the heat under the keening kettle and said resignedly, "Just leave them on the table."

ꝏ

"Gilly, Gilly, Gilly! Don't be silly, silly, silly!" called Devvy, skipping along the rain-slicked grasses that made up the back quarter of the yard.

The rain had mostly stopped and the heavy plastic of his raincoat turned his skin hot and sticky. He swiped back his hood, only to have a shower of raindrops land on his head when he ducked under a heavy branch.

"Come out!" he called, and somewhere behind him, back toward the house, he heard a car door slam shut. He dug in his pockets and pulled out a cellophane wrapped lemon drop. He unwrapped it, popped it into his mouth for a half second to get it good and juicy, and then tossed it into the grass near the briar patch. As he opened another, the bushes rustled.

"Come play, Gilly!" he called. "I've brought your favorite."

He tossed another into the briars. He dug into his pockets and felt only three more. That wasn't good. Maybe he should duck back to the house and see if Mr. Dunning had left extras. He always did. He was nice like that. But just as he turned to go, the bushes parted and Gilly stepped out. Her eyes shone with the dewiness of the misty air.

"Gilly!" he cried. "How are you?"

She didn't answer in any language he could understand, but she did make a chittering sound of pleasure as she gnawed the candy. Devvy touched her arm. It was silky smooth. She shrugged away his touch and poked through the briars for the second treat. He unwrapped a third and held it for her.

"I've missed you," he said, and then started skipping away, down to the rocky shelf below where the gray skies over Corwyn's Hollow melted into the gray ocean. He made sure to watch his footing. How many times had Mummy warned him? He remembered her story of the boy who had tumbled down the rocky crags into the surf and was lost forever.

"Are you coming?" he called, and watched Gilly take a few steps forward.

He knew she didn't like to be out in the daytime, but the sun was still hidden behind angry clouds. He tossed her his last drop, and she came forward again in this game of Lemon Drop Tag.

Devvy figured she had been quite lonely here because she had been eager to play, especially when he offered treats. And he was almost beginning to understand her funny way of talking, mimicking it, and watching her eyes fix intently as though she knew what he was trying to say. Talking with faeries was hard work, but he was sure that one day he'd master it.

ǫǫǫ

The back door slammed shut behind Devvy not long after Mr. Dunning had departed. Emily slid a plate of crackers to him as she whipped up a toasted cheese sandwich for dinner. She could still feel Lenny's spidery touch down the knobs of her spine and running through her hair.

"Are these for me?" he asked, his eyes betraying his excitement at the small dish of lemon candies on the table.

"They are," said Emily, and watched unhappily as he stuffed his pockets. She supposed it was better that she give them to him than watching

Lenny press them into Devvy's palm, like he was making some sort of greasy payment for her time.

"Don't stuff yourself on those," she said.

"They're not for me, Mummy," he answered as though she was the dullest knife in the drawer. "I share them."

"With Gilly," she mumbled. "Yes, I know. Just don't share them all so fast, right?" She pushed away an image of him bent over a basin, vomiting up chunks of yellow candies, after *sharing* them all with his imaginary companion.

"I won't. She doesn't come to see me every day."

Emily flipped the sandwich in the pan. It had gone black on one side. Angling her back so he couldn't see, she scraped it clean with a butter knife.

ººº

And so it was like that. Months went by and winter crept closer and rents came due, and so did Lenny. But Emily had no time to think of it, for it was school time again and Devvy had been sent home with letters about his clothes, his poor bucket lunches, and then at last about his behavior. At first Emily had tried to talk to him about it, about his telling stories, but the day came when she was summoned to meet his teacher.

As Emily sat nervously in the classroom, a dank affair fitting the very nature of Corwyn's Hollow, she remembered her own school days. How she had loved learning new things, reading stories of knights and princesses whisked away to better lives. Never in the stories did the princes slap their princesses or the knights demand sexual payment for chivalry. She worried at a fingernail and wondered, not for the first time, how her life had gone this far wrong.

Mrs. Beckham, Devvy's teacher, was a stout woman with iron-colored hair, and she smiled kindly at Emily from behind her very tidy desk.

"Thank you for coming, Mrs. Curtin," began Mrs. Beckham.

"Emily, please."

"Emily," she repeated. She sifted through some papers, finally settling on one that bore Devvy's crooked handwriting. "I appreciate your taking time to meet with me."

"He's shown me the letters. I'm sorry he's been a bother. He's a genuinely good boy at home."

Mrs. Beckham nodded knowingly. "They're always so good with their mums, aren't they?" An arched eyebrow made Emily's nerves hum.

"I'm not sure what you mean," said Emily, though she suspected she did and didn't like the meaning behind it.

"The boys here at school are always a bit different than the ones at home. It's not always a bad thing," she reassured Emily. "But there have been some issues."

"I know about his imagination. He's quite a story teller! I suspect he gets that from my side of the family."

"His vivid imagination comes through in his work." She slid the paper across the desk, and Emily felt color come into her face.

My mum is the best mum in the werld. She's the queen of the house, but the best queen of the werld—the best queen of all the farie—is Gilly! She has magickal eyes that see everything and teeth that shine in the light. When she talks, she talks in music.

"What a sweet story," mumbled Emily, but in her heart she felt shame and not just for the misspellings.

"It's more than that. He believes this Gilly is a living woman. He's told the other boys if they don't stop bothering him, he'll ask Gilly to…well…hurt them."

Emily's stared at Mrs. Beckham in horror. "What? No! Of course he wouldn't do that."

"I'm afraid he has. And not just the once. His behavior, while fanciful, is bordering on dangerous. He's threatening other children."

"With a faerie story?" asked Emily incredulously. "Certainly you can't think that's a genuine concern."

"It's not just that."

Mrs. Beckham opened her desk draw. Emily felt her insides twist when she heard the crinkling of cellophane. She refused to look at the lemon drops the teacher set before her.

"Devin tried to give these to the boys. He might have been trying to make amends, but then he said Gilly always came when they were out. Given his comments about Gilly harming them and then giving them these…well, it can be perceived as some kind of threat."

"Devvy wouldn't harm anyone. He's a gentle boy with a fanciful imagination."

"It seems to be more than that."

Emily was suddenly angry. "Isn't that what school is supposed to be about? Imagination? Why is making up stories in school so bad when you teach much worse stories? Charles Dickens wrote of child abuse and you teach that. Why is it wrong that my son wants to express his dreams?"

"I suspect you know why," said Mrs. Beckham dismissively. "There is a time for stories and a time for work, and there is no time for threatening harm."

"Mrs. Beckham, you said that Devvy had threatened the boys who bothered him."

"Yes, that's right."

"Why were those boys bothering my son at all?"

Mrs. Beckham blinked. Her bearing changed at once. Her lips became a thin line. "I'm not sure what you mean."

"Why are you allowing other boys to bother my son?"

"They're not, Mrs. Curtin."

"Is my son being bullied here?"

"Bullied is a strong word. Boys will be boys, and with your son's imagination—"

"You're allowing children to bother my son because he's imaginative? That doesn't seem very fair to me, Mrs. Beckham." She watched Mrs. Beckham work feverishly to get herself on solid footing, and then she did, with one pointed question.

"Mrs. Curtin, where is Mr. Curtin?"

The question was like a punch to the gut. She felt the air go out of her, watched as Mrs. Beckham rose up, ready to strike. Again.

"Perhaps a masculine figure in his life would do him good."

Lenny's grasping hands, his yellow teeth, and sour breath came to mind. Emily said stiffly, "My husband is not coming back."

"You're facing challenges. I understand," she said with sympathy as genuine as the garish yellow coloring in the lemon drops. "That can sometimes cause a boy to act out."

"He hasn't acted out," tried Emily.

"In any case, I felt it would be important to discuss this with you, so please do think about it. Hopefully you can get your son the guidance he needs. If this behavior continues, well, I'm afraid we'll have to undertake more serious discipline."

"More serious?"

"He'll be expelled."

The word horrified her. Emily stood so abruptly the chair nearly tipped over. "My son needs to not be bothered at his school. It's up to you as his teacher to ensure he's treated fairly. If you can't do that, Mrs. Beckham, I will have to bring this up with the superintendent."

"Please do, Mrs. Curtin, and we can discuss this matter in full detail with him."

It was her final salvo, and it was enough. Emily fled the room, with the word expelled ringing in her ears. Of course. Wouldn't that just be the end all? First a bad marriage, a deserter for a husband, a lecher for a landlord, and a hooligan for a child.

The shame in that thought nearly made her cry out.

How could she think that of her son? Of her dear, sweet Devvy? Of course he wasn't a hooligan. He was a child, for God's sake! And children made up stories! And he would grow out of it…with her guidance, she thought unhappily. She thought of the paddle hanging in the closet, the one Evan had used on Devvy only once before, the night before he walked out of their lives. Would she be able to wield it now? She had never had to, never wanted to, but she would do it. To save her son, she would do anything.

She arrived home and found Devvy on the sofa, chewing on a piece of toast. His eyes were red and swollen and she knew if she had to bring the paddle to her son's bottom, she would see those tears flow and it would break her heart. She wasn't ready for that.

"Devvy," she began, and he immediately began to cry. "I saw your teacher today."

"Mummy," he cried, and wrapped his arms around her narrow waist. "Mummy, Auntie Fran called."

Emily felt her insides turn icy.

"Nan died."

And at that moment, Emily felt the world go hazy, as though she was living in a nightmare from which she couldn't escape. She sank to the floor, Devvy's arms wrapped around her, and wept like a small child.

ꝏꝏ

The funeral was a sad affair, in more ways than one. Fran, Emily's older sister, took care of the arrangements with a sour attitude about having to finance the funeral herself. Emily had sat there, twisting inside, as shame forced her to whisper, "I haven't the funds to help."

Emily supposed Fran's discontent was made even more acute when, weeks later, the letter came from the solicitors' office. Emily stared in disbelief, hand shaking as she read it.

All of it, all of Mum's estate, to be sold off with the funds given directly to Emily.

Oh, Fran, thought Emily. I'm sorry. But still, her heart soared.

She thought of Lenny's hands on her thighs, prying them open like a child clawing after a Christmas present, the way his tongue would lash at her neck while she endured the act, how he had suggested—quite strongly—that she "*At least try to enjoy it.*" And so she had, making all appropriate sounds. The only blessing was that it hastened the act for him so she could get back to what she wanted to do. Which was what? Living out her days in this crumbling cottage by an unforgiving shore with a child who may or may not be right in the head?

But now…now with this letter…oh, the future seemed bright again!

She hugged the letter to her chest and looked around. No more cottage. No more wondering how she would feed Devvy. No more nights huddled in her bed, under blankets and coats, to keep warm. No more Lenny.

"Oh, Mum," she whispered to the ceiling. "You've saved our lives."

ꝏꝏ

Mr. Dunning arrived as he always did, just after breakfast on the first of the month. Emily had eagerly shooed Devvy outside, encouraging him to go and find his friend in the mists, so she could do what needed to be done.

The look of surprise on Lenny's face when she pushed him away was nearly enough to make Emily laugh.

"I don't understand," he said, hands on his bony hips.

"It's really quite clear," she said. "I've got money coming in. I'll be able to pay the rent on time. And then we'll be moving."

He blinked. "From where?"

"My mother's estate. I'll have the rent in full, probably by the end of the week."

His eyes narrowed and he smiled slyly. "You pretty girls are all the same. You think I'm going to believe that? Do you have the rent now?"

Emily faltered.

"End of the week's a long time away. And the rent is due today. You don't want me to turn you out, do you?"

"Mr. Dunning…Lenny," she tried, forcing a smile. "After all we've been through, certainly you can extend courtesy for a few days, can't you? That seems only fair."

"Courtesy is a two way road," he said, and he reached for her again. This time his hand clasped her wrist, twisting it hard, and she realized she'd gone too far.

Her leaving the village hadn't upset him; it was that she was leaving *him.*

"Let go of me," she said, and it came out in a sudden surge of anger that surprised even her.

"Pay what you owe."

"I'll pay no such thing, not anymore. I don't have to!" she shouted.

"You want your child on the streets? You want him to go hungry, the poor simpleton?" he demanded. "You think I don't know?" He smiled at the shock on Emily's face. "The whole village knows what a warped child you have, how he threatens the other boys. Good luck getting them to help you."

Steel grew in Emily's spine at the very thought of it. Her boy warped? Her dear, sweet Devvy who had endured so much from his father, the boys in school, the dire circumstances they found themselves in, and now this? She would not bear it. "Go straight to hell, Lenny," she said.

Anger flared in him, like a match being lit.

She never saw the fist. She never would have thought a man of his advanced years could be so fast. And yet…yet his hand lashed across her face, knocking her nearly to the floor. She staggered but didn't drop.

Emily touched the back of her hand to her lip. It came away bloody, and when she looked at Lenny, he looked scared at what he'd done.

"You hit me," she said and, because she couldn't resist, added, "And now I have *you.* You'll go to jail. You'll get put out of your job. You'll be the one the villagers talk about!"

"Didn't mean to," he answered, fumbling over his words. "It's just you surprised me. I mean, I thought we—you know, the two of us…

"There is no two of us," said Emily. It sounded scornful even to her, and clearly to him because the anger was back again. This time, he grabbed her arms, shook her. She cried out in pain.

"Selfish bitch! You're all the same!"

"Let go of me! My son—" She started to cry and, with clawed hands, reached his face. Two of her nails gave way. Rivers of red ran down his cheeks.

An inarticulate sound of rage came from him, shaking Emily to her core. He threw her back against the counter. She bounced off, knocking Nan's favorite pitcher sideways, and when she righted herself, she found the thick ceramic handle in her grasp. The pitcher lifted above her head, and she watched with a queer fascination as it came down on Lenny's head. He crashed to the floor, knocking the table over with him, and all Emily could wonder was "Did I do that?"

ϱϱϱ

"Gilly, Gilly, Gill—" Devvy stopped short when he heard the shriek from inside. Lemon drops fell from his hand. A tickling feeling started in his stomach, the kind he hadn't had since his dad had been around, just before he and mummy had gotten into one of their tussles.

"Gilly, Gilly…"

This time a crash sounded from the house, followed by the sound of glass breaking. He took a step toward the house, and when he heard mummy screaming, he broke into a run.

"Mummy! I'm coming!" he shouted, and the rain began to fall in sheets.

ϱϱϱ

Devvy stopped in the doorway. His mouth fell open.

"Mummy?" he asked and she was with him in an instant, wrapping her arms around him and pulling him close, the way he would nestle with Gilly sometimes in the hidey-hole. He didn't know whose arms he liked better most times, but right now, he definitely liked Mummy's better. He couldn't take his eyes off of Mr. Dunning, splayed out on the kitchen floor.

"I'm fine, love. Go outside."

He wondered at her then. She was bleeding, maybe she'd hit her head too because why would she tell him to go outside in the pouring rain without even putting on his slicker. And her eyes—they were wild and scared, like the time he'd tried to ride the ponies at the fair and one had gotten away and ran through the crowd of children. Her eyes looked like that. White and wild.

"I want to stay with you," he said, and instead of sending him away, she hugged him close.

"No, love, you should go. You should—" She stopped herself abruptly. What should he do? What should *she* do? She'd gone and killed Mr. Dunning! What would happen to her now? What would happen to sweet Devvy? She held him so tight he gasped for breath.

"Mummy, should we call the police?"

Well, of course that's what she should do. They would understand, wouldn't they? They'd see that there had been a struggle, a lovers' spat they would likely call it, though the very thought of that turned her stomach.

"I need to check on him," she whispered.

Of course that at least was the right thing to do. She unwrapped herself from her son's grip, giving him a wavering smile as she crept across the cracked and webbed linoleum. Trembling, she crouched beside him, her pale hand reaching out to touch his bald head, now slick with blood. He took a sudden, deep shuddering breath. She jumped back, nearly landing on her backside, both relieved and terrified. Thank sweet blessed mother Mary, he was alive!

"Is he all right?" asked Devvy. She smiled at him over her shoulder.

"Yes, love, he's just fine," she said. "He's going to be just—"

Lenny's hand snaked out, gripping her wrist like a vise and twisting her arms sideways. A scream tore from her throat.

"No!" she tried, but if he heard her, he didn't answer.

His teeth showed, bared like a wolf, the blood from his torn scalp running into his mouth. A line of bloody spittle ran down his chin, dripped onto the floor, filling in the web of cracked linoleum with red. "You blasted whore!" he hissed. "I'm going to kill you!"

Behind her, Emily heard Devvy mewl in fear.

"Run, Devvy!" she said. "Hide!"

Lenny's thick hand balled into a fist. The solid thump of his fist hitting her flesh was the last thing Emily heard above the slamming of the door.

୭୭୭

Devvy ran as fast he could.

But to where, he wondered. It didn't matter, he told himself. Mummy had said to run and so he would.

His feet flew over the rain-sodden grass, slipping and upending him just as he reached the briar patch.

"Gilly!" he shouted, tears and slobber mixing, his voice coming in horrible gasps. "Gilly, Gilly—" He climbed to his feet, hands on knees, at the entrance to the hidey-hole.

"Devin!"

The sound of his name made the trembling stop at once, made Devvy's breath catch in his throat. It wasn't Mummy. It was *him.*

"Come on now, lad," he called from the house. "Come back and let's have us a little chat."

Devvy ducked into the hidey hole. He buried his face in his hands when he caught the faint smell of lemon, and leaned back into the arms of Gilly, wrapping warmly around him. He tried not to cry,

"Gilly!" he said, his terror making him tremble all over. "Make him go away!"

"I hear you, boy," called Lenny, and Devvy heard footsteps grow closer.

Gilly's touch soothed him. She gazed down at him with her magickal eyes, eyes that showed Devvy the whole world in their vastness, and she turned to the mouth of the hidey-hole, to the thin legs clad in gray polyester coming closer.

"He's going to kill me," whispered Devvy, and the clacking song Gilly made stopped Mr. Dunning mid-stride.

"You're in there, boy. Just come out now…"

Gilly moved too fast for Devvy to see, her legs making mad scrabbling sounds as she burst from the hidey-hole, pushing past the briars, and launching herself a0.t Mr. Dunning. Devvy heard his surprised little "*oof!*" when he saw her.

Devvy clapped his hands over his eyes.

Against a sky of gray clouds, Gilly was a black shadow. She moved fast, faster than Devvy had ever seen her move before, and probably much faster than Mr. Dunning—or anyone—might have expected, if they could ever expect such a thing. She clacked and made her funny squealing sound, or maybe that was Lenny's horror when he finally saw what had come for him.

She spread her arms overhead, her many arms, long, fuzzy, stalk-like. Eight of them in all, some holding her bulbous body, some raised in front of her, and others feeling her way. Her wall of eyes—eight of them—sought not only the lemon drops Devvy had left in his wake, but the man with pockets stuffed full of them.

The man who had hurt Devvy.

Gilly, Queen of the Faerie Mists, rose up. Mr. Dunning's mouth turned into a giant *O* of horror when he saw it—*her*—the giant black spider with eyes that saw all and whose mouth spilled no secrets.

Lenny howled once, tried to scrabble away, but he was not as fast as Gilly's eight legs, and she was on him. There was the noise of an impotent scuffle, a grunt, and then silence from under Gilly's massive body. Through slitted fingers, Devvy saw Lenny's legs convulse, twitch once, then fall still. His body rocked gently from side to side as Gilly went about the business of ending him.

Gilly lay on him, doing what she did, and when Devvy was certain it was safe, he crawled out of the hidey-hole, over a mass of lemon drop wrappers that crinkled like new ice cracking under foot, and the remnants of a red and black checked shirt, and headed for his house. He could hear his mummy crying inside.

He touched Gilly once on her crooked leg. She chittered at him.

Devvy pressed his face against her silken face, kissed her once, and ran for home. He turned to look back once to see the soles of Lenny's shiny leather shoes disappearing into the briars.

Shelagh M. Smith teaches writing at Bridgewater State University and Stonehill College. Winner of the PEN New England Susan P. Bloom Discovery Award, her previous work has appeared in Siren, a women's literary magazine, and Embracing Writing. When not writing, she tries valiantly—and unsuccessfully—to keep up with one very busy dog and far too many cats.

JUJU
by Mary E. Stibal

When Elizabeth drove down Jerusalem Road in Cohasset, MA that afternoon and saw the flashing blue lights of two police cruisers in her driveway she automatically speeded up. Her first thought was that one of her husband Charles's security alarms had gone off accidentally. He had a thing about security, and two months ago had motion detectors installed on all doors and windows, both first and second floors, wired to their alarm company.

Still two police cruisers was overdoing it, especially for Cohasset. Their house sat literally on the edge of the Atlantic Ocean, 28 miles south of Boston in an upscale village that had minimal crime. Certainly not at a level that would require a $25,000 computerized security system, but that was Charles.

Nonetheless she careened her Audi into the driveway and had her car door open before the three cops standing by the front door, one burly, two not, could walk over. She didn't know them. Not a surprise, since she and Charles had lived in Cohasset for only three years, and never had a need to 'chat up' the local constabulary. Still, she felt a creeping dread when the one in charge, dark hair streaked with handsome gray, earnest, intense, and well, sympathetic, walked up, and introduced himself as Detective Bill Marinelli.

"Is there a problem?" she asked, and added, "I live here...I am Elizabeth Marley. Is my husband home? Charles Marley?"

When the detective asked her to step inside her own house Elizabeth knew there was a problem. A big one. The fact that their front door was already open was another. Wordlessly he led her though the foyer and into the living room with its floor-to-ceiling windows and spectacular views of Minot Light. Out of the corner of her eye she saw a band of yellow crime-scene tape across the staircase landing that led up to the library and the master bedroom.

She didn't bother asking Detective Marinelli to sit.

He said, "I am so sorry, but I have bad news." He told her that Charles was dead, although 'deceased' was how he phrased it, as if that would dull the effect. Then he added, "Your husband's body was found at the bottom of the staircase this afternoon."

Laura's heart thudded. "Dead? Charles is...dead?"

"Yes. Sarah Brown, who is I think your gardener?" He paused and Elizabeth nodded, so he continued. "She called 911 about an hour ago, and Mr. Marley was declared dead at the scene."

Elizabeth could only stare at him.

"Mr. Marley's body," he continued, "has been taken to the Medical Examiner's Office in Boston."

"Dead?" Elizabeth repeated, "My husband is dead?"

The detective said, "Yes. I am sorry, but yes. Is there someone you would like us to call?"

Elizabeth ignored the question and walked to the staircase landing cordoned off by yellow tape, and looked up. Charles had the gleaming oak and wrought iron staircase installed two years before, shipped from an 18th century monastery in Corsica. Charles was also a Napoleon buff.

She gripped the railing of the staircase. “But this is impossible. What happened? Did Charles have a heart attack…or a stroke…or what?”

Detective Marinelli hesitated. “It is too soon to know, exactly, but it appears he died from a fall down the stairs. There will of course be an autopsy.”

The next thing Elizabeth wanted to ask, although she didn’t, was the exact time of her husband’s death. When she’d last checked the time it had been 1:00 pm, exactly, just over an hour ago. She remembered because she’d glanced at her watch as she walked out of her office in Boston’s Park Plaza building.

And wished that her husband Charles would just drop dead.

She wanted to ask again if Charles was dead, but thought four times was pushing it. She assumed the police would be exact about things like that, especially where a widow was concerned. The three cops were watching her and Detective Marinelli moved closer, as if she might faint. A kind thought, but totally unnecessary.

She sank down in an armchair, staring blindly at the staircase, and the detective asked, “Are you able to drive to Boston? To the Medical Examiner's Office?”

“Drive? To Boston?” she ran her fingers through her hair, and realized her hand was shaking. “Actually no, I don’t think…”

He said, “I can take you. You’ll need to identify your husband’s body,” and Elizabeth numbly followed him outside to one of the blinking police cars. He opened the back door and she got in as if it was a taxi.

In the back seat she looked at her cell phone, still on silent from a late morning meeting, but she was too stunned to call anyone as the cruiser pulled away. Where to start? She would call Charles’s son later she decided. Elizabeth looked out the window as they drove down Jerusalem Road and wondered if the lights on the roof of the cruiser were still flashing. Probably not.

Just the night before she had told Charles in a calm, even tone that she thought they would both be happier if they separated. She didn’t mention counseling, nor did she say divorce, although that last was implicit. She just wanted out, which could hardly come as a surprise to Charles since their every conversation for the last twelve months had been rife with dislike. They’d been married just over three years, the second time for each; she a divorcee, he a widower. But she knew after six months she’d made a big mistake. He was a man who had never had an introspective thought in his life.

And she almost had to laugh thinking about it, but thank heaven she didn’t because the soft, brown eyes of Detective Marinelli were constantly flickering to the rear view mirror to see how she was doing.

Elizabeth was an art dealer at Skinner Auction House in Boston and except for the Corsican staircase, the expensive security system, and Charles’s lush rose garden in the back, all of which to be honest he had paid for, they’d been living on her income for the last two years. Not what she’d expected. He was a free-lance bio-tech writer, down to one small client now, who didn’t pay well.

But the worst part was that she was lonelier married to Charles than when she was single. And she couldn't stand it any longer, so the evening before, she'd told him she thought they should separate.

A conversation that did not go well.

He had jumped up from his chair in the dining room and snapped, "So that's what you think, is it? Really? Well then I say let's skip the 'separation' bullshit and go right to divorce. I'll ask for fifty percent of everything, and I do mean *everything.*" He waved his hand around the dining room and her gourmet kitchen, the big sweep of his hand taking in her whole ocean-front property. "And your 401K too. And I'll get half of course. I've earned it. I'll move out when I feel like it."

Charles had stalked off to the basement, and that was the last time they had spoken.

As the detective merged his cruiser onto the Southeast Expressway, Elizabeth said, "Excuse me Officer, but what time…when did it happen?"

"Based on statements, at 1:00 pm. Although the coroner will have a more exact time of death later today. Or first thing tomorrow."

Elizabeth took out her compact and checked her lipstick in the mirror, staring back at the reflection of her gray-blue eyes, dark lashes and wide-set mouth. She didn't look all that powerful, but she obviously was. Very. All she had to do was wish her husband would drop dead. And then he did. Immediately. She shut her compact and decided she was overwrought.

An hour later Elizabeth had identified the body, signed the necessary paperwork, and called Charles's son Jerome to tell him about his father. She was drained, but not from grief. She liked Jerome, a violinist with the Chicago Symphony, who was shocked yet stoic when she told him the news. She had always thought Jerome deserved a better father. Later that night they spoke again, and planned a simple yet elegant service for Charles.

Elizabeth didn't stay in her house in Cohasset that night, in fact she never stayed there again. The autopsy report released the day after his funeral concluded Charles Marley had died at 1:00 pm from a cerebral hematoma, sustained in an accidental fall down the stairs. The forensics showed he'd struck his head on a wrought iron baluster on the eleventh step of the stairwell, near the bottom of the staircase. And died from the trauma.

But Elizabeth knew the 'accidental' part couldn't possibly be true.

Charles was nothing if not agile. There was no way he could have simply stumbled down a flight of stairs and died. He was in superb physical shape, and had climbed in Morocco's Atlas Mountains just the month before. This was not a simple stumble, there was something else.

The morning after Charles died she spoke to Sarah Brown, his 'horticulturist' as he called her. Sarah said, "I am so very, very sorry. I talked to Charles upstairs a couple of minutes before…before it happened. I showed him a fungus I found on one of his Bulgarian Kazanlak roses. And then, well, he turned and fell down the stairs. Lost his balance or something."

Elizabeth pressed her, looking for a reason. "Perhaps Charles was carrying something heavy that caused him to fall, or maybe there had been a spilled liquid or something on the landing?"

"No, he just…fell down the stairs."

But when Elizabeth questioned the detective he confirmed what Sarah had said. "Your husband wasn't carrying anything at the time of his fall, and there was no substance on the upstairs landing or on the stairs themselves that could have resulted in his accident. Our investigation was thorough, and we could only conclude that Charles Marley simply lost his balance."

She didn't believe it.

Four days after his funeral service she arranged to have her belongings moved to an apartment in Boston's Back Bay, and Charles's effects shipped to Jerome. The week after that, she put her house in Cohasset on the market.

Elizabeth didn't know how to be a widow, much less the non-grieving kind. When she had identified Charles's body at the Medical Examiner's Office she had been shocked and silenced in the presence of death. It hadn't, however, make her feel any differently about her husband. She didn't like him one bit. Obituaries and eulogies can and often do err on the side of omission. What was missing from Charles's was that he was paranoid and narcissistic as well.

Still, she thought, something had happened in their house that afternoon, something significant and unexpected.

Otherwise…perhaps she had caused her husband's death.

Could that possibly be? No, that was ridiculous. But what else could it be? She didn't believe in coincidence, especially not of this magnitude. And Elizabeth was frightened at the thought that she could actually possess such a power. Which could not possibly be true of course, yet she found she couldn't pass by any mirror without stopping to stare deeply into her eyes. As if that could provide an answer. The problem was there was no one she could talk to, or at least no one who wouldn't think she was totally and completely delusional.

She didn't feel delusional. But was she—could she possibly be responsible for Charles's death?

Elizabeth supposed there was any number of women in any given year who had wished that their husband would…well… just drop dead. But of those women, how many had a spouse who had immediately, inexplicably and apparently without a reason, done just that? She thought none. Elizabeth kept telling herself she was being ridiculous, but she couldn't stop thinking about it.

A month after his funeral Elizabeth went back to their house in Cohasset just for her own peace of mind. She felt odd as she parked her car in the driveway. It was like investigating a crime inside out she thought, looking for proof that she *wasn't* responsible for her husband's death.

Inside the house the crime scene tape and the chalk marks were long gone, as well as all of the furniture, drapes and paintings. In the heavy silence she walked up the staircase and stood at the top, looking back down the flight of stairs. The view now seemed edged with danger.

As Elizabeth stood at the top of the staircase, she noticed a tiny, red light coming from a small, white box mounted in a corner of the hall, set almost as high as the ceiling. A light sensor. One she had never noticed before. For just a moment she thought it was a motion detector, then realized it would hardly be installed so high. Elizabeth stared at it again. She had been at work on the days when Charles had the new security system installed, which had taken almost a week as she recalled. She had teased Charles about it at the time, and asked if he was afraid someone was going to break into the house and steal his staircase. He had not found her comment funny. She looked at the box again, and realized it was not an alarm or a motion detector.

It was a camera.

Charles, of all things, had also had a security camera system installed in the house! A secret he'd kept from her. And the police certainly hadn't known about it either. She walked through both floors, and identified a total of eight cameras set high in the corners of the intersecting hallways, four on the first floor, four on the second. She was relieved there hadn't been one in the bedroom; but that would have been pushing it, even for Charles. No, she thought, he was just obsessed with security, and a camera system would have been a logical step for him.

But if there was a camera system, there would have to be a DVR hard drive and monitor somewhere in the house. In a closet most likely, but she'd cleaned all of them out. Thoroughly. Elizabeth checked all the closets again. Nothing. So where could it be? The only other place she could think of was the basement, where Charles kept his gardening tools. She went down to the basement and into his "fiefdom" he called it, just off the laundry. A workbench ran halfway around the room, with hooks on the walls for his array of garden tools, all gone now of course. Elizabeth got on her hands and knees and even looked under the workbench, although putting a monitor under the counter would make no sense.

She got to her feet and took a close look at the walls, and then, above one end of the bench she saw a keyhole. She looked closer and saw there was a thin seam of a wide metal door set into the wall and painted over. Elizabeth went back upstairs and got Charles's key ring, jangling with over fifteen keys, from her purse and returned to the gardening room. She started at one end of the key ring. The seventh one fit.

She opened the door and inside was a nest of electronics and a monitor and keyboard, as well as a DVR, with numbers for each camera. She turned on the monitor and after several seconds a screen came up. She looked at the login space. Charles had told her once he always used "Jerome" as a password, so she typed in his name and her heart started beating faster when another screen came up.

Elizabeth hit number five for the camera at the top of the staircase, and looked at the monitor. She punched in the date of Charles's death and 12:50 pm and hit play. There were clicks and whirrs, and for a couple of minutes she stared at the empty landing at the top of the stairs. Then Charles followed by Sara walked into view. She had something in her hand and Elizabeth clicked on zoom. Rose clippings. Of course, Sarah said she had talked to Charles about a fungus on his roses, his award-winning, rare Bulgarian roses.

ǫǫǫ

There was no sound but in the video Sarah and Charles appeared to argue, and Elizabeth saw him reach over and grab the clippings out of Sarah's hand. And she watched Sarah step back, and then Charles violently seize her arm, his face contorted in anger. And then as Sarah twisted away she gave him a mighty shove, and Charles lost his balance, tried to grab the newel post, his left arm flailing, and he plunged down the stairs.

Elizabeth was horrified. She replayed the eerily silent scene five more times and then shut it off. She went upstairs and called the Cohasset police, asking if Detective Marinelli could come over immediately.

He arrived twenty minutes later, and she played him the video clip several times. He had no expression on his face when he asked her to forward the file to the police station, took a number of photos of the landing and stairs, and left.

Early the next afternoon the detective called her. "I had Sarah Brown come into the police station this morning," he said, "and I played her the clip. She admitted she and your husband argued on the landing. It seems he blamed her for the spreading fungus in his rose bed, and he did grab her arm, which is assault by the way. She told me she was afraid of your husband, and yes, she did shove him away, but she didn't intend for him to fall down the stairs. The case is with the DA now, but your husband's death will likely continue to be ruled as accidental. Ms. Brown did call 911 immediately, but she unfortunately lied to the police about exactly what occurred. I am not sure what will happen there…if anything."

He promised to keep her apprised of any developments, and hung up. Elizabeth went to the hall mirror, and her gray-blue eyes stared back, cool and appraising. So she had not caused Charles's death by wishing it. Poor Charles. She was sad. And relieved.

At least now Elizabeth knew the truth.

That afternoon she felt like getting out of the city and drove down to Nantasket Beach in Hull. It was low tide when she pulled in and parked, the flighty seagulls winging across the air currents. Peaceful and serene. She walked along the ocean's edge for several miles, and then got in her car and headed back to Boston.

Elizabeth was in the right-hand lane on the Expressway when she was abruptly cut off by a 30-something driver in a heavy black Mercedes Benz SUV with wide tires and oversized chrome rims. She slammed on her brakes, lay on the horn, and swerved around him, avoiding a terrible accident by inches. She shot into the fast lane and as she glanced back in her rear view mirror she saw him give her the finger.

And she thought, "I hope one of your over-priced tires falls off."

Two miles later Elizabeth changed lanes and took the next exit, so she did not see the chrome rim on the black SUV's right front tire suddenly crack and the tire explode off the rim, the big SUV fishtailing into the breakdown lane, the driver shaken but unhurt. He called a tow truck on his cell phone, and a passing state police car stopped as the vehicle was being hooked onto the truck.

In his report the Massachusetts trooper wrote that the tire incident did not appear to be the fault of the driver, but was probably caused by a manufacturing defect in the rim. Rare, but not unheard of. The officer also reported that he had advised the driver to have all of his rims and tires checked out by the dealer.

Back home in Boston, Elizabeth went in her front door and walked past the big mirror in the hall with no hesitation now. Relieved that she no longer had to pause in front of every mirror and stare into her eyes.

And wonder.

Mary E. Stibal lives in Boston and in Hull on the South Shore, and consults with corporations on marketing relationships. This is her fifth short story to appear in the Best New England Crime Stories, and has just completed a mystery/suspense novel featuring gem dealer Madeline Lane, who learns the hard way that the rich are different than you and I. They will kill you if you get in their way.

OUT OF TIME
by Robin Templeton

It's amazing how easy it is to stow away almost anywhere when you're wearing an impeccably tailored herringbone three-piece suit from Savile Row. Head erect, shoulders back, I strode past both the ticket collector for the ferry and a uniformed crew member. I gave the first man a nod, and to the second I offered a slight gesture of salute. Both let me embark without a word. I quickly found a sheltered 2nd deck seat, starboard and near the bow. Perfect. I didn't need to view Hyannis Port, Massachusetts disappearing behind me, but my anger demanded that I savor my very first glimpse of Nantucket. I hadn't set foot on the island for over five years. And, with any luck, nobody would know I was visiting now.

I had chosen the earliest ferry of the day, and a dense morning fog shrouded the harbor. When a long bleat of the ship's horn announced our departure, I allowed myself to relax. My stealth mission was off to a successful launch.

Gray mist enveloped our boat, fore and aft. Within minutes, even the dock disappeared from view. Dozens of yipping and cawing gulls dove for their breakfast—ravenous wraiths as they emerged and vanished in the thickening brume. I pulled my suit jacket tighter, wishing I'd brought a topcoat. How could I have forgotten the soul-penetrating chill of the Nantucket Sound in late October? But my anger would keep me warm. That and imagining the look on my scoundrel brother's face when he realized how thoroughly I'd outwitted him.

I patted my worn leather briefcase, also perfect for my mission. It went nicely with the browns and tans in my suit and allowed me to give every appearance of a visiting lawyer or insurance broker. Perhaps a tad better dressed, but not if I were doing business with one of the wealthier families on the island. If anyone inquired, I'd say I was an estate planner. That made me smile. Yes, indeed. I was reworking the last wills and testaments of the Folger brothers—Nathan, myself, a respected art dealer in New York, and Timothy, an islander—and my no-good worm of a brother who had staged a house burglary to collect the insurance. But that wasn't the worst part. I was positive that his primary purpose in feigning the break-in was to cheat me out of a precious family heirloom.

Yes, we were descended from *those* Folgers—Peter Folger and Mary Morill, among the earliest of the Nantucket settlers as well as grandparents to Benjamin Franklin. Thomas Macy was also on our family tree along with numerous Coffins, Starbucks, Colemans, and Gardners. Our ancestors were there from the very beginning: through the negotiations with the Native American Taumkhods and the Khauds, and as part of the island's rise to whaling capital of the world. Even after the Great Fire, when we lost the whaling trade to New Bedford, many of our relatives held on and managed to survive.

Those who stayed on the island became merchants, hoteliers, fisherman, innkeepers, and handymen. My grandparents and brother, Timothy, were part of the last two distinguished groups. They'd saved our beautiful old ancestral home from creditors by turning it into a bed and breakfast.

Through the decades of lean years, our family's jewels, antiques, and real estate were sold, but the one greatest treasure remained. I could call it a pocket watch and clock casing, but what would that tell you? It was the magical, centuries-old art of scrimshaw—impossibly delicate curves of ivory carved from the teeth of harpooned whales. By itself the casing could mesmerize, but in its center was a circular hole into which a captain's pocket watch slipped perfectly, transforming the two pieces into one magnificent clock.

Both dated back to colonial whaling days when the sailors whiled away the long hours in the far Pacific by becoming expert scrimshanders. An ancient relative named Timothy Folger had carved the clock casing, and Nathan Folger, a master jeweler and clockmaker, made the exquisite captain's pocket watch embellished with whale bone, mother of pearl, and abalone—additional treasures gathered by the whalers. The perfectly paired masterworks had been owned by a Folger whaling captain, and displayed on a mantel in his ship's quarters. Each generation passed along the watch and case, telling the family stories and admiring the workmanship.

Timothy never appreciated the extraordinary beauty and historical significance of the heirlooms. The craftsmanship and artistry for both the watch and the casing was beyond anything I'd ever seen, and I'd collected ivory carvings from five continents. These intricately designed family treasures embodied the patience the sailors had learned while the great ocean churned, rolled, and determined the fate of both man and whale. It was epic—Melville knew it, Homer knew it. Hemingway and Conrad knew it.

But my doltish brother only cared about the market value of the pieces. The market value! Over and over I tried to explain that the watch and case were part of the founding of our country, part of an ancient art shared by the indigenous people and the Europeans, part of the sea, part of our very blood and sinew.

The watch and casing had remained a combined work of art for nearly two centuries. Then a ghastly mistake pried them apart.

When my grandfather died, he left no will. Poor Grandma Folger didn't know how to resolve the violent possessive argument between Timothy and me, so she gave me the watch, and my brother the case. If neither of us had any children, both pieces were to be donated to the Nantucket Whaling Museum in our grandparents' names.

Through the years, my brother wheedled and extorted money from me, threatening to sell the clock case to pay for repairs to the house. Tim knew he could sell the antique right from under Grandma Folger's nose, so I continued to mail checks.

Our last fight about the clock casing occurred when our grandmother died. I wanted to donate both the watch and the casing to the museum right then. Timothy insisted that having the clock case on the parlor mantel was an important conversation piece and part of the B&B's atmosphere. He laughed when I placed the captain's watch in my vest pocket, compounding the sacrilege by inserting a modern knockoff pocket watch into the hole left gaping in the fragile swirls of ivory. We almost came to blows over his decision. Had I not needed to get back to the mainland for a crucial business meeting, I might have killed my brother right then and there. That's how furious I was.

The moan of the ship's horn startled me. Were we nearing port? The dense fog shielded the buildings from view, but the smell of Nantucket's harbor was unmistakable—dead fish, salt air, and diesel fuel. With an automatic gesture, my hand reached for my now-missing pocket watch. Rage suffused every cell of my being. Of course the vest pocket was empty. My brother had been the one to steal it out of my suit when I was in the hospital last August. I'd seen him! That simpering wife of his held my hand trying to distract me, but I saw him go into the closet. When I was released, all of my other belongings were returned to me—my wallet, cash, and credit cards. The hospital staff knew nothing about the missing pocket watch. I didn't press because I knew who had taken it, and it wasn't anyone on staff.

After that, I left at least a dozen messages for Tim, but the bastard wouldn't return my calls or texts. Finally, I got a letter from an island attorney informing me about a break-in at the B&B and asking me to sign an affidavit testifying to the value of the clock casing. There was no mention of the watch he'd stolen from me.

And that's why I was traveling to Nantucket. If my brother had staged the B&B burglary, I had a pretty good idea where he may have hidden the watch and clock casing. If I was right, and I was sure I was, I'd be able to take possession of both items. How could he say I'd stolen something that had already been stolen? Tim's dishonesty had laid its own trap. But until the casing and watch were safely in my Manhattan apartment, I needed to move inconspicuously. Too many islanders might recognize me. And that's why I'd chosen Halloween for my mission.

The ferry docked and I made my way to the gangplank, turning up my collar to obscure as much of my face as possible. Most of the other passengers were busily collecting their luggage and children, and I slipped off the boat even more easily than I'd gotten on. My plan was to hide out on the island until after checkout time at the B&B. I knew their routine: At 10:00 a.m., guests were supposed to leave—but there were always some stragglers. At 11:00, the maid came in—probably just one because it was the slow season. By 11:30, Sarah and/or Tim would go out for groceries. That's when I planned to sneak into the house.

I stayed around the docks until eleven. I still loved the smell and feel of Nantucket. It must be in my blood. Maybe I shouldn't have been so quick to let Tim take my grandparents' house. The property would be worth a bundle if it weren't mortgaged to the hilt. But Nantucket and Timothy Folger were inseparable, and the island wasn't big enough for both Tim and me. It never had been.

Halloween had been a calculated choice for my homecoming. Both Hyannis Port and Nantucket celebrate Halloween with open shops, a town-wide parade, and everyone in town partying in masks and costumes. With luck, the veil of fog could even last throughout the day.

Despite the dreary cold, the cobblestone streets thronged with people. Some were already in costume, and retailers had bowls of candy and cookies set out for the children. I kept my head down as I made my way to Water Street.

"Nathan! Nathan Folger, is that you?"

Damn. I looked up. Owen Gardner trotted toward me dressed in faded Nantucket reds and a bulky cream-colored fisherman's knit sweater.

"Nate, you old son of a gun! I haven't seen you since your grandmother died five years ago. Tim said you had a heart attack in August. How are you doing now?"

"Hanging in there, Owen. I had some unexpected business over here, so I'm hoping to surprise Sarah and Tim. I'm heading there now."

Owen took off his Red Sox cap and scratched his head. "I saw Sarah at the grocery store a while back. And Tim's probably grabbing a beer and lunch at the Rose and Crown. Maybe you can catch up with him there."

"No, I'll just wait for him at the house. If you see him, don't tell him I'm here. Like I said, I want to surprise him."

"Mum's the word, Nate ol' chap. Hope to see you again before you leave!"

Owen faded into the mist and I hurried to the house. If both Sarah and Tim were out, I'd only have to deal with the maid. Maybe I could even spirit out the watch and case before Tim got home.

Folger Farm B & B was a bit of a misnomer since it was really an ancient whaling captain's house. The "farm" portion was a nod to my grandmother's wonderful way with both gardens and animals, and it didn't surprise me to see two fat felines—one black and white and one calico—both hunched on the front porch wicker chairs. I reached out to pet the calico and he arched his back and hissed at me. The black and white leaped off the porch and pushed his way under the crawl space. Welcome to Folger's Farm, Nathan. So glad to see you.

A mermaid figurehead held the front porch lantern. My grandparents had always kept a key on a hook right beneath her fins. It took a few minutes but my fingers managed to find it. I unlocked the door.

To her credit, Sarah had done little to change the house. Its charm was in the way it allowed you to walk back in time as soon as you entered. But most of Nantucket was like that—at least in the historic district. Predictably, the wide plank pine floors creaked noisily as I tiptoed into the parlor.

"Hello! Who's down there? Mr. Timothy? Is that you?"

I didn't answer. I barely breathed.

The woman seemed to be listening. When all was quiet I could hear her footsteps move into another part of the upstairs. My heart beat almost as loudly.

Careful to not take another step, I pivoted my body to face the fireplace mantle.

A vase of flowers had replaced the whalebone and ivory clock case. But of course it had been reported as stolen, right? That's what I was here to disprove.

The house had no basement, but it was possible he'd hidden the "stolen" items in the attic. It wasn't where I really thought they were, but I needed to make sure as soon as the house was empty. How long could I stay in the parlor before Tim or Sarah got home?

I studied the parlor walls which were covered with antique maps and sketches of the village. Some of those went back hundreds of years, too. I hadn't wanted to stay. Tim had. Now he and his wife had this house and I had my empty Manhattan apartment. Damn him. And damn the ancestors. I was going to get that watch and clock case. Maybe I'd keep both pieces—to hell with the museum.

I heard footfalls on the steps.

The best I could do for a hiding place was to crouch behind one of the wingback chairs near the fireplace. At least the draperies were shut and the room was dark.

Scarcely breathing, I watched a gray-haired woman wearing a lavender sweat suit slowly work her way backwards down the stairs. She was dusting the walnut banister. Step down, rub. Step down, rub, rub. A Pledge lemon scent wafted into the parlor and I tried not to sneeze. After she'd finished polishing, she straightened the foyer rug, put the rag into her sweat suit pocket, and extracted a key. When I heard the front door latch and the dead bolt slide into place, I allowed myself to exhale. That had been close!

Easing myself from behind the chair, I raced to the second floor. The attic door pull was to the rear of the hallway and I gave it a yank. The trap door dropped, but so did a blizzard of sawdust and mouse droppings. Typical of Tim—he inherits a multi-million dollar historic property and allows it to be overrun by vermin.

My suit was already a mess, so I gingerly made my way up the ladder. There were stacks of magazines, Christmas boxes, and a rack of old moth-eaten clothes but I wasn't seeing any evidence that the sawdust had been disturbed by anyone other than me. There could only be one other hiding place—and Tim didn't even know I knew about it.

My brother had been a thief since he was a teenager. Maybe even before. One time, after my grandmother lost a pair of pearl earrings, I followed him. It had been pretty boring—first he hung out with his friends, then he worked his busboy shift at Rose and Crown. I was about to give up when I saw him veer off the path for home and head down to the beach. Several of the islanders kept their kayaks and small boats on a protected patch of parkland. He pulled grandpa's old rowboat out and headed toward a place we called Folger Island.

Folger Island didn't really exist. Nantucket was surrounded by shoals, sandbars, and other bits of land that were at least partially underwater most of the time—Muskeget, Dry Shoal, Shiff Island, and Tombolo Point. Our self-named uncharted Folger Island was like that. Some of these areas had vestiges of ancient shacks or building foundations from long ago, but they were mostly used for fishing—or an occasional private picnic or pot party. I watched Tim row out and, about a half hour later, I saw him row back. I ran home so he wouldn't know I'd been spying on him. The next day, when I was sure my brother was at work, I took grandpa's boat to Folger Island.

It took a fair amount of searching, but I found Tim's treasure trove. Half buried, on the highest point of the island, and lashed to a bush, was a waterproof box. It wasn't locked, and when I opened it I was shocked.

Not only were grandma's earrings in there, but a whole lot more: antique candlesticks, a gold locket, a fancy looking vase, and a man's wallet--probably lifted from the pocket of a drunken tourist at the Rose and Crown. And stacks of money. There were plenty of times when I wondered what had happened to a five or a ten missing from my wallet or piggy bank, but it never had occurred to me that my own brother could be a thief.

I never trusted him again.

After letting myself out of the B&B, locking the door and replacing the key, I followed the back paths into town. My poor suit had taken a beating and I needed to change into something more seaworthy.

I found a small church thrift store run by a teenaged girl who barely looked up from her cell phone when I walked in the door. Paying cash, I purchased an inexpensive tool kit, a lantern, jeans, a faded red baseball cap, a black sweater, sandals, a windbreaker, and a well-used backpack. The store had a tiny makeshift dressing room, and I quickly made my transformation into an islander. Once I changed clothes, stuffed my suit into the backpack, and ditched my briefcase, nobody looked twice at me. All the attention was directed at Halloween—even the adults dressed up for the festivities in Nantucket.

I waited until dusk to find Grampa's boat. It was pretty beaten up, but it was still there. By nightfall, I was alone on the water with my anger, my tools, and my certainty that Tim was every bit as crooked as he'd been as a teenager. What kind of person steals from his own blood?

I rowed steadily, but as a northeasterly wind picked up, I could feel myself going off course. Turning on my lantern, I squinted into the inky darkness trying to see some sign of land ahead. What must it have been like for the ancestors who carved that clock casing when they were on whaling ships thousands of miles from home? I was scared and the lights of Nantucket weren't any more than a few miles behind me.

The bark of a gray seal was answered by a chorus of honks. Was that a beach ahead? A few more strokes and the prow of the boat scraped against sand. I jumped out and held my lantern over my head. It had been a long time since I'd seen it, but I was sure I'd landed on Folger Island.

The waves had gotten stronger, so I dragged the boat as far past the waterline as I could. Armed with the lantern, a canvas bag full of tools, a compass, and a grim determination to find my family's heirlooms, I headed toward the high point of the island.

There were signs of other explorers: cigarette butts, beer cans, joint clips, used condoms. Even Tim wouldn't be dumb enough to put priceless antiques on a lump of sand where the island kids partied, would he? But I kept going. The place I remembered was a hike, and it didn't look like the previous visitors had been interested in that form of cardiovascular activity.

The higher I climbed, the windier it got. Dune grasses grabbed at my feet and the first icy stabs of rain hit my face. "Brilliant Nathan, just brilliant," I said aloud. "You rowed an antique boat out to an uninhabited Atlantic island, and now a storm's coming up. Not one person knows where you are and you're still recovering from a heart attack."

I stopped for breath and held the lantern up again. There was something ahead—a bush and something else. Something square. Could it be? Could my brother still be using the same hiding place he used over thirty years ago?

It wasn't the same box I remembered. It was better built—fully water proof—and it was chained to the base of the bush and padlocked. I reached into my bag of tools.

After several minutes of working on it, the padlock gave way. I took a long slow breath before opening the lid of the chest.

One thing had changed since Tim's youth: he had a better eye for value. And he gave more attention to protecting his prizes. By the lantern's light, I pulled out the boxed and bubble-wrapped treasures one by one. He'd even included silicon crystals in the containers to help counteract the moist sea air.

Grandmother's gold teaspoons—they had been a wedding gift from a Nantucket mayor. A real pearl necklace that had been in the family since the 1800s. An antique revolver. Lots of antique scrimshaw. I thought my grandparents had sold these things to make ends meet. But, no, Tim just waited until their eyesight and memories failed so he could rob them.

And at the very bottom of the chest was a blue box. Hands shaking, I opened the lid. Gently removing the bubble wrap, I pulled out two objects wrapped in black velvet. One was the ivory and teak clock case. The other was a smaller box containing my watch. Tears of relief and anger poured out of me. "Tim, you son of a bitch! You thieving prick! How dare you steal from our grandparents? How dare you steal our heritage? I'm going to make sure these are donated to the Nantucket Whaling Museum, even if I have to do it anonymously and after you're dead."

I was tempted to take everything, but I wanted to be sure I was off the island safely with the watch and casing. Carefully I rewrapped my treasures in half of the bubble wrap and put them in my backpack. I stuffed the rest of the packing back in the blue boxes and returned the other items back to the chest.

The seals were barking again. I hoped they weren't by the boat. Suddenly I was exhausted and I didn't think I had enough energy to fight off a seal.

But as I made my way down the hill, I saw something else on shore. Another boat. And Tim and Sarah.

I turned off my lantern, but Tim was already walking toward me.

"Nathan, Nathan, Nathan, did you really think you could put one foot on Nantucket without a half-dozen people telling me you were here? And when I saw all that sawdust under the attic opening, I knew why you'd come."

"I just want them donated to the museum. I don't care about anything else. You helped grandma and grandpa keep the B&B going. The house is yours. And Sarah's." I turned the light back on. At least my brother didn't appear to be armed.

Tim seemed to consider my proposition. Then he shook his head. "Sorry, Nate. I have a couple of dealers making some quiet inquiries for me. Unless you can front me a half million, I'm just going to have to ask to put the watch and casing back. I assume they're in your backpack."

"A half million? My divorce wiped me out. I don't have that kind of cash."

"What a shame. Isn't that a shame, Sarah? Divorce can be so costly. And now that I have an heir coming, you really have no claim to any of the family possessions, Nathan." He patted Sarah's bulging stomach.

"But you committed fraud."

Nathan placed a powerful hand on my shoulder and pushed me down into the sand.

"Yes, it's unfortunate that you figured that out. Let me explain what's about to happen to you."

In the light from the lantern I could see Sarah pulling a syringe out of a pocket and filling it from a small vial. I struggled, but was pinned.

Tim watched her nonchalantly, then turned back to me. "Did you know that Sarah was a nurse, Nate? A nurse trained as an anesthetist? She's filling a syringe with suxamethonium chloride—SUX for short. She's going to give you a little shot in a minute that should relax you. In fact, it will relax you so thoroughly you won't be able to move. But by that time you'll be drifting out into the channel in Grandpa's leaky old boat. I just made sure it was a little leakier.

"By the time they find your body, if they find your body, it will look as if you had a heart attack and drowned. The drug will have metabolized out of your system."

Tim held a hand out to the rain. "Or, as if you got caught in one of those nasty squalls that come up so quickly on the Sound. Either way, I don't think you'll be talking to the authorities about theft or insurance fraud."

"Sarah?"

His wife started walking toward me. Then she stopped, turned around, and swung hard at Tim, ramming the needle into his arm while he held me down. He was so startled he couldn't push her off until she'd emptied the syringe.

"What the…" But already he was showing the effects of the drug and his legs crumpled beneath him.

Sarah glared at me. "Don't just stand there. Help me get him into your grandfather's boat."

I shook my head. "I don't understand."

"He doesn't love me. He never did. He just hooked me so he could have a kid. In the meantime, he's screwing anything that moves, men and women, and we're about to lose the house because of his gambling and drugs.

You said you only care about that watch and case? Well, I only care about my kid and keeping a roof over our heads. Timothy was right about one thing. Divorce is expensive."

My brother's eyes were open and filled with horror as his wife talked. But every other part of him was, as advertised, immobile.

Silently, Sarah and I carried him to Grandpa's boat. Tim made a few gurgling noises, then fell silent. Numbly, I helped Sarah push the boat into the current of the channel.

We climbed into her boat and I started rowing while she navigated. "Do you have the watch and case?" she asked.

I nodded and said, "They're in the backpack."

"Can I ask a favor?"

"Sure. You saved my life."

"Could you hold off giving the watch and case to the museum until my son is five? I want him to be able to touch them before they go in a museum case. And I want him to feel proud of his heritage."

"So it's a boy. Have you picked out a name?" What was the correct conversation to have with a woman who had just killed your brother?

"How about Peter? Wasn't he the original Folger on the island? And Ben Franklin's grandfather? I was thinking of Peter Franklin Folger. And maybe you can include his name when you donate the watch and case. It really is extraordinarily beautiful—I can't believe Timothy was selling it for whores and drugs."

Maybe this woman wasn't an idiot. Perhaps I could even help out with my nephew from time to time. But there was one thing. "Sarah, you do know that you're going to have to return the insurance money if we're going to donate the watch and case. The appraisal has detailed descriptions. As soon as the museum tries to insure it, Timothy's claim and the insurance fraud will surface."

She stared at me blankly for a minute. "But I need that money to fix up the house. Tim let it go into ruin. Turn this boat around."

"What?"

"Please, just row." I turned away from Sarah, confused as I grabbed the oars. Was she going back to try to rescue my brother?

On the third stroke of the oars, I felt a sharp jab in my left arm. I looked down as Sarah drained the syringe.

"But what…?" Already I was losing the ability to talk and my legs were going limp. I slumped into the bottom of the boat.

"I'm sorry, Nathan. I'd thought through everything else but I just hadn't figured out the insurance part. Don't worry—it won't be a bad death. I helped Grandma Folger out the same way. After all, you probably don't have too much longer to live with a bad heart."

Sarah worked the backpack off my arms and took out the watch. She wound the stem and said, "Isn't that amazing? It's still running!" She placed the watch on my chest before rifling through the rest of the pack. After she found the watch case, she resumed rowing toward Folger Island. I could do nothing except feel the roll of the sea while I watched the last minutes of my life tick off on that magnificent timepiece.

Robin Templeton is a Virginia-based writer whose ancestors helped settle Nantucket. Her short story, *The Knitter,* appeared in the 2016 Chesapeake Crimes Anthology, *Storm Warning.* Additionally, Robin's career as a photographer and experience as a private investigator formed the basis of her mystery novel-in-progress, *Double Exposure*, the recipient of the William F. Deeck-Malice Domestic Grant.

SAVING GRACE
by Gabriel Valjan

Mercy Goodfeet had passed by, and a lone delicate snowflake floated down the lane behind the young woman. The good merchant Fairebanke thought her a handmaiden of intrigue, and that delicate flake in the air, a cinder from Hell.

He had stepped away from the portal to remain unseen, when his wife, christened Rebecca, made a slight disturbance, which betrayed her presence. "You shouldn't sneak up on me as if I were prey, good woman."

"Better that you pray than vex yourself with Mistress Goodfeet. She makes her way to the woodsmen around this hour."

"I pray for her soul and for her good sense," he said as he straightened out his linen shirt. "She would better her heavenly estate and that of the community if she'd confess who got a child on her."

He allowed his wife to fix his collar. She even dared to reach up and kiss him on the cheek. "There is time yet. Rather than imperil her soul and that of her child, she'll have to reveal the father before or during childbirth. Has not her father said a word?"

"He has not, but I will not countenance rumor."

"Gossip has run that errand, dearest husband."

"You mean, amongst the womenfolk."

"And the men. The woman has suffered a terrible ordeal," his wife said.

"We share her jeopardy if she does not name the father. You have heard her father's sermon Sunday last."

"I have, good husband." She moved dishes to the cupboard. "He has reminded us yet again that the year draws to an end and that judgment is at hand." She said it without much conviction.

"You question the man's sanctity?"

"I do not. I question his analogy."

"Nonetheless, we are each responsible for a line in the ledger for our salvation. Winter is, and has always been, the Devil's season."

His wife circulated the kitchen in her pearl-grey dress. She owned four sets of clothing and a whalebone bodice. Her husband had indulged her several linen shifts. He allowed her the vain purchase of one scarlet dress for the rare occasion they traveled.

"Must you watch me?" she asked, mixing bowl in hand. "I have heard the winter sermon, but I must remind you that the Lord has given the Evil One dominion over the earth and all earthly manifestations, including the seasons."

He gave her a sharp look. Rebecca had a keen wit, but he tolerated it only insofar as she threaded and measured it with him. She was correct: fanciful whispers had found commerce among the folk in the plantation. Which inventive scandal found greater purchase was hard to discern.

Mistress Goodfeet had ventured beyond The Hedge into godless territories to bring the holy teachings to the praying Indians. Her father, the minister, had intended to reconvene with her later that spring afternoon. The

Indians had adventured out scouts, only to discover the carnage. Pequots had slaughtered everyone in the party. Her escorts, though armed, had been stripped of their weapons, then clubbed and mutilated. Two women had been in her company; they had been violated first and then butchered.

Three days later, a harried but intact Mercy Goodfeet had emerged from the woods. What had first been interpreted as a wonder of Providence had became a foul curse when she first showed that she was with child.

"I must go, for I have an appointment with the reverend," the merchant said to his wife.

The door closed behind him and more snow fell fast on his brim. He encountered Mercy. She appeared healthy and hale, though an errant ringlet evaded her linen coif, which the merchant found disconcerting. Her hair had turned red in the month after her return from her mystery in the wilderness. Some had said that it was a sign of a witch.

"Good day to you, Mistress Goodfeet. I am on my very way to your father's house."

She glanced down at the ground when she spoke. "Either let me walk ahead of you, or behind you. You endanger your good name in speaking to me in public."

"It would be uncharitable to you and your unborn child to ignore you. May I ask why you are out alone, in weather not befitting your affliction?" His eyes looked at the kindling that she had purchased. "Your father has servants bound to him to do such chores."

"They refuse me in his absence, good sir, but please do not tell my father. I wish no punishment upon them."

"But, they are indentured…" Seeing his case worthless, the merchant enjoined her to walk with him. Children were called into their houses in their wake. Mothers closed their clapboards. Men nodded to the merchant, but turned their eyes away from her. The snowfall increased.

"They do not speak to me and I was once their neighbor," she said. The merchant heard sorrow in her voice. He had bidden himself at first not to speak, but his tongue did not obey him. "You know well why they do not."

"I cannot confess. I shall not confess."

"Think not of the village, but of your father, Mistress."

"I think too much of my father."

At her door, he offered his hand for her to take the few steps with safety. "You are kind, thank you," he heard her say with a modest smile. He had known her since she was a child, but now realized how attractive she had become. He felt a natural affection for her, a genuine flow of good will, rooted in Christian benevolence. He had known her mother before she had taken ill with the pox and died, while her father was away to deliver a sermon in Salem. The young Mercy had been sent to the pest house on suspicion of the scourge; her untouched skin, fair complexion, and her growth into womanhood without any illness were now seen as further proof of her status among the damned.

Inside the parlor of the residence, he waited for Reverend Goodfeet. He bided the time regarding the graces bestowed on his comrade in faith. A horseshoe over the entrance guarded the house against witchery. He had visited the house many times. The floorboards and stout gable were of handsome wood. The chimney in the kitchen had a wide hearth, a gentle fire and a simmering kettle. He looked overhead at the timbers to hear the masculine sound, which emanated from above and then down the stairs. Reverend Goodfeet had the only two-floor property in the village. One of the selectmen had suggested that, come spring, they build a two-floor garrison against Indian attacks. The minister entered the room and they shook hands.

"Reverend. I hope that I have not arrived prematurely."

"Not at all, Samuel. Please join me in the other room. Do tell: is your wife well?" He didn't wait for an answer to ask, "Is she obedient?"

"My wife remains my blessing. I will not complain of her, or my children, for they are healthy and sound in their station."

"Excellent," the reverend said as he fetched two tankards from his cupboard. He found his jug. "We shall have ourselves a drink. I saved this batch and will nurse it through the winter." He set down the lidless silver cups and reverend uncorked the jug. "This is indeed the last batch of Rattle-Skull in the entire Bay Colony."

Reverend Goodfeet poured generous portions. The dark drink obscured the glass bottoms of their tankards. "We have known each other for years, Samuel, and I consider you a fellow in Christ, and a man upon whom God has bestowed His grace. I know that you will deny it, for modesty is your virtue, but I wish to include you in my enterprise. Please sit and listen to my proposed endeavor."

They toasted to each other's health and prosperity. The merchant Fairebanke had a gentleman's manners to stay quiet in another man's house. He abstained from another taste of his drink in order to keep his head free of its stultifying powers.

"The cold season is upon us, and it promises to be a fierce one," the reverend said with an impish glint in his eyes. The merchant had heard the slight shuffle of feet somewhere in the house. The reverend assured him of their privacy. "She may hear everything, but she won't say a word." The reverend took another hearty swallow.

"Last winter was especially harsh," Merchant Fairebanke said. He had wondered the direction and tenor of this exchange. He thought of Rebecca and how she remarked how fixed the reverend was on this theme of winter.

"Which is why winter is our ally," the reverend said.

"I fail to comprehend your meaning."

"Myself and certain men here and elsewhere in Bay Colony have designed a campaign, which I would like to petition you to join. You must take another drink before I divulge our intent and purpose."

The merchant brought the cool rim to his lips but feigned the swallow. The reverend pushed his drink forward and spoke to the merchant, hunched toward the man to intimate complicity.

"I soon plan to give a sermon to remind the congregation that we have erred from the path. I'll cite examples without any direct indictments. I'll say that we have let our womenfolk wear their hair long. I will say that I have earfuls that our younger folk have taken to riding their horses unsupervised, or that they dress above their station. We have become lax. We have failed in our compact with the Lord."

"I do not wish to disagree outright, but youth should be allowed some folly, and those fortunate to own horses are of good breeding. As for—"

Fairebanke saw the familiar raised hand, the naked gauntlet of authority. He waited.

"Forgive my interruption, good sir, but do you remember the last time we usurped heresy, when we had last turned off a Quaker from the ladder at Gallows Hill?"

Merchant Fairebanke disliked executions. He wanted his drink. He feared the scheme ahead. He said into his drink, "What have you and these good men construed?"

"Only God's rightful plan, in that we reheat the wrath between the Indians and us."

Fairebanke's eyes widened. "The garrison is but a drawing on a piece of paper; provisions are insufficient, and the Pequots are a fearsome lot."

"They attacked my daughter."

Fairebanke pushed his tankard away. "They attacked her party and committed savagery upon them, yes, but there is no evidence they harmed her. You advocate vengeance as winter breathes over the land. The timing is poor."

"One of them put a child on her."

"Then she has confessed to you? You are her father and a man of Holy Orders, but that confession has to come from her lips."

"It will not," said Reverend Goodfeet.

"She must profess it to the midwife then. It is the only way, since men are forbidden to behold the deed."

"I doubt that she will, even in that extremity of pain." The reverend stood up. He trod the floorboards as if he were behind the pulpit. Perhaps this was here he practiced his oratory, thought Merchant Fairebanke.

"The Indians are but a limb of Satan," he said. "A better triumph awaits us." The drink was working its effect. Reverend Goodfeet steadied himself on the back of his chair. "Our reward is in the taking of their land. We can seize it. We will seize it."

Merchant Fairebanke studied the reverend's face. The man's eyes were dark, his skin, pale against the white collar around his neck. The start of a sneer lifted from one end of his lips.

"You have weapons, don't you?" Merchant Fairebanke said.

"And what if I do? What if men are already on the King's Highway to this very place?" The reverend waved off the merchant. "I should not have mentioned any of this to you since you're of a reluctant disposition."

The merchant rose from his chair. He imbibed from his tankard one last time for courage. He walked up to the reverend and took the good man's tankard out of his hand. "I plead for common sense. Arms or not, confederates or not, winter is a hard time of year to mount an attack. Yes, food is scarce for the

Indians and us, but unless you have some intelligence that we are about to be attacked and sundered, then I cannot say, in good conscience, that it is worth the risk to leave our homes vulnerable for a most certain and savage reprisal. You exploit what happened to your daughter to your gain and—"

"To our gain, Merchant," the reverend said and traced his logic. "We levy the attack before they raid us. If it rights the wrongs in those spring fields then I shall have no compunction in taking the hatchet from the red men and slaying him with it. I will have a clear conscience, as you so put it."

"I charge you with but one observation, good sir. Your daughter is named Mercy, and Providence is justified that she was so named, because God or heathen showed her mercy." The short Merchant Fairebanke leveled his blue eyes with the taller man. "I have no words on the matter of paternity, unless she confesses and says it plain that she was taken…or had consented." The merchant looked away and spoke to the ground. "I must go before the weather worsens. Thank you for your hospitality. On my word, I shall say nothing of what we have discussed."

Merchant Fairebanke stepped away. The reverend seized his arm and pulled him closer. He said, "What will you have me do, Samuel? I'll tell you what I had heard happened in the woods."

Fairebanke looked down at the hand on his person. "Unhand me. Heard from whom? Her or from some fevered source?"

The reverend reached for the tankard on the table. He uncorked the jug and poured a splash of the spirit. The merchant counted the number of times he watched the freshly scraped knot of bone bob up and down.

Merchant Fairebanke put his hands around the vessel. "You have had enough."

"I'm afraid Lucifer's forces are amassed and in greater numbers than we had supposed beyond The Hedge. I'll hazard the supposition that the praying Indians are not to be trusted. They're all savages; they counterfeit our faith and keep fast to their practices. I know that from a praying Indian."

"That is distressing, but tell me what happened in the woods."

"The Wendigo got them," the reverend said, skin wan and eyes bloodshot. "I learned this from a praying Indian sympathetic to our faith and an enemy of the Pequot people. I promised him some land for his help."

Fairebanke ignored the contradiction. The savages were not to be trusted, unless they are enemies of the Pequots. "Say more of this Wendigo."

"It's an infernal spirit, a demon of sorts that goes by many names, but it possesses a plurality of awful gifts. The Pequots worship it."

The irritated eyes darted sight between the merchant and more drink. Fairebanke stood between the reverend and the jug and tankard on the table. Resigned and obstructed, the reverend conceded more details.

"The spirit is tall and thin as Death in the Book of Revelations; its hue is sulfurous and the airs about it, rank. It has antlers, a long snout, and a boar's teeth and bristles. The beast can move faster than a horse, with preternatural stealth, which is why it is mistaken for a ghost. Its inviting voice in the wind is heard before the attack. I want some more drink."

Fairebanke poured a frugal dash.

"The demon is indiscriminate in how it kills. Carnage is not its sole objective."

"Then what is?"

"Human flesh."

"A cannibal?" the merchant mused. "There must be a way to kill it." The reverend stared off into space. Fairebanke feared quiet hysteria. He repeated himself, "There must be some means to destroying it."

"There is not; to the contrary, it is half-human only in appearance. The beast has no heart and the more it eats, the more ravenous the creature becomes; it remains gaunt and murderous. I have not disclosed its most fearsome capability."

The merchant unplugged the jug, poured himself some drink and refreshed the reverend's cup before he spoke. "This cannibal demon attacked her party, yet Mercy reappeared unscathed. I recollect that she seemed immune to the feminine weakness for nerves. My apologies, Reverend, you said that this entity had another skill."

"Possession. The beast can dwell in the body of another, with no preference to sex. You can deduce the consequences should my daughter disclose the encounter in the woods. Violated or not, the creature inside her damns her. I'm certain that it will be a most monstrous birth. I'd have her give birth among the praying Indians, and if it issues forth as a grotesque creature, then I'll kill it myself."

"And if the babe is wholesome?" the merchant asked.

"Leave it with the heathens and say it died."

Fairebanke weighed what he had heard. He disliked the reverend's plan to take Indian land. The Indians could attack this winter. Starvation will alter the sanest of men. The riddle that concerned him was how to slay the unholy creature. When he exhausted his thinking on the matter, he was startled to find the reverend seated, head back and snoring.

He went to the hook next to the door for his coat. His capotain was missing. He found Mercy on the stairwell.

"Is this the hat you seek?" she asked.

He approached her with caution. "It is, and why the mischief?"

"To steal an opportunity to speak with you, as the servants are about the day with their tasks and my father is asleep from drink." She turned his hat over. "I see that your wife has sewn your initials into the lining."

Merchant Fairebanke could not remove his eyes from her rounded belly. The mound had distended her dark skirt. He tried not to contemplate how the deformity rebelled against her bodice.

"My hat, Mistress."

His hand trembled as he reached for it. His fingertips pinched the black brim, but she would not surrender the hat to him.

"You are a good man, Merchant Fairebanke. I implore you not to participate in my father's plan. I heard it all."

"All?

"All of it," she said.

The merchant could not face her. He tried a different argument. "Your father is the steward of all our souls."

"Theft damns us all, Merchant. Murder of an innocent damns us, in league with Indians to kill other Indians damns us, and if not the abandonment of a child vile, then what if he murders me?"

The merchant seized her arms and her hair fell. "Then save yourself and name the father. Innocence will prevail. Confess. Do it before he effects any part of his plot." The russet curl sat there like an upside-down question mark, a hook to distract and deceive him, he thought.

"Do you believe what he had said happened in the woods? Do you?" she asked.

"It is impertinent of you to insist on your question."

"There is much to lose, Merchant Fairebanke. The men that are in trust with this plan care nothing about me, or what had happened in the woods. I had not heard you assent to his plan, so I beseech you to step aside from the dangerous path. Think of your wife and children."

Her warm breath against his collar, her thin arms within his embrace, and that belly against him crowded his head with discordant thoughts and images.

He released her and stepped backward. She advanced one step. She was the brazen one.

"My hat, please?"

ဝဝဝ

Nobody protested the departure days after the momentous sermon. The men, most of them young and in the employ of the plantation's most prosperous men, had clasped their tearful wives and confused children.

Reverend Goodfeet waited with the other collared men on horseback. There were murmured benedictions and affirmatives among the men that they would prevail. It was better to strike first before the Indians had formed alliances. The praying Indians were not informed out of fear that they would repeat Judas in the garden. Mercy sat sidesaddle on a palfrey alone. None questioned her presence with the men. She watched the merchant comfort his wife Rebecca.

That morning the sky had been a dull gray and the sun a faint disk behind a curtain of clouds. Frost salted the ground, and the breaths of all those on the common misted. The horses turned their heads, eyes watery.

At last they moved. It was a few hours to a Pequot camp. Mercy first listened to the whispers of the men on foot speak the horrors that they would visit on the Indians. A blood lust infected them. Among her father's peers, she heard gentlemen's agreements on what crops would be planted, loans needed, as well as mutual assurances of contracts abroad. Indentured servants were promised the cancellation of their contract for this last labor.

The merchants had procured the finest black-powder rifles, bayonets fixed on them, and long knives for the purge. They would not spare man, woman, or child; those who survived were to be sold into slavery in the West Indies.

Past the hard fields, after the last bare farm and beyond the final wooden stakes that marked the boundary between civilization and Satan's forest, they proceeded into the glen. A light snow had begun to fall. The sun dimmed and a shadow fell over the land. Anxious eyes had kept vigil. Mercy Goodfeet had resolved herself to the cadence of her horse's gentle gait and the monotonous rhythm of her saddle.

A ripple of consternation passed through the men of lower rank when a shower of hail pelted them. There was talk that this was a sign that they were in the outland, in the Devil's domain. A man, a merchant who had been riding in the rear, brought up his charger to Reverend Goodfeet. He sidled his horse near the reverend, but spoke loudly enough for the good daughter to hear the troublesome news uttered to her father.

"Reverend, the foodstuffs are missing."

"Gone? How is that possible?"

"I have no idea, but some black arts are afoot here," the man said and glanced over his shoulder. He had missed her subdued smile. "These men will have no sustenance tonight. I counsel that we turn back."

"We shall not. When we rest, I will spur the men onward. We shall spare Him no quarter."

The bachelor merchant let his horse drop back. He would slip away while that early moon arched high in the afternoon sky. He galloped his way back to the village to raise alarms.

The gloom of night brought with it a shiver among the men under the bright moon. Wolves were spotted; the beasts mocked them with their yelps and panting. The men were ordered not to shoot because musket-fire would echo all around. Every treetop swayed as if they were full of demons.

Merchant Fairebanke eased his steed near her horse. She nodded her head and he, his.

"I noticed earlier that you found some amusement in the news."

"I find nothing pleasant about the lack of food. Have you forgotten that I must nourish the life within me? I'm present by another man's command."

"That man is your father, and he is your master until you have yourself a husband."

His face had intended a reprimand. She confronted him with a smile.

"That is amusing and cruel, Merchant Fairebanke. You know that a husband is not possible. You know that unfavorable possibilities await me, whether it is the Indians in these woods, these men around me, my father at the birthing stool, or the Devil himself."

"Control what you say, Mistress, and leave the rest to your Savior. I counsel you to confess the name before it is too late."

"It is already too late. You saw with your own eyes how I am perceived and judged when we left the good people. They were relieved to see me gone from their sight. Do you think I will survive this voyage?"

"I assure you that the good people of our village pray for your salvation."

"Prayer does no good out here, Merchant Fairebanke."

"Heed your tongue, for it verges on blasphemy."

"Does it, Samuel?" He had turned his head quickly upon hearing his first name. "Out here there are neither titles nor signs for the elected that will direct them to Sion's glorious gate. You are nothing more than Samuel Fairebanke, and what is that, but a name out here in this pagan paradise? The men around you place one foot in front of the other like a child who has recited his multiplication tables by rote. And yet all of you will stroke your beards and persist in calling this Babylon. Your hearts and feet move to the pulse of your greed."

The merchant sat disturbed in his saddle. He gripped the reins tight enough that his horse shook its head.

Darkness, bitter cold, and the hail that had since reverted back to snow threatened a blizzard. They would rest, but they had to move soon. Rumors about the food had become truth. The merchant assisted in her dismount. The two found solace near an oak tree. She caressed the gnarled trunk in curious appreciation.

"Your accusation of greed perplexes me, Mistress."

"Then why are you here? The enemy is not the savage. I learned that."

"So you did consort with an Indian?" he asked.

"The Pequot people saved me."

"After they killed everyone."

She said nothing.

"It is not greed, Mistress. It is preordained; we are chosen and therefore we are superior to the red people."

A commotion interrupted him. A man had thrown a rock at one of the wolves. The undeterred pack advanced, stared at them with watering mouths, when the leader stopped and sniffed the air. He yelped a painful cry and the pack disbursed with haste. The braggart declared that his projectile had defeated the hounds from Hell.

"Foolish pride," she said. "The menfolk should move and soon."

The snow abated moments later. "God approves our plan," one man said and others clapped their brethren in agreement. The men had not noticed that a thin mist had drifted in and become thicker. The horses moved, biting at their ties and then at those of their fellow beast. Some snorted, others neighed, but the consensus was that something had caused an agitation among them.

"This fog is the Devil's breath" one man had said, while another conjectured, "It is the draft from his own furnace."

A horse reared and broke free. There was a scream and then a stampede, hooves throwing clops of hard earth. In the melee the sound of men broken underfoot filled the void.

"We are sightless and without transport," a voice said in the mist.

Mercy saw shadows flash by and disappear. She called out to the merchant but he did not answer her. She braced her back against the oak tree and waited. A hand seized her. The merchant had returned. "We ought to move."

"Take faith in this tree and the moon overhead, Samuel."

She glanced up at the moon, and breathed in the mist. The oak tree, massive and ancient, moored them. A bird screeched in the distance.

"Hear that?" he asked.

"Ignore it, Samuel, and divest yourself of any interest in land, revenge, or hunger."

"You have brought this upon us," he said and stepped away. A voice was heard in the wind. Seductive and promising, it was a song Fairebanke said was from the divine choir.

"Ignore it, Samuel."

"And disdain the angels? The Lord has come to rescue us."

"I warned you."

"Warned me against what?"

"Greed."

"I suffer not of avarice," he answered. "I told you that we are predestined." The song grew sweeter in the wind. "Hear that?" he said. "You should confess so that you would be forgiven."

"Forgiven? The Wendigo came that day. Its hunger feeds on the hunger of others, for its craving is endless. When it found me it had spared me because I had no appetite in my heart."

She stared at him, her skin luminous under the lunar glare. Her hand glided over the orb of her rotund belly. "Nobody cared about my child; they consigned it to perdition."

Screams pierced the night. Bodies were smashed into trees, limbs and heads torn off. A man sprinted in front of them. A fierce growl followed him. The merchant thought that he had seen antlers. Then nothing.

"It is here," she said.

More frightful noises littered the air. The sound of bones breaking surrounded them. The mist had thickened and enshrouded them.

"Is this the demon which sired your child?" He heard nothing at first. "Mercy? Are you there?"

"Stay against this tree."

"No. I am of the elected. God protects his chosen ones."

"Farewell then," she said and whispered into his ear. "The father was my father."

He stepped back, aghast, and into the mist he disappeared.

ϱϱϱ

The young merchant who had fled the doomed party returned with elder townsmen and praying Indians; they found neither bodies in the wilderness nor a

Pequot presence at the scene. What they did discover was a lone hat, with the initials SF in the briars.

Mistress Mercy Goodfeet appeared one day with a child in another town. She was accepted as a widow. She said that her late husband was named Samuel. Her child was a healthy girl whom she had named Grace.

Gabriel Valjan is the author of the *Roma Series* from Winter Goose Publishing. He lives in Boston, Massachusetts, where he enjoys the local restaurants, and his two cats, Squeak and Squawk, who keep him honest to the story on the screen.

STICKY BUSINESS
By Bev Vincent

Edgar, Mikey and me were already at our table at the back of Marty's, our regular pub at the end of Beacon Street in Chelsea, discussing Huey's recent turn of bad luck, when Vinnie got there.

"Vinnie!" we all called out, although we were a little more out of sync than usual. There were supposed to be five of us, but with Huey in jail awaiting trial for larceny of a motor vehicle—a high-falutin' term for boosting a car—it didn't look like the whole gang was going to be together for a while. Not unless his lawyer managed to get the charges reduced to joyriding. That would have been pretty funny, come to think of it, because the reason Huey—his real name is Donald, as in Donald Duck, which is where his nickname comes from—boosted the car was so he could drive down to Chatham to see his kids. If that isn't a joy ride, I don't know what is.

Anyhow, Vinnie was late because he had a dentist appointment to get a crown on one of his teeth, which sounds a lot cooler than it really is. He was smiling and waving around a magazine. On his way past the bar, he told Holly to bring us another round, so he must've been feeling no pain, because Vinnie hardly ever treats. Not that I was complaining. Ever since we did that bank job where Joey Stefano took the fall and left us with a nice wad of cash, I've been doing better. Keeping away from the horses and the roulette wheel, most of the time. I wasn't rich—heck, I'll *never* be rich—but I was able to treat Holly to dinner every now and then, especially if I had a coupon.

Vinnie slapped the magazine on the table. It took me a while to figure out what it was, because J. Law's blonde hair covered part of the name. I have to confess—I have a major crash on Jennifer Lawrence, and she was looking mighty fine in a red dress with thin shoulder straps, showing plenty of skin and boob. She had a suggestive smile, and her hair was short and kinda wild, like she was posing outside on a windy day. I swear it was like she was looking right at me with those sultry eyes. Smoking hot. I hoped Holly didn't notice me checking her out.

In case there was any doubt, the cover said **J. Law!** in great big letters. Even bigger than the name of the magazine, which I eventually figured out was *Vanity Fair*. I'd never heard of it before, but if they thought enough of Miss Lawrence to put her on the cover, they were all right by me.

"Get a load of those," Edgar said, pointing at the magazine cover and guffawing. Of course that was when Holly arrived with our drinks. After she handed them out, she peered at the address label on the front cover. "Dr. Emil Erwin," she said. "Who's that?"

Vinnie turned red. "My dentist," he mumbled.

"Well, before you give it back to him, I'd like to look at the holiday gift guide," she said, pointing at a green banner I hadn't noticed before. She didn't look my way when she said this, but I hoped she was thinking about getting me something, even though Christmas was months ago.

After she left, Vinnie stabbed his index finger at some words near the bottom of the cover. "Get a load of *this*, boys."

I pushed my glasses up and looked where he indicated. "The Dark, Nasty Side of… Maple Syrup?!" it said. Now I'm not the smartest guy in the room, unless I'm alone in a room with Edgar, but I didn't see anything to get excited about.

"Maple syrup?" Mikey said in that falsetto voice of his. At least I wasn't the only one confused. And if Mikey and I were confused, I could only imagine what was going on between Edgar's ears.

"Maple syrup," Vinnie said, as if that answered the question. He flipped the magazine open to an article he had marked by turning down the corner of a page. One word caught my attention: "heist." Then another one: "million." Even better, that one was surrounded by the words "multi" and "dollar," even though I'm not sure "multi" is really a word.

Edgar's lips were moving as he tried to make sense of the headline, so I read it out loud for him. "Inside Quebec's Great, Multi-Million-Dollar Maple Syrup Heist." All of a sudden, I wasn't sure that dog-earing the article was all that smart. That was the kind of clue a cop on TV would be all over. I turned the page. It was a long article, but at least there were plenty of pictures. The first one showed a couple of horses in a forest pulling a sleigh with a bunch of kids in it, like something out of a Super Bowl commercial for beer.

"My dentist was running late," Vinnie said, "so I picked this up—"

"Because J. Law is on the front," Mikey said.

"Yeah, but after I read about her—"

"And drooled all over the page," Edgar said, and snorted with laughter.

Vinnie glared at him. "After that," he continued, "I found this."

None of us seemed too eager to read the article. Not only was it long, the print was really small. Besides, our beer was getting warm. "What's it about?" I asked, taking a sip.

"You see," Vinnie said, still acting all excited. "There's this place up in Quebec—"

"That's Canada," Edgar said, proud of himself.

"Yes, Canada. They store all their maple syrup in this warehouse. Everyone in the whole state—"

"Province," Mikey said. "They call them provinces up there."

"Yeah, all right. Anyhow, these guys figured out that no one was guarding the place, so it was easy picking."

"What's the big deal about syrup?" I asked. "I mean, it's just a buck or two at the grocery store. It's not like its oil or anything."

"You're absolutely right," Vinnie said. "Oil is 60, 70—sometimes as much as 100 bucks a barrel. Maple syrup's nothing like that."

I nodded, but something about the way he said it made me think I was about to be the butt of a joke.

"Anyway, the stuff you're talking about—that's fake. Sugar water. I'm talking about the real deal. They keep it on the top shelf at the grocery store, and it's expensive."

"How much?" Mikey asked.

"Five, six, ten times as much as the fake stuff."

"Okay."

"$1300 a barrel, according to this article."

We all gaped.

"Did you say…?" Mikey asked.

"Yep. Thirteen hundred bucks."

"That's a lot," Edgar said, trying to work something out on his fingers.

"Edgar, my buddy. You got that right. It's liquid gold."

ℓℓℓ

Vinnie gave us the highlights. "A lot of this is boring gobbledygook—I almost gave up. But then halfway through, it gets to the good part." He paused for a sip of beer and turned a couple of pages. "These guys stole over half a million gallons of maple syrup worth…" He ran his finger down the page. "…thirteen point four million smackeroos."

Edgar whistled and Mikey said "Holy cow" in a high-pitched squeak.

"When was this?" I asked.

"Four, maybe five years ago," Vinnie said.

"Did they catch the thieves?"

Vinnie nodded. "They got stupid. Careless. At first they took the barrels away, drained them and filled them with water, then took them back."

"Oooph," Mikey said. "Sounds like a lot of work."

"Yeah," Vinnie said. "A 40-gallon barrel of syrup weighs over 600 pounds. After a while, they started draining the barrels right there at the warehouse and didn't bother putting water in them. A guy taking inventory was walking on a stack of barrels when he knocked one over and almost fell. That's when they figured out they'd been robbed. Something like 10,000 barrels."

We sat in silence for a while, letting the story sink in.

"They're making a movie about it," Vinnie said. "With Jason Segel." He closed the magazine and we were once again treated to the smoldering gaze of J. Law.

"They should put her in it, too," Edgar said. "I'd go see that!"

We nodded our agreement, me after I made sure Holly wasn't watching. She's not really jealous, but I didn't want to ruin a good thing.

"All this talk of maple syrup reminds me of the Great Boston Molasses Flood," Mikey said.

I gave him a look. "The what?"

"You never heard about it? Happened a hundred years ago on the North End. A big tank burst and spewed a couple of million gallons of molasses into the street. It caused a su-, a su-, a whatchamacall'it…a tidal wave, except it was in slow motion, because it was, you know, molasses? The stuff was two or three feet deep for blocks."

"No way," Edgar said.

"Yeah, I saw it on *Drunk History*," Mikey said.

"I love that show," I said. "It's hilarious."

Mikey kept going. "A lot of people were hurt and, I dunno, twenty or thirty drowned. In molasses. Can you imagine that? Buildings were destroyed. Trains were knocked off the rails. It took weeks to clean up the mess. Some people say you can still smell molasses in Boston on a really hot day."

"Whoa," I said. I turned to say something to Huey, because this was the sort of story he'd get a kick out of, but then I remembered he wasn't with us. "Anyone visit Huey lately?" I asked.

"Not me," Mikey said. "I'm allergic to jails."

Vinnie nodded his agreement. "Spent enough time on the inside looking out."

I had, too, and I remembered how lonely it could get. With Huey's family living so far away, and his bad relationship with his ex, I didn't figure he was getting many visitors, so I decided to go see him the next day. It wasn't as if I had anything better to do.

We ordered another round, but I could tell Vinnie was put out that we weren't as excited by the maple syrup heist as he was, and that we were more interested in Mikey's story. He grabbed the magazine from Edgar, who had flipped back to look at pictures of Jennifer Lawrence. I didn't know what he expected. It wasn't like we could drive up to Quebec and steal their syrup. None of us could even get across the border on account of our past disagreements with the legal system. So we left it there, and that, I thought, was the end of that.

ꝏꝏ

I didn't plan to tell Huey the maple syrup story when I visited him at the Nashua Street Jail. We just ran out of things to talk about after a while. He was a bit down because he hadn't been able to get bail—stealing a car made him a flight risk, apparently—and his trial wasn't for another couple of weeks. Unless his court appointed lawyer, who was probably handling a hundred cases at the same time, found time to talk to the A.D.A. about a plea bargain.

I was up to the part where someone noticed one of the barrels was empty when I realized Huey had gotten real quiet. I thought maybe he was bored or depressed or something, so I stopped.

"Keep going," he said. "What happened after that?"

So I kept on, trying to remember all the details, but figuring it didn't really matter if I made some of them up. I mean, what difference did it make if it was $13.4 million or $14.3?

When I finished, Huey started asking questions that I couldn't answer. I wondered where I could find a copy of that *Varsity Square* magazine to send him. He'd probably like the photos of J. Law, if nothing else.

"I got a cousin," he said. "In Vermont."

"Okay," I said.

"They make maple syrup up there too," he said. "Not just in Canada. He talks about it all the time."

"Hmmm," I said, still not getting it.

"You guys can stay in his basement. I'm sure he wouldn't mind. He'll show you around. Help you case some places. I'll bet he knows all about that stuff. I'll make a few calls."

ଓଓଓ

On the drive up to Vermont in Vinnie's car a few days later, we had plenty of time to play with ideas, but we didn't really know what we were getting ourselves into, so we ended up mostly talking about movies like *The Italian Job* and *Oceans 11*. We did try to work through some rough calculations. If a barrel of maple syrup was worth $1300, maybe we could get $600 for one on the black market. If we could get ten barrels, that would be over a grand each, including Huey. It sounded like a lot of work for so little reward, though. Then Mikey said that if we broke it up into smaller lots, we could get more. After all, one of those little jugs in the grocery store went for at least $15, and there must be hundreds of them to a barrel, maybe as many as a thousand. All we had to do was find someone to wholesale it, and we were as golden as, well, as maple syrup.

We still had a few problems to sort out, like where we were going to get a bunch of empty syrup jugs, but we could deal with that later, after we had the syrup. It doesn't go bad, according to Huey, but our time was limited because the season was short. Once the farmers shipped their barrels off to market, we would be S.O.L. We'd have to wait a whole year for another chance.

When Huey said we could stay in his cousin's basement, I imagined something finished, with sofas and carpet and maybe wood paneling on the walls. But no, it was concrete floors and dust and cobwebs. After over four hours crammed in Vinnie's bucket of bolts, I'd been looking forward to a comfortable place to sleep. Silly me. Turns out, Huey's cousin's wife wasn't exactly thrilled to have four strangers sleeping in their basement, either. She gave us a few dirty looks, and her husband—his name was Chuck—an even worse one.

Chuck, who had his own troubled past with law enforcement, wasn't keen on aiding and abetting, as he put it, so we decided to get a cheap motel instead. It was a little cramped with four of us—and Edgar is as big as two people, so really like five—but it was better than the concrete floor. Plus, there was a bathroom.

Chuck agreed to give us directions to three places we should check out, but he didn't want anything to do with us after that. We spent the afternoon driving around the back roads of Vermont, using the map he drew on a scrap of paper. "Burn this when you're done," he said, which sounded paranoid and badass at the same time.

The first place we went, there were a couple of mean-looking dogs chained up in the yard, so we ruled that one out. The second place looked okay, a ramshackle building that would probably fall down in a strong wind. The third place had security cameras but no dogs, so we made that one #2 on our list. Better cameras than dogs any day. Cameras don't bite, especially if you know where they are. Besides, nobody around here knew us, except Chuck and his wife.

The next morning, we headed over to Burlington to get supplies. Mikey had a fake credit card and matching ID that he thought would be good for a day or two, so we used it to buy a bunch of stuff at Home Depot and loaded it into the back of one of those little pickup trucks they rent so you can take your lumber home.

I'd like to say our plan went off without a hitch, but I can't. It was nothing but one hitch after another. First off, we'd burned Chuck's map like he asked, but then we had a hard time finding the place we wanted to rob again. We must have driven around for an hour before we stumbled on it, mostly by accident.

Once we found it, we were able to get into the shed where the maple sugar was stored without any trouble, but it was all downhill from there. Finding the barrels was the easy part—they were arranged in a neat circle in the middle of the sugar shack. They were made of blue plastic and had numbers stamped on the side. Chuck had warned us not to take them because they could be traced back to the owner. That and the fact that they weighed a ton. Well, not a ton, but a lot. So we had these rubber tubs from Home Depot, and a bunch of pitchers to scoop the syrup out of the barrels into them. Sounded like a good idea on paper. The barrels were real buggers to get into, though, because we didn't have the right tools to break the seals. Edgar ripped them off with brute force, which meant we weren't going to be able to seal them back up when we were done.

It didn't take long to realize how much work it was going to be. We pulled our tubs up as close as we could and started scooping and pouring, but once a barrel was about a third empty, we had to lean into it and that meant getting syrup all over ourselves. Edgar tried tipping a half-empty barrel over to drain it into his tub, but it got away from him and spilled all over the floor, including on our feet.

I've never seen such a sticky mess in my life. For some reason, I couldn't stop thinking about chicken feathers blowing onto us, like someone tarred and feathered in an old movie. Every time I moved, my feet were stuck to the floor, and then the gooey stuff started working its way inside my boots, too.

We duct-taped pieces of wood to the handles of our pitchers so we could scoop more out of the barrels, and that worked okay for a while, but then we started to get so hot, sore and tired that we didn't care anymore. We were spilling as much as we were getting into the tubs, and I was sweating like a pig, which made the syrup I'd gotten all over myself runnier, so it was going down my back. I had it in my hair and up my nose—even in my ears, I think.

We emptied eight barrels before we called it quits. "Eff this, I'm done," Mikey announced, his voice squeaking with frustration. Mikey never swore, but he had substitutes for just about every curse word.

But we weren't done, of course. We still had to get our heavy tubs out of the sugar shack and onto the truck. They came with plastic snap-on covers, but those didn't work so great, especially once we started carrying them. The rubber twisted, the syrup inside sloshed around, and the lids would pop off without warning, splashing more of that sticky crap on our hands, arms, legs and feet. We finally got them all stacked up on the back of the truck, which by now was as soaked with syrup as we were.

Resting my sticky hands at the base of my aching back, I looked at the mess we were leaving behind. At least we didn't have to bother filling the barrels up with water. No one was going to have any trouble following our trail, at least as far as the truck. Our footprints were all over the place, and as the maple syrup dried, they were turning into sugary pieces of evidence. I didn't know whether the cops could collect footprints made of sugar, but we were all going to have to get rid of our boots, just in case.

Vinnie was driving, of course, and Mikey won paper/rock/scissors to get the other seat in the cab, so Edgar and I were stuck in the back with the tubs of syrup. It was a little chilly, and we were sticking to everything, but at least we were done for the night. Or so I thought.

Vinnie took it slow and easy at first, but then he got onto a paved country road and started to go faster. He must've hit a patch of ice, because suddenly we went into a skid and then the truck started spinning. The pile of plastic tubs toppled onto Edgar and me, and a couple of them broke open. I caught a wave of maple syrup right in the face, and for a few seconds I was sure I was going to die. I could only think of those poor people who'd drowned in a tidal wave of molasses a hundred years ago, and what a terrible way it must have been to go. My glasses kept most of it out of my eyes, at least.

The truck was still skidding and fishtailing, then there was a jolt and a bang, and the tailgate flew open and out went the tubs of syrup, smashing open all over the road. Edgar and I managed to hang on somehow—I think I was glued to the bed—and the truck finally came to a stop.

I sat there spluttering and trying to get syrup out of my mouth and nose. Edgar grabbed me by the arm and hauled me off the back of the truck. Mikey and Vinnie were already standing on the side of the road. One look at the truck and I knew it wasn't going anywhere. I probably should have been mad at Vinnie for getting in a wreck and destroying all our hard work, but I was too miserable.

We kicked the empty tubs into the ditch and Mikey did a quick rub-down job to make sure there weren't any fingerprints in the cab, but there was no way to clean up the back of the truck. We could only hope the spilled syrup would cover everything up.

I don't know that I've ever been more uncomfortable in all my life as we slogged through the woods, trying to keep out of sight and make our way back to the motel. It took hours, and I had syrup everywhere you can possibly think of, and I mean *everywhere*. It did not feel good, not one little bit. I've seen movies where people drip honey on each other in bed, and I'm telling you right now, that is never going to happen with me. No way, no how. Not even with J. Law.

It didn't help that Vinnie and Mikey were snickering at us most of time. They had some syrup on their clothes and boots and all that, too, but nothing like Edgar and me. Mikey kept throwing stuff at us to see if it would stick. I almost decked him.

When we finally made it back to the motel, Vinnie had a hard time getting the key card to work because it was gummed up, but eventually we got inside and stripped off our clothes. I usually don't like being naked around a bunch of guys, even friends like these. Reminds me too much of my time inside. But I didn't care about that at all. I just had to get that goop off me.

Edgar and I called dibs on the shower at the same time, and I won paper/rock/scissors over him to go first. He always picks rock. It was just sugar water, so you'd think it would come off easy with hot water, but it took a while, and even when I was done, I still felt sticky. I let Edgar have his turn, then Vinnie and Mikey washed off and I went in again. By then, there wasn't much hot water left, but I didn't care.

I'd brought a change of clothes, so I stuffed my old pants and shirt into a plastic garbage bag to wash when we got home. I probably should have thrown them away, because they would have been hard to explain to a cop if we got pulled over, but I didn't have a lot of extra money to buy new clothes. This trip had been a total bust, and I was going to have to buy new boots, besides.

We waited until daylight to head back to Boston. The early morning news started with a story about a maple syrup spill that shut down a road for hours while the fire department figured out how to clean it up. Eventually they decided to try the same stuff they used for oil spills. After the syrup soaked into it, they scraped it off the road and spread a bunch of sand that they'd have to come back later that day to sweep up. They still didn't know about the robbery, or if they did they weren't saying.

The news anchors had a good laugh over the fact that the spill had happened on Buttermilk Falls Road. One guy with very white teeth said they were putting out an amber alert for the driver of the truck. We had to explain to Edgar that was on account of the color of the syrup, but I still don't think he got it. The cop they interviewed estimated that the spilled syrup was worth over $10,000, which didn't make us feel any better. "Nothing a truckload of waffles couldn't handle," the blonde reporter in the tight blue dress said.

We were pretty quiet on the drive back to Boston. Edgar tried to make a few dumb jokes—his favorite was pointing his hand like a gun and saying "Sticky 'em up." He thought that was hilarious, and maybe it was the first time or two, but by the time we crossed the Mystic on I93, we were all yelling at him to shut up.

A few miles after the bridge, Mikey pointed at a huge IHOP sign in the distance. "Anyone up for a tall stack?" he asked with a grin.

"If you stop there," I said, "it'll be the last tall stack, short stack, or any damn stack you'll ever have. You can take that to the bank."

Bev Vincent is the author of several books, most recently THE DARK TOWER COMPANION, and over eighty short stories, including appearances in *Ellery Queen's Mystery Magazine*, *Alfred Hitchcock's Mystery Magazine* and two MWA anthologies. He has been nominated for the Stoker, Edgar and ITW Thriller Awards. "The Bank Job," featuring some familiar ne'er-do-wells, won the 2010 Al Blanchard Award. www.bevvincent.com

BEST NEW ENGLAND CRIME STORIES

NEW HAMPSHIRE

GHOSTING MRS. MUIR
by Sharon Daynard

Suzanne Muir peered out the Muddled Moose's window to the near-whiteout conditions wondering how much longer she could stretch her fourth cup of coffee. What started as a few playful flurries dusting downtown Points North's brick walkways and cobblestone streets, had worked itself into a full-fledged nor'easter that promised to bring the picturesque village in New Hampshire's White Mountains to a standstill. It was hard to believe just last week temperatures were pushing fifty.

She'd been on the receiving end of dirty looks from the diner's owner, Linda Stillwell, and a teenage waitress who remained after last call for coffee was sounded over an hour ago—back when they were all smiles, offering her a complimentary coffee to go, and yammering on about the "big one" on the way. How quickly those smiles turned to scowls as wind gusts flirted with gale force status. Their expletive-packed stage whispers made it known she'd outstayed her welcome. It was only a matter of time before they turned off the lights and told her to lock up when she was done.

She closed her eyes, took a sip of lukewarm coffee and sighed as if cherishing every overpriced drop while she wrestled with the notion of leaving with her dignity still intact. Truth was, Suzanne Muir and dignity parted ways a long time ago. As it was, she'd lost track of how many times she checked her cell for missed calls, voice messages and storm updates, and how many times her head shot up in the middle of frantically typing a text because she mistook the *jangle* of silverware thrown into a bus box for the *jingle* of the shopkeepers bell.

A tap on Suzanne's shoulder jolted her eyes open.

"Times up, Suzanne." Linda Stillwell snatched the bill from the table. "Coffee's on me. I'll even throw in a quart of the best damned corn chowder in all New England."

Suzanne forced a smile and shook her head. "I'm almost done."

"You remember my youngest, don't you Suzanne?" Linda motioned to the waitress who was too busy texting to look up. "Katie's home on winter break from UNH. She's majoring in Psychology. Katie," she called to her daughter. "A large chowder to go for Mrs. Muir."

"Thank you, Linda, but I'm—"

"Leaving," Linda finished her sentence. "Carl's not coming. Not in this weather."

Suzanne's spine stiffened at the mention of his name. "I'm not waiting for Carl."

"No? And I suppose you weren't waiting for him the day before yesterday, or the day before that. Seems to me you've been parked in that same booth the better part of a week during the lunch rush not waiting for Carl to walk through the door."

Suzanne felt her checks flush at the revelation she'd probably been the topic of conversation among patrons and staff alike at the diner. There was nothing like a desperate woman on the brink of fifty to start the Points North rumor mills churning. No doubt they'd had themselves a grand time dredging up the unfortunate bit of business with her late husband. Seven years ago might as well have been seven minutes in their petty minds.

"The only day I didn't see you sitting here was yesterday. Then again, you were probably too busy putting on that show over at the post office. Someone screw up and send you another 200 pounds of kitty litter?"

"That's not fair, Linda. That was right after Carl disappeared. I couldn't eat, I couldn't sleep, I could barely function. I accidentally ordered twenty bags of litter instead of two. I'd like to see how well you'd hold up if something happened to Katie."

Before Linda could respond, Katie placed a take-out container of corn chowder on Suzanne's table, sat down across from her, and scrolled through her cell phone. "That troll's at it again with another one-star review on Yelp. Yesterday he posted 'Given a blind taste test, it would have been impossible to distinguish the stuffed pepper soup from septic runoff if not for the Muddled Moose's signature stray hair garnish.'"

Suzanne looked at the container of corn chowder and cringed, wondering what surprises it held.

"You think that's bad, Mrs. Muir? The day before that he wrote the perfect accompaniment for the shepherd's pie was a chilled bottle of ipecac syrup."

Suzanne's head jiggled like a bobble doll. "Why would anyone say that? No one sells ipecac syrup anymore."

"Oh, he's a charmer." Linda slid into the booth next to Katie. "Last week he claimed mice all over town were throwing themselves on snap traps rather than be subjected to my bacon mac and cheese."

"Snap traps?" Suzanne shuddered, swirling the coffee in her cup.

"Bottoms up, Suzanne. Let's go."

"Please, Linda, just five more—"

"Carl's not meeting you here." Linda shot her daughter a look that begged for a cuckoo clock sounding on the hour. "Just yesterday, I heard he was living in Maine."

Suzanne closed her eyes and counted to ten before opening them. "The only place my Carl is in an unmarked grave God knows where."

Linda reached across the table and patted Suzanne's hand. "Carl's living his dream. He's been happy these last seven years. You knew he was leaving. We all did. It was all he talked about."

"Carl didn't—"

"He did. The same way your father left your mother when you were a kid. Stuff like that scars a person. Back when we were in high school you went through boyfriends like they were a bag of chips. I imagine you were the same when you were away at college before your mother died. You could have sold that empty old house and left Points for good, but instead you quit school and came back. And for what, Suzanne?"

"Well, it wasn't the coffee." Suzanne toasted Linda with her cup. "Or the company."

"You took up right where you left off in high school, drifting in and out of one relationship after the other. No one was good enough for you, either they didn't have enough money, enough of a backbone, or enough commonsense to stay clear of you from the start. And then you met sweet, harmless Carl Muir, a penniless graduate student working summer vacation waiting tables and washing dishes here at the Muddled Moose, back when my parents owned the place. I guess you didn't have a problem with the coffee or the company back then."

"Just with you, Linda."

Linda's head moved in an almost imperceptible shake as she bit down on her lower lip. "Much to Carl's credit, he wasn't interested in you or your games. But you wore him down, like you did all the others. I gave the budding romance a month tops before you grew tired of Carl and moved on to the next man. But I was wrong. The two of you weren't together two months when you and Carl tied the knot over at the town hall. To this day Suzanne, I don't know if Carl was the first decent guy that smiled in your direction or maybe it was—"

"A false positive on a home pregnancy test." Suzanne turned her attention back to the weather outside the window. "Getting married was Dudley Do-Right's idea, not mine."

Linda gave another pat to Suzanne's hand and held it there. "The point is, even back then you couldn't help how controlling you were. You were always critical of every last little flaw he had and lashing out at him because of your own insecurities. You did everything you could to sabotage your marriage and when Carl finally wanted out, you clung to him for dear life."

Katie nodded. "It's called abandonment issues, Mrs. Muir."

Suzanne jerked her hand away from Linda and wiped it with a napkin. "It's called man-opause, Katie. A few gray hairs at Carl's temples and all of a sudden he had to find himself. Some men buy a fancy car. Others have an affair. Carl didn't even have a driver's license. And as far as expertise in the bedroom went, Carl Muir was nothing to write home about."

"Suzanne…"

"So Carl decided to 'find himself' while walking the Appalachian Trail and hitchhiking across the country. Oh, he had big plans all right. He was going to take the occasional odd job along the way and record his experiences in a journal like that crackpot Jack Kerouac. He went on about it for weeks, bending the ear of everyone from the heating oil delivery guy to the Girl Scouts selling cookies outside the grocery store. He even spent a fortune on a pair of hiking books and an ergonomic backpack."

"It was hardly a fortune, Suzanne. He picked them up at a swap meet."

"Does it really matter where Carl bought them? He wasn't going anywhere. He never finished anything he started. On a whim he bought a walk-in refrigerator and a ten-burner range because he fancied the idea of turning our tumbledown Victorian into a B&B. Who in their right mind would stay at a

B&B that sits at the end of a two-mile dirt driveway in the middle of nowhere? You need binoculars to see our nearest neighbors. The B&B, like the 50s-themed bowling alley, the gourmet hotdog cart, and his novel fell by the wayside."

"Suzanne don't."

"Don't what? Push Carl off that pedestal you and everyone else put him on? "

"He gave up everything for you, Suzanne. His degree, his writing, his—"

"Carl Muir wasted twenty-two years of *my life* writing the next great whodunit. When he wasn't at the house holed up in his 'private library' with how-to books and mysteries or whittling the day away playing solitaire on his computer, he was wasting time in here drinking coffee and communing with his muses. You and the rest of the enablers in this godforsaken town kept feeding his fantasies while I was killing myself pulling double shifts. The White Mountains' answer to Arthur Conan Doyle was tweaking his two thousandth draft of *Murder in Retrospect* when he was killed. Did you ever think that maybe if Carl had a real job he wouldn't have been home that day? That he'd still be alive?"

"Carl *is* alive, Suzanne. You can't keep doing this."

"I can't keep doing this?" Suzanne's voice cracked. "You and everyone else in Points North are the ones hell-bent on keeping a lie alive. I don't know what stories your mother told you about Carl, Katie, but I can guarantee you none of them are true. My husband didn't leave on his own volition. He wouldn't have made it to the end of the driveway before he lost interest. Something happened to Carl that day. Something horrible. Our marriage was far from perfect, but I loved Carl. I searched every inch of that house for him. There wasn't even a goodbye note."

"He left divorce papers on the kitchen table waiting for Suzanne's signature," Linda added for Katie. "Carl said she could have the house and the money. He just wanted out."

Suzanne's spine stiffened straight. "How incredibly generous of him considering that house has been in my mother's family for generations. I inherited it before I ever met Carl. My name and my name only is on the deed. As for money, that was mine too."

For the briefest of moments, Suzanne's jaw clinched and her lips tightened to a thin white line, caging her words. "When I couldn't find Carl I called the police. They were useless. They rolled their eyes when I told them they needed to start a search. They didn't even bag up the bloodstained washcloth I found in his library. Chief Keller wrote it off to a shaving nick that got a bit too ambitious. A shaving nick!"

"Alright, Suzanne. I think you've staggered far enough down memory lane for one day. It's time to go."

"You're a smart girl, Katie, how would a bloody washcloth turn up in my husband's library?" Suzanne's hands slammed down on the table in response to Katie's shrug. "Because someone got sloppy cleaning up after Carl's murder, that's how. But try telling that to Keller. I waited forty-eight agonizing hours to file a missing person report. If I had to make a guess, he turned around and tossed it in the trash. All I've ever wanted was for Carl's killer to be brought to justice and for Carl to get a proper burial."

Katie pouted. Linda rolled her eyes.

Suzanne looked away, brushed her bangs from her eyes and took in a deep breath before turning back to her audience. "Months went by without a break in the investigation and then out of the blue a postcard showed up in my PO Box. On the front was a cartoon caricature of a peach picking fruit off a tree, and on the back was the inscription, *The picking's great! Carl.* My knees buckled when I read it."

"So your husband was alive." Katie looked pleased as punch.

"No he wasn't!" Suzanne picked up her coffee cup and put it down in fear her shaking hand would slosh what little was left onto the table. "I stomped up to the counter and at the top of my lungs let everyone within fifty miles know I wasn't amused. It didn't matter that I insisted it wasn't Carl's handwriting. No one listened. And those postcards just kept coming from all over the country, reaffirming everyone's belief that Carl left me."

"Suzanne..."

"Come that following February what do you think I found waiting in my PO Box? W2s from three different states with Carl's name and Social Security number on them. Carl Muir never put in a decent day's work after we married and I doubt any of that changed in the afterlife. I imagine everyone at the post office got in a good snicker while I marched to the police station, proof in hand that Carl's killer sold his identity to a migrant worker with instructions to keep his income under nine thousand dollars to avoid filing taxes. Keller wouldn't even look at the W2s. He showed me to the door. I called the IRS. Even they didn't care. Every February I get three, four, sometimes five W2s for Carl and nobody cares."

Linda slid out of the booth and signaled her daughter to do the same. "I'm sure Lester Holt and the crew at *Dateline* would be absolutely fascinated with this, Suzanne, but it's old news to the rest of us. Time to go and this time I mean it."

"I can't leave." Suzanne closed her eyes and opened them slowly. "I know he comes here for lunch sometimes."

"Carl hasn't—"

"I'm not waiting for a ghost, Linda. I'm waiting for my...boyfriend." And, as if on cue, there it was, that look between Linda and Katie. A look that might as well have been a burst of laughter. She knew the reaction the word "boyfriend" would receive. Calling him her friend, sounded too casual. Her lover, too crude. Her handyman, was such a cliché. About the only thing Suzanne knew for certain was, like Carl Muir, he was nowhere to be found.

"You have a boyfriend?" Linda's tone sounded almost mocking.

"Is that so shocking? It's been over seven years since Carl was murdered. Long enough for anyone else to be declared legally dead. And FYI,

Katie, they call that *death in absentia*. My friends at Suddenly Single thought it was time for me to move on."

Linda's brow hiked. "Suddenly Single?"

Suzanne nodded. "A support group for people who've had a spouse or significant other unexpectedly taken from them."

Linda tilted her head and gave it a shake. "And you were supposed to meet your boyfriend here today, in the middle of a nor'easter?"

"It's possible I got the day or the time wrong." Suzanne looked back out the window and let out a sigh knowing how ridiculous she sounded.

"So what you're really saying, Suzanne, is you've been stood up everyday for the past week."

Suzanne shook her head. "It's not like that. He grabs lunch here every now and then, so I thought if I—"

"Waited long enough he'd show up," Linda finished Suzanne's sentence. "I hate to burst your bubble, but it sounds like you haven't got a boyfriend anymore."

"Has he even called you?" Katie asked, motioning to Suzanne's cell. "Returned your calls? Your texts?"

Suzanne shook her head.

"He's ghosting you, Mrs. Muir."

Linda nodded. "Ghosting, aka, avoiding you like the plague."

"Ghosting? No. Blake wouldn't do that to me."

Linda's jaw went slack. "Blake Hollenbeck? The handyman?"

Suzanne nodded wondering what Linda found more incredulous, her taking a lover, or a man like Blake Hollenbeck settling for her. As far as handyman went, Blake left a lot to be desired. Her back door was still sticking, the walk-in fridge was still running too cold, and the downstairs toilet still needed its handle jiggled to stop it from running. But what Blake lacked in home repair know-how, he more than made up for with a knack for fulfilling her most intimate desires. She could live with a slow tub drain if 'getting to it later' freed up a few hours of Blake's time.

"We celebrated our three-month anniversary last Wednesday. He cooked dinner for us at my house—beef bourguignon and popovers. I made a Baked Alaska for dessert. Everything was perfect. We were making plans for a romantic getaway to the Keys."

"Maybe Blake left without you, Suzanne."

"Did you even check his Facebook page, Mrs. Muir?"

"Facebook? I don't—"

"Here you go." Katie held her cell phone out to Suzanne. "Blake's still in Points. He's got to learn to shut off the location tracker on his Facebook page. He was at the Granite Peaks hotel last Thursday and the Donut Hole on Sunday. On Monday he posted that he just missed plowing into a bull moose with his pickup on the Kanc when he was driving back from North Conway. He was here yesterday around twelve-thirty grabbing a stuffed pepper soup to go."

"Yesterday? It was so crowded I couldn't find a parking space. I left and went to the post office before heading back to work. Does your phone show where he is now?"

Katie shook her head."

"Something's wrong. Very wrong," Suzanne's voice quivered. "Blake wouldn't… ghost me."

"Go home, Suzanne. The next time Blake's here, I'll call you. How's that?"

"I can't—"

"Would you rather Chief Keller gave you a ride home, Suzanne?"

Suzanne shook her head. "You promise you'll call me, Linda? I have to talk to him."

ɷɷɷ

Suzanne Muir emptied the corn chowder into a soup bowl, ignoring the cat weaving figure eights about her ankles. She held the bowl at arm's-length, tilting her head left to right as she assessed the soup's color and consistency. It was translucent and thin, like watered-down skim milk. There wasn't even a hint of fresh cream or butter. A frown cut across her face as she held it closer and gave it a stir of her spoon. It didn't even smell like corn chowder. She counted one, two, three small cubes of potato, a dead giveaway they were canned. Instead of plump tender kernels of corn bursting with golden freshness, what there were of them were crushed and more of a mustard color. There were no sautéed bits of onions, no celery, no bits of bacon, and no course ground pepper. She didn't have to taste it to know it would disappoint. She deposited the bowl on the floor and padded down the hall to Carl's library with the hungry cat nipping at her heels.

She turned a skeleton key in the lock and pushed the library door open, sending dust and dander scurrying through the air like startled pixies seeking sanctuary in the shadows. She took a seat across from Carl's battle-scarred desk in a worn and weary leather wingback that let out a wheeze under her weight, pulled the cellphone from her pocket and entered another scathing one-star review on Yelp for the Muddle Moose for a corn chowder that even an alley cat turned its nose up at.

She looked about the room and frowned. After all these years it still stunk of Carl. The room was a mess, the same as it was the day Carl was murdered. Granted there was seven years' worth of dust covering everything including Carl, with the exception of the wingback she'd claimed as hers.

"Guess who I had lunch with today?" She waited a second or two for a response from the mummified corpse propped in the chair behind the desk. With none forthcoming she answered for him. "Linda Stillwell, the president of the Carl Muir Fan Club. She couldn't wait to bring up the kitty litter I ordered. Granted, two hundred pounds was overkill, but I wasn't sure how much I needed to mummify your body in the tub. Considering all the how-to books you read, you weren't much help."

She picked up the cat and deposited it on her lap, stroking its neck as she spoke. “That tub’s never been the same, Carl. Some of the litter must have found its was down the drain. It always ran slow, but never that slow. You remember that tub, don’t you, Carl? It’s the one I reminded you about over and over again. I didn’t have a problem with you leaving me. All I asked was for you to fix the drain and cement the dirt floor in the basement. How could I sell the house with the drain clogged and Daddy buried down in the basement? People can say what they want about my mother, but she knew what it took to keep a man.”

A smirk worked its way across Suzanne’s face before she her lips tight together and scowled, looking at him. “Two things, Carl. I asked you to do two things before you left. And you couldn’t even do that. After seven years I’d had it, Carl. I hired Blake Hollenbeck to finish what you never started. One thing led to another and we fell in love. Or at least I did. Blake was just stringing me along. He never finished any of the jobs around here that he started. Sound familiar, Carl? On our three-month anniversary he was supposed to make dinner for us. He showed up with half a container of god-dammed stuffed pepper swill from that dive. He ate the other half on the drive over here. I spent hours making a baked Alaska for dessert and he brought the soup du jour!”

She paused, took in a deep breath and let it out in a hiss. “I didn’t even hit him hard, just hard enough to knock him out. I could have called 911. I could have done a lot of things, but I put him that damn walk-in fridge of yours and locked the door. I figured come morning I open the door and we’d both have a good laugh.

“I don’t know how, but I forgot about him for a day or two and when I finally got around to checking on him the thermostat was running cold, too cold. He’d died from exposure. I know what you’re thinking, Carl, but I covered my tracks. I went to the Muddled Moose everyday, looking like a lost puppy, staring out the window, waiting for someone to take me home. I put Blake’s cell phone in a baggy and typed through the plastic. I drove all over creation in Blake’s pickup, wearing his coat and hunting cap, and cellphone in my pocket, making it look like he was having himself a great time without me. I even drove through an E-Z Pass lane knowing he didn’t have a transponder. I imagine a $26 fine is proof of life.

“And because Blake’s last meal was that awful stuffed pepper soup I had to wait until yesterday when it was back on the menu at the Muddled Moose to stage his death. Not to mention, I need the weather to cooperate with a drop in temperature. Everything just seemed fell into place with the nor’easter on the way. I drove his pickup to the top of Proctors Hill last night, propped Blake in the driver’s seat, powered the windows down, put the truck in DRIVE and let gravity do the rest. The pickup completely missed the bend at the bottom of the hill, flipped once and slammed into a stand of trees. Blake’s corpse was pretty much pinned inside the cab. He couldn’t call for help because *he* dropped his cellphone outside the Muddled Moose yesterday. I made sure I backed over it a few times in the parking lot before I headed to the post office. And low and behold, what did I find there? A post card from you that I'd dropped in the first mailbox I came across in Maine.

"I imagine the poor slob I sold your ID to will be sending another one from Florida, California, or maybe even Hawaii. That's the deal he's been living up to all these years, that and making sure his W2s keep coming to my PO Box.

"I'll be back at the Muddled Moose tomorrow, looking out that window, nursing a cup of coffee, and checking my phone for a message from Blake. I'm thinking I might even breakdown and cry my eyes out. I'm sure everyone in the diner will get a good chuckle, but it'll be worth the humiliation. And I'll keep going back to the diner and waiting for Blake until someone stumbles across his truck and finds his body. By then everyone including Linda Stillwell and her kid are going to believe he was alive and well right up until yesterday.

"Maybe I should be the one writing mysteries, Carl."

Sharon Daynard has been offered the services of a professional hit man, crossed paths with a serial killer, testified before grand juries, and taken lie detector tests. Her short stories have appeared in magazines and anthologies in the US and Canada. Her 51-word short story "Widow's Peak" received a Derringer nomination for Best Flash of 2004. She is member of the New England chapter of Sisters in Crime and a Guppy. www.sadaynard.com

BLACK ICE
by Connie Johnson Hambley

Claire Mullins-Smythe drove her Volvo wagon along winter roads, using the conditions as an excuse not to rush into another evening pantomiming a happy and supportive wife. The early spring day on Massachusetts' North Shore had been warm enough to melt snow banks into tiny rivers, but the cold night froze everything solid, leaving streaks of pavement looking wet and deceptively innocent. The car slid around a corner and she cursed her frozen world.

She wanted warmth. Not simply the outer warmth of a bright sun or a blazing hearth. Those she could purchase. The inner warmth of genuine love was much more precious to her. Tonight's celebration was a farce. As hard as she tried, she couldn't rejoice in learning that her husband will be appointed to the bench.

David Smythe was a dashing and cocky third-year law student and she was a terrified and wide-eyed first year when they met at Harvard Law. She loved him at first sight and panicked when his graduation approached and he had yet to notice her despite their many "accidental" meetings. When she finally did wedge him into a corner at a bar, he was polite enough with conversation, but his eyes never stopped scanning the room. Only when she mentioned her father was Chief Justice William Wendell Mullins did he stop his surveillance and look at her, *really* look at her. She remembered his radiance when he smiled and bought her another drink. They were married a week after she graduated law school, almost eleven years ago.

His career flourished with the assistance of her father's connections, and in the month since William's death, David barely spoke to her. She yearned for some acknowledgement she still mattered. Once David made judge, would he still want her?

The answer sent a shiver down her spine. She would have served his purpose.

She pulled into the empty garage. The house sprang to life as she pressed her code into the "Safe Haven" beta app on her cell with a perfectly manicured finger. Music blared inside and she adjusted the volume by using the sliding dot on the bar located next to the little ear icon on her screen. Lights flickered, and then stayed on. The garage door bounced only once when halfway down, rose almost all the way up, then finally eased closed. Progress. Fewer bugs this time. Maybe her client could move up the launch date of their app after all.

Before she could dictate a note, her phone vibrated in one continuous buzz. "System Alert" flashed red on the screen. A schematic of the house with text-bubble details told her someone had entered with a pass code and the security system had not been reengaged.

David. He must have parked in front in an effort to surprise her with a big celebratory dinner she had to buy the groceries for and prepare. An aversion to dining out was a quirk of his. Claire stifled the thought it had more to do with not being seen with her in public than food choice.

Her finger hovered over the "Play Video" icon then jerked to the "X" in the upper right corner. Her lip curled with self-disgust as her phone went dark. No need to check the feeds. If he was home early, it was because he wanted something and she'd put money on it wasn't her.

It hurt too much to hope, so she stopped.

With actions born from habit, she stole a quick look in the rearview mirror and gave her cheeks an extra pinch. She exuded warmth and beauty, even if she was dying a slow death inside.

She gathered up the fresh salmon with special herbs and greens, balanced the bottle of champagne against her chest, and managed to open the door to the kitchen while pressing her briefcase between her hip and the door jam.

"Please don't be afraid."

Groceries spilled to the floor as her body flinched with fright. The champagne was saved from certain death by the quick catch of a man. If the voice and the words were not enough to know he wasn't David, then his snap reflexes were. David would never help if he knew someone else would take the blame. Her eyes followed the hand. Long arm. Broad shoulders. A handsome face was surrounded by a shock of salt and pepper hair. Mostly pepper. She liked that.

"I'm sorry. Your husband gave me his keypad code to the alarm. I thought he'd tell you I'd be here." He looked around the brightly lit rooms with flickering TVs, ventilation adjusting room temperatures, and music playing from speakers. He raised his eyebrows in approval. "Pretty cool. Most of my clients want integrated systems, but they can't find one that does all this."

She swallowed back her fright and fingered the open collar of her coat. "This one's next-gen. It's not public yet. Still testing. And no, David said nothing. Is everything all right?"

"I'm Quinn Sheering of Sheering Security. Threats have been made against Judge Smythe. His firm hired me." He opened a thick leather wallet to show his ID.

She recognized his face and the name of his firm from the news. Sheering Security was one of the best in the Boston area for security services. "He's not a judge yet, Mr. Sheering. What kind of threats? When were they made? Are there any leads on who may be making them? How did your firm get involved?" She may have given up full time litigation to become chief counsel at the Cube, a high-tech start-up incubator, but she could still dig for information when she needed to.

"Call me Quinn." He picked up the scattered packages of food and placed them on the center island.

His movements were deliberate and fluid, with big-cat predator grace. He wore a dark gray wool sweater, black jeans, and boots that looked worn yet well cared for. He didn't look at her, but she could tell he was aware of everything she did. She liked that, too.

He continued. "He said he got a call three days ago, but I believe it was longer. He didn't take the threat seriously until the firm got involved when letters started to arrive. They beefed up security at the office and put a guard on him. The suspect is a past defendant on the losing end of a hacking case. The guy went off the rails. He thought he had the best lawyer ever, but the loss cost the guy his wife and family. At first the threats were directed only at David, but these arrived today." He produced an envelope from his back pocket and placed it beside the arugula.

The envelope contained a series of photographs, still warm from being held by his backside. She added one more item she liked to her list.

She spread the photographs along the cool marble. They were printed on regular letter paper, not glossy photographic paper for pictures intended to be kept, but the quality was more than adequate to get the point across. The pictures showed David in his many resplendent forms: David walking into his office building, hair windblown, and Chesterfield coat open to the elements with model-perfect panache. David taking the steps into the courthouse in twos, cell phone pressed to his ear with an urgent look of concern on his face. David leaving his tennis club, duffle bag on one shoulder, and a slender woman dressed in tennis whites on the other. His radiant smile was one Claire hadn't seen directed toward her in years. His arm cinched around the woman's waist, pulling her closer.

To anyone else, the woman would have been Claire. They had similar builds–average height with long limbs and the same auburn hair. But the woman's head was down, hiding her face, and a gold barrette Claire had never seen before pulled back her long hair. There were additional pictures of Claire, and judging by the outfits, she figured they had been taken over the past month.

The images and hand-written threat showed David and his loved one were being stalked. But to Claire, they provided one more piece of incontrovertible evidence: As well as being preyed upon by some lunatic, David was having an affair.

The last delusion of a future with David slipped away as her mouth went dry. *That effing bastard.* Her eyes widened, and her lips worked to form words her brain could not capture. There were too many layers to parse through in the few seconds it took to view the photos. "I don't . . . he didn't . . ."

Two vertical furrows formed between Quinn's brows as he continued to talk. "The firm's managing partner called me in immediately. Judge Smythe wanted to handle this on his own and not worry you."

"He's *not* a judge *yet*, Mr. Sheering," she snapped.

"Quinn," he repeated as he held up his hand to stop her protest. "He was sworn in today at a private ceremony. He said the intimidation would cease once he did exactly what he felt this guy was trying to stop." He cleared his throat and grimaced. "I'm sorry. I thought he had spoken with you."

"Has he seen these pictures?"

"No. His secretary opens all of his mail. As soon as she saw them, she brought them to the firm's managing partner."

She began to put the food away. It was another one of David's masterful moves. He was sworn to the bench because of her father's influence. Without Claire by his side, he distanced her from his success and affirmed the illusion that his ascension was on his own merits. Her mind raced through the series of facts and began to assess probabilities and likely scenarios.

One: To the untrained eye, it looked like David was protecting her. He cultivated the perception that she was still distraught over her father's death, so keeping her in the dark about the threats insulated her from worry, and being swiftly sworn in was intended to thwart the bad guy's intentions. Claire almost laughed out loud at the thought.

The theory didn't account for the woman.

Two: David was an admitted overachiever and workaholic who didn't take the threats seriously and forgot to mention them to her or to the firm until his loyal and vigilant secretary kicked them up the ladder. This was somewhat plausible since he had led such a golden life that nothing as ridiculous as a stalker would faze him. He was definitely the type to try to manage the situation on his own, so his silence would not be seen as unusual.

But, then there was the woman.

Three: With her father dead, no kids, and all love gone, she was nothing but irrelevant baggage to him. She'd place odds that the woman had a family lineage that would make the political connections of the Kennedy clan look downright paltry. Plus, David would never tarnish his perfect image by admitting to a failed marriage, so divorce was out of the question. Besides, why deplete one's assets in a divorce when the whole estate would go to him if she was the victim of a deranged killer—especially one well documented not to be him?

Add to that, a widower would need to be comforted.

Bingo.

The hairs on the back of her neck stood up.

Quinn must have mistaken her shaking hands for fear. "I've checked the grounds and the inside of the home. Judge Smythe felt you'd be safer if he stays away—"

"In an undisclosed location." Her voice shook only from the effort it took to stifle a guffaw. She wiped her nose with the back of her hand. David's "undisclosed location" would no doubt be the same address GPS coordinates showed all those nights when he said he was working late with a sensitive client. *God! What a fool!* She hated to cyber snoop, but the technology made it so tempting, and easy. Besides, it was David who first introduced her to "People Placer," saying he felt more connected to her when they were apart when he could see where she was. Her last hope of love died.

"I know this is a lot to take in." Quinn's voice was even and low, filled with empathy and concern.

"Y-yes. It is." She kept her back to Quinn as she slipped off her coat and threw it on the chair, using the moment to compose herself. David was setting her up. A deranged killer was stalking them. Perfect.

When she was ready, she turned around, wringing her hands and breathing rapidly. "What does David want me to do? Should I stay here? Should I leave? What does David think?" She opened her eyes wide and searched Quinn's face for clues.

"He said you should go to the chalet and hole up there until this blows over. I'm to drive you myself and provide 24/7 surveillance."

She was about to answer when a drip of water fell on her forehead. It was joined by another before a steady stream of water poured from the ceiling.

"Damn it!" She pulled out her phone and jabbed and swiped at its screen while hurrying up the stairs to the master bedroom suite. Quinn followed on her heels. Water overflowed from the Jacuzzi and flooded the bathroom floor. She stopped him from entering. Her phone sounded a long buzz and "System Alert" flashed. The text bubbles outlined a leak and a power issue. A few more swipes at the screen and the water stopped flowing from the custom-forged copper waterfall spout. The lights flickered off. She turned on her flashlight app and directed the beam to each faucet and drain in the bathroom, then looked at her phone again. Just the tub was activated—much better than the last time when the shower and sinks turned on, too.

"What's going on? I checked the upstairs when I arrived, and there was no water running." Quinn was suitably confused. And impressed.

"It's part of the upgrade to Safe Haven once we get it programmed right. What could be better than coming home to a hot bath when you don't have to wait for the tub to fill?" She beamed. It was her idea because long soaks were something David loved. She was going to present it to him as an anniversary gift. The geeks at the Cube were like kids in a candy store when she told them they could use her house for any experiments they wanted.

They may have been great programmers, but as electricians, they sucked. The whole suite was dark with just enough light coming from the hallway to see her way around. She reached toward the tub to empty the drain.

Quinn grabbed her arm. "If everything's wired, is it grounded?"

"Who knows," Claire said, voice flat. She confirmed the circuit to the Jacuzzi pump was off. "Let's dry things up. Hand me a towel?"

He obliged and spread extra-thick bath towels on the floor. In a few minutes, they had everything mopped up. He looked over her shoulder with interest as she pulled up the circuit breaker schematic and tapped the "Reset" icon. The lights turned on and valves whirled. Once back in the kitchen, she determined the ceiling would survive its water damage, but would need to be repainted, and made a note to have the system checked.

Quinn brought the conversation back on point. "Okay, then. What did you decide to do? Judge Smythe was adamant you'd be safer out of town. He says the chalet in New Hampshire would be the safest place for you."

She stopped a smile from twitching the corner of her mouth. "Of course. That's exactly what I'll do."

He visibly relaxed. "That's good. The police know who's behind the threats, so it won't be long before they track him down and arrest him. But it could be a day or two. Did you want to pack some things?" He waited a moment for a response. "Mrs. Smythe? Claire?"

"Oh, I'm sorry. There's just so much to think about. Yes. I do need a few things. I won't be long." Within twenty minutes, she emerged dressed in jeans, boots and bulky sweater, carrying an oversized purse and rolling a small suitcase behind her.

Quinn began the drive north. The patches of black ice absorbed his attention. Occasionally, he tried to make small talk or to ask for directions, but Claire was busy with her phone and tablet, and gave only sparse and polite answers.

"I'm sorry. I'm just letting people at the Cube know I'll be working remotely for a few days." She fumbled with cords, devices, and chargers.

He nodded his understanding, and within two hours they passed Loon Mountain and shortly after that he parked beside the chalet. She waited in the car as Quinn walked the area. Deep banks of snow had frozen and thawed to piles of white corn, and Quinn skidded and slid over the glaze of ice. His flashlight's beam shone deep into the woods and reflected so brightly off the ice, the whole interior of the house seemed to be lit.

The chalet was the only major asset David brought to their marriage and more than once she had to beg him not to put it on the market. Perched high on a hill in the Kancamagus Pass, it offered spectacular views of the valley and was the perfect spot for evening cocktails. She threw her heart and soul into redecorating it and made sure to keep David's memories intact. Pictures from his childhood dotted the walls, and framed portraits of the two of them from their courtship and beyond were on coffee tables and bookcases.

The post-and-beam structure was primitive. They spent many hours and sent too many emails to count planning its complete renovation, but only got as far as the coats of paint she applied. More than once they had to resort to using the ancient gas stove for heat when the electricity failed. But, she loved their cozy adventures even if David seemed to loathe the place. Spotty cell service helped limit intrusions from the outside world, making it her sanctuary in times of stress.

Tonight the chalet felt different. Were chairs moved? Had someone been there? She turned on heat and lights, noting a subtle shift in the air. Quinn tossed his belongings on the sofa and went into the kitchen to put their takeout food on plates.

They jumped when the landline rang. Claire grabbed the phone off the wall in the kitchen. She cradled the handset between her ear and shoulder as she tapped the screen on her cell.

"Oh, David! Are you safe?" The sound of his voice made her weep. Quinn put his head down and walked to the other room giving her privacy as she talked about the events of the day and congratulated him on his swearing in. "Yes. I'm alright. I'm more worried about you. You sound so stressed." Her own voice was a tight wire. "We've settled in for the night. I'll be fine." She listened for a beat. "I love you, too, Darling. Good-night." As if in a dream, she slowly replaced the handset in the cradle.

A wave of fear and grief washed over her. She clutched her hand to her stomach and stifled a dry heave. A tear escaped and ran down her cheek before she had a chance to wipe it away. She pushed Quinn away when he approached her. "I'm sorry. I thought I could stay here, but I can't. Everywhere I turn I see David and it makes me worried sick. Would it be alright if we stayed at an inn I know of just a little farther up the highway?"

Quinn resisted at first, but acquiesced when he called and found the inn had no other guests for the night and rooms were available. He made reservations for two rooms under names she didn't recognize.

He responded to her raised eyebrow with, "Standard procedure when providing security and maintaining privacy."

She went room to room and turned off most of the lights and lowered the heat. He waited for her at the door as she wiped down the counters one last time and opened and closed the sliding doors to the deck.

"Fluky lock," she said as they left.

Claire slept soundly, snuggled deeply under the inn's goose down duvet. Even the sound of an explosion and sirens filling the valley didn't disturb her. Only urgent knocking on her door woke her.

"Mrs. Smythe! Claire! Open the door!"

She wrapped herself in a robe and shuffled to the door. Quinn stood there. Stubble darkened his face and weakened her knees.

"Innkeeper said it was a nearby chalet. Gas leak."

"Ours?"

"The explosion took out the phone lines in this section of the pass. Can you see your chalet from here?"

Claire motioned him to her balcony. A thick plume of smoke rose where her chalet once stood and the woods burned. He caught her by her elbows as her legs buckled and helped her into a chair. He shook his head as he spoke.

"I can't find my phone. Do you have yours?"

Claire nodded weakly and began to search her luggage. "I thought it was here. Maybe it's in the car?"

"I checked already. It's not."

"I must have left it in the chalet!" She shook her coat as if the phone would appear like a dove by a magician's sleight of hand. "No way is this a coincidence," she said, holding back tears. *David tried to kill me! David wants me dead!*

"I agree. Only David knew we were there," he said. "We must have been followed."

She let another possibility stay unspoken. Maybe David let her be tracked. She gripped her hands together to stop their shaking. "Maybe it's better if whoever did it thinks he was successful."

Quinn considered this. "The area is swarming with firemen and investigators. With the threats documented against you and the judge, I'll bet the suspect will be arrested soon."

"Give the police time to do their work. It's not even 9 AM." She stretched her toned leg out of her robe. She watched his eyes follow the curve of her calf to her thigh.

"True," he said, voice trailing in thought. "I'll drive to a phone."

"That lunatic could be anywhere!" she gasped, her voice tight with panic. "We're safe here, aren't we?" *What would David be thinking right now? That arrogant S.O.B. would only need to hear the chalet exploded to believe I was dead.* She let the top of her robe open an indiscreet amount.

Quinn nodded slowly. "We can stay put until we know more," he said.

It didn't take much to convince Quinn, and the innkeeper was happy to have cash-paying guests midweek and late season.

Quinn insisted Claire stay inside and seemed to enjoy an assignment that required no more of him than to walk the grounds once an hour and to pick up the extension of the phone in the lobby to see if service had been restored.

A patch of warm spring sunshine invited her to curl onto a couch. She motioned for him to sit beside her. "Tell me about your work," she purred.

Quinn was more talkative when the conversation was work related. He had an easy manner and quick wit and worked at getting her to relax. They began to enjoy one another's company, and as the hours passed, she could see him struggle to maintain a professional distance.

"My other clients have experienced an overzealous fan or two, but this guy was really crazy. It was like someone intentionally antagonized him," he said.

Claire knew how David could get under someone's skin. "You know, a couple of start-ups at the Cube are working on apps that could use your help. With your experience and insights into what wealthy clients want, you could really make an impact. They have a decent budget for outside consultants, so you'd be paid well for your time."

"Some of my clients earned their fortunes designing programs and apps."

"No reason you shouldn't have a shot at the big money." She sighed and looked out the window.

It wasn't until the evening that they were startled by the ringing of the telephone. Quinn nearly leaped for it in a rush to check in with the office.

Quinn finished his phone call. "The police arrested the guy around noon. They had an APB out for the suspect's car. It was tagged going through the EZPass lanes on Route 93 during times that coincided with being able to set up and return from the explosion. They found maps, a gun, pliers, camera and pictures of you and David in his car. They notified David of his arrest."

She sat up. "They did? What time?"

Quinn shrugged. "Immediately afterward. No later than, say, one o'clock. I'm sure he'll be relieved to hear from you."

"Won't your office call him?"

Quinn smiled. "I think he'd want to hear the news directly from you. Don't you?" He handed her the inn's phone. "Oh, and the local cops found my cell phone in the woods near the chalet. I must have dropped it."

He handed her the phone. She hesitated, fumbled as she dialed, then waited. After a few moments she hung up and tried another number, nearly dropping the phone from her shaking hands. Failing again, she tried a third. "David? Pick up the phone! It's me, Darling. I'm fine! I'll be home soon to tell you all about it." She smiled her brightest as she placed the phone back in its base.

"I guess we should go," Quinn said.

Claire stood and straightened her shoulders. "Yes. I guess you're right."

An hour later they were in Quinn's car driving slowly along the roads of the Kancamagus Pass slicked with black ice. They both sighed with relief to hit the salted highway.

"It's late and I'm starved. Would you mind if we grabbed something to eat first? There's a little diner in Rowley that makes great pie. How about a slice of banana cream and a coffee before we get back? They'll be fast and it's my treat." She looked at him with gratitude. "It's the least I can do to say thank you."

They sat at a corner booth in the empty diner. Claire excused herself to the ladies room to freshen up. She reached into her purse, pulled up the bottom lining, and brought out her phone. Quinn hadn't noticed the one she used at the chalet was an old phone of hers she activated with her current number on their way north. She had retrieved it from her bottom desk drawer when she packed. It had fewer features than her current phone, but excellent GPS capabilities. What would the geeks call a phone to be used once and discarded? A burner. David would have seen her location on his phone's People Placer knowing she would never be far from her cell and the hacker had more than enough skills to follow her. David's call to the chalet's landline double-checked her location. That call was meant to seal her fate, but it sealed David's instead. She left the burner on the kitchen counter, fully charged and turned on. All she needed was time.

She turned the water on in the sink, slipped the battery into her cell phone, and waited for it to power up. It was a risk, but she knew David would be too self-congratulatory to look at her cell phone usage once events unfolded. She keyed in the activation sequence and the phone came to life.

People Placer showed the history of David's movements. He had left his "client's" location around the time he would have learned of the arrest, and went straight home. Maybe alone. Most likely not. She deleted her one voicemail message without listening to it. She activated her Safe Haven app. All signals were good and strong.

She flushed the toilet and checked the video feed. Her blood chilled to ice. She tapped the screen and waited. Her phone began one long, continuous buzz. Her head dropped and shoulders sagged as a wave of nausea sloshed in her gut. This time, she didn't bother to turn the phone off as she slipped it back into her purse.

By the time she settled back into the booth, the pies had arrived, piled high with meringue and whipped cream. Quinn's coffee was almost gone and hers was cold. She motioned to the waitress for a fresh cup and to warm

Quinn's. They chatted and planned to meet again next week so he could be introduced to the Cube's associates.

When they arrived at her home, David's car was parked in front of the house. A red Audi Claire had never seen before was in the garage. When they entered the kitchen, a steady stream of water flowed from the ceiling. They ran through the house and up the stairs, following a trail of clothes that started with shoes and shirts, progressed to boxers and bra, and ended with the gold barrette.

Quinn was in front. He held her back from entering the suite, but she could see clearly into the bath.

David and the other woman never made it into the Jacuzzi. In a tableau of thwarted connubial bliss, they lay, naked and sprawled, with their bodies wrapped together. David must have reached out to the spout to steady them on the slippery floor. His hand completed the circuit and allowed a jolt of electricity to fry them both in the midst of their blazing offense.

Claire pulled in the corners of her mouth to prevent a satisfied smile.

CONNIE JOHNSON HAMBLEY began to steadfastly plot her revenge against all bad guys, real and imagined, at the ripe age of six when an arsonist torched her family's farm. When receiving her law degree didn't provide satisfactory tools for revenge, she turned to fiction writing and became immediately satisfied with the varied ways to kill and torment evildoers. Her third thriller in *The Jessica Trilogy, The Wake*, joins *The Charity* and *The Troubles,* which won the 2016 Best Fiction at the EQUUS Film Festival in New York City. Her short story, "Giving Voice," appears in *New England's Best Crime Stories: Windward.* Connie is a board member and Featured Speaker of Sisters in Crime New England.

AN OMINOUS SILENCE
by Edith Maxwell

Silence, both peaceful and ominous, jolted me awake. I lay in the upper berth in the Grand Trunk Line sleeping compartment I shared with my midwifery apprentice, Genevieve Rousseau, who still slept below. Our next scheduled stop was at the Canadian border shortly after dawn. But it was still dark, and the car was not rumbling and clacking along the tracks, nor swaying to and fro as it had since we'd boarded in Portland, Maine, yesterday evening.

Rummaging under my pillow, I retrieved both spectacles and pocket watch. The low light from outside the privacy curtains illuminated the watch just enough to show the time: five in the morning. What? When I peeked behind the window shade the porter had pulled down the night before, I understood. I knew it had been risky to travel from our coastal town south of Portland to Montreal in March, a time when winter still held the region in its chilly grasp. I'd been invited to a gathering of midwives, though, and I'd very much wanted Genevieve, originally a French-Canadian herself, to meet several famous teachers in our field.

It appeared we would arrive late. All I could see outside was white. Clumps of snow sticking to the glass. Snowflakes blowing in the wind. White bulky monsters of snow-covered pines standing sentry against a dark sky.

Perhaps an avalanche here in the White Mountains had covered the tracks. Or had an unpredicted storm blown in? Possibly both. I fought down a moment of panic. I had no idea how long it would take the railroad to clear the tracks, or if help could even reach us. What if the train exhausted its supply of food and water, or of coal? No. I shook my head. This was 1890 in New Hampshire, after all, not a century earlier nor out west on a northern prairie. Modern towns were everywhere. We wouldn't be stranded for long.

The sensible thing in this silence would be to go back to sleep, but my concerns had me too wrought up to do so. Instead I pulled on my dress and shoes and climbed quietly down the cloth ladder.

"What time is it?" Genevieve asked in a sleepy voice.

"Five. I couldn't sleep, but you should."

She nodded and rolled over.

My woolen shawl wrapped around my shoulders, I slipped through the heavy curtains into the aisle. If I could find a porter, I might be able to learn something about our situation.

I passed the curtain-shielded berths holding a very pregnant French-Canadian wife and her maid. A grief-stricken Marie-Claire Peel had told me last night that her father had passed away suddenly and she was traveling home from Maine to Quebec to be with family. Her maid traveled with her, as did her rather overbearing American husband, Vernon Peel, a banker in Portland who occupied the adjacent berths. I'd told Mrs. Peel I was a midwife, and if she had any worries about her condition, she was welcome to solicit my assistance. Mr.

Peel, a florid, breathless man, had snorted. "She'll have a proper doctor when her time comes, not some country midwife."

I had smiled. "I'm sure she'll be well looked after." While Mrs. Peel looked to be far along in her pregnancy, we expected only a fifteen-hour train ride. I very much doubted she'd be in labor before we arrived in Montreal.

I shrugged off the memory. Curious. Not a porter in sight, nor any other passenger. I made my way down the passageway between the curtained-off berths. Yesterday I'd had to proceed with care, making sure the movement of the train didn't send me careering into the wall or a fellow traveler. Not today. A snore followed by a snort drifted out of one compartment, while in another a child whimpered. The scent of warm human bodies held a backdrop of soot.

At last I spied the black-jacketed porter, Spencer, who stood conferring with a passenger.

"Excuse me, Spencer. Can you tell me what has happened, please?"

"We're stuck in the snow, Miss Colby," Spencer said. "We're in a cut, there's a slide just ahead, and the tracks are covered by five feet of new drift." He was a man well along in years, with a trim build, neat silver hair, and a quiet manner.

The other man, both unshaven and uncombed in contrast, nodded gravely. I'd seen him in the café parlor car after dinner, but I hadn't been introduced to him. At first he'd been carousing at the bar with Vernon Peel and then had argued with him in a belligerent tone.

"And the driver can't push through the drifts?" I asked, although the answer seemed obvious.

"No, miss. One foot, two feet, certainly. Not five."

"How shall we be rescued, then?" I tried to keep concern out of my voice.

"I could go out there and commence to shovel, if that'd help." The passenger spoke with breath reeking of stale alcohol through his grin. His high collar had sprung free of one button and rubbed against his neck.

"Now, Mr. LeMoyne, that won't be necessary," Spencer said. "When we don't arrive on time, Boston & Maine will send out train plows and meet us from the nearest maintenance station up ahead and possibly from the one behind, as well. Both of which I'm afraid are some distance away, and they can't begin until the sun comes up. We've also sent out a couple of men to make the trek to the nearest town. They'll telegraph word of our predicament and rescued we shall be."

"As you wish." The passenger glanced at me "Adoniram LeMoyne, miss. At your service." He made a mock bow. "But you can call me Ade. All my friends do."

"I am Catherine Colby. I'm pleased to make your acquaintance, Mr. LeMoyne." I watched him lurch down the corridor, weaving back and forth as if the car was still moving. I hoped he was headed for his compartment to sleep off the drink. Could he possibly have been imbibing all the night long?

I decided to continue to the café car to see if I could scare up a cup of coffee so early. I'd almost reached the passageway to the next car when I heard running footsteps. Mr. LeMoyne came sprinting toward Spencer. I hurried back that way.

"Help!" His voice was low and urgent as he grabbed Spencer's arm. "Come quickly. He's dead!"

ooo

I stepped back from Vernon Peel's still form in the bottom berth. I'd checked his neck for a pulse, but his already cool skin had told me the verdict. Crowded behind me were a hand-wringing Spencer, who'd gladly accepted my offer of help, and a distraught Adoniram LeMoyne.

"Yes, I'm afraid he's dead," I murmured. But why, how? I wouldn't be surprised if heart failure caused his demise. With his red face and breathless manner, plus his girth, he'd clearly been a man to ignore his own health. Rather than a person who enjoyed long walks, fresh foods, and abstinence from intoxication, Mr. Peel looked like a man who indulged in rich dishes, tobacco, and drink. To wit, a pewter tankard from the bar lay abandoned at the end of the berth.

I turned and surveyed my companions' faces. "Were you sharing this compartment with Mr. Peel?" I asked Mr. LeMoyne.

"Why, yes."

A nod from Spencer confirmed it.

"I'd just come in to take my sleep and there he was," Mr. LeMoyne went on. "I'd met him on the platform in Portland and he invited me to ride with him, since his wife had a separate compartment with her maid. I'd decided to take this trip at the last moment but could secure only a common coach ticket, not one on the sleeping car. Vern and I are old friends, and we..." He shaded his eyes with his hand and turned away.

"I'll have to inform Mrs. Peel," Spencer murmured, his brow knit and his eyes tense. "And the police, when we make contact with the outside world again."

"The police, you say?" Mr. LeMoyne whirled, suddenly over his grief. "Why on earth, man?"

"It's procedure, sir. An unattended death while in transit always demands notifying the authorities."

Mr. LeMoyne's sorrow had looked genuine, but he now seemed alarmed at the prospect of police. Why? My mind went to work on that one. Perhaps the death hadn't been from natural causes. What if someone on the train had murdered Vernon Peel in his sleep? Adoniram himself had been arguing with his so-called friend just last night. Vernon could have other acquaintances on the trip, as well. My brain now began to sort through the possibilities.

Spencer cleared his throat. "Miss Colby, I wondered if you might accompany me to notify Mrs. Peel. Considering her delicate condition, I'm afraid learning of her husband's demise might cause her extreme distress."

"Of course I will. She's just next door, isn't she?" With the way sound traveled through the curtains, I'd be surprised if she hadn't heard.

"Yes, miss." He closed the curtains in front of the berths.

Heads with wide eyes had popped out between other curtains in the car, but Spencer admonished them all to go back to sleep, that everything was under control.

Marie-Claire stood in front of the adjacent berths, clutching a wrapper that barely stretched around her nightgown. Her dark eyes were wide, her petite features drawn into a mask of horror. She searched our faces. The stern visage of Eugenie, her maid, appeared from the upper berth above Marie-Claire, framed by the curtains.

"Mon Dieu, what has 'appened?" Marie-Claire's gaze fell on Adoniram. "Mister LeMoyne, who is dead?" The word "who" came out more like "oo."

"Mrs. Peel, perhaps you would like to sit down first," I ventured.

She stared at me. "Who are you again?"

"Catherine Colby, midwife. We met in passing last evening."

She nodded. "But I must know now, who is dead?"

"I regret to inform you, ma'am, that your husband became deceased during the night," Spencer said gently.

Marie-Claire's hand tightened on her shawl until her skin was the color of bleached linen, but she didn't sway. She shook her head, fast. "It must be a mistake. Mr. Peel cannot be dead."

"I'm afraid he is." I also spoke in a soft voice.

She nodded twice, slowly, making a tsking sound. "It was his heart. I told him. Now you must show me." She lifted her chin.

Eugenie murmured something to Mrs. Peel in French. I'd been studying French, because I was often called to attend the births of French-Canadians in my town, but I didn't catch what she said.

"Non, Eugenie. I will go."

"Very well, Madam."

Spencer offered his arm, but the new widow padded past him and slid open the curtains. I watched as she knelt in front of the berth and crossed herself. She stroked her husband's forehead, speaking privately to him. She clasped her hands and lowered her face, still murmuring. She touched her fingers to her lips and then to his before turning a wet face to gaze at Spencer.

"Now I need the help, s'il vous plaît." She extended her hand for Spencer to help hoist her up. "Why the train is not moving? We must bring home my husband's body."

Spencer explained about being snowed in. Eugenie shouldered past me, now fully dressed in her severe black dress, her slate-gray hair pulled back in an equally severe knot.

"Come and lie down, Madam. This is a terrible shock." She helped Marie-Claire back into her berth even as Spencer closed the curtains on the late Vernon Peel.

ooo

I sat with my coffee in the café car gazing at the snowy wonderland. It didn't seem so wonderful now we were stuck in it. Adoniram LeMoyne stood at the bar, one foot on the brass foot rail, a tankard in front of him. Ale for breakfast, no doubt. I wouldn't mind a drop of it, myself, but decided to stay with the stimulating effect of coffee for now.

I considered Mrs. Peel's reaction to the death. She had seemed sad but not surprised that her husband was gone, and had not appeared as overcome with grief as some widows I'd seen.

My thoughts moved to Mr. Peel himself. How had he died? His wife certainly thought it was from heart failure. But yards from me stood a man who shared the compartment, who'd had a public and loud dispute with the deceased. I needed to get back to the body to check, in the absence of police, if any clues remained as to Vernon's manner of death. We'd not even checked for a wound on his body, blood on the back of his head, or any puncture marks. I knew from reading Pinkerton's stories that people were murdered in all kinds of ways beyond the obvious ones of gunshot and stabbing. Perhaps Spencer could be convinced to allow me some further investigation, despite the cordage he'd strung in front of the curtained berths and a neatly lettered sign that read, "Keep Out." If it was a crime scene, it was hardly well secured.

In the meantime, I'd see what I could find out from Adoniram. I drained my coffee and approached the bar. "I'm very sorry about the death of your friend, Mr. LeMoyne." I slid onto a stool next to him.

"Thank you, miss."

"Tell me how you knew Mr. Peel?"

"We were Harvard men together, of course. Drifted apart a bit in recent years, don't you know, but when I saw him there on the platform it was like no time had passed." He shook his head in a sad gesture. "I hate the thought that the last words we exchanged were angry ones."

"I saw a bit of that exchange. What was your dispute with him?"

He gazed at me with watery, bloodshot eyes and upended his tankard into his mouth before answering. "You might have noticed he's had a bit more, ah, success than I myself have achieved. I merely asked for a small loan to tide me over until a big business venture comes through, but he was having none of it. Got quite self-righteous, going on about morality, the evils of gambling, and such. Not to speak ill of the dead, of course."

"Of course not." What he described didn't seem like the kind of argument over which to murder someone, but who knew? "Are there other acquaintances of yours here on the train? From your Harvard days, I mean?"

"Not that I've seen. But if they haven't come into this car, I wouldn't have then, would I?" He gestured to the bartender. "Fill 'er up my man, will you?"

The door to the car burst open. Genevieve rushed toward me, her shawl and her red hair flying behind her. "Come quickly. Mrs. Peel is having pains!"

ეეე

After I took a moment to wash my hands and grab the birthing kit with which I always traveled, I hurried to Marie-Claire's side. On the way from the café car I'd instructed Genevieve to wash up and tidy her appearance. I'd need her assistance if the pains turned out to be true labor. I didn't know if Marie-Claire had received antenatal care, or if this was her first child or her fifth. It didn't matter. If her baby and her body had chosen today for the birth, today was when it would be.

But how could we possibly help her give birth in a space essentially open to all the other passengers. I'd stopped Spencer. "Is there somewhere we can move Mrs. Peel? It appears her baby is on its way and she needs privacy."

His eyes went wide, but being the competent man he was, I saw the wheels turning in his brain.

"I might have an idea."

Several minutes later we were blessedly ensconced in an empty but luxurious private car. Spencer had said the railroad was transporting it to Montreal for its new owner. Marie-Claire lay on the hastily made-up berth at the end of the car with Eugenie hovering nearby.

"I need light," I told Eugenie. "Please raise the shades and turn up the lamp." I perched on the edge of the berth even as Marie-Claire let out a cry. I quickly noted the time.

"Ça fait mal," she wailed. "Miss Colby, it hurts."

"And I am here to help you." When the pain seemed to have passed, I palpated her belly with both hands, glad to feel a fetus of a hearty size. "Good. The baby is head down and in an advantageous position. I'll listen to his heart now." I drew out my Pinard horn and pressed it against her belly, listening through the other end to a good fast heartbeat. "All is well. Tell me when your baby was supposed to arrive."

"Not until next month. Will he survive if he comes now?"

"Not to worry. It seems of a healthy size for this stage. Let us wait and see if the pains--"

She cried out and I checked the time again. Two and a half minutes since the last one began.

I glanced up. "Does she have other children?" I asked Eugenie, who stood with hands tightly clasped. "Have you ever assisted at a birth?"

"Oh, no, miss. This is her first. And I have no experience with such matters as childbirth." From the set of her mouth, it looked like she wasn't interested in having any, either.

I sat with Marie-Claire for the next hour as her pains grew closer together and more intense. I checked the entrance to her womb and found it well along the path to being fully open. I asked Eugenie to fetch Genevieve for me and told the maid she might as well go and breakfast, that we would be fully occupied here.

"Mrs. Peel, ça ne vous dérange pas?" You don't mind?

Marie-Claire just waved the question away. "Vas-y." Go ahead.

After her maid left, she grabbed my arm. "I never wanted a baby," she said in a hoarse whisper. "But Mr. Peel, he forced himself on me, said we must have children. Now he's dead and anyway I will have one." She wiped away a tear. "It was a terrible marriage, Miss Colby. Eugenie, she saw my suffering." She let out a deep grunt. "Here is another."

Genevieve slid through the door, sleeves pushed up. "What can I do?"

I stood and spoke in a low voice. "First, please go to the café car and bring me a pot of boiled water."

"All right."

I returned to Marie-Claire's side. Had she devised a way to do away with her husband here on the train? Genevieve returned with the pot of water and an odd look on her face.

"Stay with her a while, please," I said. "The contractions are intensifying, but her womb is not yet fully open. I'll return in just a few minutes."

ꝏꝏ

I reached over Mr. Peel's body and opened the shade. I knelt in the still-ominous absence of train noises, my gaze traveling over every square inch of the berth. Luckily Spencer had not objected to my request to investigate. I'd reminded him he was too busy to guard the scene, and until the police arrived, the berth was woefully open to being tampered with. I'd ducked under the cord and closed the curtains after me.

Vernon lay fully dressed except for tie and jacket. I opened his shirt and saw no bullet holes or blood on him anywhere, nor bruises. With some difficulty I half-rolled his heavy inert body away from me, but the back of his head and neck were intact and blood-free. I let him roll back. When he did, his head followed all the way to face me, and with his eyes still open, it was not a pleasant sight. I pushed his head gently back and drew my hands over his lids. I sniffed, detecting a noxious odor in the air. Was it male sweat combined with death, or something else? A poison? I leaned in and smelled Vernon's face near his mouth and nose. That was where the scent originated.

I sat back on my heels. His body was still pliable, so his death had not been early in the evening, but I already knew that. Perhaps the bartender could tell me what time Mr. Peel returned to his compartment.

I reached for the tankard and sniffed it, detecting the same unpleasant smell. If Vernon's death had not been a natural one, poison might well be the culprit. And if it hadn't been injected, this cup could be very important evidence.

Concealing the mug in my skirts, I hurried back to my compartment. It was past time for me to return to Mrs. Peel, to the car that had now become a birthing chamber.

When I did, Genevieve had her hands full. She was stroking Marie-Claire's forehead, urging her not to push despite the guttural noises the mother-to-be was emitting. The look my apprentice gave me was both exasperated and grateful. I quickly mouthed "Sorry" to Genevieve and washed my hands at the washbasin in the corner.

"Mrs. Peel, it sounds like you're ready to birth your child. I'll check the opening as soon as this pain has passed." I waited until she closed her eyes and lapsed into heavy exhausted breathing before sliding my hand and arm into her passageway. Good. A full fist's worth. I nodded to Genevieve as I wiped off my hand on a piece of linen. "Boost her up. Let's meet this baby."

Genevieve gently assisted Marie-Claire to assume a more upright position with bent knees.

"With the next pain, I want you to push with all your might." I had a fear, with her expressed unwillingness to assume the mantle of motherhood, that she might hold back the birthing process without meaning to. I'd seen women do it before.

My fears blessedly did not come to pass. By the time an hour had elapsed, Marie-Claire held a small but healthy daughter. My simple birth kit had sufficed, with Genevieve's help, and the birth had proceeded with no problems. The new mother gazed with surprise at the blanketed newborn girl in her arms, an infant watching her with the calm dark eyes of all healthy humans at the fresh age of ten minutes old. Marie-Claire looked up at me.

"C'est ma fille. Ma chérie fille." A tear escaped her eye.

"Yes, she's your dear daughter." Genevieve wiped away a tear from her own cheek.

"What will you name her?" I asked, glad she'd birthed a girl. She might have grown to resent a male who would only remind her of his father.

She looked back down at the baby. "I should name her Verna, after her Papá. But I will not. She will be called Marie-Reine. She is a princess now, but she will rule her world when she is grown. No man will make her do nothing she does not want to."

"It's a lovely name." I stood. "Genevieve will help you with your first suckling. I'll be back."

"Wait, Catherine." Genevieve took me aside and whispered in my ear.

I narrowed my eyes and nodded once. "Very interesting." At her curious expression, I added, "I'll explain later." When I re-entered our sleeping car, I faced a crowd of female passengers even as a noise outside the window grew louder. Was this racket our rescue?

"Well?" one matron demanded. "Safe passage for the two?"

"Yes." I smiled.

A girl piped up. "Is it a son or a daughter?"

"A healthy baby girl and a healthy new mother."

A round of clapping subsided only when Spencer appeared at the end of the car, announcing, "The plow is coming!"

A cheer went up as I rushed to speak with him. "Spencer," I called.

He turned and waited until I caught up with him. "I need to inform all the cars," he said. "Can this wait?"

"No." I lowered my voice to a murmur. "I believe I found evidence of poison in Mr. Peel's compartment. As soon as worldly possible, I need to speak with police."

He looked aghast. "Do you mean murder? On the Grand Trunk Line?"

"I do."

໑໑໑

I led a ruddy-faced police officer to the café car. Once the track was clear, our train had proceeded as far as the nearest town, then waited while the authorities were fetched. I'd explained my find as well as what Genevieve had overheard. After their searches, the police had asked me to take them to the murderer.

Now I pointed to Eugenie. "Her."

"Miss Eugenie Villeneuve," the officer said, placing his hand on her shoulder. "We have reason to believe you caused the death of Mr. Vernon Peel."

The clatter of silverware and the buzz of conversation in the car hushed. All eyes were on the stern-faced maid.

Eugenie's face went as white as her collar. "I most certainly did not."

"The bartender has confirmed that you brought a last cup of rum punch to Mr. Peel in his berth last evening. The cup left at his feet has the distinctive virose odor of digitalis, which can be fatal in large doses, particularly to people with heart disease. And we have located Mr. Peel's vials of that same medicine in your own luggage."

Would he mention what Genevieve had told me, which I'd passed on to the officer? My apprentice had heard Eugenie muttering in French to herself in the cafe car when she'd gone to fetch the water. The maid had been thanking God for digitalis.

Eugenie pushed to standing and spit out a stream of French I could only assume were curse words I hadn't yet learned. She switched to English, her face now aflame. "He was an awful man. He abused Madam. He tried to force himself on me, too, but I fought him off. He deserved to die!"

"Miss Villeneuve, you are under arrest for the murder of Mr. Peel." The officer snapped handcuffs on her and led her away.

I supposed the police would question Marie-Claire as to whether she had put Eugenie up to the murder. I hoped that the new mother, who'd discovered unexpected joy with her baby, was innocent and that her maid had acted alone. I didn't blame Eugenie for her anger, but murder was not the way to achieve justice.

The silence, no longer ominous, disappeared as the train began to rumble and clatter once again toward Montreal.

Agatha- and Macavity-nominated and national best-selling author **Edith Maxwell** writes the Quaker Midwife Mysteries, the Local Foods Mysteries, and award-winning short crime fiction. As Maddie Day she writes the popular Country Store Mysteries and the new Cozy Capers Book Group Mysteries. She is president of Sisters in Crime New England, lives north of Boston, and blogs at WickedCozyAuthors.com and elsewhere.

AFTER I DO
by Peggy McFarland

Evie parked behind Rocko's truck, irritated he hadn't moved it from the prime spot closest to the door. It didn't look like he'd taken the Camry out for a spin today either.

A wasp lazily hovered over the molding carpet rolled in Rocko's truck bed. She'd have to warn Rocko before he hauled a load to the dump. Which, by the looks of the carport, he hadn't begun tackling that chore. It would take more than one trip to get rid of all the yard bags of rotting leaves, broken patio furniture and rusting vehicle parts. Like Rocko would haul anything today. City Hall had closed at four, and he still hadn't registered the truck. Now he'd have to wait the weekend, and she'd have to remind him again on Monday. Then, he'd accuse her of nagging. Another week got away from him. Another year had gotten away from her.

Evie drummed her fingers on the steering wheel. She could back out of the driveway now, take a road trip until her credit card maxed, and then settle where she landed. Be rid of him, without a confrontation. But she would have to be alone forever, since she would remain Rocko's wife.

Divorce was a stigma; that's how she was raised. You started something, you finished it, especially if you started with "I do." Her grandmother had upheld her commitment to her alcoholic husband. Her mother too, with her serial cheater of a husband. Rocko wasn't an alcoholic and wasn't a cheater; he wasn't a bad guy at all. He just wasn't... the one.

She inhaled, then blew out a slow breath. "I can do this." The rearview Evie didn't look convinced. Her friends said, stuck in an unhappy marriage was just as much a statistical cliché as divorcée.

Evie glared at her reflection. "I can. I will."

ϙϙϙ

Disturbed blared from the Bose docking station. The sink overflowed with dishes. Rocko stood at the stove stirring. Evie plopped the case of Dasani and groceries on the table. "You got that babe?" Rocko shouted.

Evie fumed as she shut off "The Sound of Silence." She pulled out a chair, kicked off her pumps, and rubbed her sore left foot. It hurt worse than the right one. "Babe, can you get me a couple Tylenol?"

"Oh-no. No headache for you tonight."

Rocko made a big deal out of running down the hall, banging and dropping things from the hall closet, shouted, "Got it!", then came back with the medicine bottle. He pretended the child-proof cap was too much, got it opened and flung it behind him, then shook out two tablets. He knelt on one knee and presented her his open palm. "The Lady's Headache Cure."

He wore his "Will Cook For Sex" apron. Evie shuddered. How could she admit to Rocko he didn't do it for her anymore? "Can I have a water?"

"What about those in front of you?"

Evie inhaled, counted to five, exhaled. "Right."

She should say something now, while she was irritated. Anger gave her courage. Evie rifled through her purse.

"Whatchya got there?"

Evie let go of the envelope. Not yet. "Just my receipt." She took it out and looked at it. "Damn! I forgot to pay for the water."

"The water police are going to nab you."

"They might." How'd she not pay for those? Because she'd been distracted by the lawyer's appointment, stuck behind the harried mother with the squalling toddler, then irritated by the cashier who scratched her pimples and rolled her eyes instead of scanning groceries with any sense of urgency. "I'll have to go back and pay."

Rocko snickered. "I think Market Basket won't miss the four dollars."

"That's not the point. It's stealing." Evie got up and went to the sink. She got out a glass and ran the faucet.

"What *are* you doing?"

Evie inhaled, counted to five, exhaled. "Taking the Tylenol."

"Don't tell me." Rocko ripped the stiff plastic and took a bottle out from the case. "You can't drink one of these because you didn't pay for them?"

"I was raised better than that." Evie downed the tablets, drank the tap water, then placed the glass gently on the counter. "Karma's a bitch. You never know what could happen if you drink stolen water."

Rocko uncapped the bottle, raised it to her in a *cheers* gesture, and guzzled the contents. "Ahh." He wiped his mouth, then froze. A fake-panicked look crossed his face. He held up one hand, pounded his chest with his other, shook his head, then dropped both arms and grinned. "Nope. Nothing bad happened."

There was a time when Evie would have laughed at his sophomoric wit. She forced a half-smile at him, wished she lived with a grown-up, and then turned down the burner under the bubbling pot. "What's this?"

Rocko crossed the kitchen. "I made gravy."

"I see. What is it?"

He blew on the contents of the wooden spoon and held it out to her. "Taste."

He'd gone heavy on the garlic. He'd sweat that out his pores later, stinking up the bedroom. Yet, he had made dinner.

Rocko cooked instead of registering his truck or cleaning the carport or any of the chores he'd promised. Now she had a messy kitchen, and he'd expect kudos for "being considerate."

"So?" he asked expectantly.

So I want a divorce. Once she blurted those words, Evie would feel better. Or so her friends said.

Evie opened her mouth. "Delicious."

ΩΩΩ

Rocko came to bed wearing his Fred Flintstone "I'll Make Your Bedrock" boxers and a cloud of Listerine. Evie forced herself to smile at his dancing eyebrows. Foreplay used to be more than puns and mouthwash.

He shut off the overhead light, turned on the "sex light," a red nightlight in the corner, and snaked onto the bed. Evie raced through her excuses—too tired, had a headache, too bloated—but his hand caressed her through her panties before she chose one.

"I made dinner." His hot breath, once a turn-on, now tortured her ear.

"Yes, you did."

After dinner, Rocko had disappeared into the basement to work on his Lego stop-motion film. Evie practiced her speech while doing the mound of dishes—how had pasta sauce required six pots? By the time she'd scrubbed spatters off the stovetop, the backsplash, the walls, and the counter, she was too drained for a confrontation. Tomorrow, she promised. When she was fresh and could be rational.

Now, Rocko nuzzled her neck while his fingers explored under her panties and Evie had to delay this. "How'd your filming go?"

"I'm nailing it. Like I'm gonna do to you."

Evie shifted away from him. "Is there any prize money?"

"Hmm, hmm," Rocko murmured, pulling her closer. "A Lego shopping spree."

"That's not money."

"*Mucho* Legos."

"Great. Build us a two-car garage out of Legos."

Rocko stopped caressing. "You have a problem with my Legos? You said you didn't mind."

"That's not—"

"I could be like other husbands, and go out with the guys, spending all my time on sports or drinking, but I don't. I come home to you."

"I know—"

"It's my only outlet."

"Cleaning the carport could be an outlet."

Rocko flopped onto his back while he emitted a put-out sigh. "Not that again."

Evie allowed him to pout a moment. Now would be a good time. "Rocko, I have something—"

"You know I can't get that stuff hauled until the truck is registered."

"Why didn't you take care of that today?"

"You sure know how to kill a mood." Rocko got out of bed and shut off the sex light. He squeaked out an extended garlic fart. He climbed back in, yanked the covers over himself and turned his back to her. Evie swallowed, as best she could while holding her breath. Now was not a good time.

There was never a good time.

"Rocko?"

"Goodnight."

"I want to talk—"

"Too late."

Evie inhaled, blew out a slow exhale. "I want a divorce."

Rocko flung himself upright and switched on the overhead. "What?"

"I don't love you anymore."

ǫǫǫ

Rocko argued with her almost till dawn. She offered to sleep in the spare room, but he'd pleaded with her to uphold their commitment. His dejected expression was too much. She swallowed her refusal. He spooned her, said she was his best friend, they could—had to—make this work. He promised he could change. Be a better man.

Evie closed her eyes. At least she'd deflected sex.

ǫǫǫ

Evie woke to the roar of the lawn mower, the smell of fresh cut grass and gasoline, and an empty bed. He'd let her sleep in.

She did her morning bathroom ritual, then went to the kitchen. Coffee was made. The first time she'd ever woken to fresh coffee. A torn notebook page sat next to her mug. Rocko professed his love, his commitment, his devastation that she hadn't even tried to fix things before they'd become so badly broken. He would be a better man.

The mower silenced. Evie sat at the kitchen table and gazed out the window. Rocko rolled the mower to the carport. He stopped, stared at the contents, hung his head.

The papers remained in her purse. She would either have to commit to staying or commit to leaving. Rocko grabbed the closest yard bag of leaves, and lifted. The bottom fell away. His swears carried on the breeze.

What ever happened to *if you love something set it free*? Could her feelings change toward him? Rocko could do everything right, yet he'd still be Rocko.

The urge to flee overwhelmed her again, as it had yesterday. She got up and paced. She would miss her family, her home, her life.

Outside, Rocko carried a bag to the back of the truck and placed it next to two others. He was trying, she had to give him that.

Evie finished her coffee. She would do the right thing, and try the counseling. Like he'd shouted last night, in the middle of his devastation, maybe she wasn't a peach to live with either. She could try to fall in love again. He'd insisted this was his house too—he would not leave. She wasn't a quitter. They'd committed to a lifetime. He could change. She had to give him a chance. Give *them* a chance.

"Goddamn mother-fuckin' cocksucker, SHIT!" The screen door slammed open, and Rocko charged past Evie, slamming her into a wall.

She rubbed her shoulder. Irritation flared. What didn't go right for him now? He could be such a baby when it came to actual work. Rocko banged things in the hallway. She marched to him. "What is it?"

"Wasps," he rasped. He clutched his throat with one hand, while his other raked the contents of the closet. "Where…is…it?" He gasped between words.

Oh shit, oh shit, oh *shit!*

"Let me." Evie guided Rocko to the living room, then hurried back. She yanked out towels. One of his injectors *was* in here. She'd seen it last time she'd cleaned the closet. Rocko's pseudo-Tylenol-chivalry last night had destroyed all semblance of organization; it was total chaos.

Evie shoved aside the milk carton shaped box of Epsom salts, clattered Pepto-Bismol and Tums containers. Cold medicine flew off the shelf, as did triple antibiotic cream and tightly rolled ace bandages. No EpiPen.

The next shelf she pulled out a catch-all basket. Evie dropped down to the floor, blew a greasy strand of hair away from her eyes, and swiped through travel-sized samples, toothbrush holders, cough drops, sunblock bottles and aloe cream…the yellow, gray and white box wasn't there. Not in the basket, not in the medicine cabinet. Where was it?

"I can't find it! Is there one in your truck?"

Evie didn't wait for a response. She ran outside. The wasps, she was supposed to warn him yesterday, but had let the divorce papers, the parking situation, the carport, the water, the *everything* distract her. It was her fault. She had to find his shot.

She jerked open the passenger door of the truck. The rusty hinges groaned. Three slams, then the glove compartment opened.

Cloudy, brown liquid oozed inside the EpiPen. Gone bad. Expiration date, two years ago.

Evie sped back inside. Rocko had fallen off the couch. He lay on the floor. Tears stained his bloated face, a symptom of anaphylactic shock. Was he still breathing? His eyes fluttered open.

"Hang in there baby, I'll find it!"

Evie searched the closet again. She stood on tiptoes and swept her arm across the shelves. Her fingers touched the hard edges of a box. She slid it forward.

.03 Epinephrine. How had she missed it on her first search? The phrase "till death do us part" echoed.

She pulled out the auto-injector. Clear liquid, expiration date a year from now. She had moments to decide.

"I can't find it!" Evie shouted.

She should call an ambulance. She should have called before searching for the EpiPen. She panicked, that's what she'd tell anyone who implied she'd done wrong.

Evie went to her purse. Under the divorce envelope, she found her phone. She dialed the three digits, and went to the living room.

Rocko's open, wet eyes accused her in their sightlessness. She touched his chest. He wasn't struggling, wasn't heaving, wasn't moving... wasn't breathing.

Through hitching breaths, she gave the dispatcher the information. She hung up the phone, retrieved the box with the auto-injector and instructions, and then went out the side door to the carport. She bit her wrist to stifle her sobs, and checked the area for nosy neighbors. No one was outside.

Evie stuffed the torn-up divorce paperwork along with the good EpiPen deep inside a rotting leaf bag. She took the expired one with her, and knelt beside Rocko. Evie waited for the paramedics and their official confirmation of death.

Peggy McFarland has completed her debut novel, *Bar None,* and is currently in the process of seeking an agent. Her short stories have appeared in several Level Best Books anthologies, as well as *Shroud Magazine*, *Uncle John's Bathroom Reader*, and in many other print and online venues. When not writing, she manages a restaurant in Chelmsford, is trying to get better at posting to social media, and is surprised at how complicated bed shopping can be.

RHODE ISLAND

FARM TO TABLE
by Shawn Reilly Simmons

"Where's the ball?" Ramon growled, wiping a sheen of sweat from his upper lip.

"Under that one," Brad said, darting his eyes to the wooden cup in the center. He twisted his arms against the ropes that held him in the chair.

"Wrong," Ramon said with a sneer, flipping it over to reveal nothing but the greasy tablecloth underneath.

"Wait, I was sure it was that one," Brad said. "Give me another chance."

Ramon sucked his teeth and lifted the cup on the left, revealing the scarred wooden ball. He put it back on the table and slid the cups over the tablecloth again.

"Which one now?" Ramon said. He pulled the gun from his waistband and placed it on the table.

"I have an idea," Brad said, panic speeding his words. "Why don't you give me three out of five guesses."

Ramon rolled a toothpick into the corner of his mouth. "Why should I do this?"

Encouraged, Brad spoke even more rapidly. "Because, you know. Fairness and all."

"You think it's fair to sleep with another man's wife?" Ramon said, his brow darkening. He laid his hand on the gun and rubbed the silver barrel with his index finger.

"In all fairness, I didn't know she was married," Brad said, slipping on his best salesmen's smile. "I thought she was just the maid, you know, coming to clean my room."

"Still," Ramon said, considering. "You might have reasoned she was someone's wife, seeing as she wears a ring."

Brad laughed a little too loudly. "Right, Ramon, that's right. You got me there. I should have asked about that before—"

"You slept with her," Ramon said, glaring.

"Look, Ramon, man to man. Sofia didn't tell me she was married, and we've fun. It's not like I've been forcing her into bed all weekend. That should count for something, right?"

Ramon gazed at him, a faint smile playing at his lips.

"Actually, it's more her fault then mine when you think about it," Brad reasoned.

Ramon's smile disappeared and he sat forward. "Say that again and see how things go for you, tourist."

The color drained from Brad's face and he jerked against the ropes, the legs of his chair lifting off the floor. "Is this really the punishment for accidentally having an affair while on business in Providence?"

"Yeah, it is." Ramon picked up the gun and pointed it at Brad's forehead. "Farm to Table is a family run business."

"Again, I didn't know. What can I do to make things up to you? I'm more than happy to leave quietly and never come back," Brad said, his voice trailing off as his eyes flicked to Ramon's gun.

"Tell you what. Choose correctly, and I'll only break your arm. Pick the wrong one again and *poof*, no more smooth talking salesman," Ramon said.

Brad looked around the dingy basement of what he once thought of as a quaint seaside bed and breakfast. "Why did you bring me here? You could have just shot me in my room."

"You've already made enough of a mess. Besides, we got good people checking in tomorrow. Also, it doesn't work that way," Ramon said, placing the gun back on the table.

"What doesn't work what way?" Brad asked, motioning with his eyes at the cups. A mouse scurried across the floor and Brad lifted his polished loafers in the air.

Ramon smiled, revealing three gold front teeth. "You know how many wandering businessmen come and stay here, thinking they can do whatever they want, just because they're away from the missus for a few days? I bet no one will even miss you, you don't come home."

"They'd miss me," Brad said quietly.

"Doubtful," Ramon said, yawning. "Don't worry, if you don't survive the game, I'll let the little lady know exactly what you were getting up to during your stay at our place."

"I still don't get what you're doing with this game. It's not a gamble if I lose either way. You could just—"

"You want me to shoot you right now?" Ramon asked.

"No! I just don't understand why this is happening," Brad said.

"You're a smart guy. Figure it out," Ramon said, crossing his arms tightly at his chest.

"Figure what out?"

"Look, stop asking so many questions," Ramon said, exasperated. "This is how I like to do it."

"Do what?"

"Shut up and choose a cup," Ramon said, failing to hide his irritation.

"Shuffle them again," Brad said. "We've been talking too long. It's not fair."

Ramon blew out a long sigh and slid the cups around. "Pick one, traveling salesman."

Brad cleared his throat. "That one," he said, and darted his eyes to the right.

Ramon upended the cup and revealed the ball, rolling slightly back and forth on the tablecloth.

Brad's eyes grew wide. "I found it!"

"Nice job," Ramon said. "I'm happy for you. Disappointed I only get to break your arm, though."

"Wait!" Brad said. He scraped the chair across the floor and jerked his shoulders from side to side, struggling to free himself from the ropes. Ramon stood up and shoved Brad's shoulders, tipping the chair backwards. Brad and the chair crashed against the concrete floor.

"Stop!" Sofia shouted from the doorway. Her face was in shadow, the light from the hallway outlining her shapely figure beneath her cotton maid's uniform.

"Sofia, help!" Brad shouted from beneath Ramon, who stood over him grasping his lapels.

Sofia went to the table and picked up the gun, raising it steadily at the men. "Stop this, Ramon. Sit him up," she said in an even voice. Ramon stood up and pulled the chair upright with Brad still attached, setting it down on all fours with more force than was strictly necessary. He stood behind the chair, his hands laying heavily on Brad's shoulders.

"Sofia, thank God you found us. Get me out of here," Brad said, relief flooding his face.

Sofia aimed the gun at Ramon's head. "Did he find the ball?"

"Yes, after a few tries," Ramon said. "He was very bad at guessing. I gave him extra chances."

"That means it's my turn this time," Sofia said. She lowered her aim and pulled the trigger. Brad's eyes grew wide and he looked down, watching the blood spreading across his dress shirt.

"Ramon, did you know that Brad is the top salesman for his company? He's in the million dollar club," Sofia said, her accent rolling through her words.

"A big shot, huh?" Ramon asked.

"With just two hundred in cash and a maxed out credit card on him." Sofia sniffed and pulled Brad's wallet from the pocket of her apron.

Brad's eyes glazed over and he began to fade, his confusion morphing into understanding.

"And this," Sofia said, flipping open the worn leather wallet to reveal a picture of Brad standing next to a tall brunette in a wedding dress. She tossed in on the table and slipped the gun into her apron pocket. "Time to get back to work," she said to Ramon, who followed her out the door and closed it behind them.

Shawn Reilly Simmons is the author of the Red Carpet Catering Mysteries, which are inspired by her experiences as an on-set movie caterer. *Murder on the Rocks*, the fifth book in the series, will be released in February 2018. Shawn serves on the Board of Malice Domestic, is a founding member of The Dames of Detection, a co-editor at Level Best Books, a member of Mystery Writers of America, Sisters in Crime, and the Crime Writers' Association in the U.K. Her short stories have been published in a number of anthologies, most recently "Burnt Orange" in *Passport to Murder: the Bouchercon 2017 Anthology* (Down & Out Books), and "The Prodigy" in *Mystery Tour*, the 2017 CWA Anthology (Orenda Books).

www.ShawnReillySimmons.com
@ShawnRSimmons
Facebook: @RedCarpetCateringMysteries

THE MURDEROUS TYPE
by Andrew Welsh-Huggins

O'Malley's knees ached worse than ever as he huffed and puffed up the stairs to the third-floor apartment. Eileen was right, as much as he hated to admit it. He was a pig. Like the night before when he ordered the extra-large coffee cabinet at Big Alice's. She'd harangued him all the way home to Cranston until his head throbbed at the thought of the Red Sox tickets he'd given up that evening. Like she should talk, anyway. She wasn't the slip-of-a-thing girl he'd married, not by a long shot. She was her mother, is what she was. Come to think of it, her mother also thought he was a pig.

He reached the upper landing and paused to catch his breath.

"You OK?"

He glanced at the patrolman in the department-issue brown uniform. Impossibly young looking. And something funny about his eyes. O'Malley couldn't figure it for a moment. Then it came to him. The kid actually cared.

"I'm fine." Still breathing hard.

"You sure?"

"Nothing retirement won't fix. Whaddya got?"

The patrolman glanced through the apartment door. "White male. Landlord gave the name as Edmund McCurdy."

"What's wrong with him?"

"He's, ah, dead."

"Believe that's already been ascertained, Officer"—he peered at the patrolman's badge—"Donatelli. Any idea how he got that way?"

"Looks like he was shot, sir. In the head. As far as we can tell."

"We?"

"Me, and the neighbor who found him."

"Where's he now?"

"She, sir. Back downstairs. I told her to wait in her apartment. She was kinda upset."

"Maybe because she did it?"

"I don't think so."

"Why not?"

"She doesn't seem, ah, the murderous type."

"They never do, Donatelli."

"No, sir."

O'Malley brushed past the patrolman. The apartment door opened onto a small living room. The man lay on the floor face down, blood pooling around his head like a scarlet halo, body positioned as though he'd been walking out of the room when he was shot.

"He was like this, when she found him?"

"Yes, sir."

"What was she doing up here?"

"Trying to borrow sugar, I believe. The door was partly open."

"Borrow sugar? At this time of day?" It was almost ten o'clock.

"She's a student, sir. Ris-dee—Rhode Island School of Design," he added quickly, as if O'Malley wouldn't have heard of the place. "She does watercolors."

"You seem to know a lot about her, Donatelli."

"Just trying to be thorough."

"Don't jump to any conclusions. Understand? Don't ever forget that."

"No, sir," Donatelli said. O'Malley searched the patrolman's eyes for signs he was humoring him. What's a fat pig know, anyway? But the boy's face was guileless as a priest after mass.

ᘓᘓᘓ

Edmund McCurdy was from Upper Arlington, Ohio, wherever the hell that was, according to his license. The apartment was sparsely furnished, to put it mildly. A couch and chairs Goodwill wouldn't have taken. Mismatched utensils and only two plates. A turntable and a few record albums—Paul Simon's *Graceland* the only one O'Malley had heard of. No TV. A bookshelf stuffed with paperbacks by writers he'd also never heard of. Roth. Tyler. Atwood. Whatever. On the top shelf a framed color photograph of a girl—dark, bobbed hair, friendly smile, freckles. Attractive in a Midwestern, girl-next-door kind of way. Picture watermarked with the name of a photo studio. High school senior portrait? Daughter? In the bathroom a few toiletries along with an out-of-place matching blue washcloth and towel, thick and luxurious. Perhaps brought from a much nicer bathroom in Upper Arlington, Ohio. A copy of the *Providence Journal* magazine on the floor next to the can, pages wrinkled from shower steam. A neatly made twin bed in the bedroom. The sheets and blankets Ann & Hope quality. So not brought from home. A book called *Beloved* on the cheap nightstand. Easing onto his knees with a grunt, O'Malley needed less than fifteen seconds to find the strip of condoms and the tube of K-Y in the Tupperware box under the bed. So McCurdy read books nobody'd heard of and had himself some fun. Case was practically solving itself.

ᘓᘓᘓ

"No trouble, no trouble."

"Heard you the first time," O'Malley said.

The landlord, a Cape Verdean named Ramos, stood on the porch casting nervous glances at the interior stairwell. He was dressed in heavy dark work pants and a blue long-sleeve shirt with his name stitched over the breast pocket. His accent someplace between Portuguese-Creole and "I don' know nothing." The bright red house was a triple-decker, like all the houses on the street, homes tall and solid and honestly built as nineteenth-century sailing ships. The street a spur running off Hope. Big with the university crowd.

According to Mr. Ramos, McCurdy called to inquire about the apartment in July, answering a classified ad in the ProJo. He paid a security deposit, first and last month's rent without complaint, and moved in August 1. Mr. Ramos wasn't sure what the man did.

"Any visitors?"

"Just his daughter."

"Daughter?"

"She go to Brown. That's what he say."

O'Malley thought of the picture on the bookshelf. He didn't relish another trip up those stairs. He looked in vain for Donatelli. Where the hell had the patrolman gotten to? He thought of the condoms under the bed. Sighing, he described the girl in the photograph to Mr. Ramos.

"That's her. She is here many nights."

"Nights?"

"That's right." Mr. Ramos glanced inside again. "What about the blood, on carpet? The security deposit no cover—"

"You're sure she was his daughter?"

"That's what he say."

"She's a Brown student, and she's visiting him at night?"

"Yes."

"Ever stay the *whole* night?"

"Maybe." Reluctantly. "I cannot be sure. I go to work early. Go to bed early."

"Where?"

"I clean. At Providence Ring."

"The jewelry factory? On Taunton?"

"Grosvenor."

"Clean, like the rings?"

Mr. Ramos shook his head. "Clean the floors. The bathrooms. Every day. Very dirty."

"You sure this girl was Mr. McCurdy's daughter?"

This time Ramos wouldn't meet his gaze. "That's what he tell me. No trouble. No trouble."

O'Malley started to ask another of the three dozen questions crowding into his head. The arrival of the crime scene guys interrupted him. Bureau of Criminal Investigation. About time. "Don't go anywhere," he said. He waved at the technicians. He followed them up the stairs, wheezing as he went. He stopped to catch his breath on the second floor landing beside an opened apartment door. He heard a familiar voice inside.

He found Donatelli sitting in a wooden chair in the apartment's sunny kitchen. He was speaking softly to a woman sitting opposite him. A canvas was propped on an easel beside the woman, the painting a swirl of yellows and reds and greens that seemed like nothing at first but then shaped itself into what even O'Malley recognized as a street scene in Fox Point down by the river. Pretty good, actually. The woman had thick dark hair and eyes the color of olives. She was wearing a white smock daubed with paint that failed to disguise a figure O'Malley would have walked up and down three flights of stairs for all day long. She looked a little weepy. He cleared his throat. The woman sniffed as she looked up at him. But Donatelli started.

"Detective," he said, standing. "This is Julia. She's the one…"

"Who found him?"

"She's very upset. I was just—"

"I can see what you're doing. Time to go."

"Where?"

"College Hill."

"What about—?"

"Keil called in sick and Koller's working a suicide at Blackstone Park. You're with me the next few hours."

"If you really—"

"Thank you for your assistance, miss," O'Malley said to Julia. If he'd had a hat he would have tipped it.

"Nice of you to comfort a witness like that," O'Malley said as they stepped outside. "Especially a witness like *that.*"

"Just trying to help, sir."

"Yeah. I can see that."

ϱϱϱ

O'Malley got the other uniforms started on canvassing, then ordered Donatelli to the Brown University security office. He told him to show the girl's photo around as a start. See if he could find out who she was. Then he drove back downtown to 209 Fountain. Once in his second-floor office he eased himself into his chair, scrounged an incident form and piece of carbon paper, fitted them into the typewriter and started to hunt and peck.

Halfway through Brogan sauntered in. "Your old lady called," he said, dropping a pink message slip on his desk, the fake-wood top stained with coffee cup rings and marked with cigarette burns. "Wants you to swing by Antonelli's, pick up a chicken."

"Thanks," O'Malley said, not looking up.

"Maybe you could get some milk and toiletries too, long as you're doing the grocery shopping," Brogan said with a smirk. O'Malley flipped him off. It was just like Eileen to call and leave a message like that, knowing he'd get his chops busted by the other detectives. But it was just like Brogan to be a dick about it, too.

Finished, O'Malley picked up the phone book and flipped through until he found the map with the U.S. area codes. He called 216 for Cleveland and 513 for Cincinnati, with no luck. Finally, he located Upper Arlington in the 614 area code. It was near Columbus. A place he'd actually heard of. Ohio State football, right? The operator gave him information for an Edmund and Melissa McCurdy on Patricia Drive. O'Malley wrote down the number, thanked the operator, and hung up. He looked at the seven digits and then at the phone. What was the call he was about to make? An inquiry? A death notification? Those were supposed to be in person, but how to handle a case like this? He could call the locals, but who knew how long it would take to get an officer to the house, assuming they'd even do it.

"Hello?"

A woman's voice, picking up on the fourth ring.

"I'm trying to reach Melissa McCurdy."

"Yes. This is she."

O'Malley identified himself.

"Is this about Charlie?" she said. Her voice suddenly small, like a young girl's.

"Charlie?"

"My husband. Is that why you're calling?"

O'Malley glanced around the office. Looked at the Block Island-shaped hole in the opposite wall. Thought of Julia, the RISD student who'd found the body. Recalled her figure. Her eyes the color of olives. Flashed to Eileen, and her mother.

"I was inquiring about an Edmund McCurdy," he said, carefully.

"That's him. Edmund Charles McCurdy. He goes by Charlie. Has something happened?"

"He's, ah, living in Providence. That's correct?"

"Yes. As far as I know."

"As far as you know?"

"Is this about her? It is, isn't it?"

"Her?"

"The girl. Jennifer." Her voice so quiet now O'Malley was having a hard time hearing.

"Who's Jennifer, ma'am? If I may ask."

A pause. "His girlfriend, if you must know. Jennifer Ratliff."

O'Malley thought of the girl in the photo. Just a kid. And what had McCurdy's license said? Forty-two years old?

"When was the last time you saw your husband, Mrs. McCurdy?"

A deep sigh traversed the telephone lines between Patricia Drive in Upper Arlington, Ohio, and Fountain Street in Providence. "The night before he left. When I told him what a fool he was."

"Mrs. McCurdy, is there anyone there with you?"

"There?"

"In your house."

"No. The kids are at school and I'm cleaning up. If you could just tell me why you're calling—"

No way around it, apparently. "I'm sorry to have to tell you this. But your husband was found dead this morning. It appears he was shot."

"Shot?"

"That's right. I'm sorry."

"Oh, God," Melissa McCurdy said.

After he hung up, O'Malley stared at the phone for a long minute. That girl, McCurdy's lover? A Brown student? Not even half his age—

The phone rang, interrupting his thoughts.

"It's David," the voice on the other end said. "Officer Donatelli."

"Yeah?"

"I'm at the security office. Nobody knows the girl. They're checking with the student life office. Trying to match pictures."

"Skip that." O'Malley told him about the call to Ohio. He gave him the girl's name.

"OK," Donatelli said, sounding a little disappointed. "I'll call you right back."

ooo

O'Malley left his unmarked Plymouth Fury in front of the Brown bookstore on Thayer and crossed campus to the girl's dormitory. He tried not to stare at the co-eds lounging under the trees on the warm day. He'd only been on campus a few times in his life and always felt out of place. The red brick buildings and brilliant green lawns looked like something transplanted from an England that only existed in the movies. Very expensive movies.

Donatelli met him outside New Pembroke hall along with a dour woman who introduced herself as Mrs. Lowell from Student Life.

"Is it possible to do this someplace less public?" she said. She was wearing a tweed jacket, white blouse, matching tweed skirt and heavy, brown shoes that brought to mind muddy equestrian fields.

"Like where?"

"An office, perhaps? It could be upsetting to the students, seeing…this." Her eyes on Donatelli's uniform.

"Give 'em something to write home about," O'Malley said, going inside.

They found the girl in a room halfway down a second-floor corridor. The hall smelled of disinfectant, pizza and perfume. A stereo blasted from two rooms down. *"Walk like an Egyptian,"* a singer crooned. O'Malley knocked and went inside.

He recognized her right away. Sitting on the bed, looking bored. The girl in the picture: no question. Jennifer Ratliff. Except she looked even younger in person. Girlfriend? Really? To her right, reading a magazine at a desk, another girl about her age. Blonde, flat-chested, perfect white teeth. Blue top, tan shorts, red sweater thrown jauntily around her shoulders. Beside Jennifer sat a woman who could have been her much older and more exotically dressed twin. Curly, black hair springing in all directions. Red floral dress like something you'd order from a glossy catalog. Lots of jewelry, starting with the pearl necklace. The detective introduced himself. The woman rose. "I'm Angelica Ratliff. I'm Jennifer's mother."

Interesting. "You're, ah, visiting?"

"Yes."

"From Ohio?"

"That's right."

"And you are?" He directed the question at the blonde.

"Missy," the girl brayed. "I'm her roommate."

"What's going on?" Mrs. Ratliff said. "Why are you here?" O'Malley ignored her and looked at her daughter.

"Jennifer."

She looked up, still bored.

"I need to ask if you know an Edmund McCurdy."

The girl froze mid-yawn. He might as well have asked her to take all her clothes off.

"Miss?"

"Um, yeah." Eyes darting between Missy and mom.

"May I ask how?"

"I—"

"Charlie McCurdy took advantage of my daughter," Mrs. Ratliff said, locking eyes with the detective. "Filled her head with ideas. Misled her. Then he followed her here out of some misplaced notion of *love*." The word spat like an obscenity. "She's only eighteen, for God's sake."

Age of consent, O'Malley thought, glancing at Mrs. Lowell. The student life administrator was glowering at the girl.

"When was the last time you saw Mr. McCurdy?"

"I'm . . . I'm not sure," Jennifer said.

"Mr. Ramos, his landlord, said you were there frequently."

"Well, we couldn't, you know, be *here*." A weak flip of her right hand to designate the dorm room.

"He was demanding," Mrs. Ratliff interrupted. "Psychologically controlling. That's why I came out. Something had to be done."

"When did you arrive?"

"Tuesday."

So two days ago. "Did you see McCurdy? Once you got here?"

"Me?"

"That's right."

A pause. "I went and talked to him yesterday," Mrs. Ratliff said. "I gave him a piece of my mind. Told him this had to stop. That he was ruining Jennifer's life. I told him if he didn't—"

"Didn't what?" O'Malley said sharply.

"If he didn't leave her alone he was going to regret it."

Jennifer stared at her mother. "Mom. You didn't . . . I told you."

"Told her what?" the detective said.

"I told you I could handle it." A flood of tears suddenly streamed down the girl's pale face. "I thought I could."

"What's this all about?" Mrs. Ratliff said. "It's immoral, what this man has done. But unfortunately, not illegal." Then something like hope crossed her face. "Except maybe in Rhode Island?"

"Jennifer," O'Malley said, watching the girl's face carefully. "I'm afraid I have some bad news."

Mrs. Ratliff agreed to accompany Jennifer back to the station to answer some questions. With Donatelli beside him taking notes, O'Malley pieced together the back story.

Edmund "Charlie" McCurdy and his wife lived three doors down from the Ratliffs. Jennifer babysat for their kids from time to time. McCurdy was a lawyer in a medium-sized firm in downtown Columbus. More to the point, he was a frustrated writer whose wife refused to hear any talk of him quitting his job to pursue his dream, even though his sole output from what O'Malley could gather appeared to be a half-finished manuscript and a bunch of notes. Jennifer by contrast was bright, well-read, and more than willing to listen to Charlie dream. Listen with benefits, apparently. They'd fallen in love as she read her poems to him. He'd left everything behind to follow her to Providence when she got into Brown.

O'Malley shook his head. Just when you thought you'd heard it all.

Apparently he still hadn't, he thought, as he asked Mrs. Ratliff to repeat what she'd just said.

"You heard me. You know who I'm talking about?"

Of course I do, O'Malley said to himself. Of course I know who the Old Man is. The boss of bosses, sitting up on Federal Hill, running the entire New England mob out of a dusty storefront. Who didn't? Around Providence, it was like asking if you knew who Santa Claus was.

"What's he have to do with any of this?"

Mrs. Ratliff sat back, beaming with unmistakable pride. "I'm not originally from Columbus, you know. I grew up in a place called Youngstown."

O'Malley rubbed his face. "Steel mills?"

"Once upon a time. Not now. But plenty of the same kind of men, if you catch my drift."

"I have no idea what you mean," O'Malley said.

"My maiden name is Cappocia. People in my family know other people. The connections run deep. Frankly, I was happy to get away from it all, after I went to Ohio State. But it's hard to escape. And family looks out for family. Especially when someone in that family's being preyed upon."

"Mrs. Ratliff," O'Malley said. "Are you telling me—"

"I'm not telling you anything, detective. That's all I have to say. And now I'd like the opportunity to call a lawyer."

Outside the interview room, O'Malley leaned against the wall in the poorly lit hallway.

"Did she just say what I think she said?" Donatelli said.

"What do you think she said?"

"She, ah, sounded like she was taking responsibility for ordering a hit on Mr. McCurdy. For, ah, being with her daughter."

"That's what it sounded like to me, too. But remember what I said before, about jumping to conclusions."

"OK."

"So before we do anything else, we need to run an errand."

"An errand? Now?"

"Now. The Mrs. wants a chicken from Antonelli's."

ợợợ

They made one stop first. The San Gennaro Social Club sat midway down Atwells Avenue on Federal Hill. Its pink stucco walls gave it the look of a building perpetually bathed in the light of the sun setting over the Mediterranean. O'Malley walked under the entrance's white canvas awning and pulled open the wooden door, heavy and ornate as the top of a sarcophagus. Donatelli followed a step behind, visibly nervous.

Inside the windowless club it was dark and cool. It took the detective a minute to adjust his eyes to the velvety shadows. He'd been inside once or twice before, but only at night. It didn't matter. San Gennaro's was like a cave. The light and the temperature didn't change, day or night. On the other side of the room three men looked up from a table. They had short, black hair, five o'clock shadows at noon and shoulders as wide as feedbags. They were dressed as if they were just coming off eighteen holes. Or from digging eighteen holes. Two of them stared daggers at O'Malley. One of them nodded. He didn't nod back.

"Detective." A tall, thin, deeply tanned man in a tailored pin-striped suit materialized before them. He took O'Malley's right hand in both of his. His fingers were draped in enough gold rings to outfit a winning Super Bowl team. It was not the Old Man, of course. O'Malley only merited a lieutenant. He believed he was just fine with that.

They sat at a table covered in thick white cloth, set for lunch. Red napkins like folded-up pennants at each setting. The club bartender approached and set down three thick-cut glasses of dark liquid. He smiled pleasantly and wished them a good day. He was the size and build of two mailboxes stacked one on top of the other with a face like a side of beef pulled from a fire just in time. The lieutenant offered a toast. They clinked glasses and sipped. Donatelli choked slightly. O'Malley savored his.

"So," the lieutenant said. "What can we do for you, detective?"

O'Malley explained why they were there. He played it straight. No point bullshitting or pussyfooting around. When he was finished the lieutenant laced his gold-laden fingers together and set his hands on the table as if he were praying up the street at Church of the Holy Ghost.

"Cappocia?"

"That's right."

"And you said the name of the deceased is McCurdy?"

O'Malley nodded. "First name Edmund. Goes by Charlie."

"The girl is a first-year student. You're sure about that?"

"Yeah." What difference did that make? But no point asking.

"If you'll excuse me a moment."

"Yeah, sure."

The lieutenant walked to the table where the three men were sitting. He whispered in the ear of the man closest to the kitchen. The one who'd nodded at O'Malley. After a moment he stood up and both men disappeared into the back.

"What now?" Donatelli said in a low voice.

"We wait."

"For what?"

"For information. Or for the feds to kick the front door down and ask us what the hell we're doing here."

"Are you—"

"Relax. I'm kidding, mostly. Ever been to Antonelli's?"

Donatelli shook his head.

"You're in for a treat. They wring the birds' necks right in front of you."

It wasn't a long wait. Just enough time to finish the drinks a sip at a time and admire the plaster statuary placed in discreet nooks around the room like confiscated museum pieces.

"Detective O'Malley?" The lieutenant back at the table, his face a stone.

"Yeah."

"No one is familiar with a Mrs. Angelica Cappocia Ratliff from Youngstown, Ohio."

O'Malley nodded. So she'd been bluffing, for whatever reason. Big surprise. But they'd had to check it out.

The lieutenant cleared his throat. "However."

"Yeah?"

"The girl. Her daughter?"

"Jennifer."

"She has a roommate, I believe."

"That's right."

"Melissa Alden? Missy?"

O'Malley recalled the flat-chested blonde with the perfect teeth and jaunty sweater. How would someone at the San Gennaro Social Club know about her?

Dumb question.

"Yeah. That's her."

"The Aldens of Newport, if I'm not mistaken. Missy has a brother, also at Brown. Penfield."

"Penfield?"

"Penfield Alden III."

"What about him?"

The lieutenant leaned forward and whispered in O'Malley's ear. He might have been murmuring accolades about the day's wedding soup. Except that he wasn't.

"You're certain—" the detective said.

"We appreciate you coming directly to us with this information," the lieutenant interrupted. "I trust you'll remember our cooperation in the future."

A minute later O'Malley and Donatelli stood outside the club, blinking as their eyes adjusted to the September sunlight.

"'The Aldens of Newport'?" O'Malley said. "Ever heard of them?"

"Sure. They have one of those mansions. And a yacht that's like the size of the Queen Mary."

O'Malley glanced at him. "You've never been to Antonelli's but you've heard of the Aldens of Newport?"

Donatelli shrugged. "They're real famous. They're in the paper all the time. And besides, my mom and my sisters always did the shopping."

"Famous for what?"

"Famous for how rich they are, I guess."

ooo

"No trouble, no trouble," Mr. Ramos said.

"Shut up," O'Malley said. "You're not in any trouble. At least not yet. It's a simple request."

"I no—"

"You clean floors at Providence Ring, right? No different. Just push the mop up and down the hall like normal. You're invisible to these kids. Trust me."

They set him up on Jennifer's hallway. It didn't take long. A thin, lanky young man sauntered up half an hour later and ducked into the dorm. Five minutes later Mr. Ramos emerged.

"That's him."

"You're sure?" O'Malley said.

"Sure."

"Why?"

"I see him. He comes twice with the girl. A red BMW, both times. You no see that kind of car on my street very often."

O'Malley and Donatelli marched inside. They were too late. Penfield Alden III had ducked out the other door.

"Find the lady. Mrs. Lowell," O'Malley growled. "Kid like that has more than one hidey hole."

Sure enough, they located him an hour later in a pastel blue clapboard house on Benefit Street. The in-town residence of the Aldens of Newport, O'Malley figured. A house that was already fifty years old when his relatives were eating grass to keep from starving during the potato famine. The boy answered the door wearing a blue monogrammed button-down shirt, tan khakis and deck shoes. No socks.

"Yes?" he said, in a tone that implied that craftsmen entered in the rear.

"Avon calling," O'Malley said.

It didn't take long. All he'd done, Alden insisted, was to give Jennifer the gun. Something a friend of a friend helped him acquire. Who apparently knew a guy who came under the jurisdiction of people at the San Gennaro Social Club. She told him she was just going to scare the guy. Said she was tired of

McCurdy. He was so *old.* Said she wanted to spend time with her new love, Penfield Alden III.

" 'I love you, Penny,' " Alden said, recounting their last conversation.

"Let's go," O'Malley said, forcing the boy to his feet. "I'm not sure how much more of this I can take."

ϙϙϙ

"I'm guessing he gave her a million reasons to fall in love with him," O'Malley said as they left booking. "Two million, maybe. Yacht like the Queen Mary, right?"

"Bigger than anything in Ohio," Donatelli said. "That's for sure."

In the interview room at 209 Fountain, Jennifer Ratliff aged considerably as they explained the situation to her, her face hardening like concrete setting up in the cold. The Midwestern friendliness vanished, replaced by a stare O'Malley had seen in girls who weren't quite from next door.

"You've got this all wrong," her mother said in the next room over, when they broke the news to her. She tugged at O'Malley's sleeve. "I'm a Capoccia! From Youngstown! I'm the one you want!"

"You should be careful about telling tales, Mrs. Ratliff," the detective said, shaking her loose. "I know you were only trying to protect your daughter. But sometimes stories go places you can't anticipate."

ϙϙϙ

"You did good," O'Malley said, back in the detective bureau. "Grab a beer over at Christopher's, when we're done? You've earned it."

"Maybe some other time," Donatelli said. "I'm, ah, meeting someone."

"Who?" O'Malley said, curious. Even a rookie like Donatelli had to know it wasn't an idle invitation. Downing a few at the department watering hole with his seniors and all that.

"Julia," the patrolman said, turning a color close to the stucco walls of the San Gennaro Social Club. "The girl—"

"The girl who found McCurdy. Yeah, I remember." O'Malley allowed himself one last recollection of the artist's figure, poorly hidden under the paint-spattered smock. "Sure she's your type? RISD, right? College girl. All, you know . . . " He made a fist with his right hand and cocked his pinky up.

"I'm taking classes too."

"College classes?"

Donatelli nodded.

"Where?"

"Rhode Island College. At night. I should have my degree in another year and a half. I took an art history course last spring. It was kinda interesting. That's what I was talking to her about, this morning."

College, O'Malley thought to himself, driving home a couple of hours later. The chicken from Antonelli's packed in ice on the front seat beside him.

Way too late for dinner, which he knew he'd hear about. He shook his head. He'd gone through the academy with guys who hadn't finished high school. Wave of the future, he guessed. He stopped at a red light. He pondered how a fresh-faced girl from Ohio had managed to ruin so many lives at such a young age. Charlie McCurdy, a dreamy, horny idiot. Penfield Alden III, a rich, horny idiot. The light turned green. O'Malley passed Star Market and thought about stopping and picking up a tub of coffee ice cream. He thought better of it and kept driving. Eileen was right. He was a pig. He needed ice cream like a hole in the head. Well, maybe not the best analogy, he considered, turning on the radio to see how the Sox were doing.

Andrew Welsh-Huggins was born in Providence, grew up in western New York State and now lives in Columbus, Ohio, where he covers criminal justice issues for The Associated Press. He is the author of nonfiction books on the death penalty and domestic terrorism and also writes the Andy Hayes mystery series about an ex-Ohio State quarterback turned private eye.

BEST NEW ENGLAND CRIME STORIES

VERMONT

MAIDSTONE
by Maia Chance

A lady living in one of our obscure New-England towns, where there were no servants to be hired, at last, by sending to a distant city, succeeded in procuring a raw Irish maid-of-all-work, a creature of immense bone and muscle, but of heavy, unawakened brain. In one fortnight she established such a reign of Chaos and old Night in the kitchen and through the house that her mistress...dismissed her. What was now to be done?[1]

Brigit, the previous maid-of-all-work, never left Gardiner Farm. This I understood by my second hour there.

One hot July afternoon I arrived on a milk wagon come from Littleton, all of my earthly belongings in dented bandboxes and worry riding high in my throat. Mrs. Gardiner herself met me at the front door, a forbidding figure in black bombazine. Her eyes skimmed me down and up like a ladle on cream. "You appear ladylike enough. Tall as well, and modestly dressed, but you're very slender. You wrote in your letter that you were strong."

"I am strong, ma'am."

"Then come in. The work has fallen behind."

I bobbed my head.

She led me into her large white farmhouse on the hill. Along the way to the kitchen, I saw Brussels carpets, framed engravings, satin wallpaper, a desk piled with papers, but no other human beings.

"Here is the kitchen," Mrs. Gardiner said. "Brigit left it in chaos, as you can see, and I am too occupied with my writing for domestic chores."

"No one else lives here?" I asked. "Such a large house—?"

"I supposed the milk wagon man would have told you. Don't they all gossip? Gardiner Farm is a model scientific farmstead. It does not produce. I experiment."

My mouth fell open a little; I could not help it.

"Close your mouth," Mrs. Gardiner said. "How coarse you look. I engaged you because you wrote that you were presentable enough for indoor work."

"I am!" I lowered my voice. "I am, ma'am." Mrs. Gardiner's advertisement in the *Mirror and Farmer* had appeared like a heavenly gift only one day after Papa died and his farm was seized. Losing this position was unthinkable. I must be allowed to stay on.

Mrs. Gardiner said, "I am writing a book, an instructional manual, about the correct and scientific arrangement and management of the home. It is my hope that someday even a large farmstead like this one might run like clockwork, with only occasional interventions from the lady of the house. How impossible that seems at times. Clean this mess up, and then you may take your things—" Mrs. Gardiner looked at the bandboxes heaped in my arms with distaste. "—up those back stairs to the attic. The maid's room is there."

Mrs. Gardiner left, and I cleaned the kitchen. Oh, I know how to clean. Until the previous week, I had kept Papa's house and cooked for a clutch of farmhands, too. I scraped vegetable peels, egg shells, and spongy apples into a pail and hauled it all out to the pig pen. I swept a month's worth of ash from the fireplace and scoured the draining board. I mopped the floor. I scrubbed the table. The only thing I left untouched was the stove.

I had never seen such a stove. Scrolled iron feet supported hulking, boxy, black metal shapes. I recognized the round hobs on top and doors that might've led to ovens or coal burners. Yet an unfamiliar oval tank teetered up on one side, and mysterious cranks, bins, and knobs protruded as unevenly as a town seen from afar.

As I worked, I was gripped by the sensation that the stove was watching me. So monstrous and authoritative it was that, as foolish as it sounds, I dared not raise my eyes.

Once the kitchen was clean, I took my bandboxes up to the stuffy, bare-raftered attic. A dormer overlooked kitchen yard, outbuildings, tumbly stone wall, maple forest. A narrow bed hunkered under the eaves. Why was the floor dusty around the bed? The dust was white and fine, like chalk from a schoolroom slate.

I set down my bandboxes, sank onto the edge of the bed, and pressed my eyes into my palms. No. I would not think of Papa's face subsiding into his skull. I had yet to weep for him and moved forward as though floating, my memory clipped short, unsure if I could trust my eyes.

I looked up.

One floorboard didn't lay flat, and its nails were gone. Fingerprints smeared the white dust.

I waited a moment. Then I knelt, and pried up the floorboard. Underneath, arranged between cobwebby floor joists, were a girl's things. Dingy petticoats and a patched nightdress. A tarnished looking glass in a brass case. A crackled picture, perhaps torn from a book, of a Madonna cradling an oversized baby. Many-times-laundered handkerchiefs. These were the private things of a girl without a wardrobe or chest. The things of a penny pincher who never got rid of anything, but mended, darned, patched, and made do until there was nothing left with which to do it.

Someone like myself.

And I, well, I would never leave my precious threadbare things behind. Not even if I'd been commanded to leave in a hurry.

What, then, had befallen Brigit?

After extensive inquiry and many personal experiments, the author has found a cooking-stove constructed on true scientific principles...Of this stove, drawings and descriptions will now be given.

Mrs. Gardiner said to me, "Girls, fleshly girls—even girls such as you, Hattie, although I observe that you are singularly graceful—girls stumble about, making errors and messes and neglecting thrift, and meanwhile there is always more and more work to be done. Machines do not have weak minds or weak backs. They are strong and steady. Mr. Clay designed this stove to my own specifications." She ran ink-stained fingers over the hob, as though caressing a pony. "Mr. Clay built it, too, at his own foundry on the other side of the village. It is opportune that he has recently come to live in this obscure place—he was a famous mechanic in the City of Spindles. This stove is the only one of its kind. You are a very fortunate girl to have the privilege of using what is, in truth, a scientific implement."

"Oh," I said, willing myself not to back away from the crouched metal fiend. "Yes. Thank you, ma'am."

"Here is the dinner menu, to be ready at seven o'clock." Mrs. Gardiner passed me a piece of paper overlaid with handwriting so elegant it was almost illegible. Letter by letter, words assembled: shell bean succotash, roast beef, biscuits, yeast rolls, poached pears, cherry pie.

"Are you expecting company, ma'am?" I asked.

"No, you foolish girl. This is so you may practice with the stove. I shall taste each dish, and the rest will go to the hogs. Now pay attention. I'll show you how to operate the stove but once. Here—" She swung open a drawer on the stove. "—is the fire box—you must add more coal. Do not use wood—we do not burn wood at all in this household, and in fact, you are forbidden to enter the woodshed. Is that clear?"

"Yes, ma'am."

"Mr. Clay, you see, is experimenting with the construction of a mechanical wood-splitter, and it is dangerous."

"Yes, ma'am, that does sound dangerous."

"I have already fetched the roast—there it is on the draining board. All of the other food stuffs for this meal will be found in the pantry. The coal is in the cellar." Mrs. Gardiner opened and shut stove compartments, explained that the big tank heated hot water for washing up, showed me the built-in spit roast on one side and the baking compartment on the top, the closet for warming plates, the box for ash, and the damper cranks. "It is exceedingly scientific," she said as she left, "and thus it does not require further explanation. Please serve dinner in two hours."

With shaking hands, I loaded the fire box with coal and got it lit. While I waited for the contraption to grow hot, I opened the kitchen door to admit fresh air. I made the pie crust. I managed to impale the roast on the spit only after dropping the whole slippery thing on the floor (I prayed that Mrs. Gardiner didn't hear the thump), and I began the cherry pie filling. But although I knew the receipt by heart, the sticky crimson mixture bubbled up too hard, scalding the back of my hand. I shouted and dropped my spoon.

I bent for it. I raised my eyes.

There was a man in the kitchen door. Tall. Dark tousled curls, sparkling jet-bead eyes. Smiling at me.

"Pardon me, miss," he said. "I heard you cry out—are you all right?"

"Yes, it's…" I picked up the spoon, straightened. "This stove frightens me a bit. I feel as though it wishes to master me, rather than the other way around."

The man laughed. "Clever phraseology for a maidservant—I suppose you're Mrs. Gardiner's newest?"

"Yes. Hattie." Stop. I'd made an error. This man was not a farmhand or someone here to prune the apple trees. His clothes were fine, his voice cultured. Mrs. Gardiner might dismiss me for overfamiliarity.

I turned to the stove to find golden-pink bubbles frothing over the side of the pot. I grabbed the handle, burned my palm, the pan clanged to the floor, and pie filling burst up and out like a dahlia blossom.

"Look what I've made you do," the man said, stepping forward. He took some cloths from the table and crouched to help me sop up the mess. I worked quickly, embarrassed by his large warm presence. "I am Mr. Clay, by the by," he said. "I work for Mrs. Gardiner."

"But aren't you a mechanic? That's…" My cheeks grew hot. "I did not mean to insult your stove, sir."

He smiled. "My true work lies in inventing new contraptions for the bobbin mill up the road—making faster, more efficient, more reliable machines seems to be my row to hoe. The stove was but a minor project, a diversion for me and a favor to Mrs. Gardiner."

"Like the other machine in the woodshed."

His eyes flicked. "Mrs. Gardiner spoke of…the mechanical butter churn?"

"A wood splitter."

"Ah. Yes, that as well. Mrs. Gardiner is inordinately fond of mechanical inventions, and she has a zeal for system and order."

"I suppose that's why the last maid, Brigit, left in such a hurry."

"Did she? Yes, Mrs. Gardiner is difficult to please, and I did gather that Brigit and my stove never made friends. There. The floor is as clean as a slate." Mr. Clay stood. "I am so glad to have made your acquaintance, Hattie. Good luck—oh, and shut the smaller flue a little. You've got to suffocate that thing."

ℚℚℚ

I woke at dawn, as was my habit, and dressed quickly, standing atop the loose floorboard that hid poor Brigit's things.

The kitchen was more tidy than I remembered having left it. Had Mrs. Gardiner gone over my work, flicking crumbs, straightening canisters, polishing knives? Would she tell me I was inadequate and send me on my way? I had, in the end, mustered the dinner she'd requested, even the cherry pie. She'd tasted each dish without comment, and I'd scraped it all into three slop buckets after. But she could change her mind.

Unsure of what my day's chores were, I went to the room where I had seen Mrs. Gardiner's desk, in the hopes that she would be there. She was not.

Sunbeams lit up her stacks of papers. I glanced over my shoulder; I crept to the desk. The page on the blotter read:

In a work which aims to influence women to train the young to honor domestic labor . . . there is special reason for explaining the construction of the muscles and their connection with the nerves...Fig. 53 represents the muscles of the arm after the skin and flesh are removed. They are all in smooth silky cases, laid over each other, and separated both by the smooth membranes that encase them and by layers of fat..

"Hattie!" Mrs. Gardiner said sharply.

I turned, my heart jigging. "I only—"

"Quiet! If you wish to keep this position, you must be extraordinarily helpful. Is that clear?"

"Yes, ma'am."

"You are first to make a circuit of the henhouse, spring house, root cellar, and keeping room to collect the foodstuffs required for the day's meals, for which I left a list in the kitchen. The keeping room is adjacent to the woodshed. Mind what I said about the woodshed."

ooo

First I went to the root cellar, built into a slope out back. In that cool, vaulted chamber I gathered Winesap apples, sand-packed parsnips, a linen-wrapped cheese, and salt pork plucked from murky brine. Inside the spring house, a pipe poured icy water into a trough from which I took jugs of cream, milk, and a crock of butter that were keeping fresh. Then the henhouse, where I deftly stole eggs from the fluttering, irritable girls.

I tried to pet a hen because you see, I was famished with loneliness and despite all of that nice stored food, I saw no one else at Gardiner Farm. Who milked the cows and made the butter? Who slaughtered the hogs? Who mowed the hay field?

The hen pecked my wrist so hard, a spot of blood beaded.

The woodshed and attached keeping room stood in the shade of girthy oaks. What a prodigious amount of firewood the farm must have gone through in its heyday. For while most farms thereabouts had only an open-air shed stacked with split birch, maple, and beech logs, this woodshed was the size of a six-horse stable. Double doors shut out the day.

I stepped from the gaudy sunshine into the shade, blinked at the contrast, swatted a black fly at my neck, and opened the keeping room door.

All was cool and dim and fragrant. Paper-lined shelves held wrapped hams and bacon slabs. Pallid, bumpy Hubbard squashes lurked in baskets like eyeless ghouls' heads.

Dangling from ceiling hooks were the head cheese sausages Mrs. Gardiner had requested for the midday meal. I reached for one and the waxy marbling of its casing called to mind a human arm, a girl's arm, fair, unblemished, and dizziness rippled from my skull to my tailbone.

Brigit. Where was Brigit?

Behind a well-stocked shelf, a thread of light shone between two planks.

The woodshed—that was what lay on the other side.

I moved aside a slab of bacon, and put my eye to the crack.

"I believe if you agreed to go for a walk with me, Hattie, I could show you far more agreeable beauty spots. The millpond up the road, for instance, is thought picturesque by the locals."

I rounded and pressed my shoulders to the shelf. "Mr. Clay! I was only—I was—there was an insect, and I feared it would spoil the hams."

"I didn't suppose nice Yankee girls were so adept at lying." Only half of his face was illuminated. The cleft in his chin was bottomless. "And you *are* nice, are you not, Hattie? So graceful. Did your mother lecture you on deportment? Require you to walk about with a book upon your head?"

"No," I whispered. I unhooked a head cheese sausage and placed it in my basket. Mr. Clay had not moved from the doorway.

The offal scent of the head cheese rose up, over-salted and musky. I said, "Mrs. Gardiner won't be pleased if breakfast is late."

"I don't suppose you please her much at all," Mr. Clay said. "You're too pretty. Mrs. Gardiner isn't partial to the pretty ones."

"Please, sir, I must—"

Mr. Clay stepped aside with a conjurer's sweep of the arms.

I squeezed past him and out into the insect-humming day. As I went, I saw the white dust on his bare fingers and shirt cuff.

ℓℓℓ

The next morning, I ventured into the keeping room again, this time for some bacon.

That crack between the wall boards had been sealed up with tar.

ℓℓℓ

Many days passed. Solitary days. I cooked lavish meals for the hogs and kept the house spick-and-span while Mrs. Gardiner wrote at her desk.

I was only nineteen, so you cannot think too poorly of me if I borrowed Brigit's tarnished looking glass to make my hair pretty for Mr. Clay. Yet during those days, I never saw him, nor another soul besides Mrs. Gardiner. Sometimes I felt that I was being watched—by that hulking stove, by the darting boot-button eyes of the hens, by the knots in the floorboards—yet I reckoned that it was only my loneliness and grief. I wondered if I *wished* to be watched.

And fresh milk and cream appeared every morning in the spring house, someone changed the hens' nesting box straw, and a hog disappeared from the pen, but I was afraid to ask my mistress who did all of that work overnight, and each evening I was too exhausted by my own chores to stay up and keep watch.

On the second Sunday, I walked a mile downhill through fields and forests to Maidstone Meeting House. Mrs. Gardiner was not a church-goer, it seemed, for she was bent over her writing desk when I left.

Maidstone was but a dozen white wooden buildings clustered together like ducklings on the river bank. Below its sharp steeple, the meeting house's chalky rectangular face looked as though it was missing something, like its eyes or a nose. It was cool inside, with bobbing hats, and somber homespun on every pair of shoulders. I slid into the last pew beside a rosy plump woman with a straw bonnet.

The young, tightly-combed minister emerged, all in black. He expounded upon sin and guilt until a strand of his oiled hair came loose across his forehead and his voice quavered with indictment.

"Satan's machinations are more clever, and blacker, yea, blacker, than you will ever be able to foresee," he said, his voice dropping at last to an exhausted chant. "Beware! For unless you repent and find your home in the bosom of the Lord, Satan will steal your life and your soul." The minister's gaze shot out across the congregation and hit me so sharply, my body felt all lit up and my heartbeat sliced my chest.

The rosy plump woman was called Sarepta, she told me outside in the sunshine, and when she learned that I was the new maid-of-all-work at Gardiner Farm, she said, "Oh, you poor thing, you must be perishing for someone to talk with! I'll walk with you as far as the ridge—let us walk by way of Bobbin Mill Road. It's so much cooler up there, and prettier, too. You may see the mountains from end to end."

"All right," I said. A friend would be nice. Nicer than spiteful hens.

We set out on a different road, alongside a gushing stream and a stone wall. Sarepta was juicy with gossip and self-revelation. She was childless, she told me, and her husband helped run a milk train to Boston. She did not ask many questions and I was simply glad—almost tearfully glad—of human company.

"There is the bobbin mill," Sarepta said, stopping to catch her breath at the top of the hill. She pointed to the unpainted wooden building across the stream. "I used to work there, before I was wed."

A green pool poured over a ruler-straight weir. Across the way, water splatted in rhythmical bursts on the turning wheel.

"Mr. Clay works there?" I asked.

"Mr. Clay! You've met him? All of the mill girls are aflutter about him—not you, too? They say he left behind many broken hearts in the City of Spindles. He has broken hearts here in Maidstone, as well." Sarepta laughed. "The mill girls say that this pond is haunted by the spirits of lovesick maidens. Perhaps some of Mr. Clay's admirers will end up here."

"Drowned? Did the maidens drown *themselves*, or—?"

"Why, little Hattie, what a fancy you have."

I thought of Brigit—how could it be avoided? I said, "The maid before me at Gardiner Farm. Brigit. Did you know her?"

"Brigit, yes. I mean, only a little. She lasted but a month—no, perhaps even less. Mrs. Gardiner can't keep on maids. It's those newfangled experiments and gewgaws of hers, and they all say Mrs. Gardiner finds endless fault and after a while she begins to slap them—ah, poor Hattie, you are nodding. Don't say she strikes you? That you'll be leaving soon, too?"

Across the millpond near the overgrown bank, something protruded from the water. My breath ceased. *An arm. A girl's arm—*

No. Only a tree branch.

I looked away. "I worry that something befell Brigit. Some…misfortune."

"Misfortune? Why, she rode the train back to Boston. She'll be better off there. Irish girls—papists, you know—they never take to the countryside. Boston is better for Brigit. Those Irish that keep arriving by the shipload, they aren't like us. They don't know how to keep a house. All they eat is potatoes, and the babies! All the babies they have, one after the other." Something flinty had crept into Sarepta's voice, and my soul, which had been reaching out, over-eager, for a friend, shrank back like a poked snail.

"Brigit left her things behind," I said. "In the maid's room. Nothing valuable, but surely they were valuable to *her*. To return to the city empty-handed, without even a nightgown?" I watched the millpond's aching slide to the edge of the weir.

"Well, I don't know, you silly goose," Sarepta said, her tone light again.

"Did Brigit…was she pretty?" Mr. Clay had said that Mrs. Gardiner didn't like pretty maidservants.

"Pretty!" Sarepta laughed. "Not at all. Short and heavy, with immense feet and an earthy complexion—and she did not bathe enough. She had dust on her—dust!—as though she'd been rolling about in flour like a fryer chicken."

Dust.

Sarepta and I bade each other farewell, and I continued toward Gardiner Farm.

I cooked a Sunday supper for the hogs that afternoon, with apple brown betty for dessert. The weather was already too thick, and the beastly stove made the kitchen hotter than Tartarus. I kept the kitchen door open wide as I dashed about my work, kneading, chopping, wiping, stirring, prodding, flipping.

How long he had been watching me, I couldn't say.

A great oak tree stood outside the kitchen door with shady lawn beneath, and Mr. Clay sat leaning on the trunk with a sketchbook on his knee.

I froze at my work when I saw him.

"I hoped you wouldn't ever notice me," he called with a smile. He shut the notebook, stuffed it into a knapsack, got to his feet, and mounted the porch. "You are a captivating study."

"I didn't know you were an artist, Mr. Clay."

"One must have some respite from all that metal and grease, don't you think?"

"Could I offer you a cold drink, Mr. Clay? Cider?"

"I don't believe Mrs. Gardiner would approve of her maidservant entertaining a gentleman in the kitchen. Come for a walk with me, Hattie. Have you seen the millpond? It is very cool there, and pretty."

How comely his face was, the faint sheen of sweat on his sunburned cheekbones, the luster of his dark eyes. A fearful plum pit hardened in my belly, but my cooking was done an hour early and I would—*must*—ask him about that white dust.

So I dampened the stove, placed my biscuits in the warming oven and a clean cloth over my brown betty, and I set out on the road with Mr. Clay. As we went, I felt Mrs. Gardiner watching us from the house. I knew I would lose my position when I returned.

The damp cottony sky enfolded us as we walked. Bruise colored clouds cartwheeled over the mountains, and thunder grumbled. The insects in the fields on either side of the road buzzed louder. The bird twittering died. I watched the toes of my battered boots appear and disappear from beneath my kicking skirt hem. I bundled up all of my courage.

"Mr. Clay," I said, "what is…from whence comes the white dust?"

"White dust?" He hitched the knapsack up on his shoulder. "The dust! It comes from my foundry. Or, to be exact, from plaster castings. First I take many, many plaster castings of my object to capture its precise geometry, and from these plaster castings I make the sand castings for the metal pieces I require."

"And Brigit helped you with your work?"

"Brigit was extraordinarily helpful."

"Which is why she left so much plaster dust in the maid's room."

"Did she? Then I reckon so."

"But where has she gone?"

"To Boston, my dear."

I stopped walking. The first raindrops stung my face. "I have been so afraid."

"Don't be afraid—although your timidity is in truth part of your charm. You are a faultless New England type, Hattie, do you know it? The quintessence of all that is lovely about the mill girls I saw in Lowell, fresh girls come down from the hills in their headscarves, ever so lightly freckled by the sun—" He brushed his knuckles over the bridge of my nose. "I long to capture it. That fluid grace. Discover its formula and find a way to make everything move like a song, as you do."

Suddenly, I was in his arms and his mouth was pressing upon mine with a violence that stole my breath. Something hit the road, and Mr. Clay and I split apart. Afire with shame, I took another step back. Mr. Clay crouched to gather up the knapsack and notebook that had tumbled free.

Inky lines blurred with rainwater, but I knew it was a drawing of me. No, not a drawing, but a *diagram*. Labeled. Precise. With the lines and arcs and Fig. 1 and Fig. 2 that I had seen in Mrs. Gardiner's manuscript, in primers, and in pamphlets about livestock.

Captured in paper and ink: the formula for my grace.

"You have been watching me for many days," I said.

Mr. Clay, still crouched, looked up at me with eyes as alien as a goat's.

"Brigit never returned to Boston," I said. "That white dust—she was coated in white dust, her things, the maid's chamber. You took plaster castings of…of her body? Her face? And then? *Then?*"

"In the end, we required a cast of Brigit's face, and wet plaster does have a way of seeping into eyes, nostrils, and mouth." Mr. Clay's voice was flatter than before, as though he had grown bored. "There are worse ways to die."

I turned and dashed up the road, which was now speckled dark with rain, toward Gardiner Farm.

Was Mr. Clay's cruelty the result of his time spent in the City of Spindles with those hundreds—thousands?—of mill girls, working fibers at their machines for ten hours every day of the week? How it never mattered that their wrists throbbed or that their fingertips went raw? All that mattered—Mr. Clay knew, all of Creation knew—was that the girls did not cease, that they never, ever ceased, and if they did, another girl, just the same, would seamlessly step in to fill her place.

I skidded across the muddy kitchen yard to the woodshed, dragged open the double doors which were, to my wonder, not locked, and at first I laughed up into the diluvial clamor of the sky, for I believed that all of those lurking shapes inside were only piles of firewood.

"Not one of them suitable for indoor work," Mrs. Gardiner said behind me, her voice cutting through the downpour.

I didn't turn. My raggedy breaths shook my shoulders, and I wiped rainwater from my eyes. Now I could see that the lurking shapes—ten, twelve, or more of them—were moving.

A shape on a stool plunging a butter churn by its knee. Another bent over a table with a rolling pin, rattling wood against wood. Still another swishing a broom. One, in the dimmest corner, swinging a silver hatchet up, thumping it down onto a wooden block, swinging it once more aloft.

Maids. Only maids. And yet their motions—rigid, graceless, rhythmical, with a lack of both yield and variation—made my heart shrink to a stone.

"Hattie," Mrs. Gardiner said. "Hattie, Mr. Clay and I wish for you to be extraordinarily helpful."

What was now to be done? Forthwith came into the family-circle a tall, well-dressed young person, grave, unobtrusive…with all the modest self-possession of a lady. The new-comer took a survey of the labors…and, looking, seemed at once to throw them into a system; matured her plans, arranged her hours of washing, ironing, baking, cleaning; rose early, moved deftly…The work seemed to be all gone.

[1] Note: Block quotes are excerpted from The American Woman's Home, Or, Principles of Domestic Science by Catherine Beecher (New York: J. B. Ford and Company, 1869).

National bestselling author **Maia Chance** writes mystery novels that are rife with absurd predicaments and romantic adventure. She is the author of the Fairy Tale Fatal, Discreet Retrieval Agency, and Agnes and Effie mysteries. A resident of Vashon Island in Washington State, she plays laundress and cook to two imperious children and a cat, and takes secret solace in chocolate, good books, and vintage cocktails.

VOICES CARRY
by Dayle A. Dermatis

If I didn't have such an aversion to group showers and scary women's prison wardens named Elsa, I would totally kill my parents right about now. I would beat them about the head and shoulders with my French horn.

Except I don't want to damage my French horn. Hm. Let me work on that plan.

They had to drag me to this hick town in the middle of nowhere, where in order to be in high school band, you had to be in *marching* band, too, performing at the football games everyone else cared about. That's how I ended up stomping in a prescribed pattern around the middle of a wet field of crushed grass while the trombone player behind me kept taking an extra step and nailing me right between my shoulder blades.

I don't think anyone in the metal bleachers even noticed us. (Greenville Central School: Too cheap to have bleachers on both sides of the field.) Certainly they didn't make much of a noise until the short-skirted cheerleaders bounded onto the field as the band was leaving.

The school was apparently also too cheap to dry clean the rented blue-and-white band uniforms, because mine smelled faintly of the last person to have worn it. The chin strap of the Marge-Simpson-hairdo hat dug into my chin.

Wooh. Go Mountaineers. Rah.

There's very little color here in October, despite the name; even the famed flaming southern Vermont leaves were muted and depressed under the lowering grey clouds. It might snow tonight. *Snow*! Jeezus.

You know what's on the Welcome to Greenville website? Pictures of cows. And tractors. And old people crossing the street.

After safely stowing my French horn and hat in the band room, I returned to the game. The players, all hulked out in their gear, were trotting across the weird red track material that ran in an oval around the field to get to their starting positions. I just wanted a hot chocolate to warm me up before half-time, when we had to march again.

"Who are we playing against?" I asked Herman who, despite having lived here his whole life (and his father is one of the janitors, because name your kid "Herman" and then *kick him while he's down*), cares even less about the game than I do.

Herman plays tenor sax. He's one of those guys who'll probably be quite attractive as an adult, but right now he has to suffer through scattered acne, spindly legs, and a kind of a pointy head. We kissed once, decided it wasn't going to work, and now he's pretty much my only friend here in hell.

It's not like I'm Prom Queen material, anyway.

He squinted, his breath coming in clouded puffs, and tucked his hands in his armpits. "Arlingsburg, I think."

Arlingsburg, which is apparently code for Impossibly Podunk Town. As if Greenville is some kind of metropolis. In both places, people shove half a bathtub upright into their front yards to make little shrines. Seriously. Kill me now.

Kill me now was my last thought before we found the dead body under the bleachers.

An older guy (a live one, not the body) was down under there, too, in the soda-cup- and napkin- and condom-littered place, looking just as shocked. He had a camera around his neck, a battered silver flask in one hand, and a reporter's notebook sticking out of the multipocketed khaki vest he wore over a thick, dark green, wool fisherman's sweater.

Without moving from where I'd stopped, I rested a hand on the icy metal strut next to me and leaned closer for a better look at the body. Him, I recognized.

Male, mid-30s, slender build, wire-rimmed glasses. Brownish hair with bits of dead brown leaves sticking in the dried blood over his right ear.

Mr. Lundy, our English teacher.

Well, that sucked.

Beside me, Herman said, "Uh…should we do something?"

"No," I said. "He's dead."

"How do you know? I mean…."

Because dead bodies aren't like you see on TV, where a live person is playing dead. Even if the actor is stellar and doesn't twitch an eyelash, no matter how much makeup you pile on 'em, they still don't look really dead.

I'd been with my grandfather when he died. He was on palliative care, finally comfortable thanks to the morphine. When they say cancer eats away at you, they aren't kidding—that's about as apt a description there is. Grandpa was sunken, the liver spots on his head visible now that his white hair was patchy and lank. His jaw had fallen open as he drifted asleep on the good drugs, as if he didn't have the energy to close it.

My dad had taken my mom down to the hospital cafeteria for coffee. I'd listened to her complaining about the hospital cafeteria coffee as they walked away, her voice and heel-clicks fading.

So I was holding Grandpa's hand—I swear he squeezed it once or twice that afternoon, even if he never opened his eyes—and reminding him of the funny family story about the enormous ceramic ALF and the burnt-orange velour sofa, and I was laughing as I told it, and then I realized he was gone.

I think he wanted to know I was happy before he could let go. I think he wanted all of us to be happy, so I hope he didn't hear my mother complaining about the goddamn coffee.

But when I say he was gone, he was *gone*. What was on the bed was an empty shell. Not asleep; not really, really still. Just no longer there.

My parents came back and my mother said "Oh God" and my father said "I'll go get someone" in a whisper (because, why? to not disturb Grandpa's resting in peace?) and I started to tear up and my mother said, "We'll cry when we get home."

And I thought, WTF is that all about? But I didn't cry. That's not what we do.

I didn't cry at the funeral, either, because they said not to.

Then I was never able to cry later, at home or anywhere.

The hospital room had resounded with silence. The metal bleachers overhead now thrummed with people stomping their feet and cheering. Apparently our team had done something good.

The older (live) guy—maybe in his forties? I don't know. I couldn't see any salt-and-pepper hair under his brown knit pea cap—tucked his flask into one of the many pocket in his vest and started taking pictures.

"What the hell are you doing?" I demanded.

"I'm a reporter with the *Bennington Banner*," he said, as if that made it okay.

He stepped closer and I said, "Don't contaminate the crime scene!" Because yeah, I do watch those stupid forensic shows, even if you know that the person they're talking to at the ten-minute mark is the killer, and you can figure out by minute forty-three why and how he dunnit.

The older guy stepped back. He dug into yet another pocket and fished out his cell phone. "I'll call 911," he said.

Above us, the crowd roared again.

"This is really going to piss everyone off," I commented. "Because I think we're winning."

ϱϱϱ

The police kept us there forever, asking questions. I was torn between wishing I'd been able to get another hot chocolate, because I was freezing, or being glad that I hadn't, because I really had to pee.

At least I hadn't had to march in the now-cancelled halftime show. I'll take my blessings where I can find them.

As soon as they released us, I made a beeline for a Porta-Potty. I'd've rather waited until I got home, but that wasn't going to happen.

My parents stood *right outside*. They'd had to be there while I was questioned, and now they were sticking to me like gum on the bottom of my shoe.

Unfortunately, this meant that I could hear them.

"I wish she hadn't had to see that," my mother fretted.

I had told them I was fine, but of course they hadn't listened.

"I wonder what happened," she went on.

"Well, wasn't he one of the…you know…them?" my father said.

"Oh, right," my mother said.

Holy shit. I felt like the top of my head was going to blow off and explode the Porta-Potty. Mr. Lundy was dead and all they cared about was that he was gay? And were they assuming that's why he was dead?

I wanted to shout at them for being so ignorant, but we just didn't talk about these things. I knew they'd ignore me. So I just growled under my breath, shoved my earbuds in my ears, and played Holst's "The Planets: Jupiter" really loud all the way home.

Loud is, after all, the only way to listen to "Jupiter."

Except my hands did start shaking, once we were in the truck. Yes, we own a dark grey Ford; apparently it's the law in the Green Mountains that you have to own a truck. Because we had to get firewood and take our own trash to the dump. The dump where, on summer evenings, I am not kidding, it's a pastime to sit and watch the black bears.

And my parents *chose* to move here.

Anyway, I started to think about Mr. Lundy, and a part of my brain thought, hm, this is what delayed shock must feel like, because I couldn't get my hands to stop shaking and "Jupiter" sounded even louder than I'd set it, and the back of my mom's headrest, with the little tear where my dad had caught it with something, seemed especially in focus.

It's not like I'd known Mr. Lundy very well or anything. He'd been my teacher. But he'd been nice, in that way some adults are nice to teenagers, treating those of us with brains like we *have* brains.

Once he'd figured out that I actually *liked* to read (and read something other than *Twilight*. Please.), he started recommending books. *The Princess Bride* (far superior to the movie). *The Last Unicorn*. Anything by Neil Gaiman.

Mr. Lundy's chin had been a little weak, and he'd worn glasses, and had nondescript sandy brown hair, and I don't know whether he was gay or not. But I was pretty sure he didn't deserve to die.

ଌଌଌ

The reporter guy called me the next day. His name was Joe Dashnaw and he was normally a sports reporter, although he had co-written the front-page story. I knew all this because although my parents tried to keep it away from me, it wasn't hard to find the morning's paper in the pile next to the kindling for the woodstove in the family room.

"I can't talk to you without my parents present," I told him, which he should've remembered from yesterday.

"Off the record," he said. "I'm just curious if your memories of the incident match mine."

Well, of course you are, you bonehead. If you hadn't been drinking....

But the police hadn't said we couldn't talk to each other, and I was bored, so I said okay.

I went into the family room, where my father was dozing in the tan recliner we'd bought for Grandpa a couple of years ago, before he got really sick. A golf game was on low, and my mother was leafing through a *Better Homes and Gardens*. She and my dad had had a fight about her huge stash of them and whether we were going to truck two decades' worth of them with us to Greenville.

I think she won, and they're in the basement somewhere. She'll never go back through them, mark my words.

I told them I was going to walk to Stewarts for some ice cream.

My mom frowned, setting the magazine next to her on the black leather sofa. "I don't want you walking anywhere alone," she said.

"Okay," I said. "Herman will go with me."

That roused my dad. He lowered the foot rest of the recliner. The springs inside twanged.

"I'm not so sure you should be spending so much time with this Herman," he said.

Oh for crying out— "He's just a *friend*," I said.

"Oh, George, it's fine," my mother said.

As if my mother would even know if we were doing it. She once said she didn't understand the purpose of premarital sex. And that, my friends, was the entirety of conversations we've had about the matter.

I was already texting Herman, and fifteen minutes later he showed up on my doorstep, and off we went.

It's probably stupid to go out for ice cream in October, but it felt warmer today because the sun was actually out, and ice cream is ice cream after all.

Stewart's Shops were unique to the area. The chain sold gas and some basic groceries; there was some sort of Milk Club where if you bought ten cartons of milk, you got a free one. They still used index cards to keep track.

They also sold their own ice cream, in gallons or in cones or cups. Each shop had a couple of Formica tables. Mr. Dashnaw was sitting at one, and raised a hand when we entered.

I ordered Adirondack Bear Paw (vanilla, caramel, and cashew crunch) in a cup, because someday I'll escape this godforsaken place and I won't be able to have this ever again. Herman hesitated, and I knew it was because he didn't have the money. So I ordered him a Black Raspberry and told him he owed me one.

We slid onto the curved, hard orange bench across from Mr. Dashnaw. He had a cup of coffee cradled between his hands. He looked better today that he had yesterday. His eyes were brighter, somehow, and he just seemed less…rumpled.

"Do the police have any leads?" I asked, and realized I sounded like a bad cliché.

Mr. Dashnaw shook his head. "Not really. Autopsy said he was hit on the back of the head. You know, they say most people are killed by someone they know."

What did that mean? His partner? A closet gay-basher?

My hands started to shake again, and I stuffed them between my thighs, as if I were trying to warm them.

"I didn't see any footprints," Herman commented around a mouthful of ice cream.

The ground under the bleachers was patchy dead grass, hard-packed mud, and scattered trash. But I remembered when we walked under there that I'd been kicking at the clumps of grass, upturning them, and there had been other areas of fresher mud.

"I don't think he would've just been hanging out under there," I said.

"Maybe he was dragged there."

"Didn't he jog on the track after school?" Herman asked. I turned and stared at him.

He shrugged. "Sometimes I stay late and my dad drives me home when he's done work."

Come to think of it, Mr. Lundy *had* been wearing sweatpants, a hoodie, and sneakers. That hadn't even occurred to me until now.

Mr. Dashnaw asked if we knew about Mr. Lundy's home life, which we didn't. We talked a little more and then he said, "Thanks, kids. This might be the break I need. I'm really sick of sports reporting."

And I thought, awesome. Someone's dead and it's a way to further your career? But of course I didn't say it aloud, except to Herman, on the way home.

When I got home, my mother said, "Mrs. Fessette said she saw you at Stewart's talking to that reporter."

Crap. I *suck* at lying. I always end up with a big goofy grin on my face. "Yeah, he was there," I said. Truth. "He's really a sports reporter." Also truth.

I thought about Mr. Lundy, dead, and I didn't smile.

"I just don't want him upsetting you," my mother said.

"I'm fine," I said. Okay, that was a lie. But it was the kind we told each other all the time.

ɷɷɷ

I couldn't fall asleep that night, no matter what type of music I listened to: baroque, rock, country. Tears clung to the back of my throat, scraped the backs of my eyes. Maybe if I slammed my hand in a door, I'd be able to cry.

No, then I wouldn't be able to play French horn. Have to work on that plan, too.

ɷɷɷ

Tuesday night was the viewing, at the Brown Funeral Home in Bennington. The main part of it had been an old house, and they'd tacked an extra part on, or maybe extended to meet up with the carriage house, hard to tell. It was painted white, with a zig-zag stone-edged walkway for people who couldn't get up the stairs.

I guess a lot of old people go to funerals. Now there's a depressing thought.

Inside was slate-blue acanthus-leaf wallpaper and gilt-framed paintings and dark wood furniture. It smelled overwhelmingly of flowers, all the different scents jumbled up and cloying.

Mr. Lundy's partner wore a new-looking dark suit, but the toes of his loafers were scuffed, and his hair was messy. I realized I recognized him: he owned the only used bookstore in Bennington, a tiny place jammed full of books, with a rickety staircase that I was always sure was going to come crashing down under my weight and that of the volumes stacked along the edges.

We shuffled through the line. I looked at Mr. Lundy in the coffin. He looked worse than when we'd found the body, I thought. Now he looked waxy, fake.

We got to Mr. Lundy's partner, and I realized I didn't know his name. His eyes were red around the edges, but he managed a smile when I told him Mr. Lundy had been my teacher and I would miss him. I wanted to tell him about the books he'd recommended, but I couldn't. It was like I was suddenly, stupidly shy. But I couldn't get the words out; they stuck with the tears in my throat.

My father shook his hand, his voice hearty, as it always was when he was uncomfortable. My mother simply descended into unflinchingly polite mode, overemphasizing to convey fake emotion.

I wanted to kick them in the shins.

My mouth was dry, so I took a bottle of water and stood off to the side with Herman, who'd ridden with us. His hair was slicked over and he looked uncomfortable in his dress pants, which were a little short, and white shirt.

I tried to drink, but had trouble swallowing.

The reception line dwindled, and Mr. Lundy's partner sat down in a corner with people he obviously knew well. I wanted to leave, but my parents were talking to the Fessettes, and when my mother gets talking, God help us. Eventually my father would get bored and start poking her in the waist with a finger to get her moving.

Mr. Lundy's partner covered his face with his hands, and I saw his shoulders shaking.

Something hurt, deep and sharp in my stomach. Not exactly like wanting to throw up, not like appendicitis. More like something cracking, breaking.

And that's when I cried. Not for me, because I hadn't known Mr. Lundy all that well, but for his partner. For his parents. For the people who loved him, because he was gone and they would never have him again.

Then I realized I was lying to myself. I was crying for them, but I was also crying for me—for Grandpa.

My mother hurried over and put her arm around me. "No, no," she said. "You're not supposed to be sad."

Which was a stupid thing to say, and it only made me cry harder. She started digging in her voluminous purse for a Kleenex, but I knew all about her scary, crumpled, holey Kleenexes, and I squirmed out of her grasp and reached around for the handy box nearby. Funeral homes clearly buy them in bulk at Sam's Club, and for good reason.

My father said, "Maybe it's time to go," and I said, "I have to go to the bathroom," and that made them happy because at least I wouldn't be making a public scene anymore.

Nobody spoke on the drive back to Greenville, through the dark and the cold. Herman patted my hand, and I suddenly gripped his, glad for his touch.

No, not that way.

ᘐᘐᘐ

The police figured out that Mr. Lundy had been killed by a transient, a drug addict who'd approached him for money. The guy had been living in the woods on the other side of all the sports fields, and that's where they found him.

The fact that he'd been so close to the school was some scary shit. I half-thought my parents were going to decide Greenville wasn't any safer than anywhere else we'd lived, but we'd moved here for my father's job, and the guy had been passing through, apparently. Headed south, where it's not so freaking cold.

My parents don't say anything about me losing it at the funeral home. They're probably not going to like it when the essay I wrote about Mr. Lundy gets published in the *Bennington Banner*, because I mention his partner. They're not going to like the fact that I've realized that I maybe have a crush on a girl.

But you know what? I can talk about it with somebody else.

Because life is too short not to cry and not to say what's in your heart.

Bestselling author **Dayle A. Dermatis** saw her story "The Scent of Amber and Vanilla" shortlisted for *The Year's Best Crime & Mystery Stories 2016*. Her latest crime fiction is gothic paranormal mystery *Waking the Witch* and short story "Bothering With the Details," forthcoming in *Hitchcock's*. Sign up for her newsletter (and get free fiction!) at www.dayledermatis.com.

NEW ENGLAND

HARD AS GRANITE
by Charlotte Broadfoot

The glistening outcrop was 'flattish' but not smooth enough to agreeably accommodate her back and buttocks, which body parts she wriggled and shifted into imagined hollows, aiming for the most comfortable position possible. Last year's bathing suit, grown too tight with a summer's growth spurt, and a thin old beach towel afforded little insulation between the tanned skin, gangly bones and the unforgiving stone. She didn't mind though—the rock reminded her of home (Chester, Vermont) where granite had always been a construction staple.

Regardless of the discomfort, she'd claimed ownership of this private space for herself. Spread-eagled on the faded terrycloth, face raised to the robin's egg blue sky, Minnie reveled in the strong July rays beating down on her and warming the spackled rock about her. The heat and light bounced off the inside of her tightly closed eyelids. Transparent specks seemed to float in a red-orangish medium neither liquid nor solid, behind the inner eye-lid wall...almost like bubbles from a bubble-wand. *Floaters*, Tray had once dubbed the phenom with his greater knowledge and experience.

She sighed in contentment. A slight breeze wafted the scent of spruce and pine, in combination with the fermented lake smell; (rotten logs, water lilies, shore birches and cedars.) Somewhere in the distance she could hear the murmur of voices. She scowled suddenly at the sound of a nearer, heavier tred in her direction, and then the sound of silence? She *would* not open her eyes.

"You g'wan now Sylly. Don't you even think about it, if you want to see tomorra..."

She was tempted to squint open just one eye but decided not to give him the satisfaction. This was *her* spot. Her small hands fisted, ready for a fight. She waited, a tight breathless little ball, but when nothing else occurred, she took it that Sylly must have moved off and out of her personal space.

Minnie exhaled, much relieved. Feeling deliciously wrapped in solitude again, she settled her mind and focussed on the sound of friendly, small waves lapping at the base of the rocky incline she'd expropriated. Her mind lazily jumped along the agenda she'd already set for the day. *Another full day on the water, probably in a row boat, some swimming for sure—maybe even some jump offs with the boys from this very spot—oh, and a turn at fishing of course. Later, perhaps hunt down a salamander in the woods.*

Her heart bounded with youthful exuberance. How awesome to be away from the heat and cement of the city, all the usual routines.

Absence from friends makes the heart grow fonder her mom had paraphrased. Yes, in a couple of weeks she'd look forward to going home to play with Ella and Cindy, but right now she wanted to indulge what her father, shaking his head in mock disapproval, referred to as her *tom boy tendencies*.

Well, Mom and Dad too busy relaxing themselves the one time of the year they could, wouldn't be on her tail all the time here. '*Walk don't run*' or '*A lady doesn't cross her legs like that*!' '*Pull up your socks; pull down your skirt, for*

Goodness sake." Her dad's favorite? '*Straighten up there, Missy. Shoulders back, head high, chin up.*' As if she was a soldier for Pete's sake.

Muffled sounds emanated from the Lodge fifty yards distant, reminding her that her mom would be just starting to get her younger sister Carrie up and ready for the day. Her dad, freshly showered, would be already sitting out on the flame-red Adirondack chairs, drinking his first coffee of the day, chatting and laughing with some of the other guests, and her brother would be thinking up some hare-brained scheme with Sylly, this year's best friend from…*where was it—Maine? New York State?* Somewhere relatively close by, for he and his family to be cottaging here on Lake Champlain.

None of Sylly's history was important enough for Minnie to dwell on. Sylly wasn't *her* friend and her brother Tray, older by two years, spent more time with him than her anyway. Tray made sure to call Sylvano by his full name, glaring at Minnie every time she thrust in her blade with *Sylly*, turning away just in time with nose-in-air so her brother couldn't see the jealousy or hurt in her own eyes. (Tray hadn't yet used the one comeback that would have devastated her and won *that* war*: Hermione!)*

They had been at the old-fashioned Wampanoag Lodge (locally referred to as the Landlubbers Inn) in the Champlain Lake Valley country for five days now. Minnie ticked off the years on her fingers. As a family, they'd been coming there for three weeks every summer ever since Tray was a baby, so ten years; all *her* life, in other words.

As they didn't have a camp yet of their own, like practically all her other friends back in Chester, the rambling old gabled structure was almost like a home away from home in the summer. Minnie loved it all, from the creaky old staircase and the transoms above the doors to the guest suites (no air-conditioning), to the balding lawns with their jutting granite and quartz outcrops and the root strewn path between the maples and hemlocks winding down to the boathouse, dock and swimming platforms. If there was a heaven for a precocious eight-year-old, this was it!

"Minnie. Min---nie! Breakfast!"

Mom wouldn't brook any rebellion when it came to nutrition, but once she'd had her eggs, bacon, pancake and sausage with side of jam and toast and juice, Minnie'd be free until lunch. Even if Sylly *had to* come along, she and Tray would probably be going out later to fish the shoreline in one of the old rowboats or a canoe, so there was the afternoon to anticipate too.

She hoped it would be the canoe. It'd be great to tip it over, watch Sylly flounder in the waterlilies like the useless sunfish she thought him to be. (The pert nose sniffed at the thought of the beautiful little fish that annoyed *real* fisherman particularly.). She bet Sylly would be afraid of leeches too—she'd had to put a worm on his hook for him the first time they fished off the dock. Maybe she'd get some mileage out of *Champ* the Lake's own 'Nessie Monster' next time they all went swimming. She'd have to remember that one. She *almost* felt a twinge of guilt, but it passed.

Sitting in the dining room, Minnie looked around for one of the other guests—Mr. McEvoy. This was his first year here. Right from the get-go, she had noticed he stuck to himself. As unofficial *Lodge Greeter* (and due to the dirth of kids her own age this year) she had befriended him, playing the odd round of shuffleboard or horseshoes in the play area on the other side of the Lodge.

At first, he seemed a bit standoffish, reluctant to encourage her, but when they were alone he seemed to enjoy her company and as he did not seek much contact with the other adults, Minnie felt she was rather special. Not that they said too much to each other—just sat in companionable silence, or played the odd game of checkers on the *wrap-around* if the weather turned.

"What are you hanging around with that 'Slob-ovian' for?" Tray had demanded archly one day. She'd come out with some defensive remark in retort, but Tray's bad opinion did carry some weight. Naturally she'd never say so. It prompted her to take stock. She couldn't really defend even to herself Mr. McEvoy's pocked face or porky profile with low belted pants holding up a beefy paunch. Patently un-ironed summer shirts opened in a wide V at the neck, revealing thick wiry tuffs of greying hair. He was shiny and balding on top, and had a very bad habit of not connecting with his eyes, which were bulbous, lighted sometimes with an odd expression that would flash for an instant and be gone.

Minnie put his slightly unkempt appearance and unsociability with the other Lodge guests down to the lack of a wife. It seemed obvious. Nobody to look after him. Her mom, however, had dismissed him summarily as a 'Traveling Salesman,' whatever that meant.

Minnie continued to see Mr. McEvoy as a compromise when no other playmate was available, but she also felt with all her good nature that Mr. McEvoy needed a friend, and she could be that, especially when Tray and Sylly didn't want her around, as was the case now. However, as she glanced over the dining room, Mr. M was nowhere to be seen either.

Minnie shrugged. It was 8:30 am and breakfast having been disposed of as fast as possible, Tray had tapped Sylly on the shoulder and they had disappeared into the woods on the property, probably to make a fort of dead branches. Perhaps she would sneak up on them later, rushing their defences like Captain Blood, but right now Minnie was annoyed. It was still early and good for fishing, before the real heat of the day sent the fish down to cooler depths. *Time's a-wastin'.*

She excused herself from the table. Mom was taken up too much lately with two-year-old Carrie to notice her leave—which was what she wanted. Sauntering out onto the wide porch, seeing the odd couple around the umbrellaed tables or a lone reader absorbed in their book on a striped hammock, the way appeared clear to make for the water. Minnie was an intelligent and independent child and her parents, while not uncaring, just expected she could take care of herself. The only thing she had been forbidden to do was to take out a boat on her own, even though *she* knew she was quite capable.

So, the second her striped rubber thongs hit the ground, she was off and running over the haphazard bouldery lawn, around the granite hilltop on which the Lodge perched, down the side path, through the sun-speckled forest, jumping breathlessly over root and stone, until at last landing with a thump onto the floating dock. Joy bubbled up in her like an underground spring. She knelt and peered over the side of the dock rungs, tracing her mirror image in the water with her fingers. The water was cool and refreshing to the touch. It was an almost bright mustard colour from the sun-splashed sand particles and algaed-rock beneath, the shallow shore giving way to the deeper blue water at the far end of the long wooden dock. A few minnows and sunfish darted around the piers, but if they were still feeding Minnie reasoned, so would the perch and pike, maybe if lucky, even a bass. Tray had taught her well.

The fishing equipment was kept in the boathouse, a long tall rectangular board-and-batten structure anchored to the rock face behind and on stilts well into the shallows at the front. It had large double doors opening from the side onto the main dock and a single door at the back. The wooden floating dock itself ran along the front and curved around the back in an inverted 'L.'

A rainbow of canoes was stacked on ledges inside—red, green, blue. Lovely old rustic 'time immemorial' paddles were stuck, blade up, in a huge old iron cauldron by the door. Some of them had faded images on the blade. There were only two small windows in the boathouse that looked out on the lake side—probably a winter provision—the result being that it was dark and a bit musty inside. It was quite the transition to step out of the burnished sunlight into the darkness of the interior. Minnie had had to refocus her eyes a bit.

The child heard in the back of her mind her mom's instruction: '*Always wear a life jacket down by the water*,' but the old PFD's that had never been replaced in a couple of decades and probably *way* past code now, were too bulky for a kid used to free range of movement. Anyway, Minnie considered herself an excellent swimmer, having been baptized by water from the age of two. She knew the Lodge's shoreline like the palm of her hand. No worries there!

She went to get the fishing pole she always considered had her name on it, though in fact, any guest could use it. It had the quick-release cast mechanism she preferred, and the red casement of the reel appealed to the 'girly' side of her, an element she had not really acknowledged yet, it being so far removed from a life of sun, sand, and swashbuckling.

Busy as she was, untangling some of the 6-lb test line on the rod (*Who HAD used her rod last?)* she was aware through peripheral vision of a shadow in the doorway. She took no real notice though until its creator moved. Looking up, framed in the doorway was the missing Mr. McEvoy. Her face brightened.

"Hey, Mr. McEvoy, didn't see you at breakfast."

Mr. McEvoy didn't seem to be as surprised to see her as she was with his appearance. He peered at her, then looked thoroughly behind him, finishing with a full sweep of the interior of the Boathouse. He seemed to be satisfied, but *of what* she wondered?

The smile pasted on the man's face rang false to the inherent honesty of an eight-year-old. The hairs on Minnie's neck rose unbidden with a vague, uncomfortable feeling that stiffened her whole body. An unknown but ancestral fear sent out paralyzing tentacles. Some of the reaction must have registered on her face, because his settled into a grimace.

He stepped purposefully into the dark of the boathouse, and spoke her name softly—*Hermione*—almost calling her in the way you would to a reluctant pet.

The oddness of his manner spoke volumes to Minnie, alerting her but still without knowing the exact cause of her fear. McEvoy took another stride inward and stopped, pretending she knew, to be looking at the canoes on the walls but edging forward, closer.

Instinctively, Minnie put a rack of 7-horsepower trolling motors between herself and him. She still had the fishing pole in her lax hand, unsure whether to drop it or not.

The boat house which had been a friendly retreat before, now seemed too dark, perilous even. In a small thin voice she tried to inject with some veritas, she ventured, "Oh, I think I just heard my Mom calling..." and made a step to indicate her response.

Mr. McEvoy also took a step, blocking her trajectory. "Really?" came the soft rejoiner. "I didn't hear anything, Hermione. We're quite a long way from the Lodge down here, you know."

"No, I did!" she babbled. "I did; I'd better go…"

"I can't believe a big girl like you would tell tales, Hermione." The wounded voice became cajoling. "Wouldn't you rather show your old friend…the canoes? I have a game I could teach you too." The smile on his face did not match the queerly glittering eyes, and so unruffled was his tone, it was almost hypnotising.

Minnie's breathing had become unaccountably rapid, and her eyes darted around the boathouse in a scared, random manner. She felt talking filled the weighty space.

"Um…can't. Tray and Sylvano (for once she drew out the name) are coming down to fish." She waved her rod wanly, as proof.

"I don't think so, Hermione." McEvoy took a tentative step. "I saw them take off to the woods earlier, and they were whooping like Cowboys and Injuns—not our sort of entertainment, is it?" This comment was accompanied with a conspiratorial shake of the head, and a rather dramatic sigh.

All Minnie knew, she didn't want to play *anything* with Mr. McEvoy, and that realization came almost too late as the bulky man launched himself around the bottom end of the engine rack, stretching out an arm and trying to catch hold of her. Without thinking, she jabbed the point of the rod into his face, dropping it while he pawed the spot on his cheek fiercely, cursing. She fled towards the open door at the back, having the intuition to grab a standing paddle on the way out.

In seconds Mr. McEvoy was after her, the two facing off at the end of the portion of the floater dock that curved around the back of the boathouse. Minnie was trapped by the rock face at her back. She still hadn't a clue what was transpiring or why; she only knew, like any feral animal, that she was in extreme danger—of something. The paddle was long and awkward for a child her size, but she held it like a barrier between them. The dock rolled a bit with waves from a powerful motorboat that had passed recently, the boards soaked by the 'curl.'

"This wasn't the game I had in mind," Mr. McEvoy puffed rather crossly, glancing furtively in a 180-degree turn. "But I do think you know, we *will* play that game." (The quiet tone had gotten lower and more insistent.) "I'll teach you the rules." He put his finger to his lips for *silence.* "Our secret—you can't tell anyone. You like secrets, don't you? All kids like secrets."

He was about fifteen feet away, making a slow determined approach toward Minnie, patience at an end. It was his attitude that triggered the paddle, almost of its own volition, to bear down squarely and hard on the crown of his head when he lunged.

The power of an eight-year-old however, even with adrenalin pumping, wouldn't have been enough to deter such an advance. It was a happy circumstance therefore that a slippery dock proved to be Mr. McEvoy's undoing. Even though her strike was not a Viking thrust, it pushed McEvoy off-centre and because, unlike Minnie, her assailant was wearing inappropriate dock wear (laced-up brogues with smooth leather soles), he had no traction whatsoever on the wet and slimy boards.

With an astonished look on his face, he slipped off the dock, arms flailing and failing to purchase anything to stop the momentum, falling hard over the side into the lake. Minnie witnessed his head striking the granite rock by the wooden foundation. She saw blood spurt. The 'O' formed by his pursed lips matched the one on hers, but it was *his* mouth, gaping, that quickly filled with water. The surprise in his eyes followed her even as he sank and the water closed over him.

Minnie dropped the paddle in the water as if it were a hot iron, but her feet would not move from the spot, and neither could she call out. It was not long before the corpulent body of Mr. McEvoy was soon bobbing up in the water, between the dock and the rock, like one of her fishing accessories, the iconic red and white floater.

The sun now seemed harsh, scorching and relentless and yet Minnie felt cold and tremulous. Her feet were leaden but she managed to walk past the bobbing body, arms outstretched in front and back, hugging the wall of the boathouse. As she rounded the corner, nobody in sight, she looked for the secondary, less used path up to the Lodge, that wound up through rocks and to the back of the property.

She sprinted up it as if the devil were right behind her and only stopped, gasping from the run and climb, at the top of the hill, at the same rocks she'd been sunning on in the morning. Drained, she could not seem to get warm. When she looked at guests in hammocks, or quietly conversing in the garden chairs, it all seemed so unreal. She sat down on her rock, now unmindful of the rough surfaces abrading her bottom. Clasping her knees with scrawny arms grasping tight, chin perched atop, unblinking eyes looked out over the endless lake vista.

Finally, someone must have gone down to the docks for a swim. Suddenly there was a big hullabaloo with people running about, calling for an ambulance, emergency, and then after that hushed tones and whispers.

"Looks like he meant to go canoeing or something, slipped on the dock, and hit his head. Shame when you're on vacation, right?"

She saw her own dad talking to an elderly couple, then look her way and say to the owner of the Lodge just passing, "Mr. Faraday, best not alarm the kids. Don't let anyone go down there for now." And he waved at Minnie, a sort of paternal pretend- heartiness. Minnie remained rooted to her rock like one of the small hemlocks that grew impossibly out of the cracks.

The emergency crew came by boat from the nearest marina with their siren blaring. She viewed their arrival from her rocky perch over the lake, and after an hour or so, she saw them leave with their baggage. She did not join the crowd or ask any questions, even when Tray and Sylly came to find her, babbling with excitement over the horrible death of a guest.

Everyone was withdrawn at dinner that night in the Lodge, her parents presuming her quiet demeanor extended from her comradeship with the deceased, and so beyond a little pat on the head for commiseration, they left her in silence.

She went to bed early and again, as everyone had been affected by the commotion, it was not seen to be unusual. Carrie was asleep already, so she turned herself to the wall and pretended to be asleep when her Mom eventually came up to bed. Her Dad was bunking with Tray in another room at least some of the time—and she could hear them all talking out in the corridor when she did fall asleep.

But next morning, when Minnie made her way to her special rock, the sky wasn't as blue, the stone was rough and scraped her skin, the water seemed to stretch far, far away—a bleak gray. She was filled up with a greyness herself she couldn't explain, and questions so deep she didn't know what to do? Eventually though, she knew she needed her Mom.

Not seeing her Mom outside with some of the other lady guests, she tore across the lawns, into the Lodge and up the main staircase. The three of them, Mom, Carrie and she shared the larger family suite. Her Mom had just put Carrie down in the Lodge's rental crib, and Mom was folding clothes.

"Mom!"

"Hmmm. Yes?" Mom continued her task without looking up.

"Mom?" Minnie tried again, her voice ladened with uncommon angst.

Mom looked up this time. "Min, what is it?"

Minnie knew what had happened was bad. She regarded McEvoy's death as awful, but essentially it was his own fault and since she did not regard her own actions as anything other than self defence, she would never mention her part in any of it. There was something however, even worse, she didn't understand. How could she put into words, describe a fear she knew nothing about?

Mom took a stab, although on the wrong track. "Is this about Mr. McEvoy?"

Minnie nodded at first, then abruptly shook her head. In a long shuddering breath, she stammered, "I don't think Mr. McEvoy was…nice.'

"What?" said Mom. Her quizzical expression showed that this was not what she had been expecting.

Minnie stared at the ground and repeated, with a bit more conviction. "…nice."

This time Mom grabbed Minnie's shoulders gently, and lifted her daughter's chin up with her fingers to stare into her eyes. She studied their depths, evidence of an age-old betrayal: hurt, alarm, sorrow.

"Did he ever do anything to you, Minnie—that you didn't want him to do?"

Mom's heart was racing now, but she tried to keep her voice calm and natural. Minnie remained like a stoic statue in her grasp, but when she uttered a low 'no' Mom expelled a long deep relieved breath. Then, with a mom's intuition, "But…he wanted to?"

"I…think so," came the small, uncertain response.

Then her Mom clasped the innocence to her heart, kissing the top of Minnie's head, trying to wrap her arms as tightly around her as she could. For a minute they held the comforting, protective embrace.

Mom unwrapped first, and drawing Minnie down on the bed with her, began tracing a pattern on the old chenille bedspread to minimize the horrific discovery for both. As she traced, she slowly found the words, trying to both warn and balm at the same time this headstrong independent daughter and prepare her for a life in which the sun would not always be so bright or all-encompassing.

Charlotte Broadfoot resides in London, Ontario (Canada) dividing each year quite simply into six months of winter writing and six months of beachifying, trekking, and vengefully weeding invasives from her garden palette. She is currently engaged in developing her new *Winter Whinging* blogging website beachcombersbookery.com and absolutely thrilled that "Hard as Granite" has been included in the *Snowbound* anthology.

Made in the USA
Middletown, DE
08 May 2018